MIKE CAVALLARO's

NICO BRAVO

AND THE TRIAL OF VULCAN

:01

First Second

NEW YORK

Firšt Second

Published by First Second
First Second is an imprint of Roaring Brook Press,
a division of Holtzbrinck Publishing Holdings Limited Partnership
120 Broadway, New York, NY 10271
firstsecondbooks.com
mackids.com

Library of Congress Cataloging-in-Publication Data is available.

Our books may be purchased in bulk for promotional, educational, or business use.
Please contact your local bookseller or the Macmillan Corporate and Premium Sales Department
at (800) 221-7945 ext. 5442 or by email at MacmillanSpecialMarkets@macmillan.com.

First edition, 2022
Edited by Mark Siegel and Dennis Pacheco
Cover design by Kirk Benshoff and Sunny Lee
Series design by Andrew Arnold
Interior book design by Mike Cavallaro
Color by Jeremy Lawson and Mike Cavallaro

This book was written and drawn on park benches and kitchen tables, aboard trains,
and in cafés and bars, on an iPad Pro using Clip Studio Paint, and colored in Adobe Photoshop.

Printed in China by 1010 Printing International Limited, Kwun Tong, Hong Kong

ISBN 978-1-250-21887-2 (paperback)
1 3 5 7 9 10 8 6 4 2

ISBN 978-1-250-22045-5 (hardcover)
1 3 5 7 9 10 8 6 4 2

Don't miss your next favorite book from First Second!
For the latest updates go to firstsecondnewsletter.com and sign up for our enewsletter.

TO DAD

PART 1:
THE BEGINNING OF THE END.

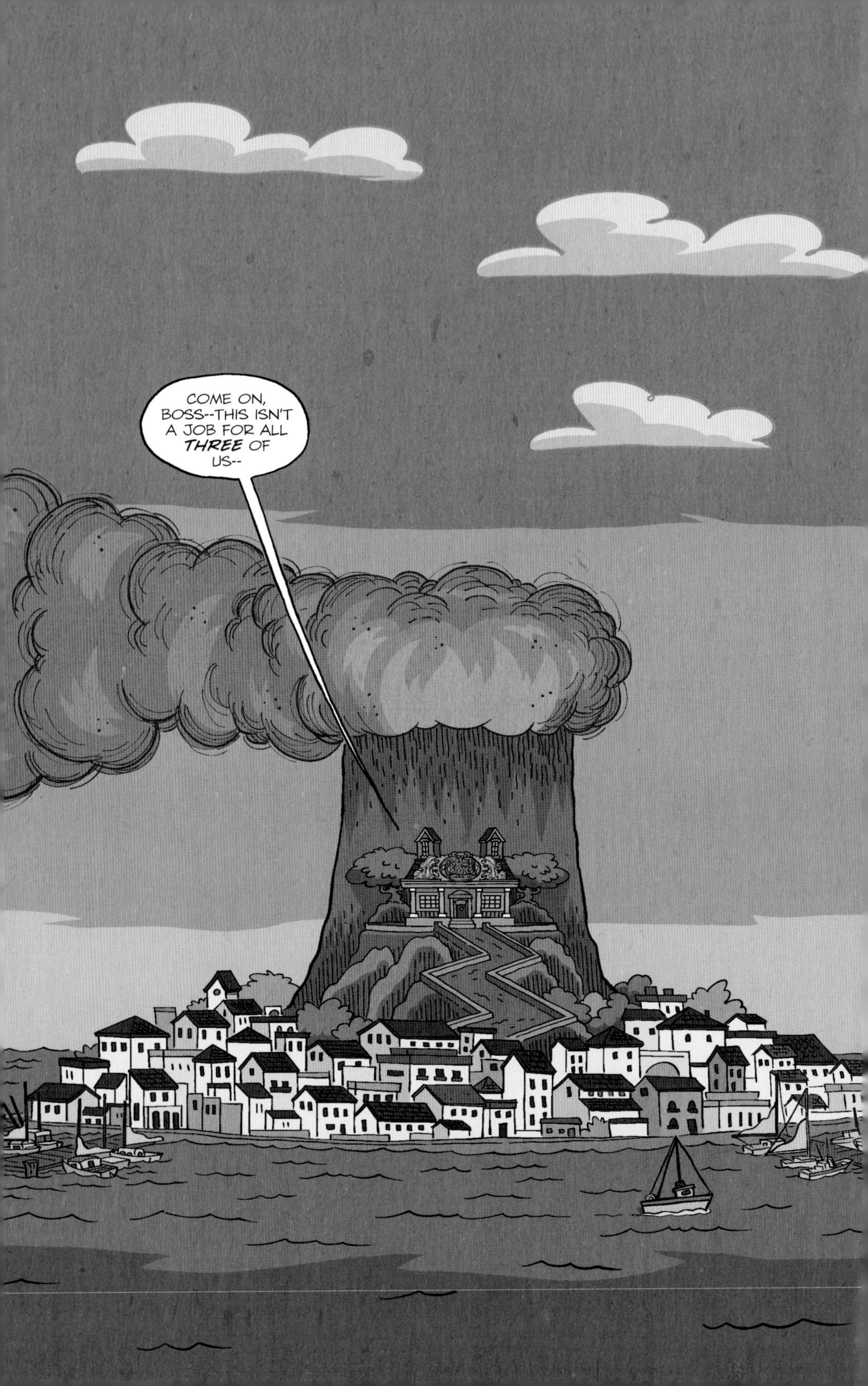
COME ON, BOSS--THIS ISN'T A JOB FOR ALL ***THREE*** OF US--

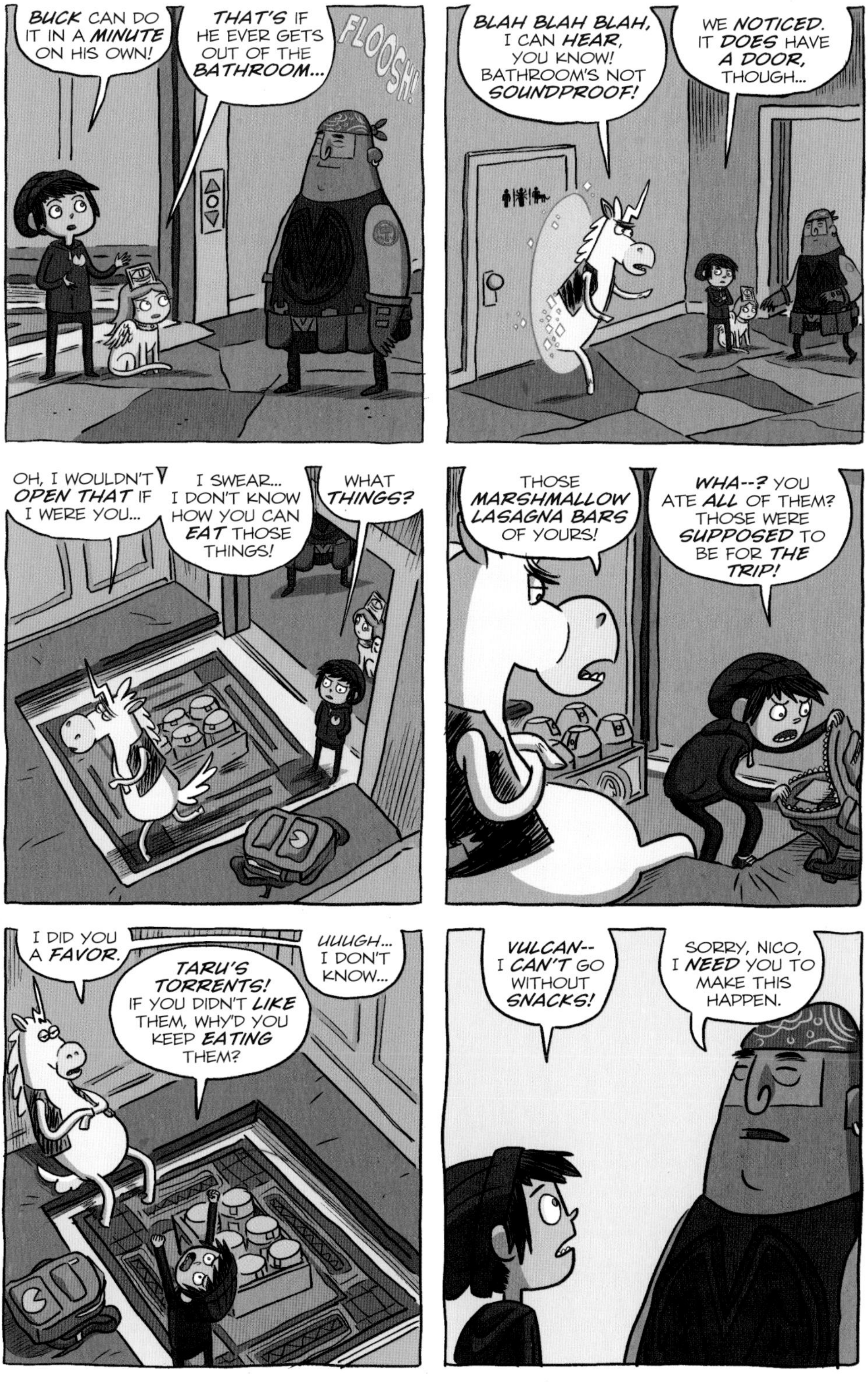

BUCK CAN DO IT IN A MINUTE ON HIS OWN!
THAT'S IF HE EVER GETS OUT OF THE BATHROOM...
FLOOSH!
BLAH BLAH BLAH, I CAN HEAR, YOU KNOW! BATHROOM'S NOT SOUNDPROOF!
WE NOTICED. IT DOES HAVE A DOOR, THOUGH...
OH, I WOULDN'T OPEN THAT IF I WERE YOU...
I SWEAR... I DON'T KNOW HOW YOU CAN EAT THOSE THINGS!
WHAT THINGS?
THOSE MARSHMALLOW LASAGNA BARS OF YOURS!
WHA--? YOU ATE ALL OF THEM? THOSE WERE SUPPOSED TO BE FOR THE TRIP!
I DID YOU A FAVOR.
TARU'S TORRENTS! IF YOU DIDN'T LIKE THEM, WHY'D YOU KEEP EATING THEM?
UUUGH... I DON'T KNOW...
VULCAN-- I CAN'T GO WITHOUT SNACKS!
SORRY, NICO, I NEED YOU TO MAKE THIS HAPPEN.

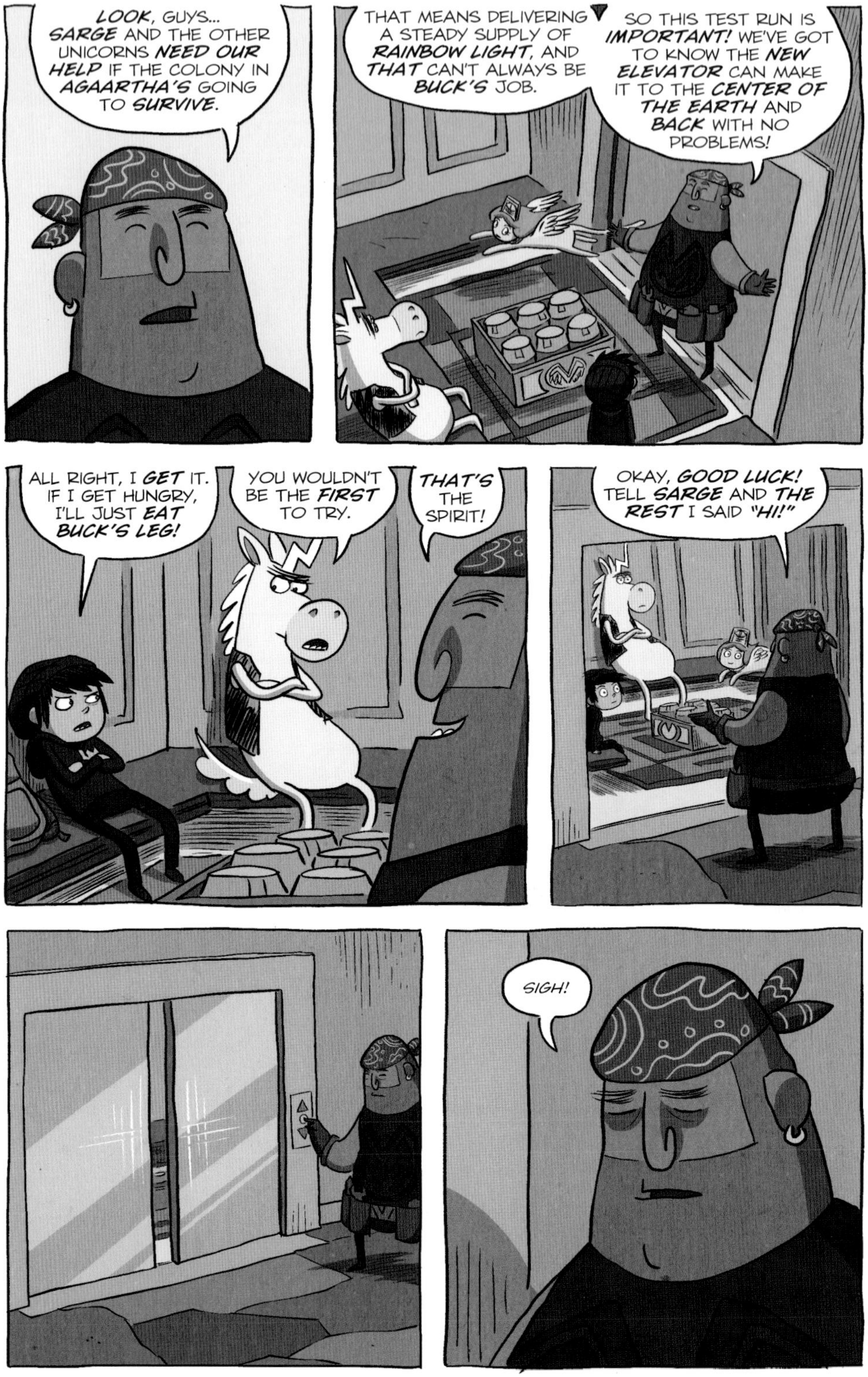
LOOK, GUYS... SARGE AND THE OTHER UNICORNS NEED OUR HELP IF THE COLONY IN AGAARTHA'S GOING TO SURVIVE.
THAT MEANS DELIVERING A STEADY SUPPLY OF RAINBOW LIGHT, AND THAT CAN'T ALWAYS BE BUCK'S JOB.
SO THIS TEST RUN IS IMPORTANT! WE'VE GOT TO KNOW THE NEW ELEVATOR CAN MAKE IT TO THE CENTER OF THE EARTH AND BACK WITH NO PROBLEMS!
ALL RIGHT, I GET IT. IF I GET HUNGRY, I'LL JUST EAT BUCK'S LEG!
YOU WOULDN'T BE THE FIRST TO TRY.
THAT'S THE SPIRIT!
OKAY, GOOD LUCK! TELL SARGE AND THE REST I SAID "HI!"
SIGH!

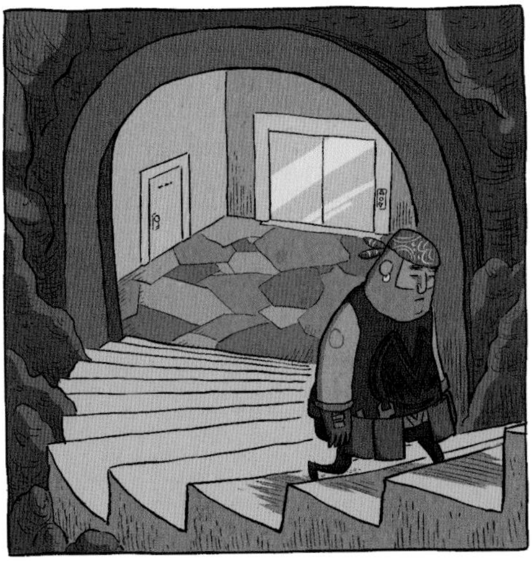
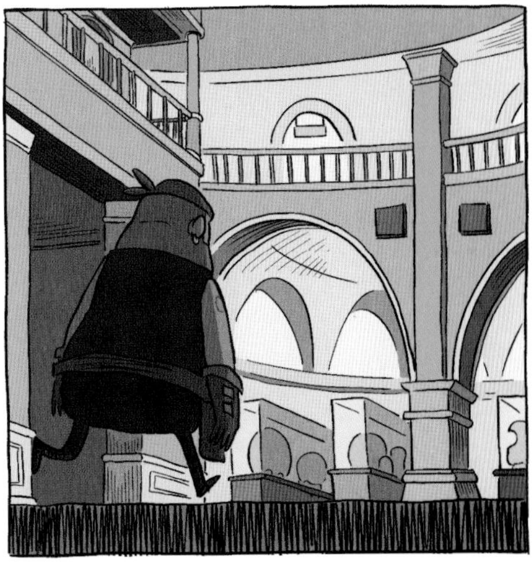
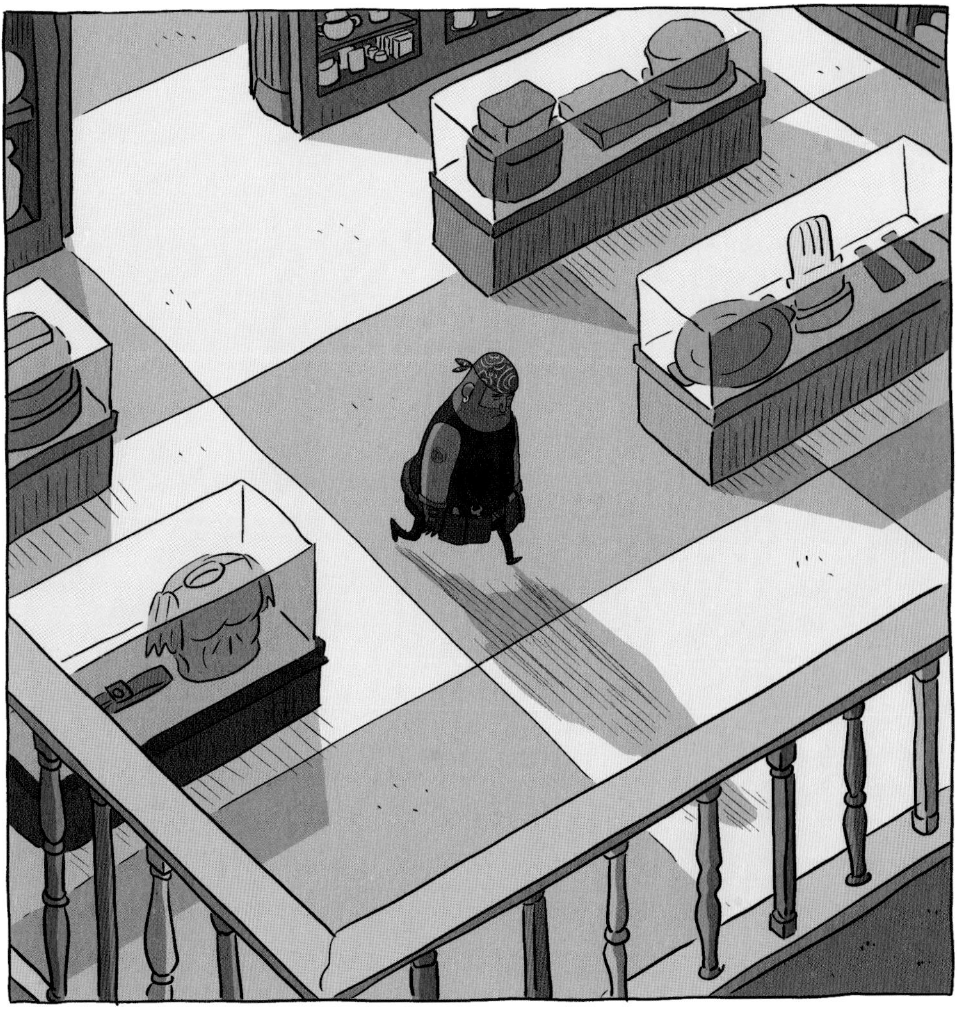

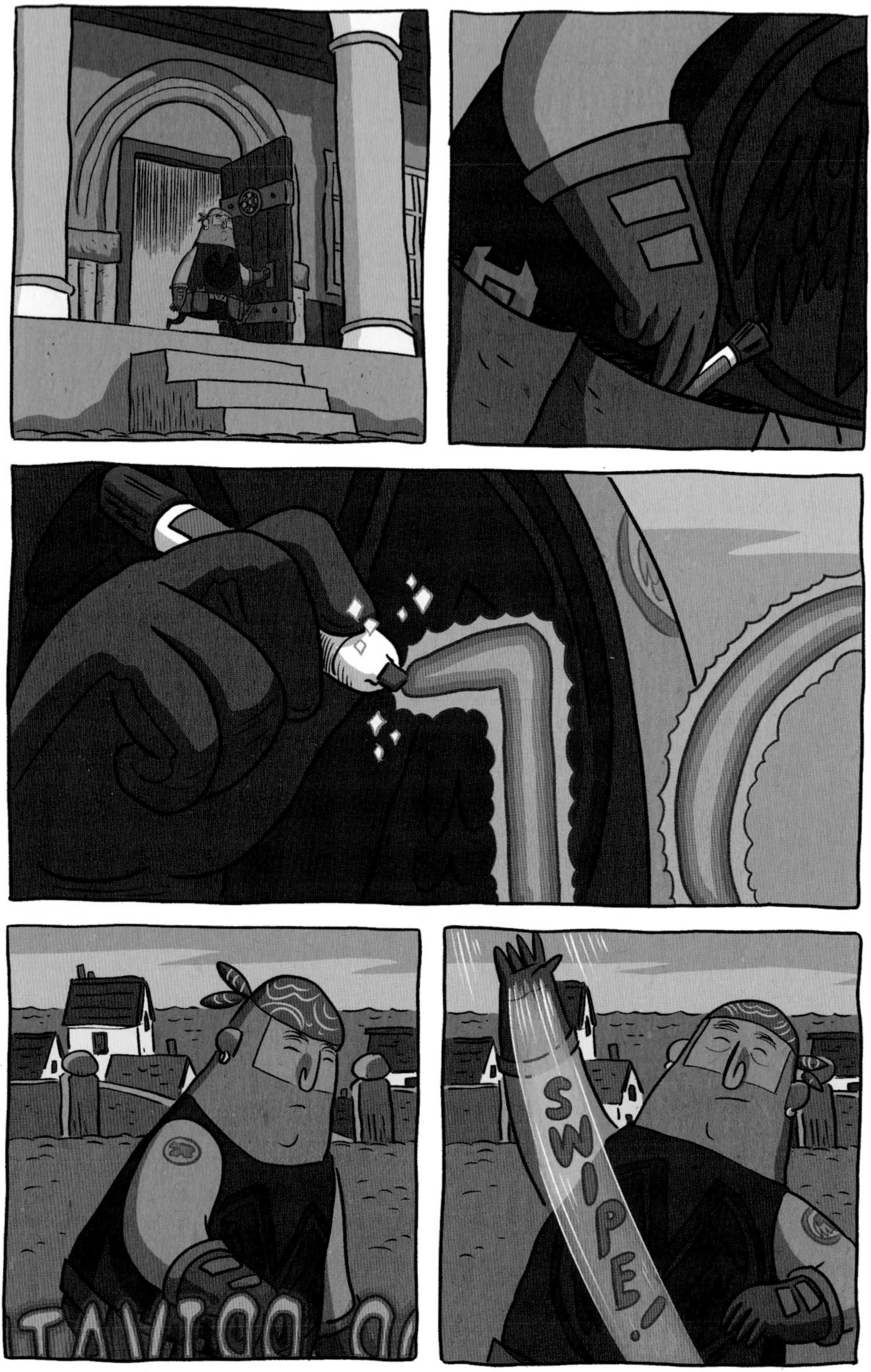
SWIPE!

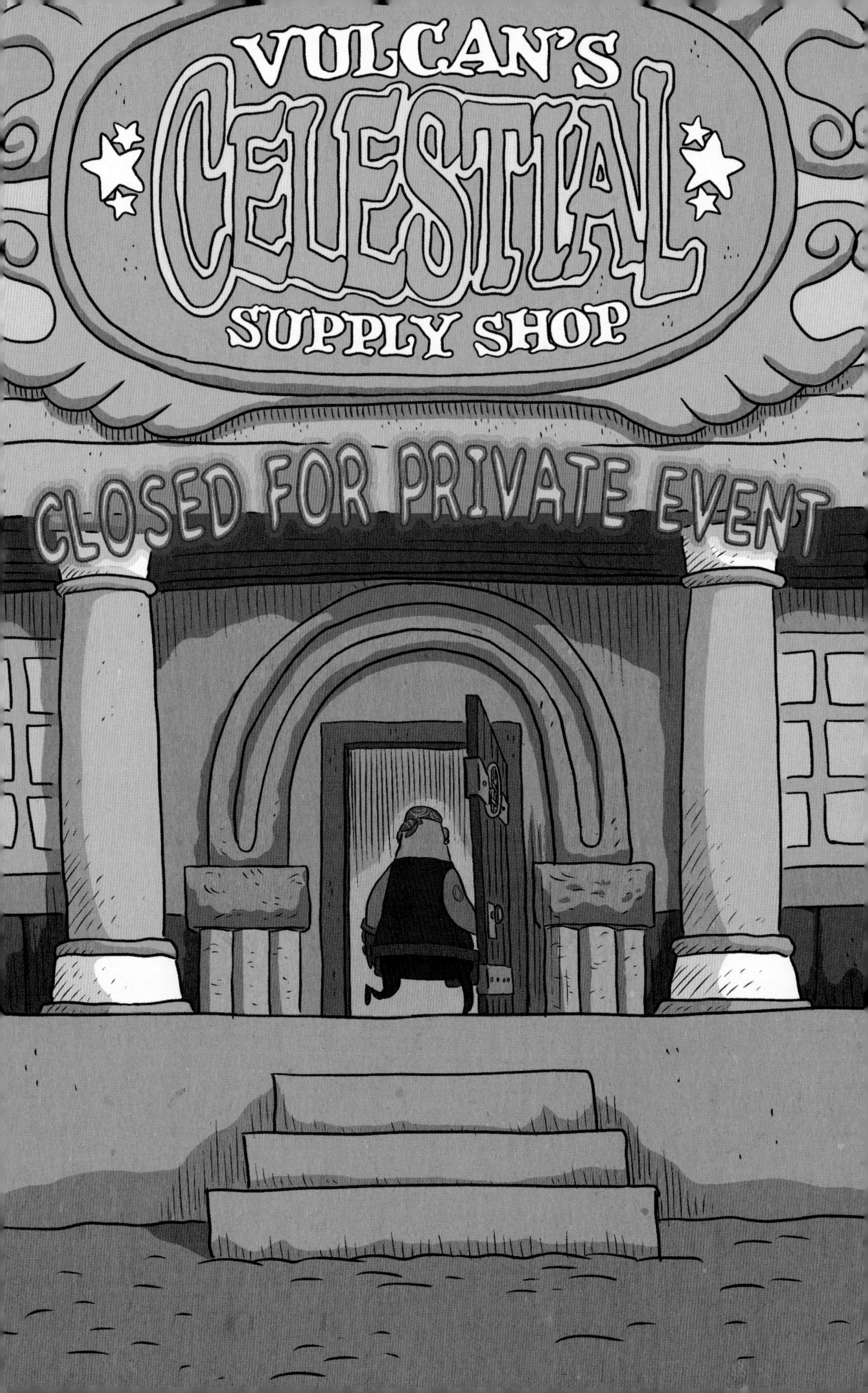
VULCAN'S CELESTIAL SUPPLY SHOP
CLOSED FOR PRIVATE EVENT

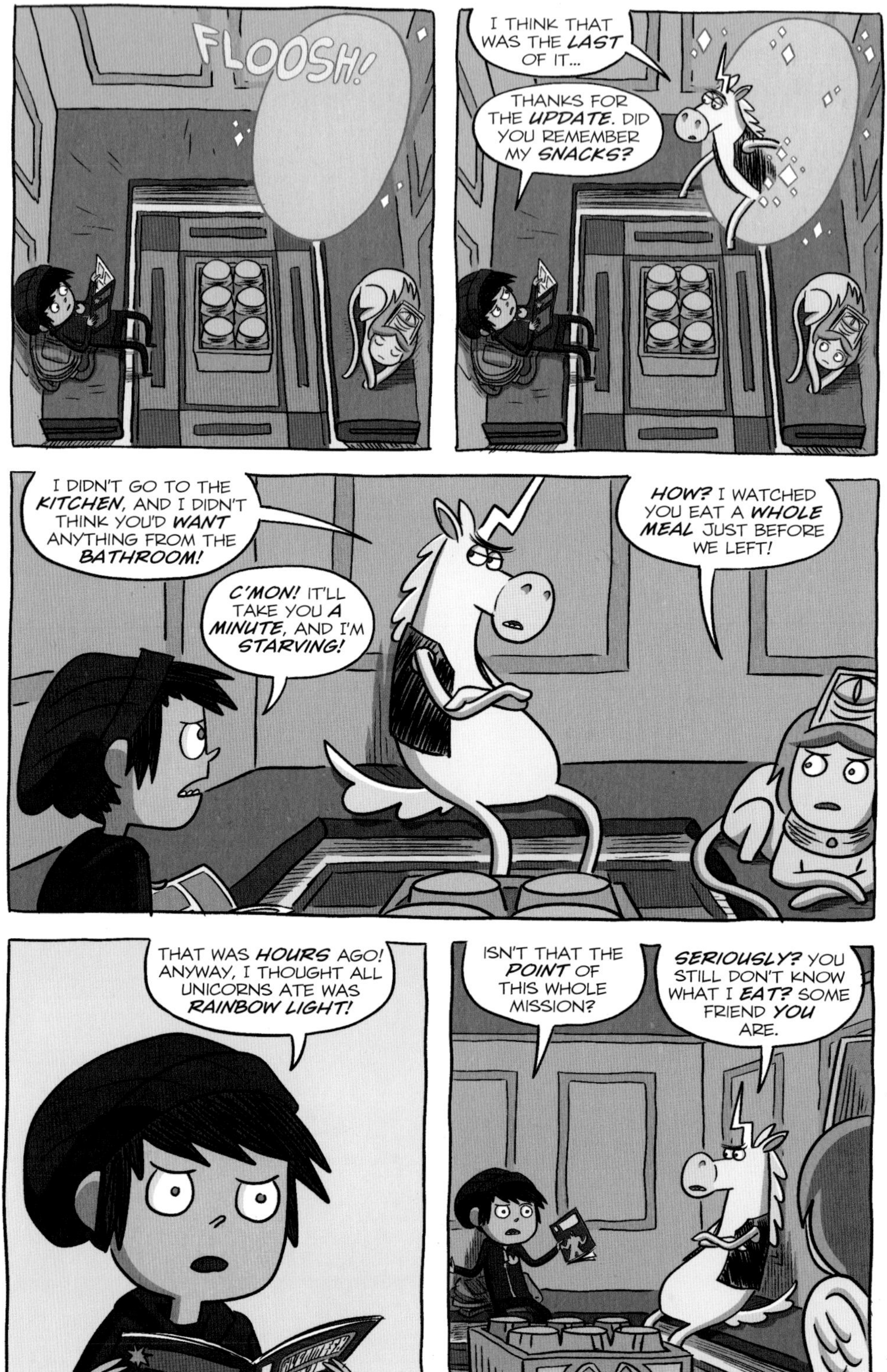
FLOOSH!
I THINK THAT WAS THE LAST OF IT...
THANKS FOR THE UPDATE. DID YOU REMEMBER MY SNACKS?
I DIDN'T GO TO THE KITCHEN, AND I DIDN'T THINK YOU'D WANT ANYTHING FROM THE BATHROOM!
C'MON! IT'LL TAKE YOU A MINUTE, AND I'M STARVING!
HOW? I WATCHED YOU EAT A WHOLE MEAL JUST BEFORE WE LEFT!
THAT WAS HOURS AGO! ANYWAY, I THOUGHT ALL UNICORNS ATE WAS RAINBOW LIGHT!
ISN'T THAT THE POINT OF THIS WHOLE MISSION?
SERIOUSLY? YOU STILL DON'T KNOW WHAT I EAT? SOME FRIEND YOU ARE.

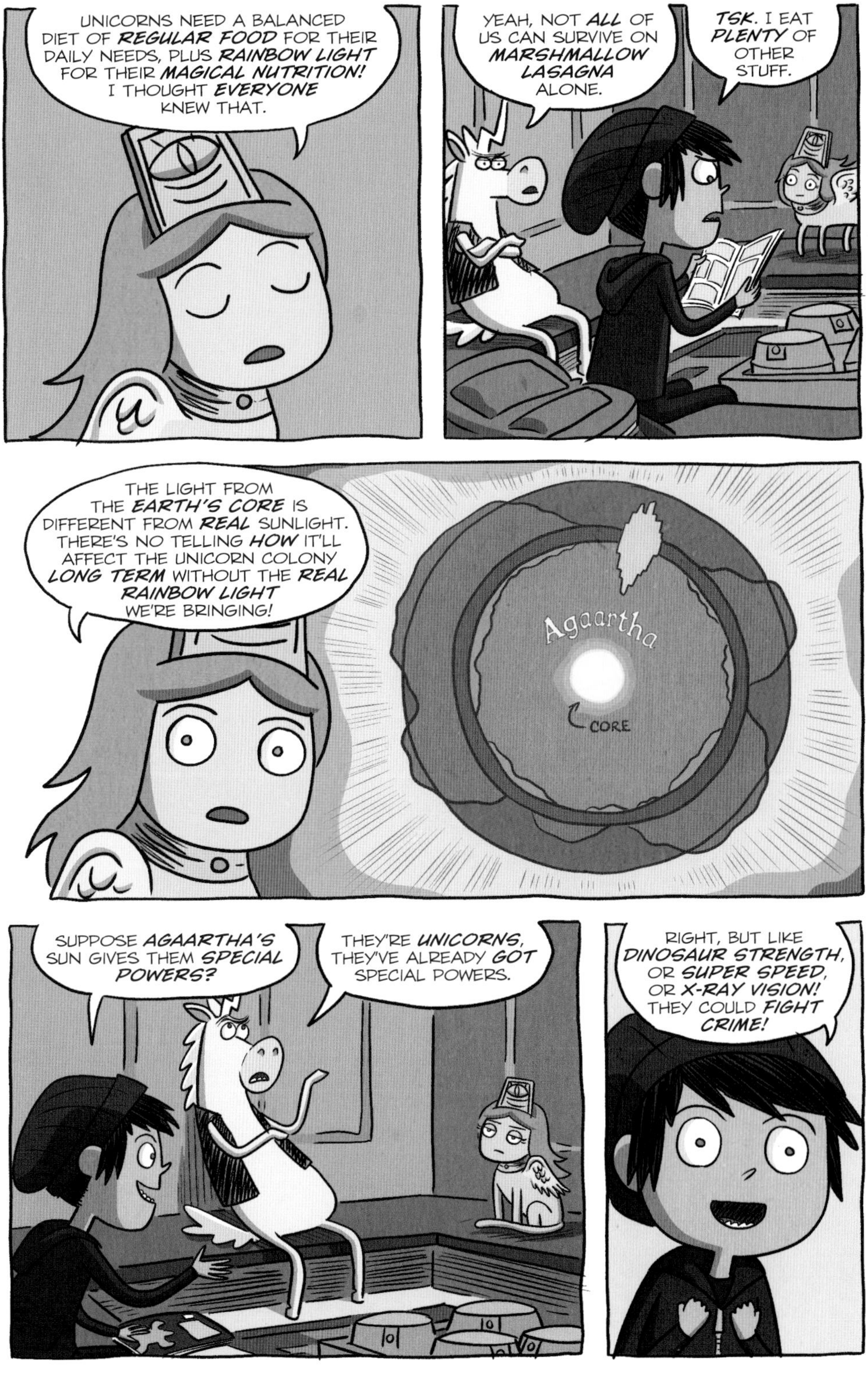
UNICORNS NEED A BALANCED DIET OF REGULAR FOOD FOR THEIR DAILY NEEDS, PLUS RAINBOW LIGHT FOR THEIR MAGICAL NUTRITION! I THOUGHT EVERYONE KNEW THAT.
YEAH, NOT ALL OF US CAN SURVIVE ON MARSHMALLOW LASAGNA ALONE.
TSK. I EAT PLENTY OF OTHER STUFF.
THE LIGHT FROM THE EARTH'S CORE IS DIFFERENT FROM REAL SUNLIGHT. THERE'S NO TELLING HOW IT'LL AFFECT THE UNICORN COLONY LONG TERM WITHOUT THE REAL RAINBOW LIGHT WE'RE BRINGING!
Agaartha
CORE
SUPPOSE AGAARTHA'S SUN GIVES THEM SPECIAL POWERS?
THEY'RE UNICORNS, THEY'VE ALREADY GOT SPECIAL POWERS.
RIGHT, BUT LIKE DINOSAUR STRENGTH, OR SUPER SPEED, OR X-RAY VISION! THEY COULD FIGHT CRIME!

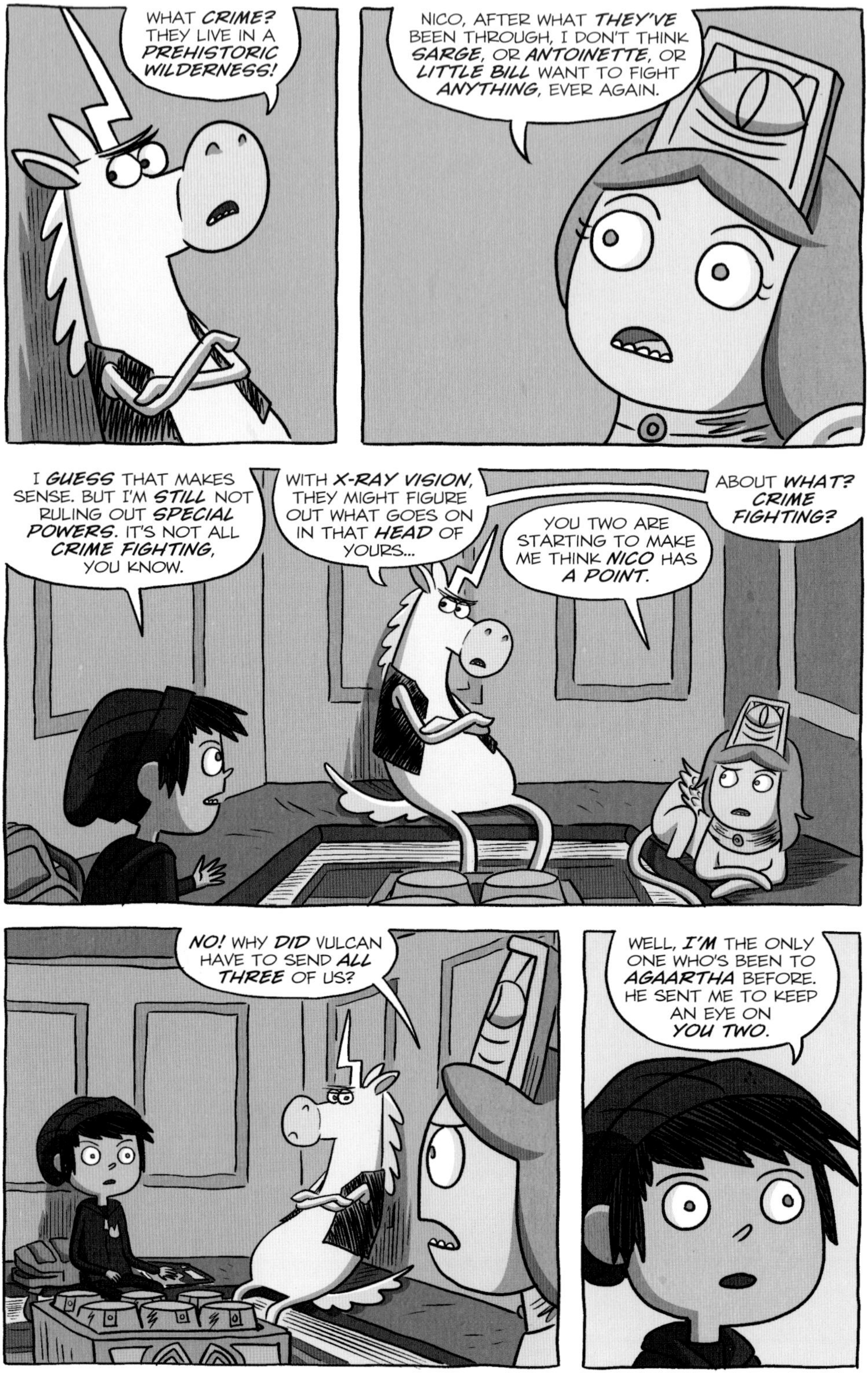
WHAT CRIME? THEY LIVE IN A PREHISTORIC WILDERNESS!
NICO, AFTER WHAT THEY'VE BEEN THROUGH, I DON'T THINK SARGE, OR ANTOINETTE, OR LITTLE BILL WANT TO FIGHT ANYTHING, EVER AGAIN.
I GUESS THAT MAKES SENSE. BUT I'M STILL NOT RULING OUT SPECIAL POWERS. IT'S NOT ALL CRIME FIGHTING, YOU KNOW.
WITH X-RAY VISION, THEY MIGHT FIGURE OUT WHAT GOES ON IN THAT HEAD OF YOURS...
ABOUT WHAT? CRIME FIGHTING?
YOU TWO ARE STARTING TO MAKE ME THINK NICO HAS A POINT.
NO! WHY DID VULCAN HAVE TO SEND ALL THREE OF US?
WELL, I'M THE ONLY ONE WHO'S BEEN TO AGAARTHA BEFORE. HE SENT ME TO KEEP AN EYE ON YOU TWO.

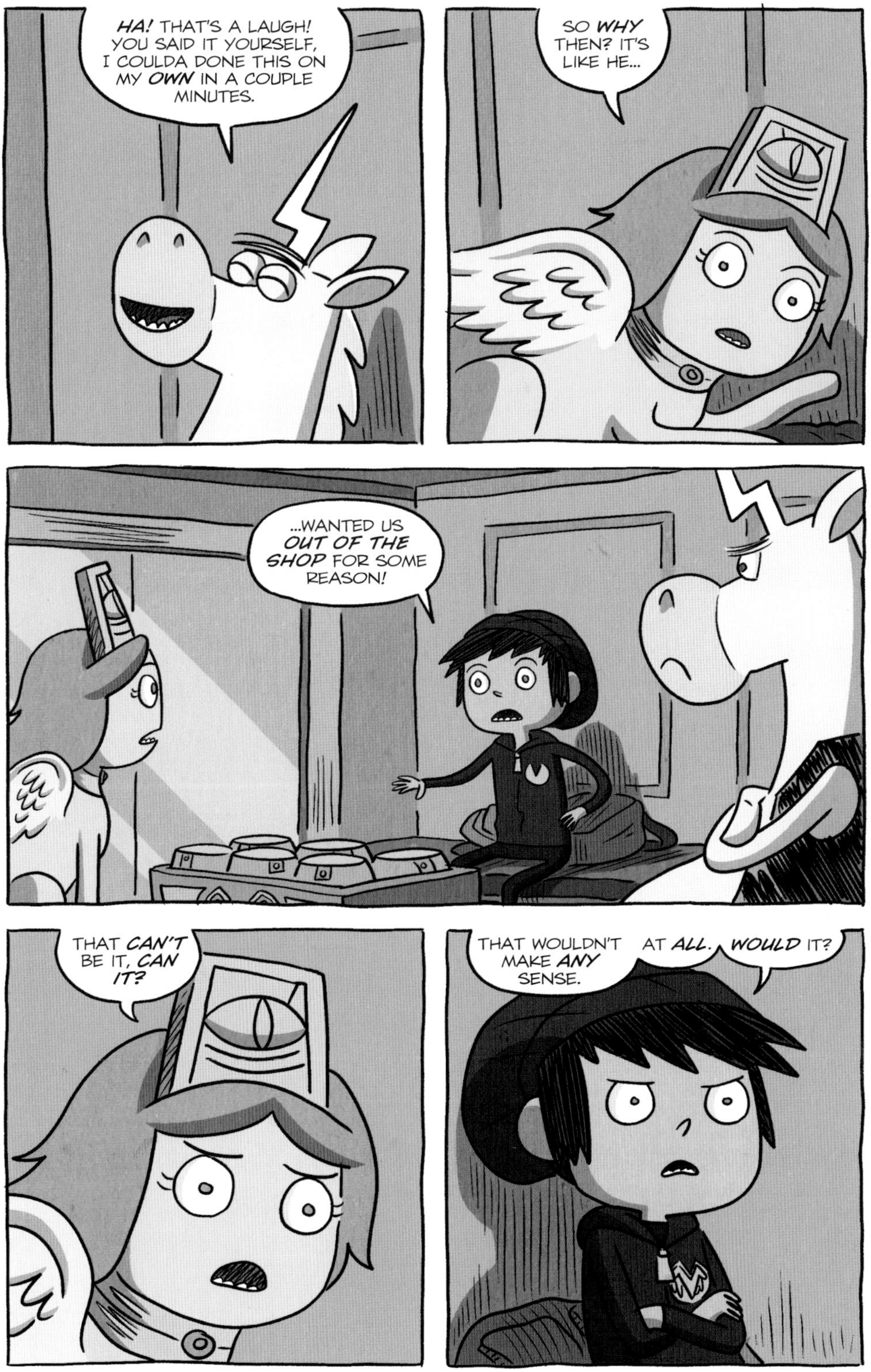
HA! THAT'S A LAUGH! YOU SAID IT YOURSELF, I COULDA DONE THIS ON MY OWN IN A COUPLE MINUTES.
SO WHY THEN? IT'S LIKE HE...
...WANTED US OUT OF THE SHOP FOR SOME REASON!
THAT CAN'T BE IT, CAN IT?
THAT WOULDN'T MAKE ANY SENSE.
AT ALL.
WOULD IT?

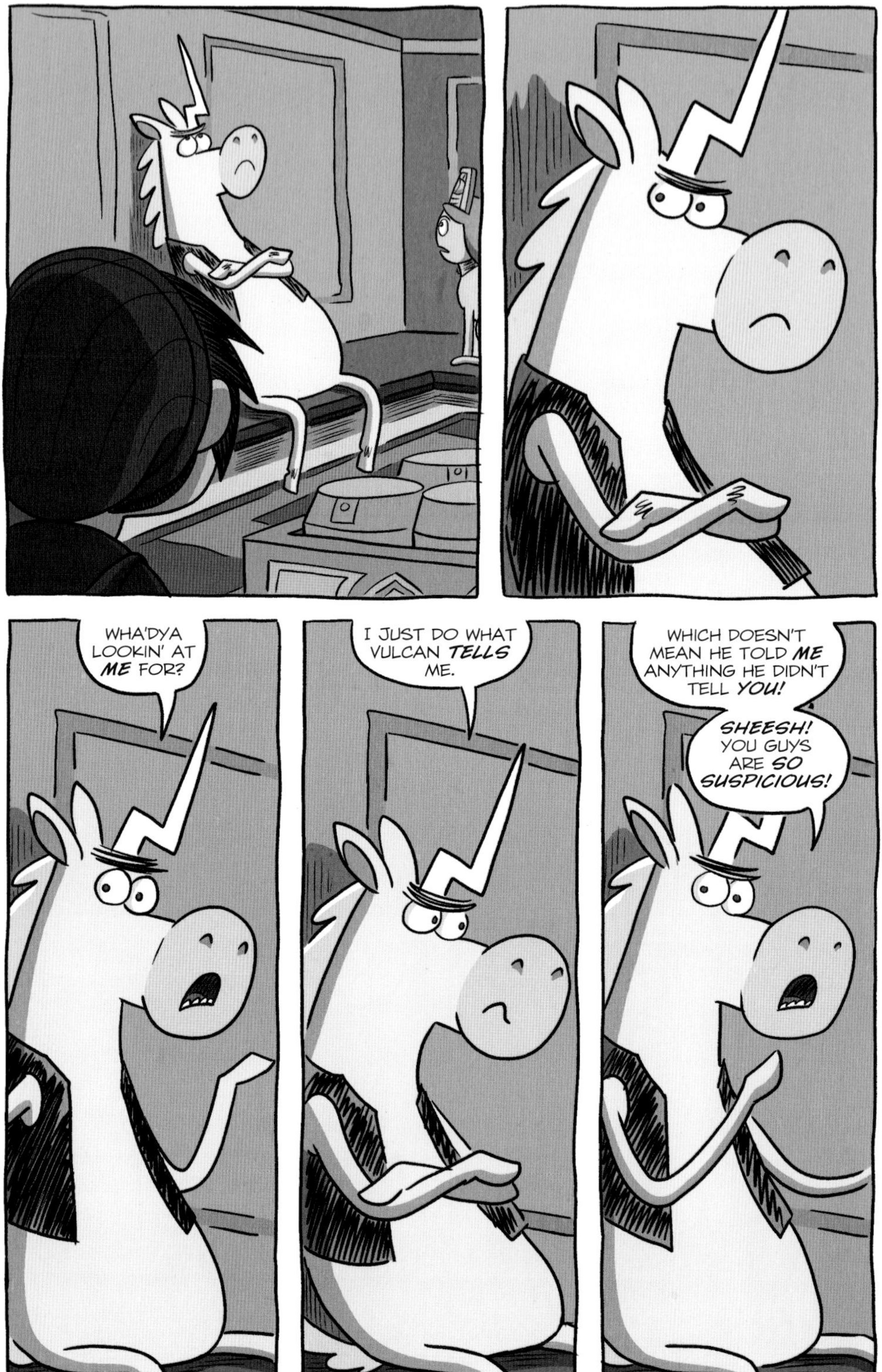
WHA'DYA LOOKIN' AT ME FOR?
I JUST DO WHAT VULCAN TELLS ME.
WHICH DOESN'T MEAN HE TOLD ME ANYTHING HE DIDN'T TELL YOU!
SHEESH! YOU GUYS ARE SO SUSPICIOUS!

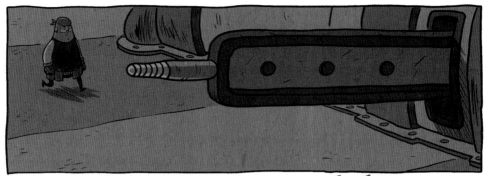

KLAANG!

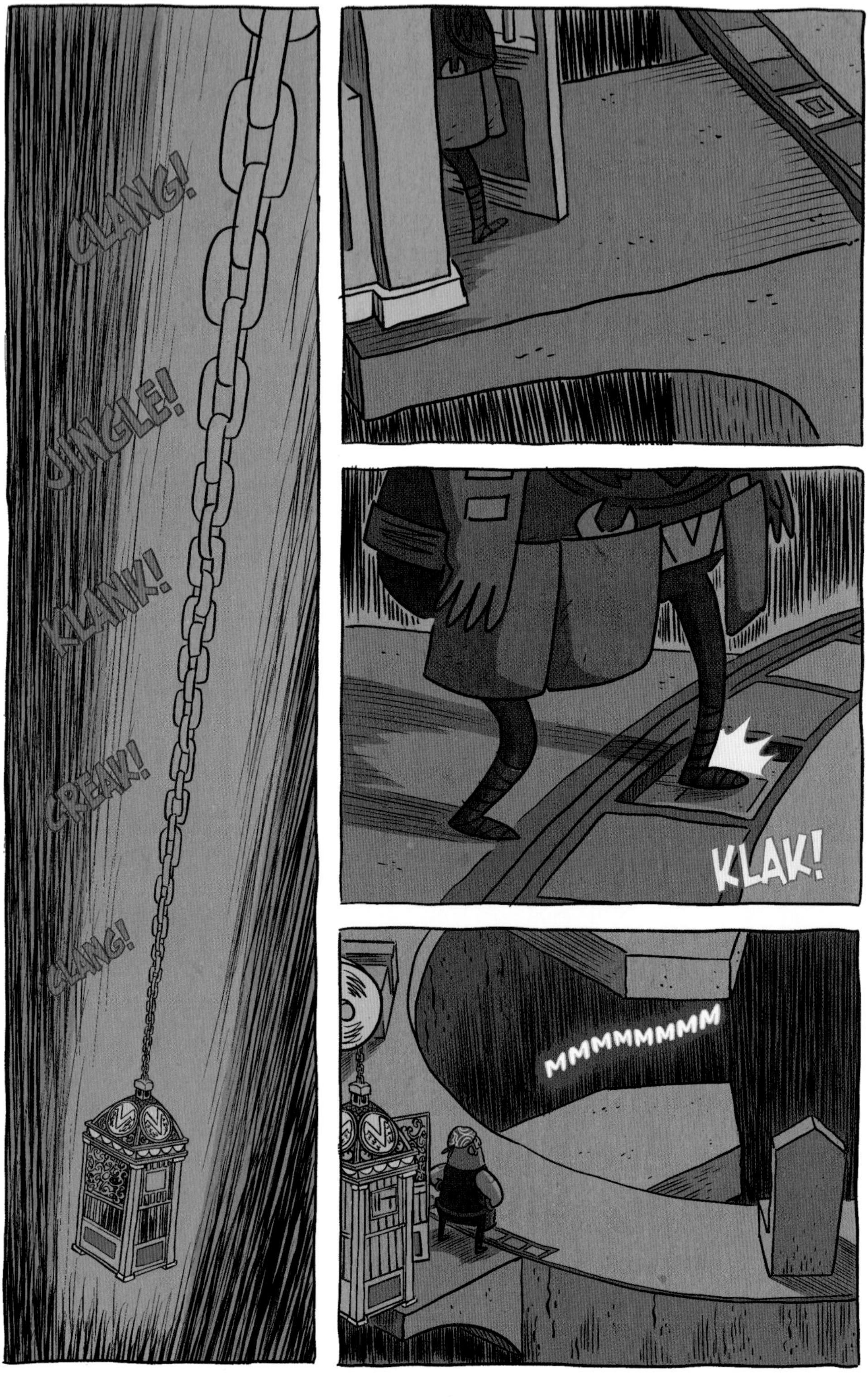
CLANG!
JINGLE!
KLANK!
CREAK!
CLANG!
KLAK!
MMMMMMMM

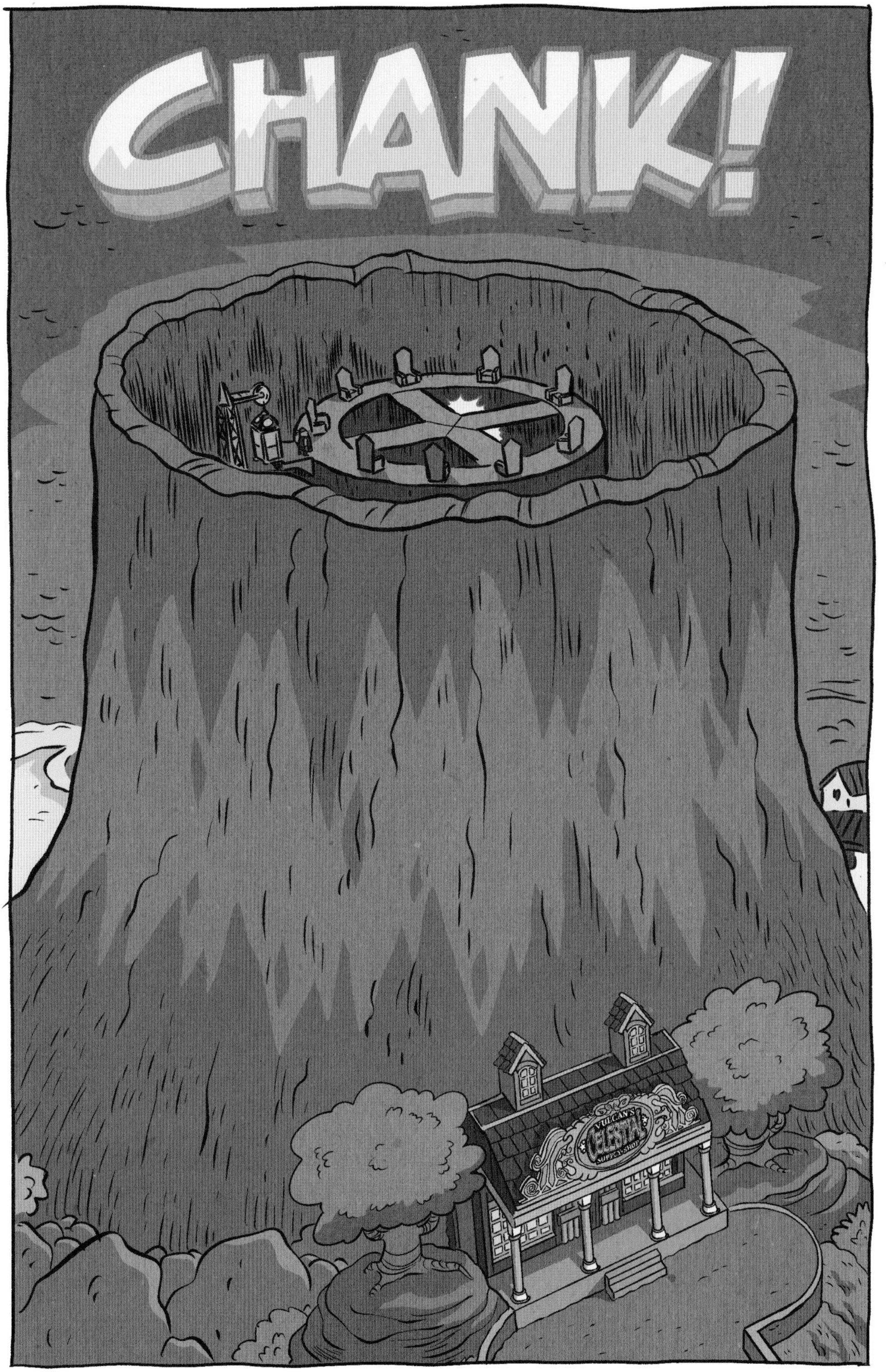
CHANK!
VULCAN'S
CELESTIAL
SUPPLY SHOP

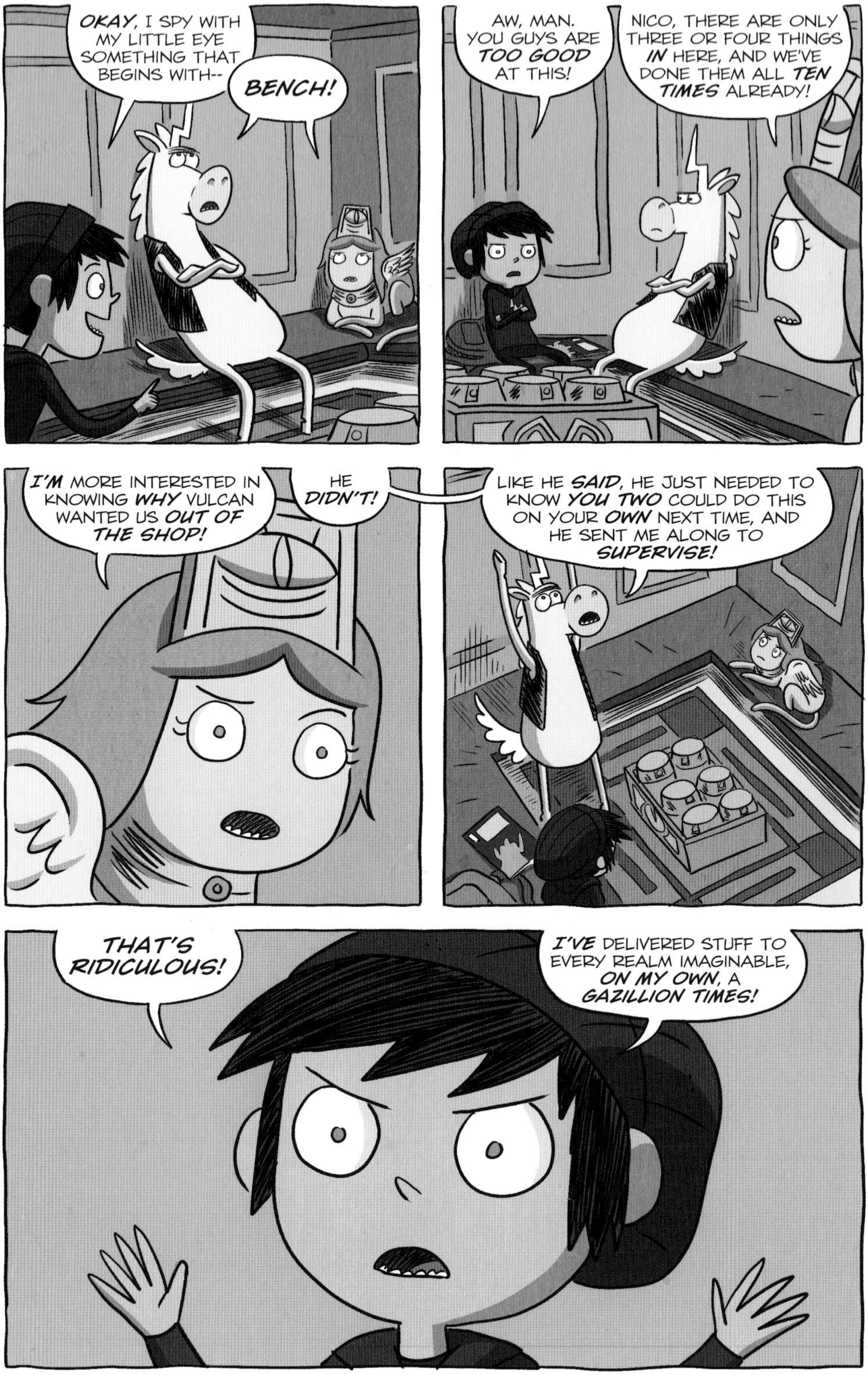
OKAY, I SPY WITH MY LITTLE EYE SOMETHING THAT BEGINS WITH--
BENCH!
AW, MAN. YOU GUYS ARE TOO GOOD AT THIS!
NICO, THERE ARE ONLY THREE OR FOUR THINGS IN HERE, AND WE'VE DONE THEM ALL TEN TIMES ALREADY!
I'M MORE INTERESTED IN KNOWING WHY VULCAN WANTED US OUT OF THE SHOP!
HE DIDN'T!
LIKE HE SAID, HE JUST NEEDED TO KNOW YOU TWO COULD DO THIS ON YOUR OWN NEXT TIME, AND HE SENT ME ALONG TO SUPERVISE!
THAT'S RIDICULOUS!
I'VE DELIVERED STUFF TO EVERY REALM IMAGINABLE, ON MY OWN, A GAZILLION TIMES!

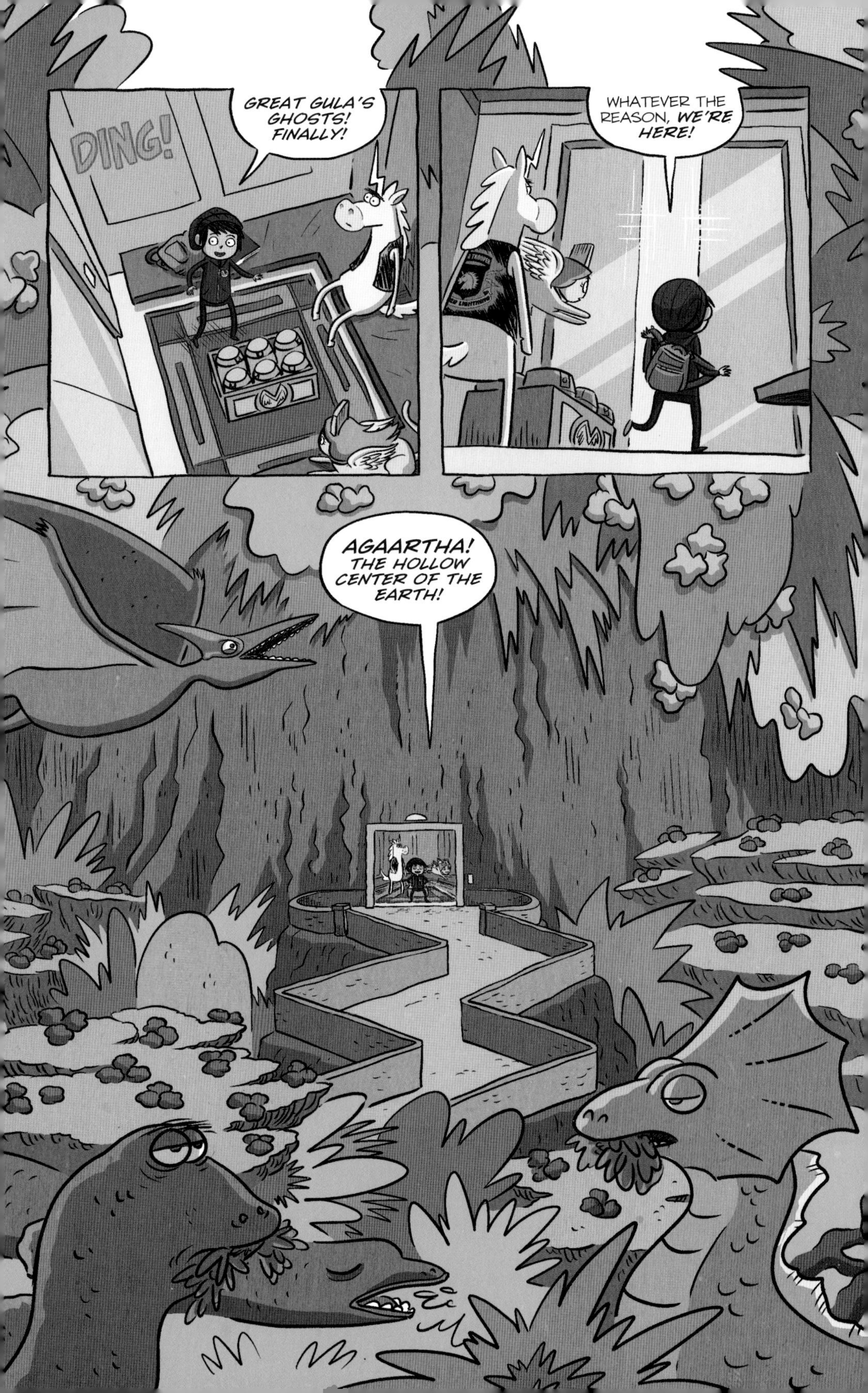
DING!
GREAT GULA'S GHOSTS! FINALLY!
WHATEVER THE REASON, WE'RE HERE!
AGAARTHA! THE HOLLOW CENTER OF THE EARTH!

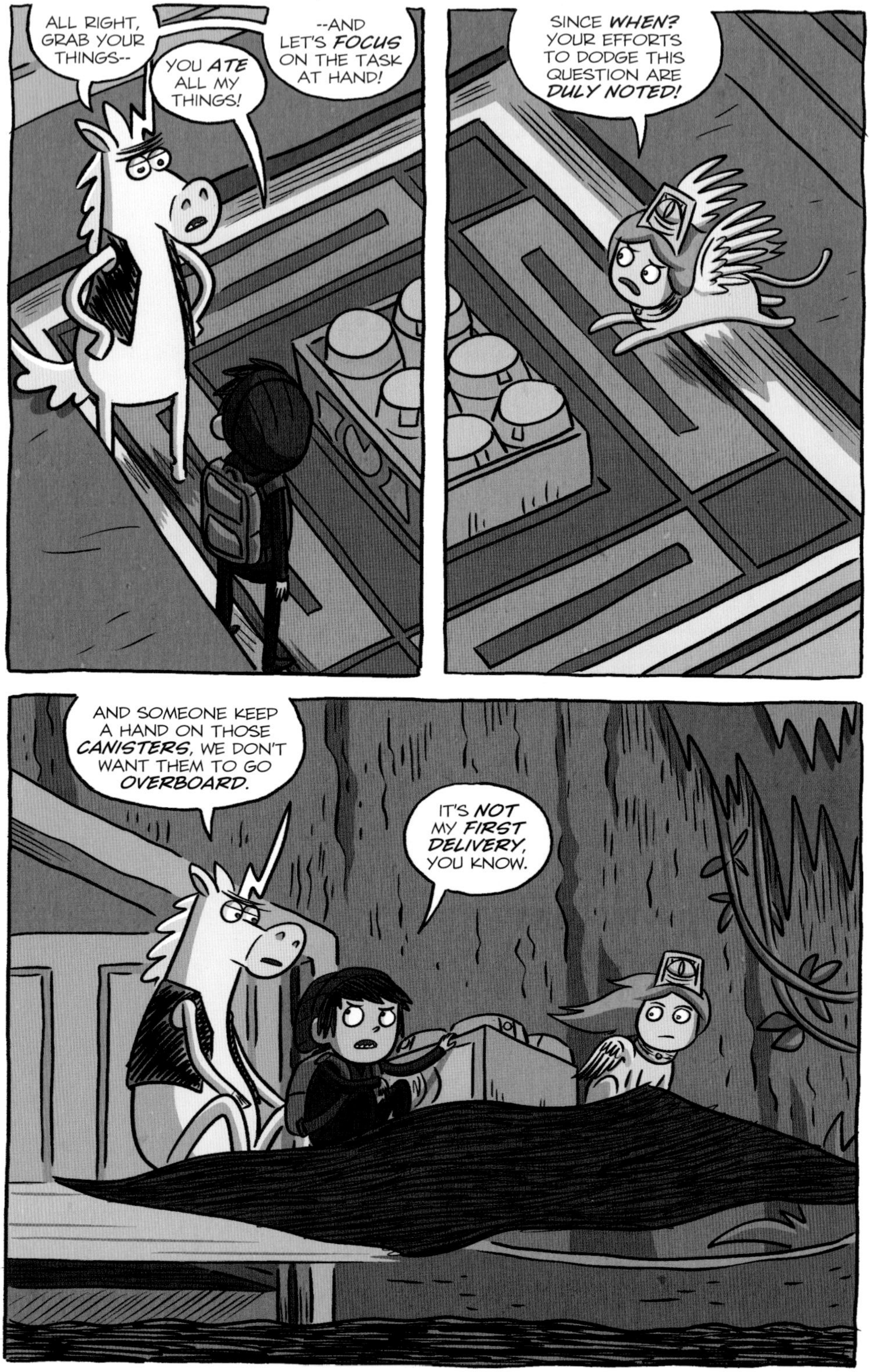
ALL RIGHT, GRAB YOUR THINGS--
YOU ATE ALL MY THINGS!
--AND LET'S FOCUS ON THE TASK AT HAND!
SINCE WHEN? YOUR EFFORTS TO DODGE THIS QUESTION ARE DULY NOTED!
AND SOMEONE KEEP A HAND ON THOSE CANISTERS, WE DON'T WANT THEM TO GO OVERBOARD.
IT'S NOT MY FIRST DELIVERY, YOU KNOW.

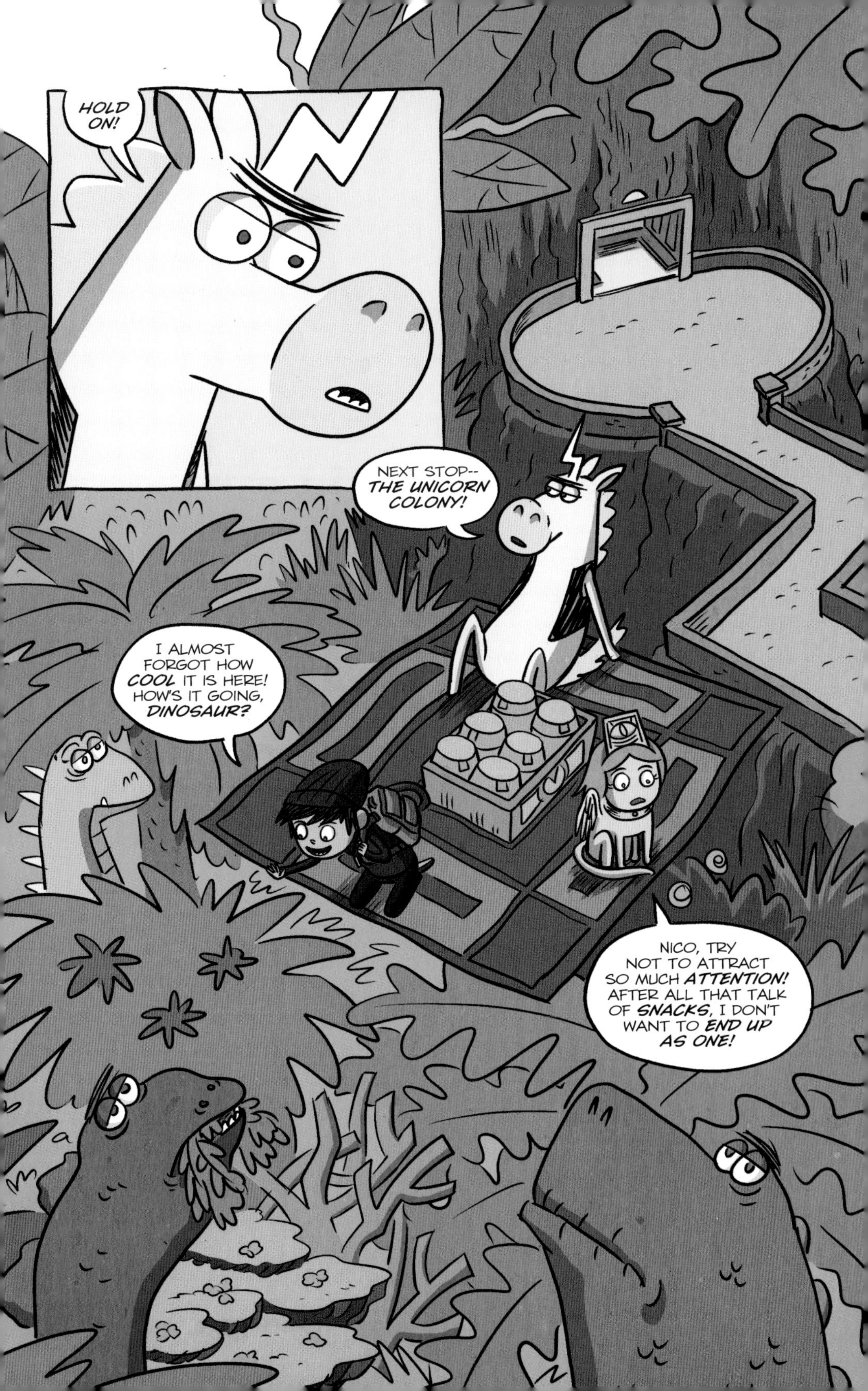
HOLD ON!
NEXT STOP-- THE UNICORN COLONY!
I ALMOST FORGOT HOW COOL IT IS HERE! HOW'S IT GOING, DINOSAUR?
NICO, TRY NOT TO ATTRACT SO MUCH ATTENTION! AFTER ALL THAT TALK OF SNACKS, I DON'T WANT TO END UP AS ONE!

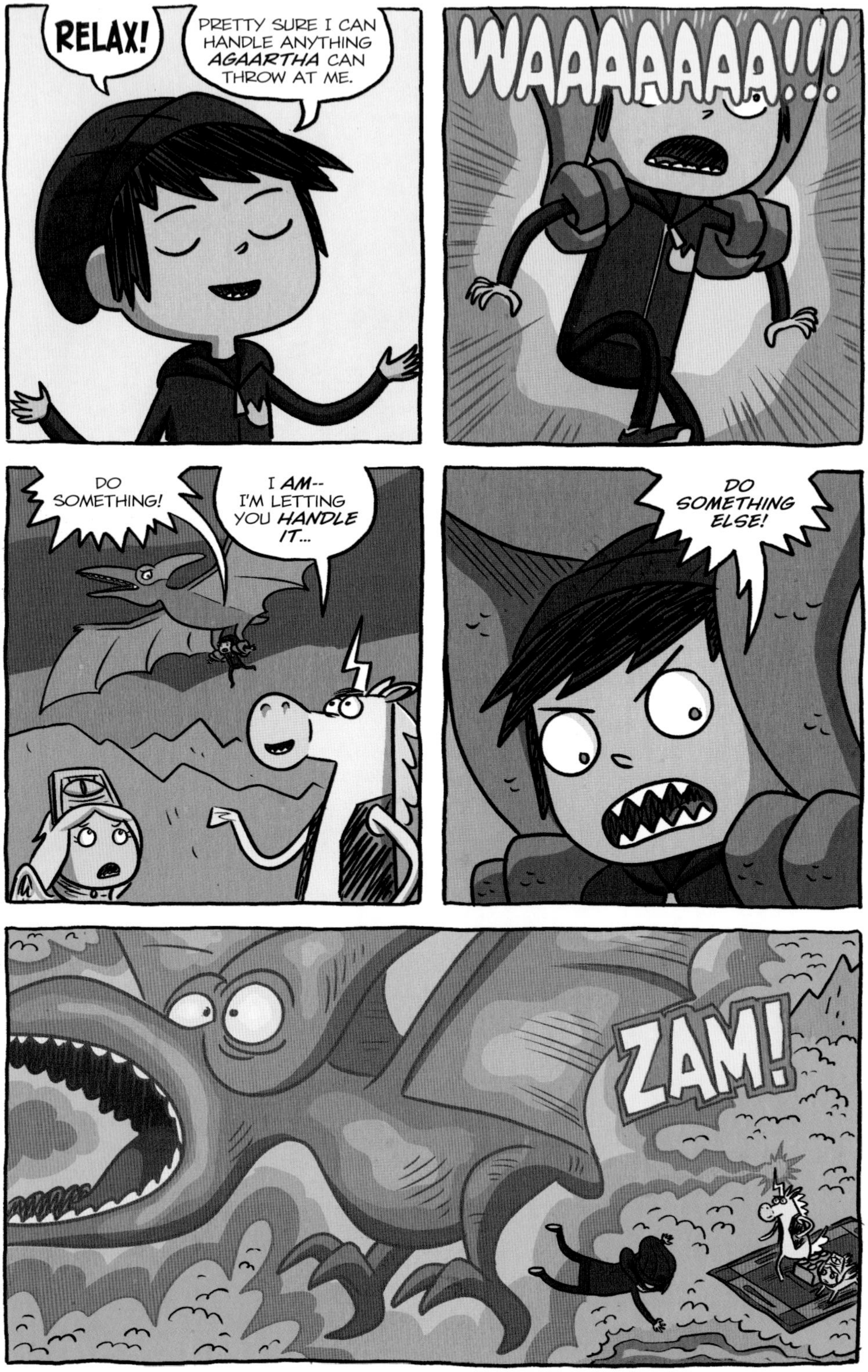
RELAX!
PRETTY SURE I CAN HANDLE ANYTHING *AGAARTHA* CAN THROW AT ME.
WAAAAAAA!!!
DO SOMETHING!
I *AM*-- I'M LETTING YOU *HANDLE IT*...
DO SOMETHING ELSE!
ZAM!

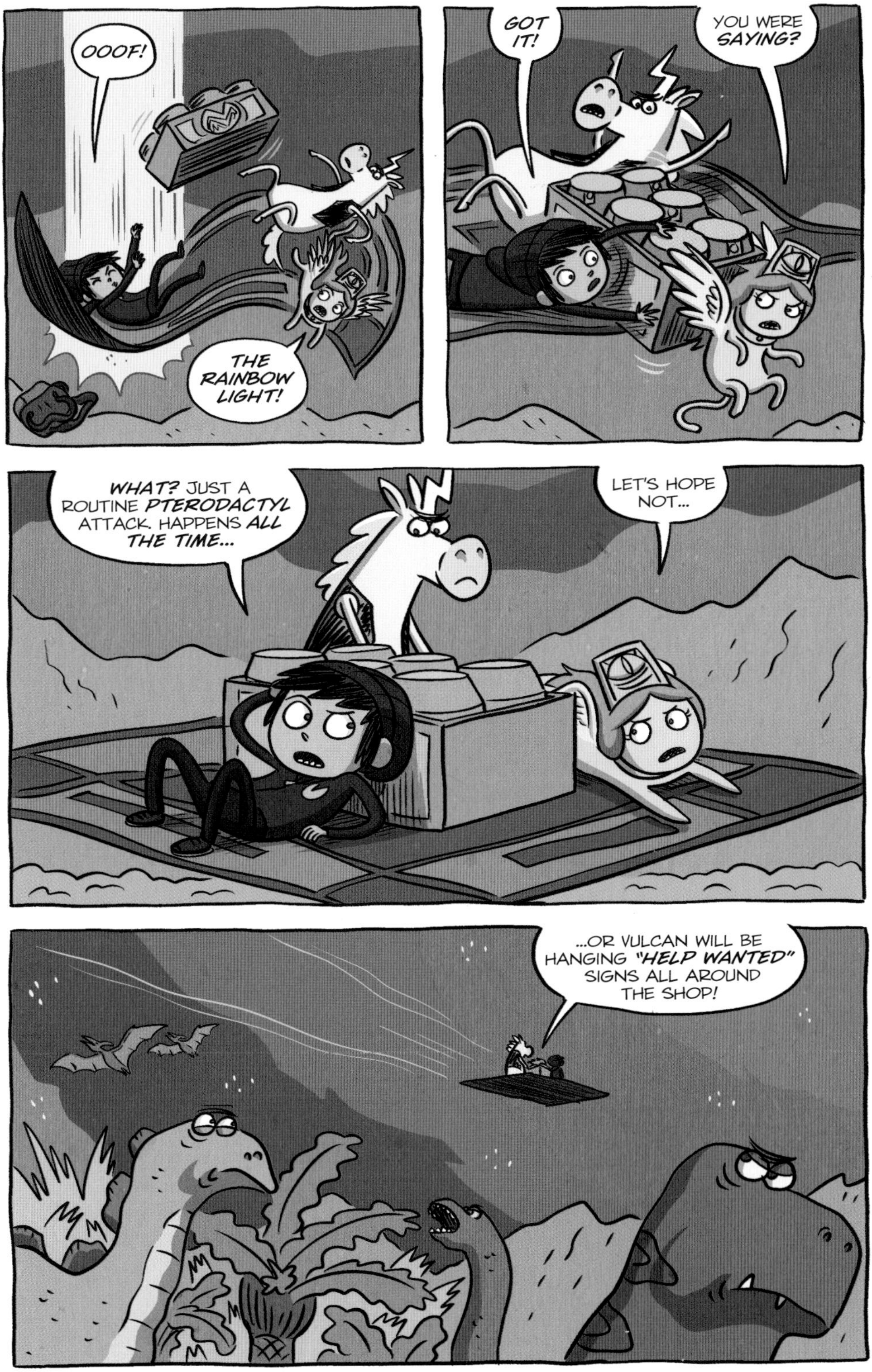
OOOF!
THE RAINBOW LIGHT!
GOT IT!
YOU WERE SAYING?
WHAT? JUST A ROUTINE PTERODACTYL ATTACK. HAPPENS ALL THE TIME...
LET'S HOPE NOT...
...OR VULCAN WILL BE HANGING "HELP WANTED" SIGNS ALL AROUND THE SHOP!

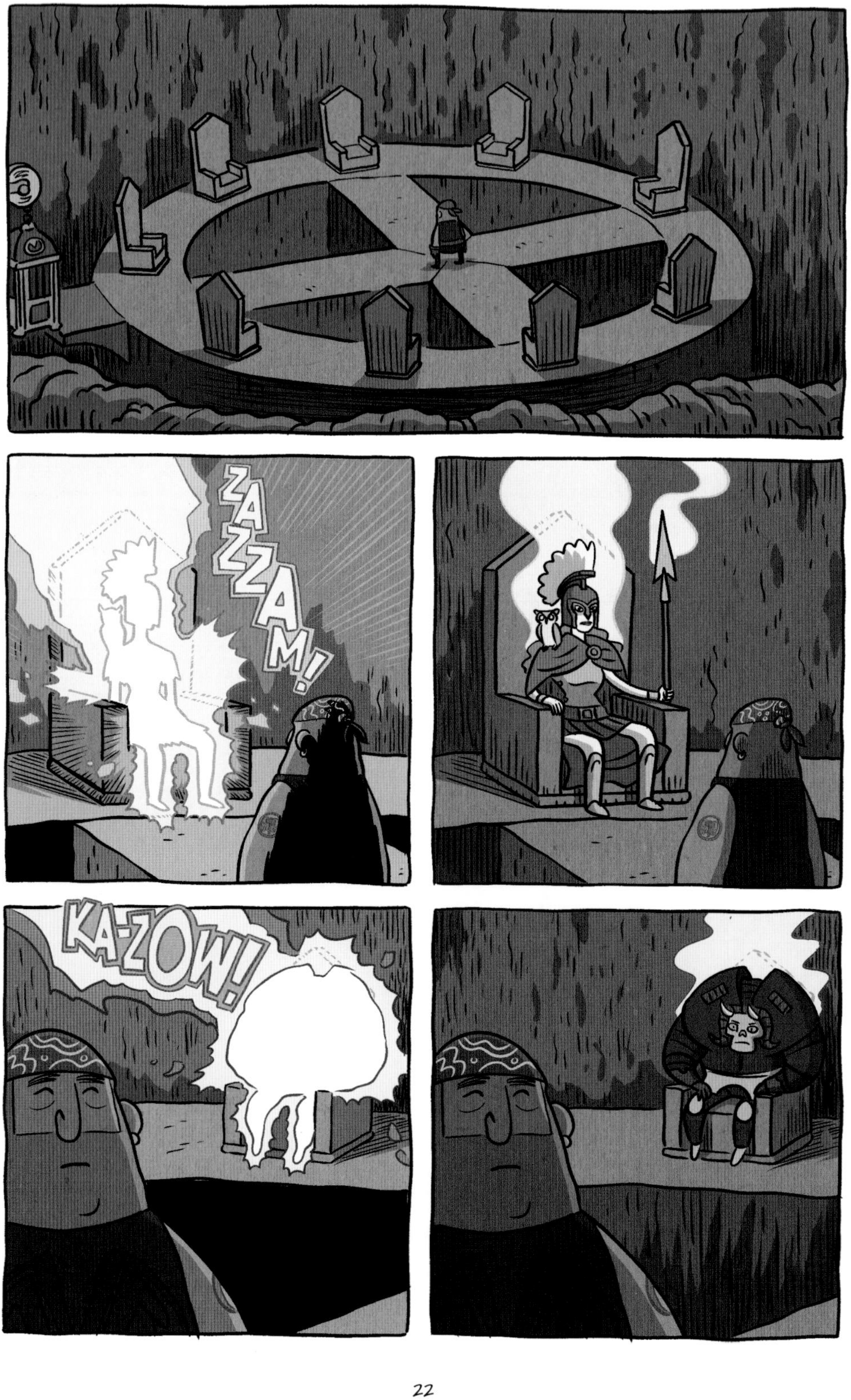
ZAZZAM!
KA-ZOW!

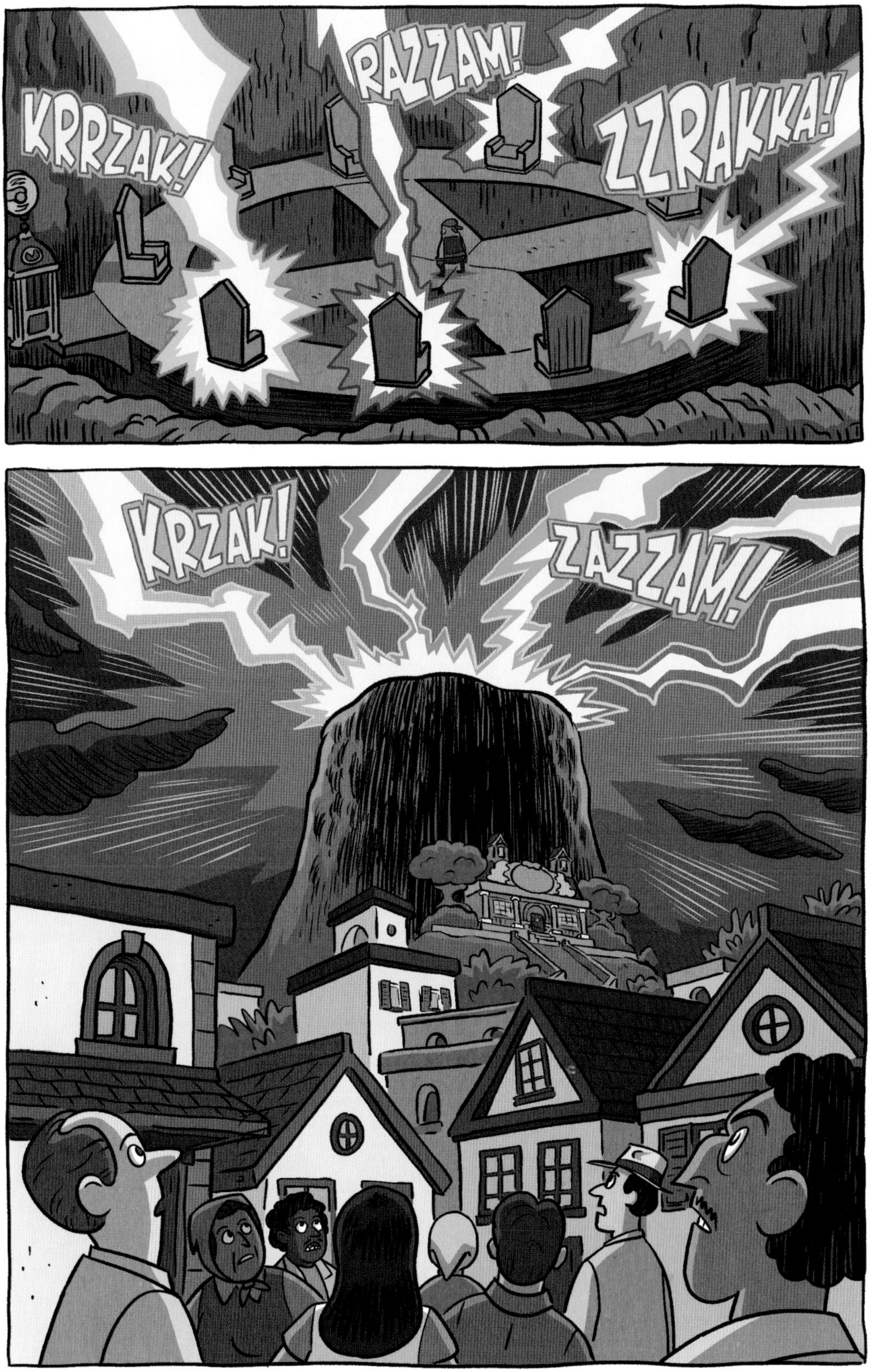
KRRZAK!
RAZZAM!
ZZRAKKA!
KRZAK!
ZAZZAM!

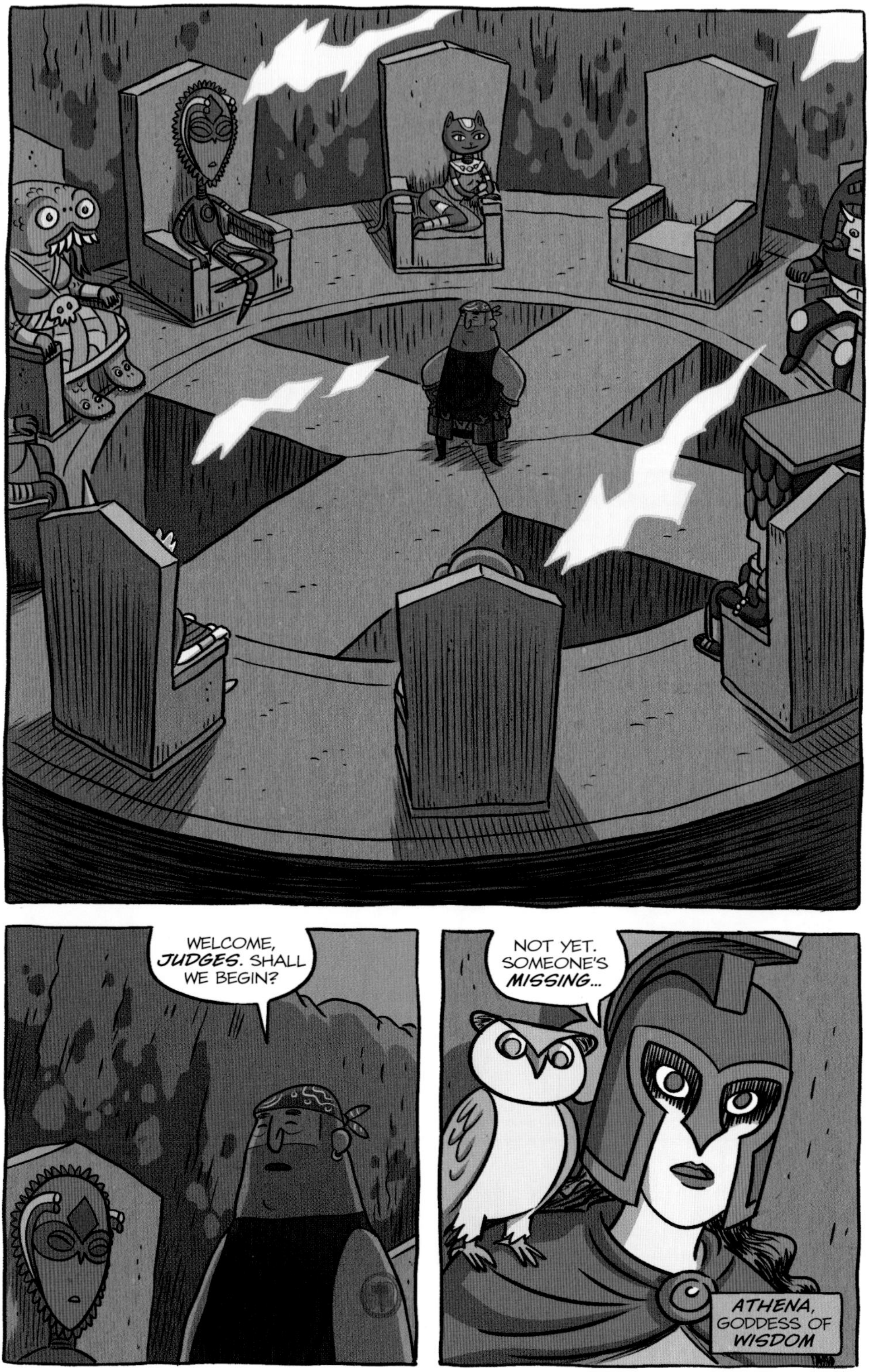
WELCOME, JUDGES. SHALL WE BEGIN?
NOT YET. SOMEONE'S MISSING...
ATHENA, GODDESS OF WISDOM

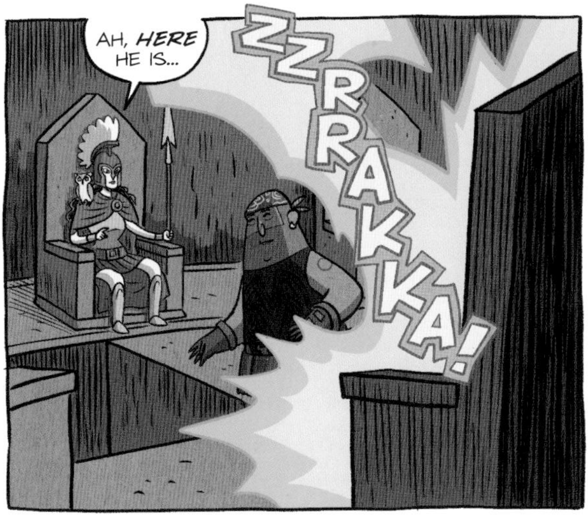
AH, HERE HE IS...
ZZRAKKA!

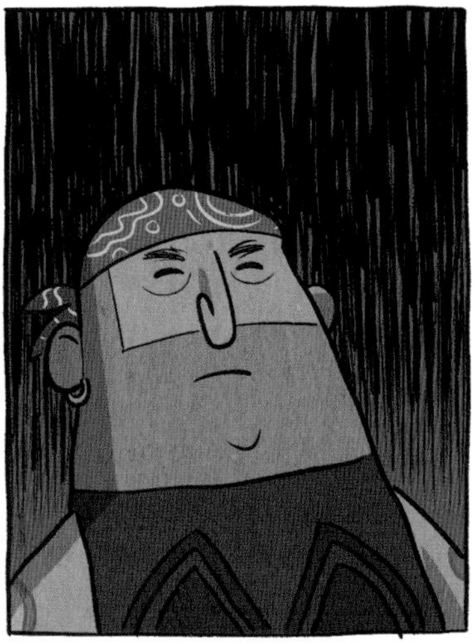

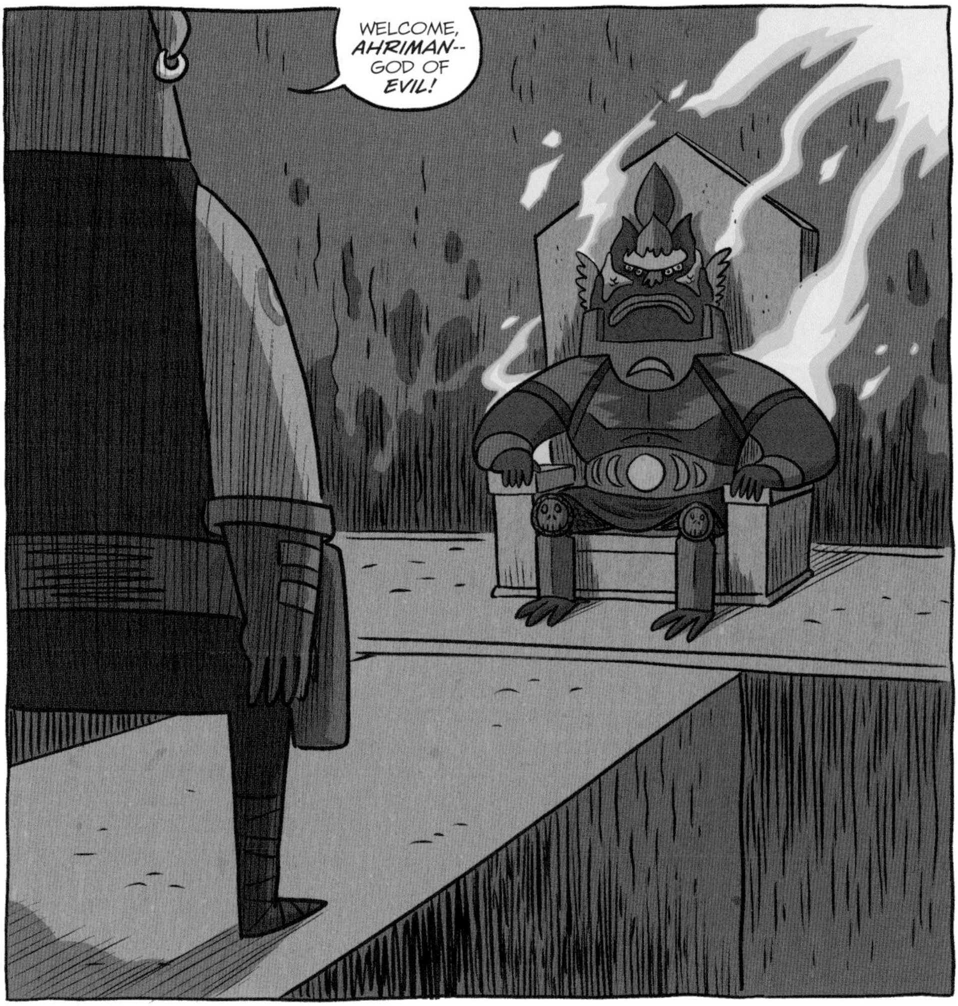
WELCOME, AHRIMAN-- GOD OF EVIL!

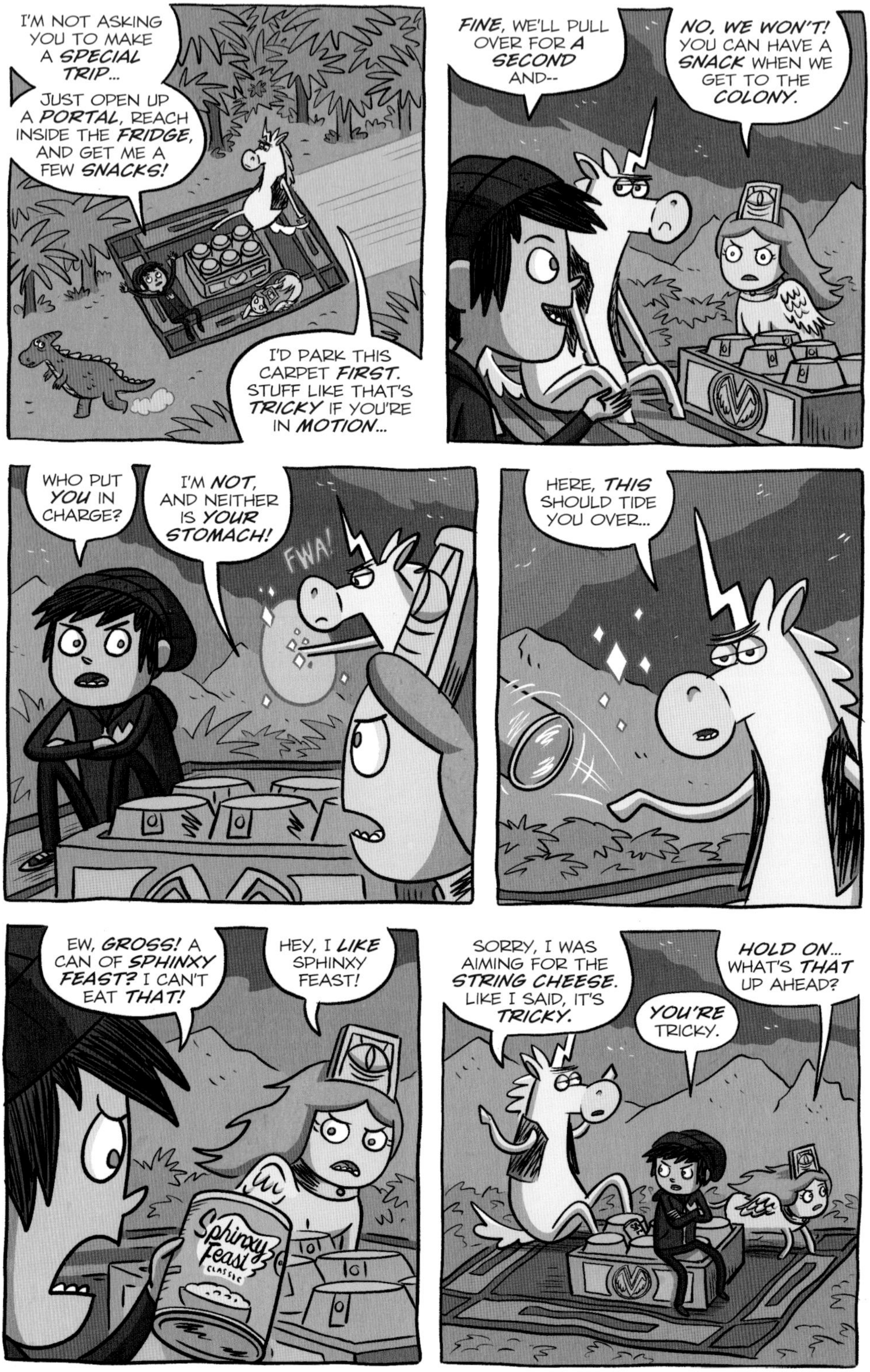
I'M NOT ASKING YOU TO MAKE A SPECIAL TRIP...
JUST OPEN UP A PORTAL, REACH INSIDE THE FRIDGE, AND GET ME A FEW SNACKS!
I'D PARK THIS CARPET FIRST. STUFF LIKE THAT'S TRICKY IF YOU'RE IN MOTION...
FINE, WE'LL PULL OVER FOR A SECOND AND--
NO, WE WON'T! YOU CAN HAVE A SNACK WHEN WE GET TO THE COLONY.
WHO PUT YOU IN CHARGE?
I'M NOT, AND NEITHER IS YOUR STOMACH!
FWA!
HERE, THIS SHOULD TIDE YOU OVER...
EW, GROSS! A CAN OF SPHINXY FEAST? I CAN'T EAT THAT!
HEY, I LIKE SPHINXY FEAST!
Sphinxy Feast
CLASSIC
SORRY, I WAS AIMING FOR THE STRING CHEESE. LIKE I SAID, IT'S TRICKY.
YOU'RE TRICKY.
HOLD ON... WHAT'S THAT UP AHEAD?

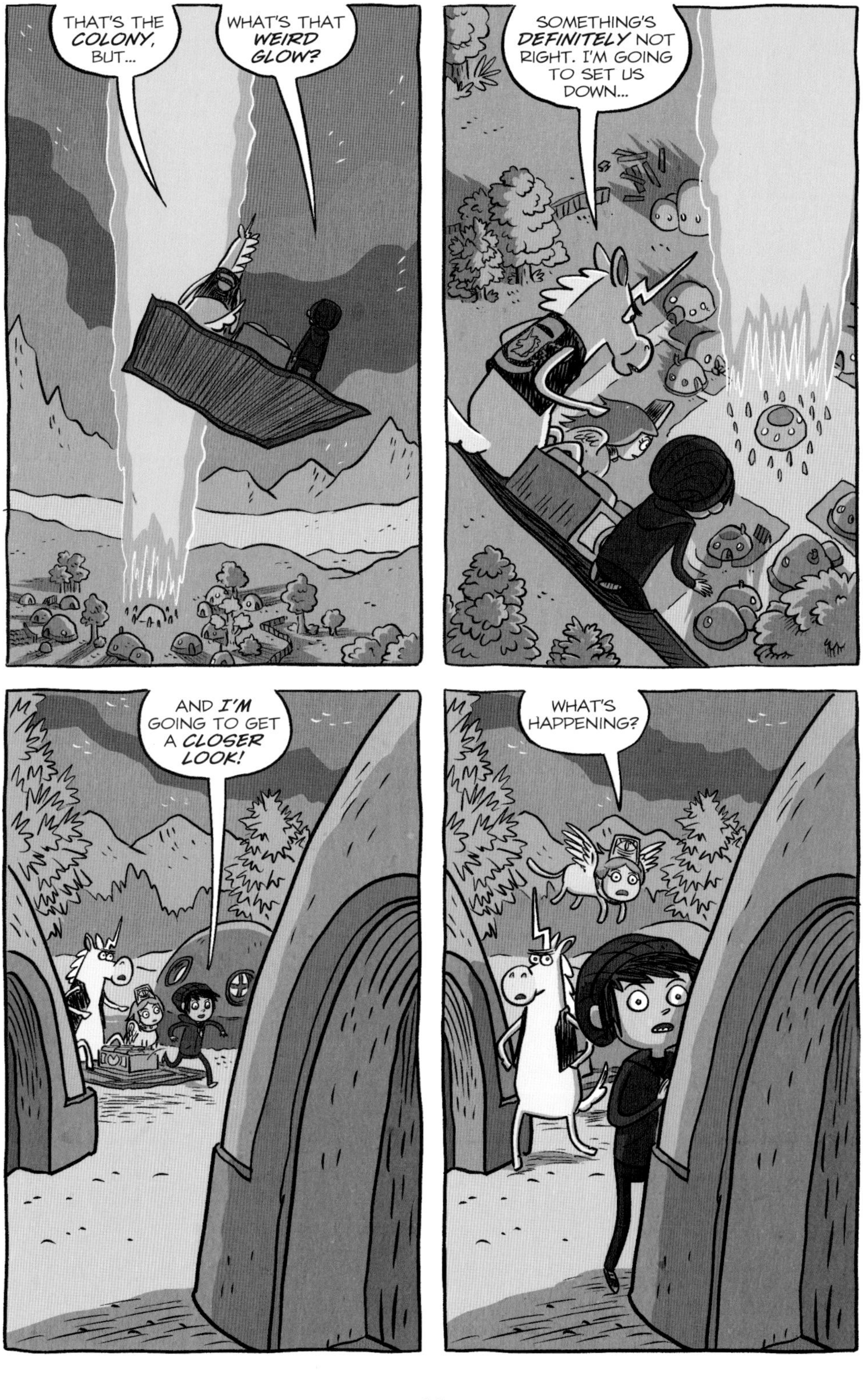
THAT'S THE **COLONY**, BUT...
WHAT'S THAT **WEIRD GLOW?**
SOMETHING'S **DEFINITELY** NOT RIGHT. I'M GOING TO SET US DOWN...
AND **I'M** GOING TO GET A **CLOSER LOOK!**
WHAT'S HAPPENING?

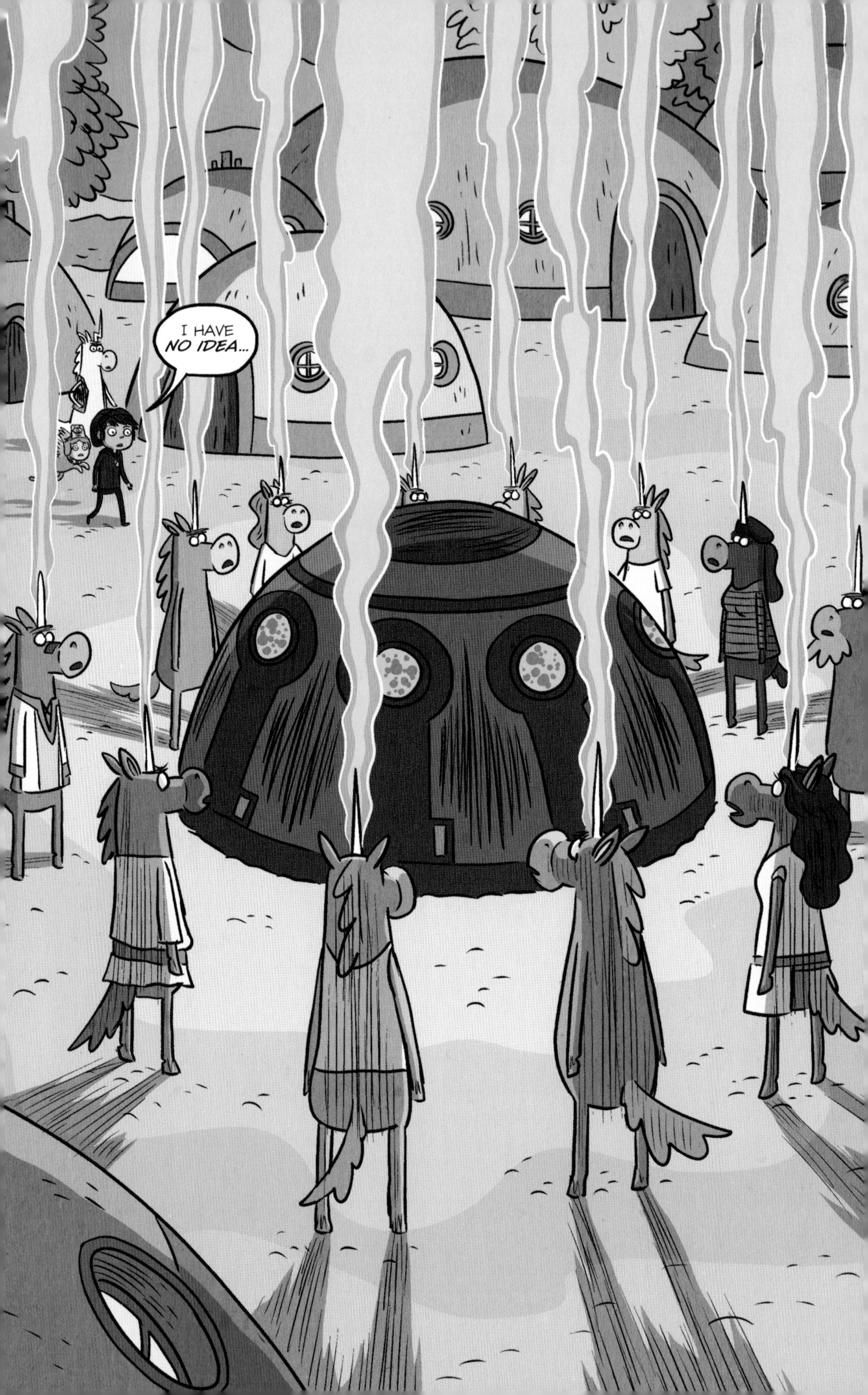
I HAVE *NO IDEA*...

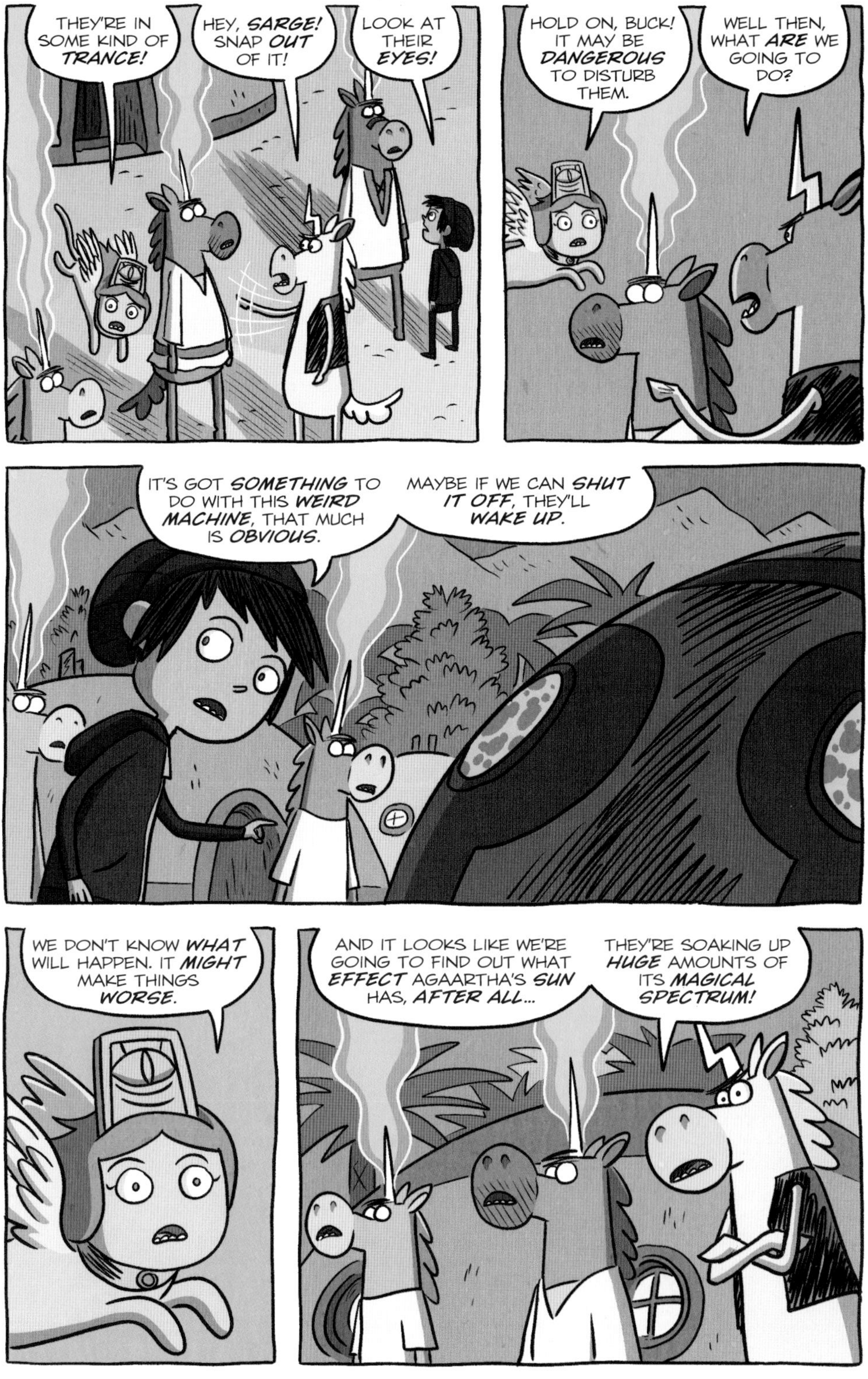
THEY'RE IN SOME KIND OF TRANCE!
HEY, SARGE! SNAP OUT OF IT!
LOOK AT THEIR EYES!
HOLD ON, BUCK! IT MAY BE DANGEROUS TO DISTURB THEM.
WELL THEN, WHAT ARE WE GOING TO DO?
IT'S GOT SOMETHING TO DO WITH THIS WEIRD MACHINE, THAT MUCH IS OBVIOUS.
MAYBE IF WE CAN SHUT IT OFF, THEY'LL WAKE UP.
WE DON'T KNOW WHAT WILL HAPPEN. IT MIGHT MAKE THINGS WORSE.
AND IT LOOKS LIKE WE'RE GOING TO FIND OUT WHAT EFFECT AGAARTHA'S SUN HAS, AFTER ALL...
THEY'RE SOAKING UP HUGE AMOUNTS OF ITS MAGICAL SPECTRUM!

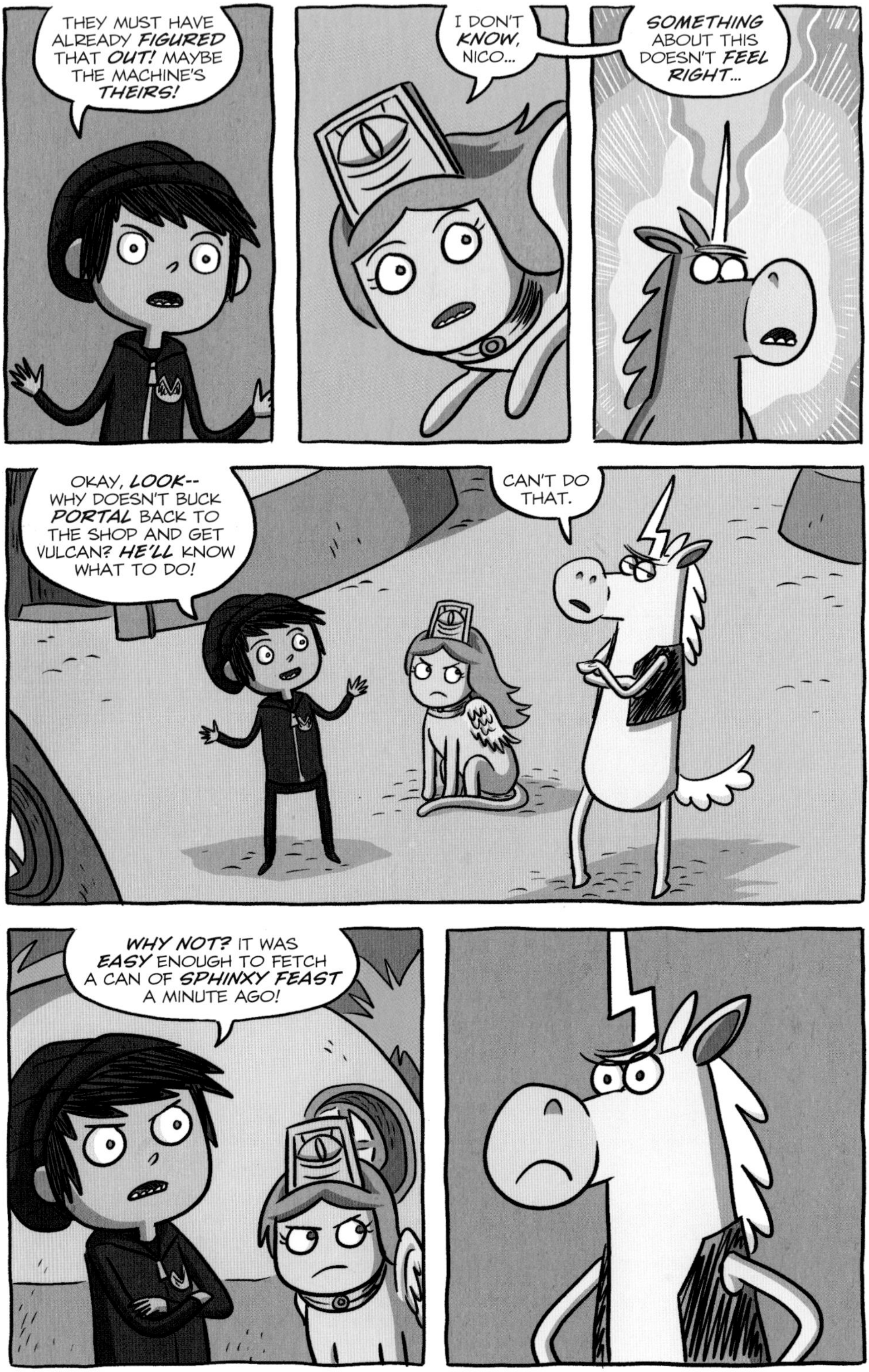
THEY MUST HAVE ALREADY FIGURED THAT OUT! MAYBE THE MACHINE'S THEIRS!
I DON'T KNOW, NICO...
SOMETHING ABOUT THIS DOESN'T FEEL RIGHT...
OKAY, LOOK-- WHY DOESN'T BUCK PORTAL BACK TO THE SHOP AND GET VULCAN? HE'LL KNOW WHAT TO DO!
CAN'T DO THAT.
WHY NOT? IT WAS EASY ENOUGH TO FETCH A CAN OF SPHINXY FEAST A MINUTE AGO!

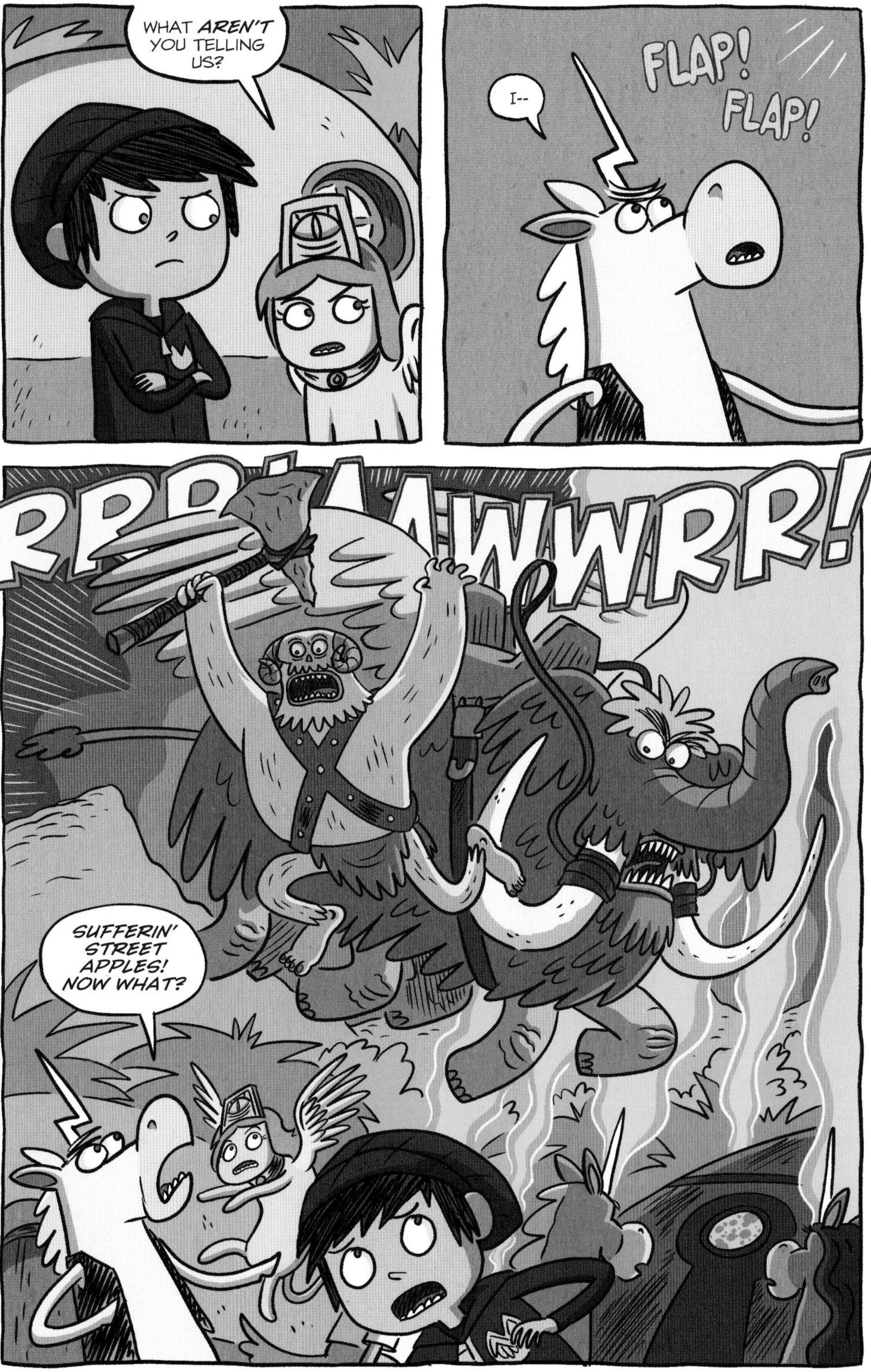
WHAT *AREN'T* YOU TELLING US?
I--
FLAP! FLAP!
RRRAAAWWRR!
SUFFERIN' STREET APPLES! NOW WHAT?

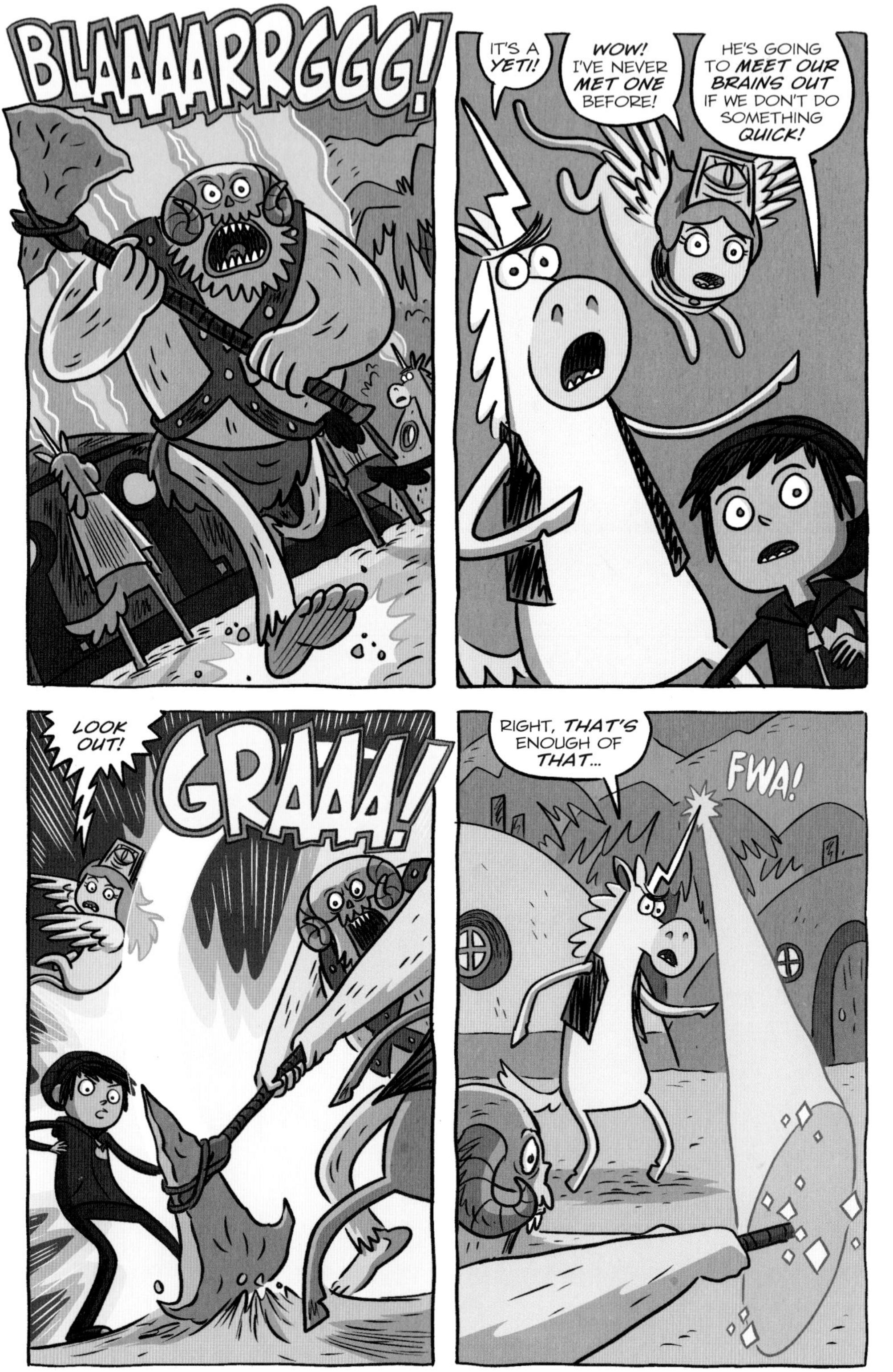
BLAAAARRGGG!
IT'S A YETI!
WOW! I'VE NEVER MET ONE BEFORE!
HE'S GOING TO MEET OUR BRAINS OUT IF WE DON'T DO SOMETHING QUICK!
LOOK OUT!
GRAAA!
RIGHT, THAT'S ENOUGH OF THAT...
FWA!

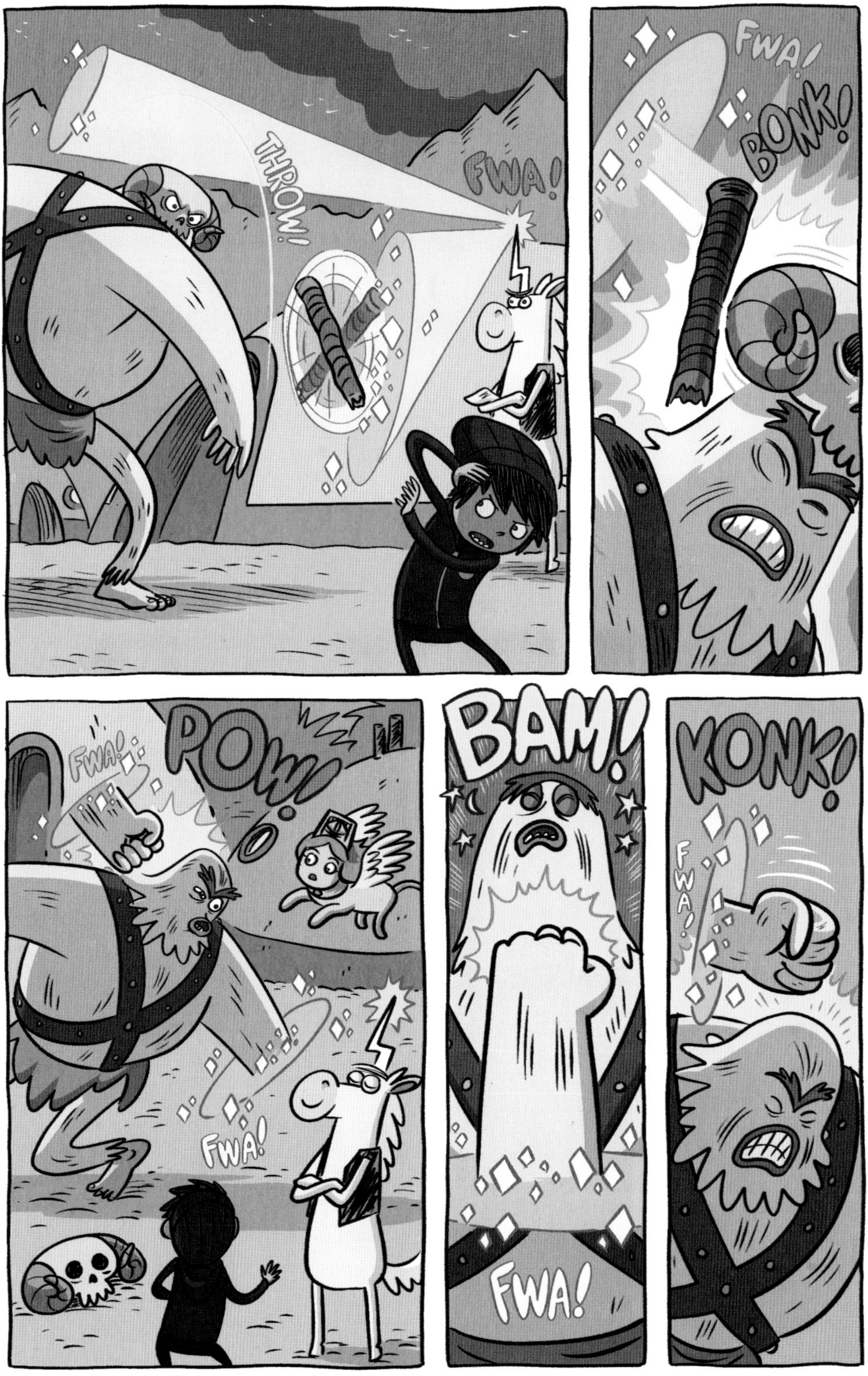
THROW!
FWA!
FWA!
BONK!
FWA!
POW!
FWA!
BAM!
FWA!
KONK!
FWA!

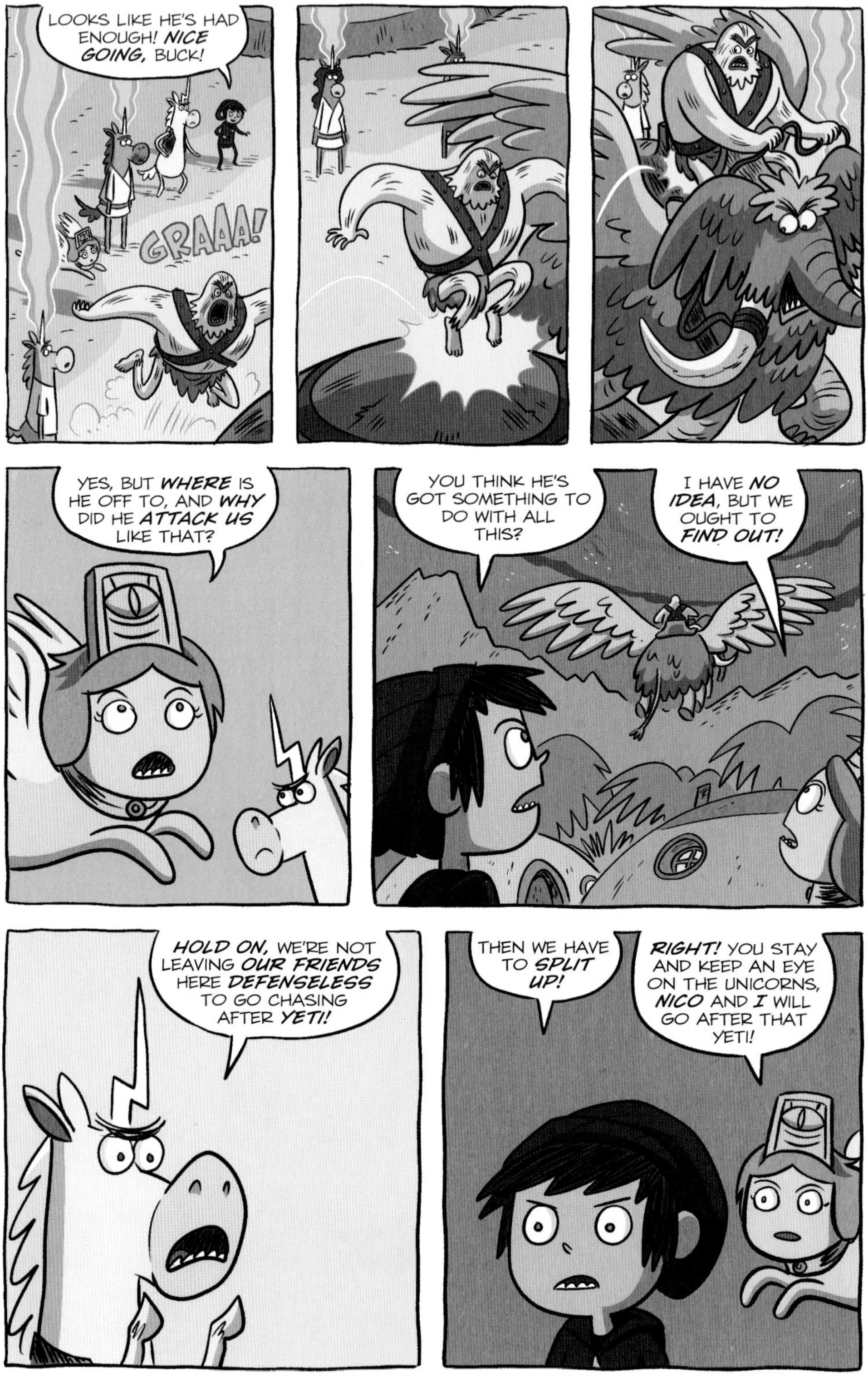
LOOKS LIKE HE'S HAD ENOUGH! NICE GOING, BUCK!
GRAAA!
YES, BUT WHERE IS HE OFF TO, AND WHY DID HE ATTACK US LIKE THAT?
YOU THINK HE'S GOT SOMETHING TO DO WITH ALL THIS?
I HAVE NO IDEA, BUT WE OUGHT TO FIND OUT!
HOLD ON, WE'RE NOT LEAVING OUR FRIENDS HERE DEFENSELESS TO GO CHASING AFTER YETI!
THEN WE HAVE TO SPLIT UP!
RIGHT! YOU STAY AND KEEP AN EYE ON THE UNICORNS, NICO AND I WILL GO AFTER THAT YETI!

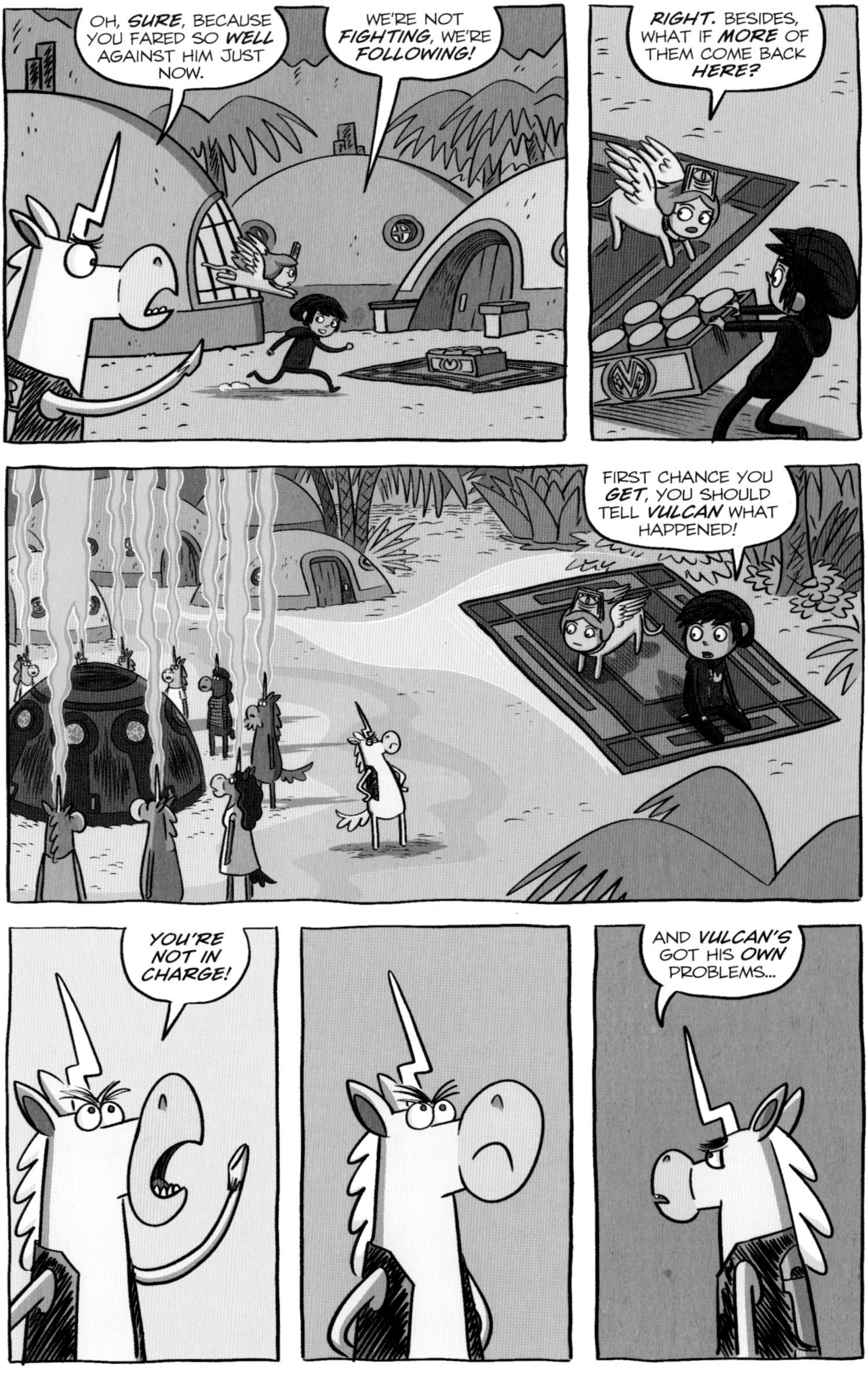
OH, SURE, BECAUSE YOU FARED SO WELL AGAINST HIM JUST NOW.
WE'RE NOT FIGHTING, WE'RE FOLLOWING!
RIGHT. BESIDES, WHAT IF MORE OF THEM COME BACK HERE?
FIRST CHANCE YOU GET, YOU SHOULD TELL VULCAN WHAT HAPPENED!
YOU'RE NOT IN CHARGE!
AND VULCAN'S GOT HIS OWN PROBLEMS...

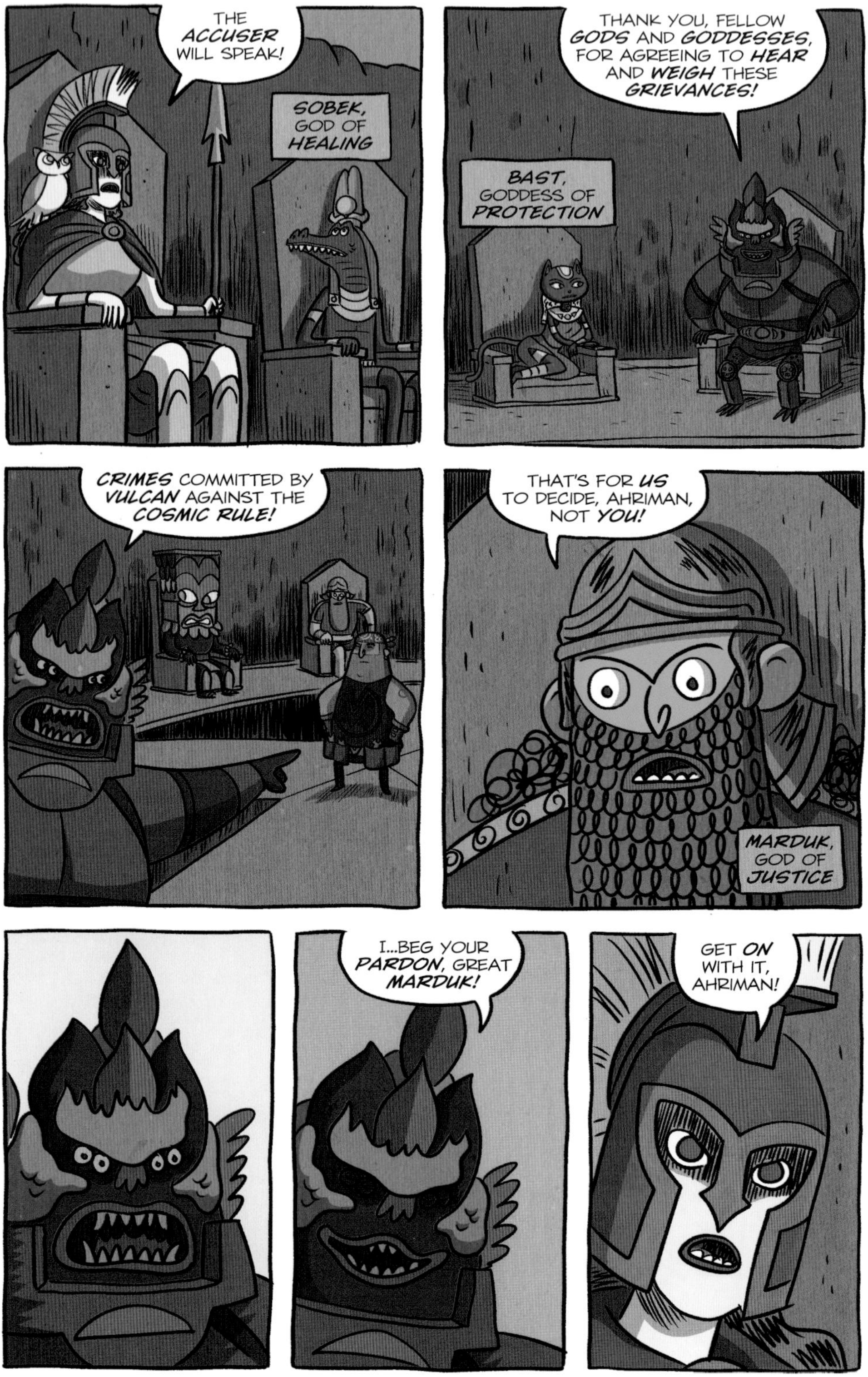
THE ACCUSER WILL SPEAK!
SOBEK, GOD OF HEALING
THANK YOU, FELLOW GODS AND GODDESSES, FOR AGREEING TO HEAR AND WEIGH THESE GRIEVANCES!
BAST, GODDESS OF PROTECTION
CRIMES COMMITTED BY VULCAN AGAINST THE COSMIC RULE!
THAT'S FOR US TO DECIDE, AHRIMAN, NOT YOU!
MARDUK, GOD OF JUSTICE
I...BEG YOUR PARDON, GREAT MARDUK!
GET ON WITH IT, AHRIMAN!

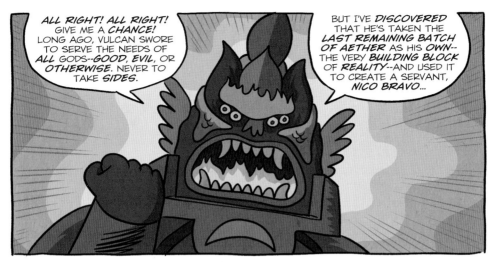

ALL RIGHT! ALL RIGHT! GIVE ME A *CHANCE!* LONG AGO, VULCAN SWORE TO SERVE THE NEEDS OF *ALL GODS--GOOD, EVIL,* OR *OTHERWISE.* NEVER TO TAKE *SIDES.*

BUT I'VE *DISCOVERED* THAT HE'S TAKEN THE *LAST REMAINING BATCH OF AETHER* AS HIS *OWN--* THE VERY *BUILDING BLOCK OF REALITY--*AND USED IT TO CREATE A SERVANT, *NICO BRAVO...*

...WHO *SECRETLY* ENFORCES *VULCAN'S WILL* OVER *OURS!*

VULCAN IS A *THIEF* AND AN *OATHBREAKER!*

HIS *POSSESSIONS* SHOULD BE *FORFEIT--*

--AND HIS CREATION *DESTROYED!*

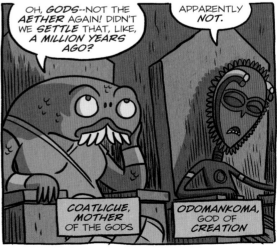

OH, *GODS--*NOT THE *AETHER* AGAIN! DIDN'T WE *SETTLE* THAT, LIKE, *A MILLION YEARS AGO?*

APPARENTLY *NOT.*

COATLICUE, MOTHER OF THE GODS

ODOMANKOMA, GOD OF *CREATION*

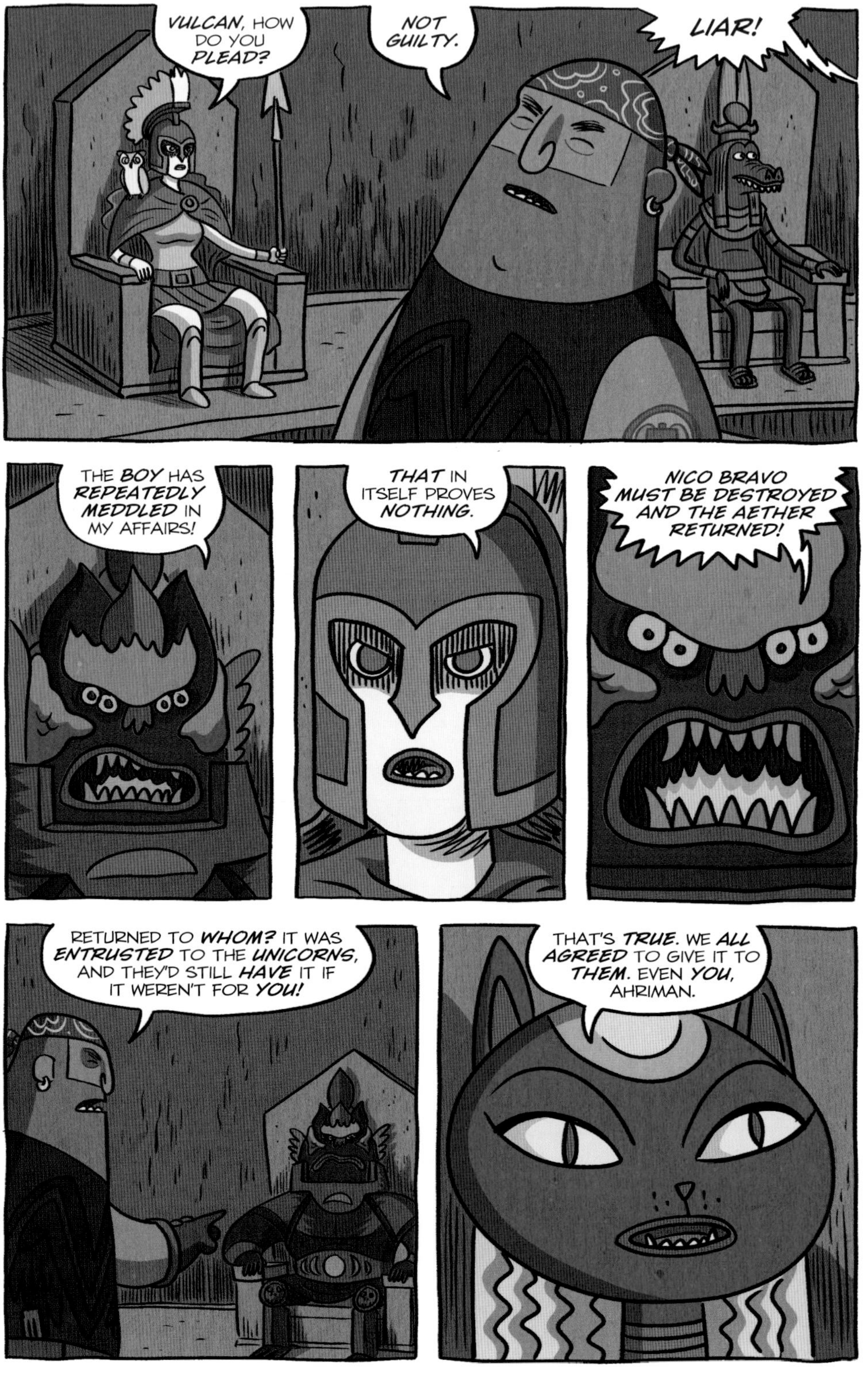
VULCAN, HOW DO YOU PLEAD?
NOT GUILTY.
LIAR!
THE BOY HAS REPEATEDLY MEDDLED IN MY AFFAIRS!
THAT IN ITSELF PROVES NOTHING.
NICO BRAVO MUST BE DESTROYED AND THE AETHER RETURNED!
RETURNED TO WHOM? IT WAS ENTRUSTED TO THE UNICORNS, AND THEY'D STILL HAVE IT IF IT WEREN'T FOR YOU!
THAT'S TRUE. WE ALL AGREED TO GIVE IT TO THEM. EVEN YOU, AHRIMAN.

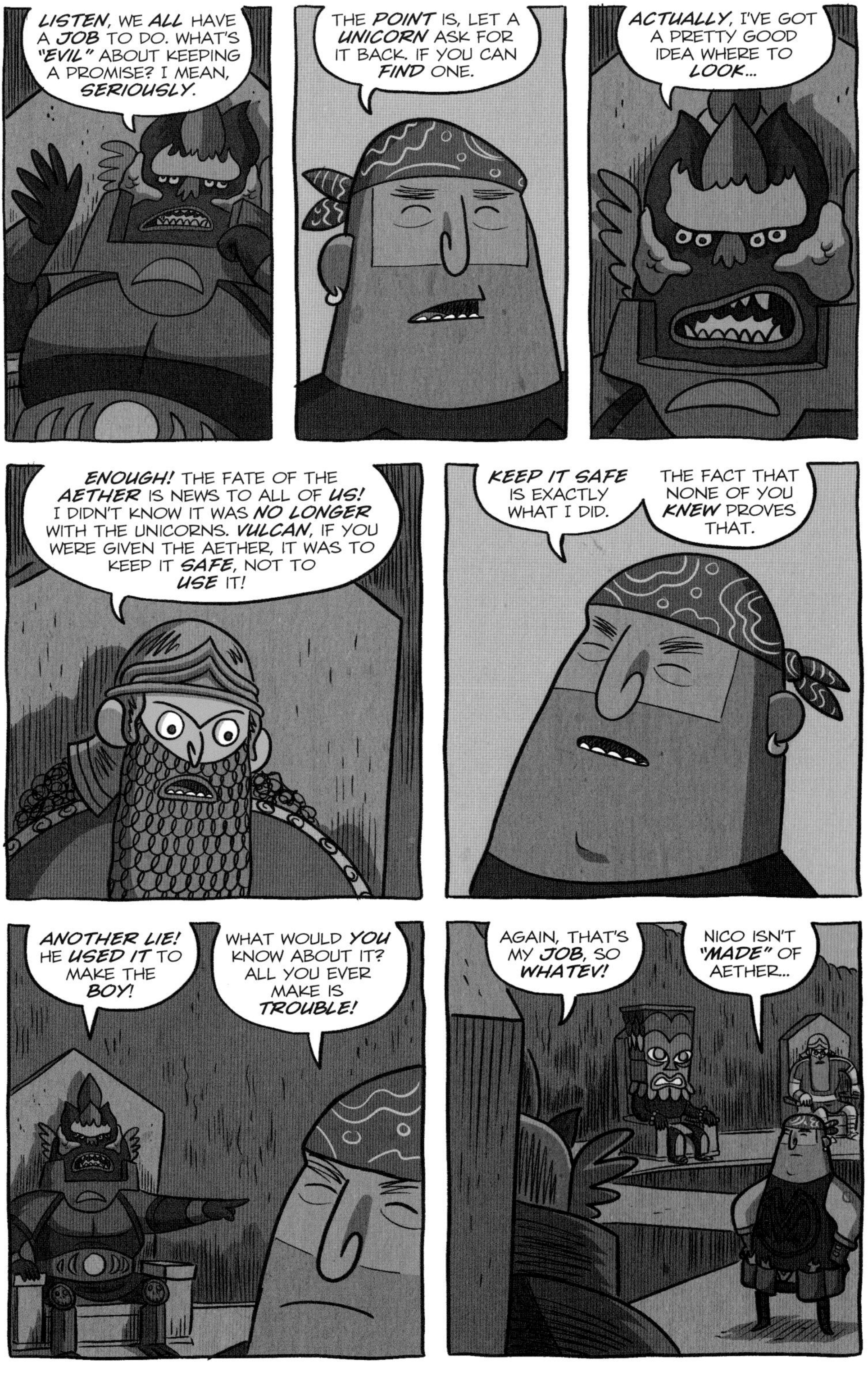
LISTEN, WE ALL HAVE A JOB TO DO. WHAT'S "EVIL" ABOUT KEEPING A PROMISE? I MEAN, SERIOUSLY.
THE POINT IS, LET A UNICORN ASK FOR IT BACK. IF YOU CAN FIND ONE.
ACTUALLY, I'VE GOT A PRETTY GOOD IDEA WHERE TO LOOK...
ENOUGH! THE FATE OF THE AETHER IS NEWS TO ALL OF US! I DIDN'T KNOW IT WAS NO LONGER WITH THE UNICORNS. VULCAN, IF YOU WERE GIVEN THE AETHER, IT WAS TO KEEP IT SAFE, NOT TO USE IT!
KEEP IT SAFE IS EXACTLY WHAT I DID.
THE FACT THAT NONE OF YOU KNEW PROVES THAT.
ANOTHER LIE! HE USED IT TO MAKE THE BOY!
WHAT WOULD YOU KNOW ABOUT IT? ALL YOU EVER MAKE IS TROUBLE!
AGAIN, THAT'S MY JOB, SO WHATEV!
NICO ISN'T "MADE" OF AETHER...

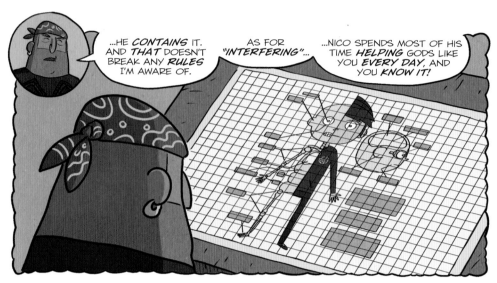

...HE *CONTAINS* IT. AND *THAT* DOESN'T BREAK ANY *RULES* I'M AWARE OF.

AS FOR *"INTERFERING"*...

...NICO SPENDS MOST OF HIS TIME *HELPING* GODS LIKE YOU *EVERY DAY*, AND YOU *KNOW* IT!

THAT'S TRUE! I MISSED AN ISSUE OF *GILGAMESH 5000*, SO *NICO* LOANED ME *HIS* UNTIL THE *REORDER* CAME IN!

ARES, GOD OF *WAR*

YEAH, I'D BEEN USING THE WRONG *MANTICORE OIL* FOR *YEARS* UNTIL *NICO* POINTED IT OUT.

LAST YEAR, I WAS GOING TO BUY THIS SMALLER, CHEAPER *LITTER BOX?* BUT *NICO* TALKED ME *INTO* GETTING THE *DELUXE*. BOY, WAS *HE* RIGHT! *FIVE STARS!*

WELL, *YIPPEE* FOR ALL OF YOU! ALL HE'S EVER DONE FOR *ME* IS *MESS THINGS UP*, AND I THINK HE DOES IT ON *PURPOSE!*

THAT'S THE THING--ALL *ANY* OF YOU *EVER* THINK ABOUT ARE *YOUR PLANS!* YOU USE *MORTALS* HOWEVER YOU WANT. SAME GOES FOR THE *AETHER*, AND *EVERYTHING ELSE*. YOU *NEVER* WONDER IF MAYBE THEY HAD ANY PLANS OF THEIR *OWN!*

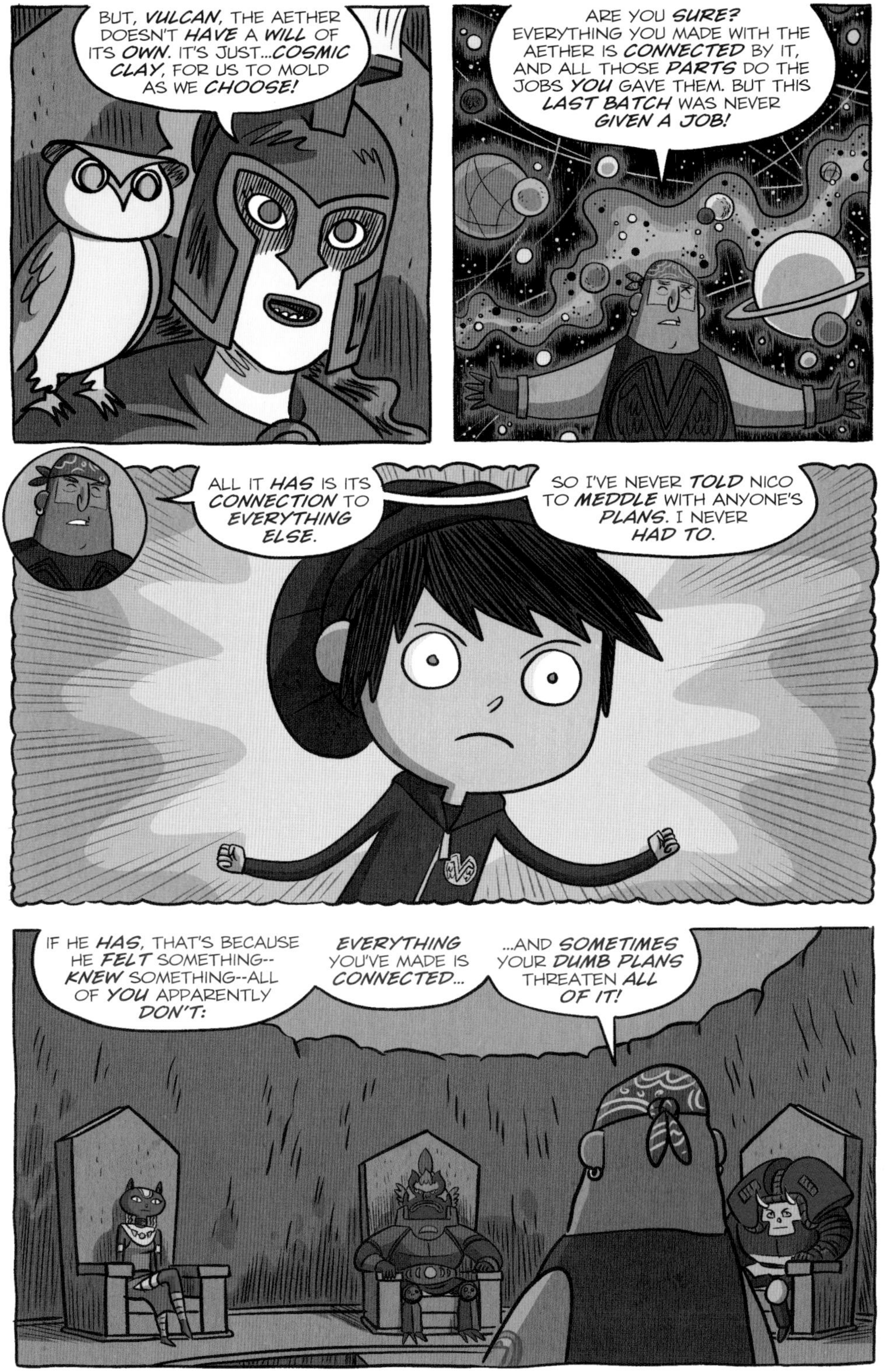
BUT, VULCAN, THE AETHER DOESN'T HAVE A WILL OF ITS OWN. IT'S JUST...COSMIC CLAY, FOR US TO MOLD AS WE CHOOSE!
ARE YOU SURE? EVERYTHING YOU MADE WITH THE AETHER IS CONNECTED BY IT, AND ALL THOSE PARTS DO THE JOBS YOU GAVE THEM. BUT THIS LAST BATCH WAS NEVER GIVEN A JOB!
ALL IT HAS IS ITS CONNECTION TO EVERYTHING ELSE.
SO I'VE NEVER TOLD NICO TO MEDDLE WITH ANYONE'S PLANS. I NEVER HAD TO.
IF HE HAS, THAT'S BECAUSE HE FELT SOMETHING--KNEW SOMETHING--ALL OF YOU APPARENTLY DON'T:
EVERYTHING YOU'VE MADE IS CONNECTED...
...AND SOMETIMES YOUR DUMB PLANS THREATEN ALL OF IT!

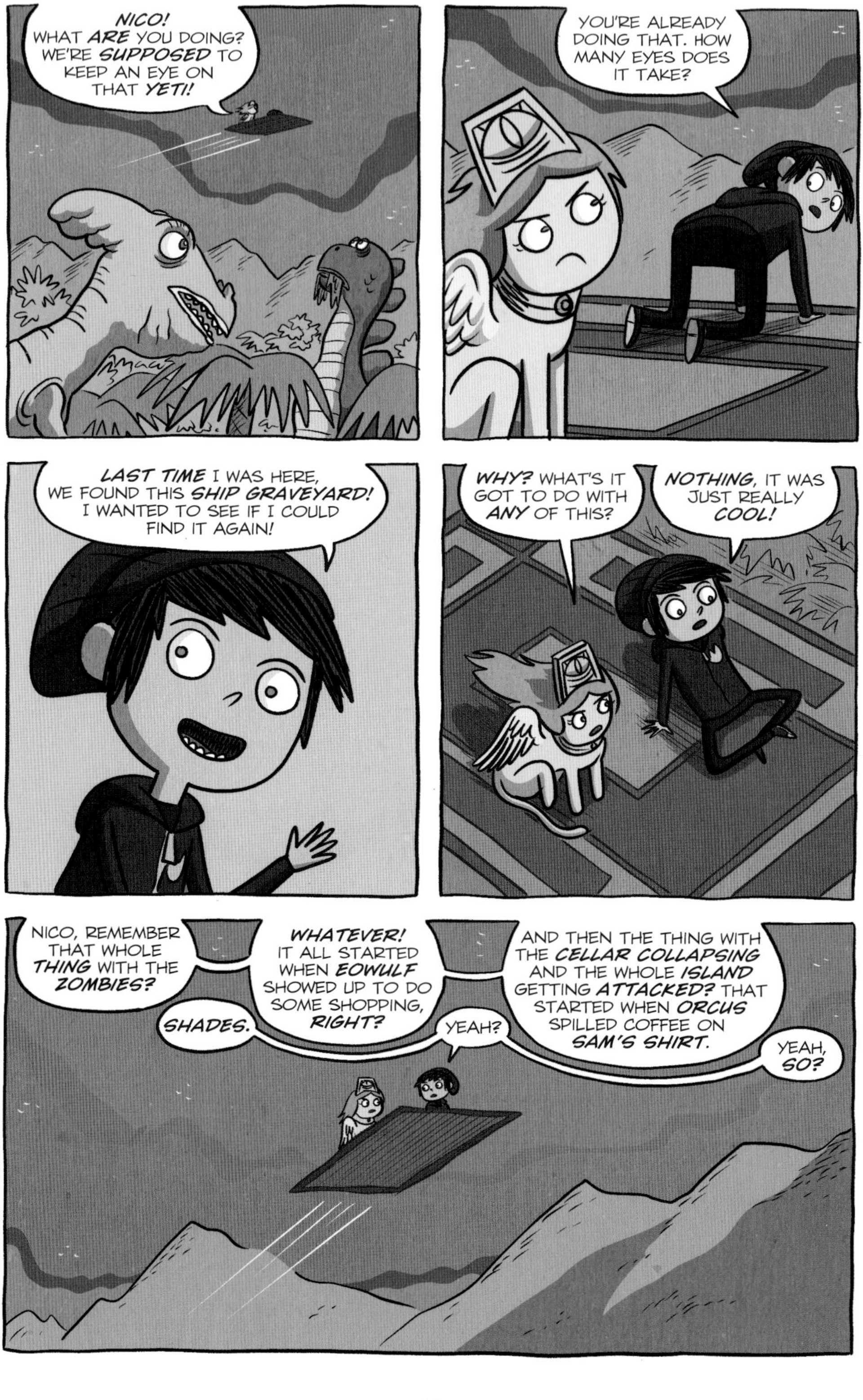
NICO! WHAT ARE YOU DOING? WE'RE SUPPOSED TO KEEP AN EYE ON THAT YETI!
YOU'RE ALREADY DOING THAT. HOW MANY EYES DOES IT TAKE?
LAST TIME I WAS HERE, WE FOUND THIS SHIP GRAVEYARD! I WANTED TO SEE IF I COULD FIND IT AGAIN!
WHY? WHAT'S IT GOT TO DO WITH ANY OF THIS?
NOTHING, IT WAS JUST REALLY COOL!
NICO, REMEMBER THAT WHOLE THING WITH THE ZOMBIES?
SHADES.
WHATEVER! IT ALL STARTED WHEN EOWULF SHOWED UP TO DO SOME SHOPPING, RIGHT?
YEAH?
AND THEN THE THING WITH THE CELLAR COLLAPSING AND THE WHOLE ISLAND GETTING ATTACKED? THAT STARTED WHEN ORCUS SPILLED COFFEE ON SAM'S SHIRT.
YEAH, SO?

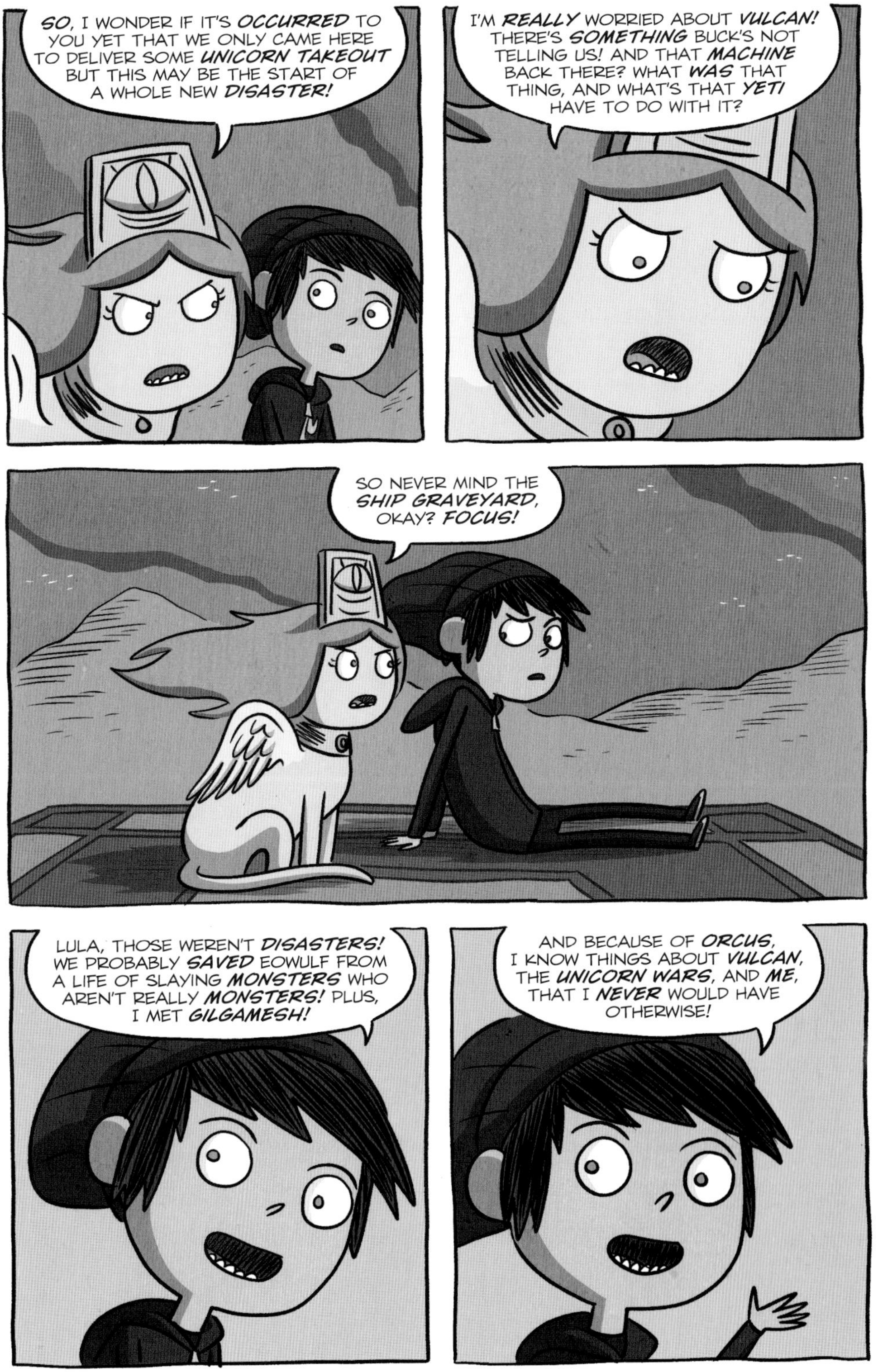

SO, I WONDER IF IT'S OCCURRED TO YOU YET THAT WE ONLY CAME HERE TO DELIVER SOME UNICORN TAKEOUT BUT THIS MAY BE THE START OF A WHOLE NEW DISASTER!
I'M REALLY WORRIED ABOUT VULCAN! THERE'S SOMETHING BUCK'S NOT TELLING US! AND THAT MACHINE BACK THERE? WHAT WAS THAT THING, AND WHAT'S THAT YETI HAVE TO DO WITH IT?
SO NEVER MIND THE SHIP GRAVEYARD, OKAY? FOCUS!
LULA, THOSE WEREN'T DISASTERS! WE PROBABLY SAVED EOWULF FROM A LIFE OF SLAYING MONSTERS WHO AREN'T REALLY MONSTERS! PLUS, I MET GILGAMESH!
AND BECAUSE OF ORCUS, I KNOW THINGS ABOUT VULCAN, THE UNICORN WARS, AND ME, THAT I NEVER WOULD HAVE OTHERWISE!

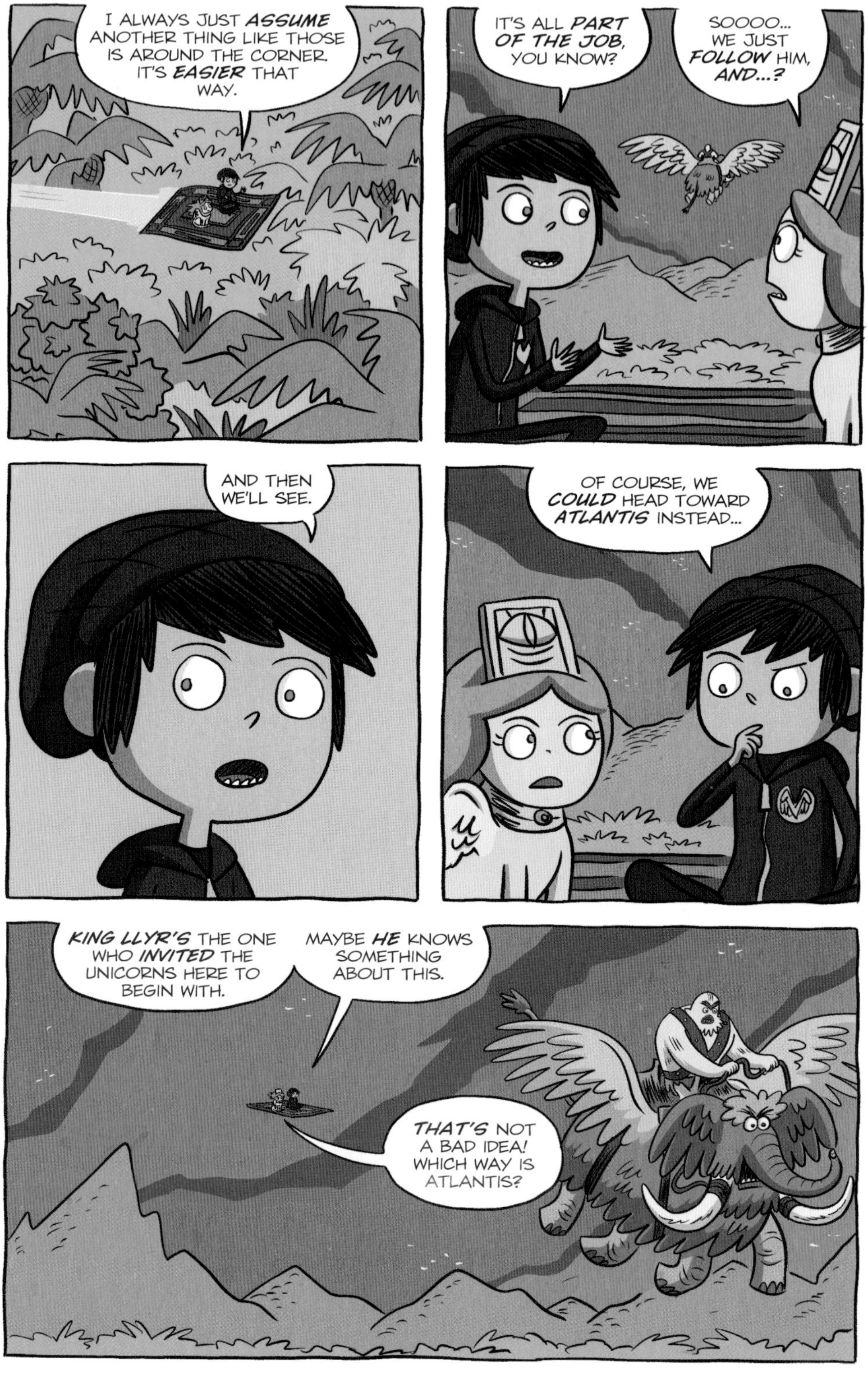
I ALWAYS JUST ASSUME ANOTHER THING LIKE THOSE IS AROUND THE CORNER. IT'S EASIER THAT WAY.
IT'S ALL PART OF THE JOB, YOU KNOW?
SOOOO... WE JUST FOLLOW HIM, AND...?
AND THEN WE'LL SEE.
OF COURSE, WE COULD HEAD TOWARD ATLANTIS INSTEAD...
KING LLYR'S THE ONE WHO INVITED THE UNICORNS HERE TO BEGIN WITH.
MAYBE HE KNOWS SOMETHING ABOUT THIS.
THAT'S NOT A BAD IDEA! WHICH WAY IS ATLANTIS?

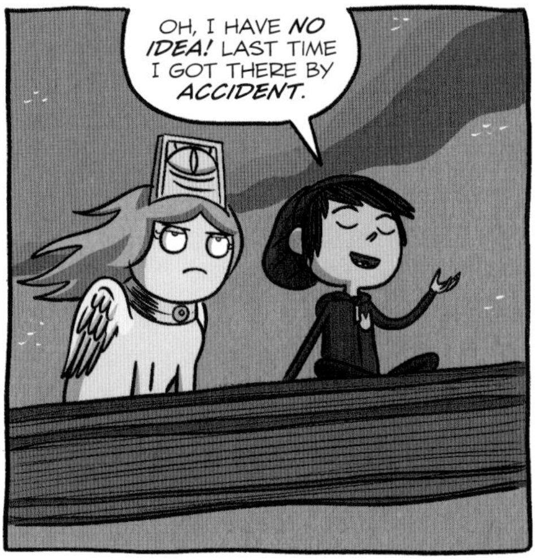
OH, I HAVE **NO IDEA!** LAST TIME I GOT THERE BY **ACCIDENT**.

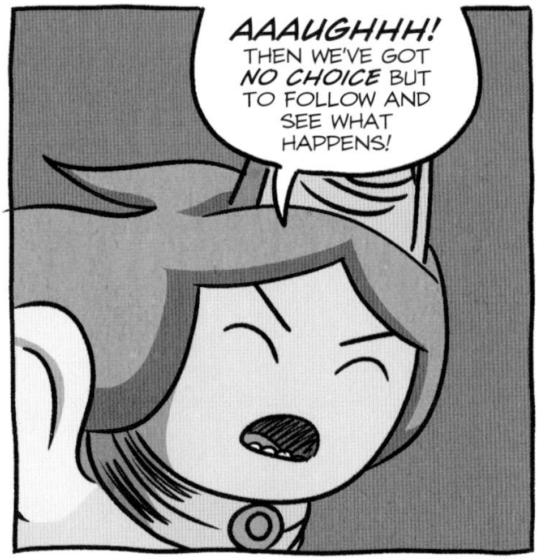
AAAUGHHH! THEN WE'VE GOT **NO CHOICE** BUT TO FOLLOW AND SEE WHAT HAPPENS!

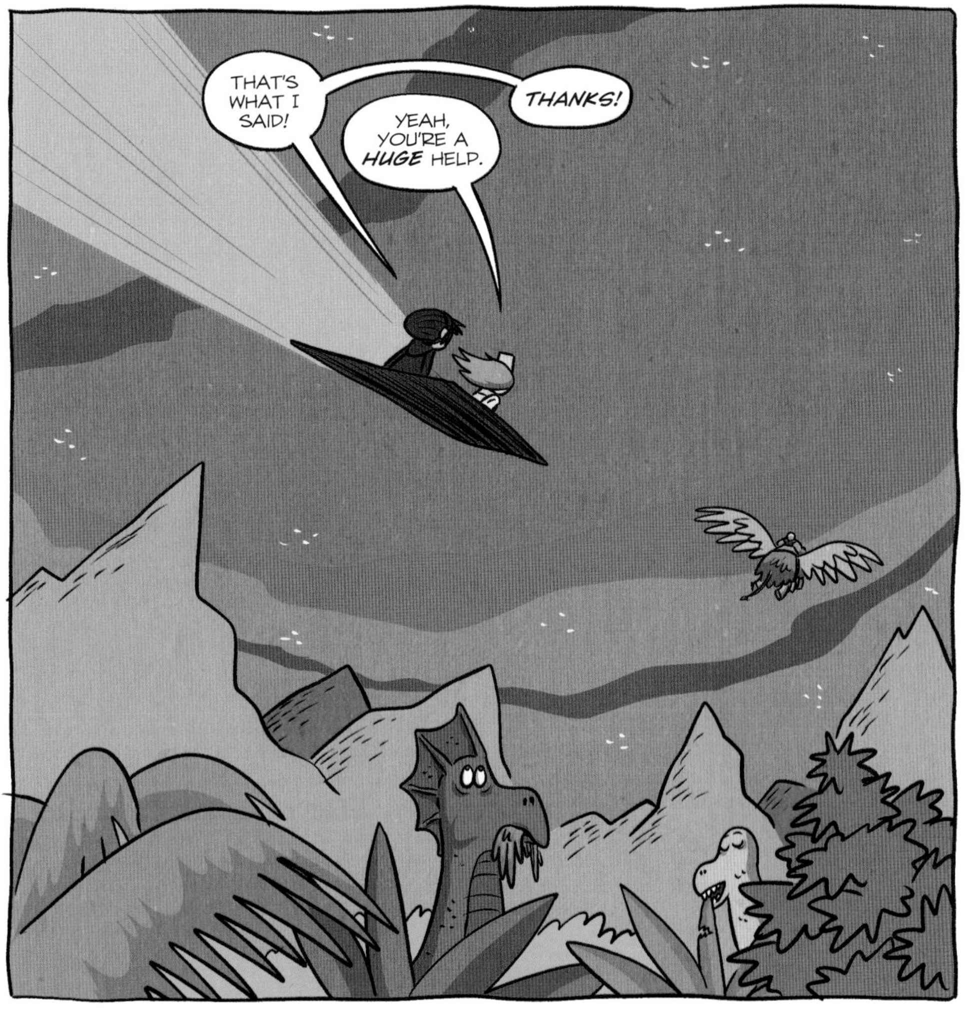
THAT'S WHAT I SAID!
THANKS!
YEAH, YOU'RE A **HUGE** HELP.

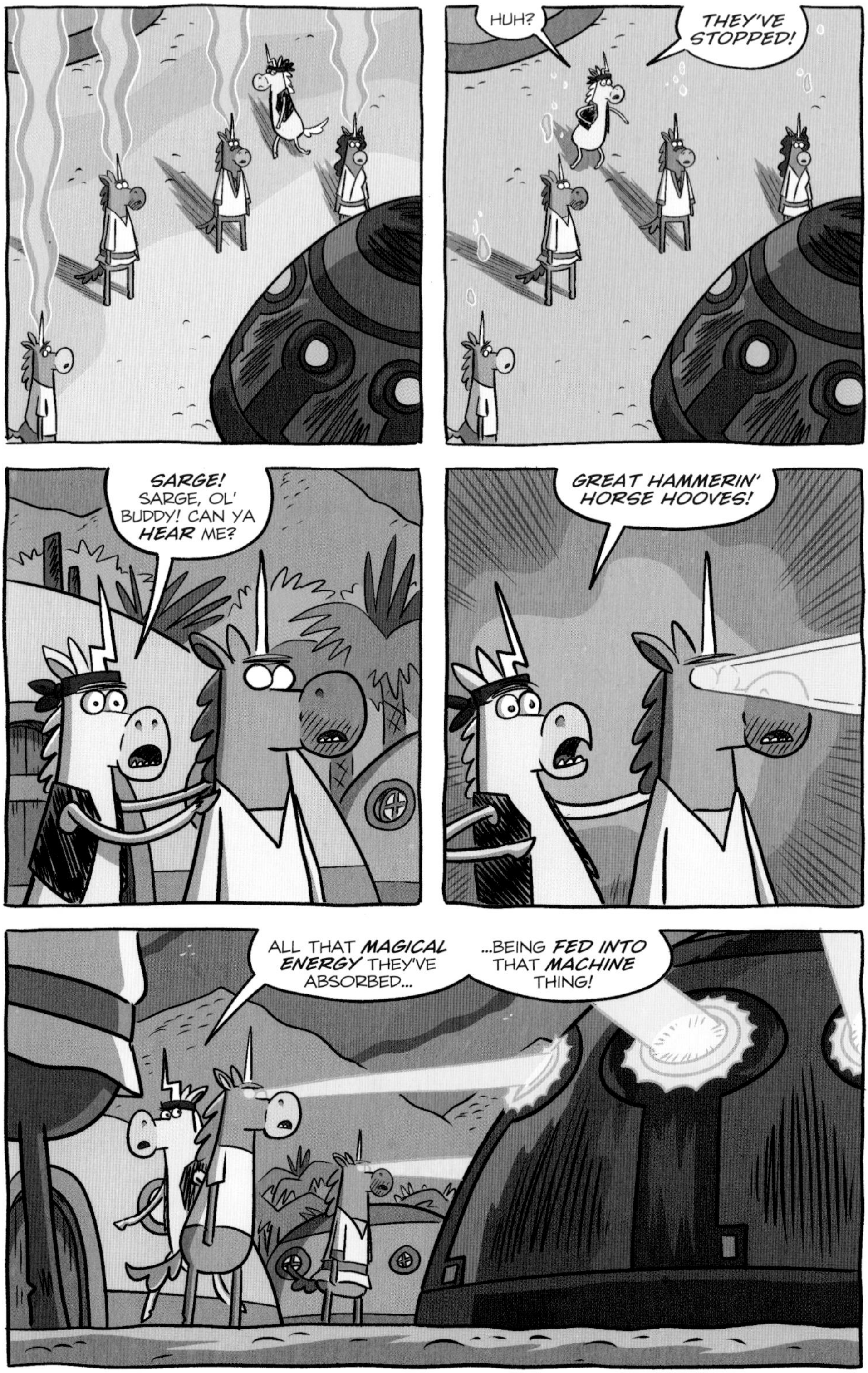
HUH?
THEY'VE STOPPED!
SARGE! SARGE, OL' BUDDY! CAN YA HEAR ME?
GREAT HAMMERIN' HORSE HOOVES!
ALL THAT MAGICAL ENERGY THEY'VE ABSORBED...
...BEING FED INTO THAT MACHINE THING!

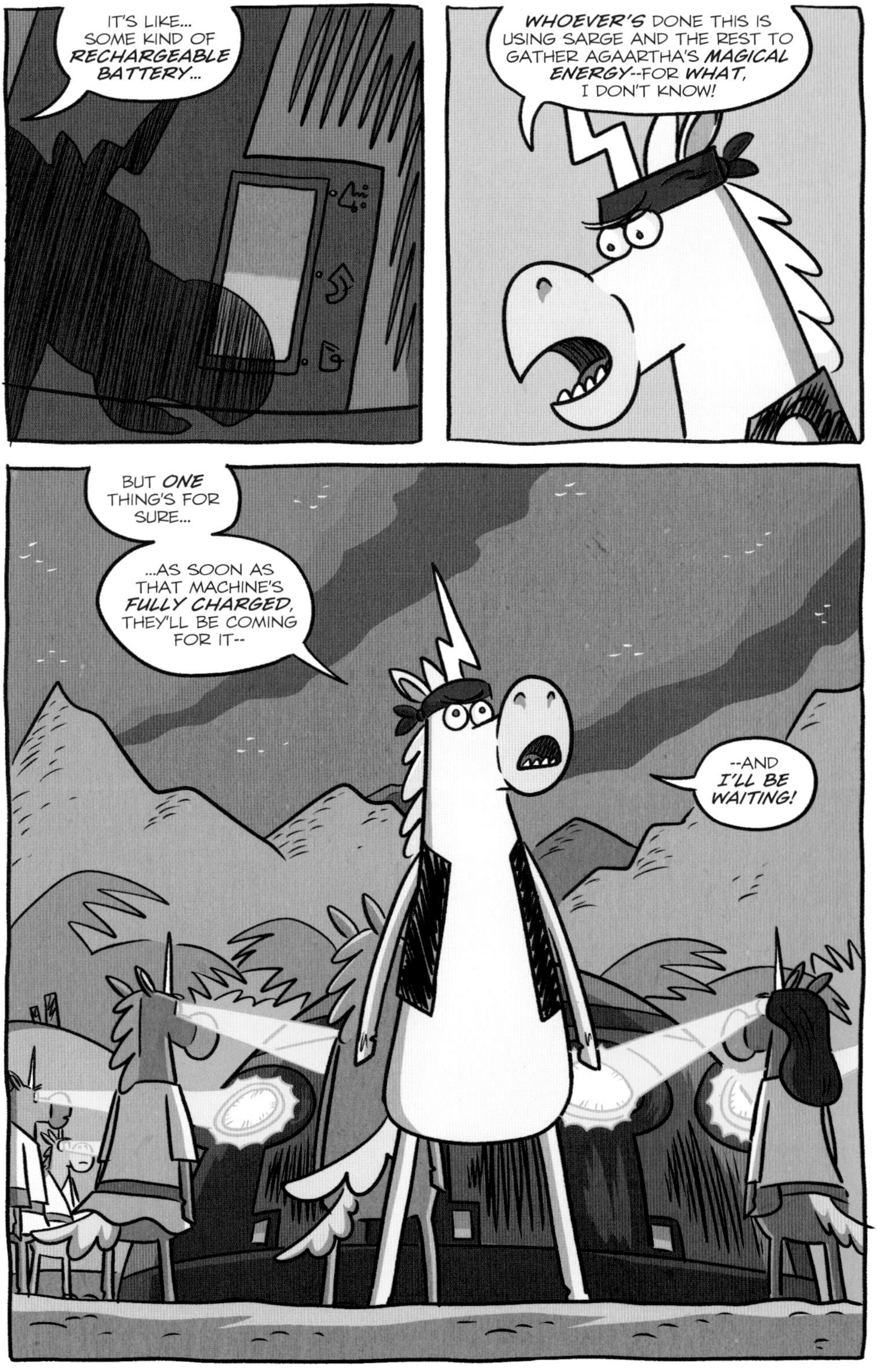
IT'S LIKE... SOME KIND OF RECHARGEABLE BATTERY...
WHOEVER'S DONE THIS IS USING SARGE AND THE REST TO GATHER AGAARTHA'S MAGICAL ENERGY--FOR WHAT, I DON'T KNOW!
BUT ONE THING'S FOR SURE...
...AS SOON AS THAT MACHINE'S FULLY CHARGED, THEY'LL BE COMING FOR IT--
--AND I'LL BE WAITING!

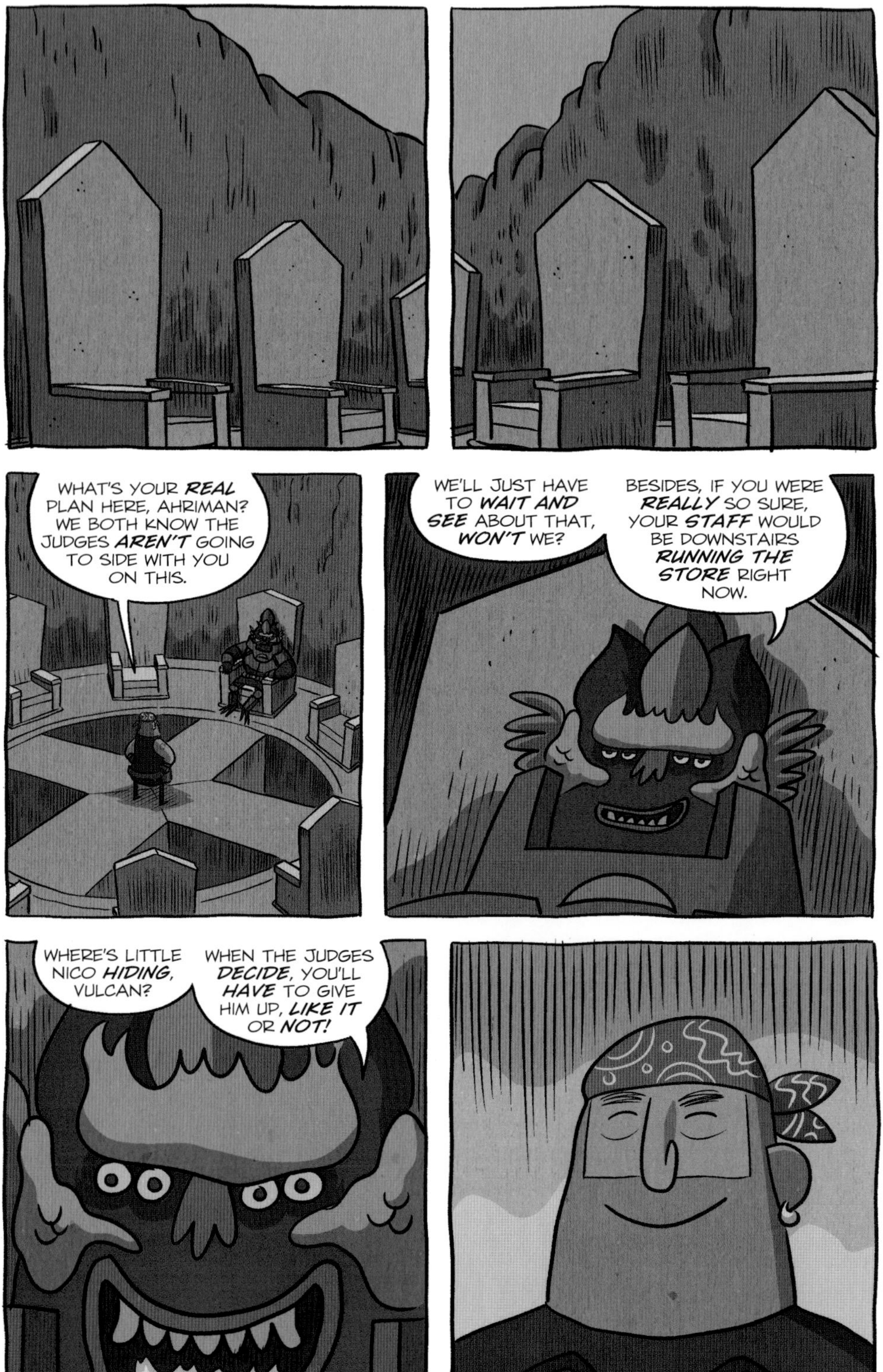
WHAT'S YOUR **REAL** PLAN HERE, AHRIMAN? WE BOTH KNOW THE JUDGES **AREN'T** GOING TO SIDE WITH YOU ON THIS.
WE'LL JUST HAVE TO **WAIT AND SEE** ABOUT THAT, **WON'T** WE?
BESIDES, IF YOU WERE **REALLY** SO SURE, YOUR **STAFF** WOULD BE DOWNSTAIRS **RUNNING THE STORE** RIGHT NOW.
WHERE'S LITTLE NICO **HIDING**, VULCAN?
WHEN THE JUDGES **DECIDE**, YOU'LL **HAVE** TO GIVE HIM UP, **LIKE IT** OR **NOT!**

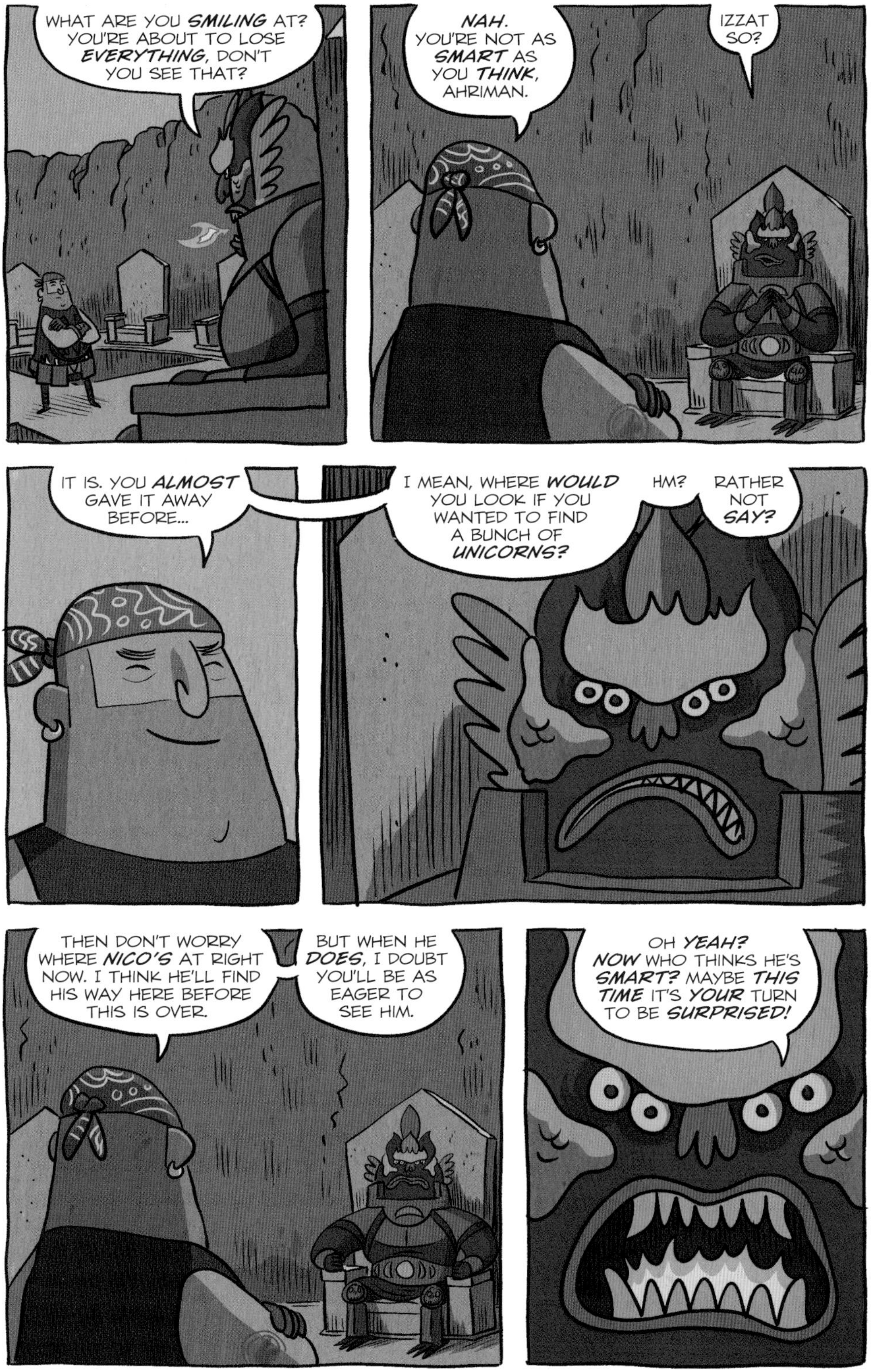
WHAT ARE YOU SMILING AT? YOU'RE ABOUT TO LOSE EVERYTHING, DON'T YOU SEE THAT?
NAH. YOU'RE NOT AS SMART AS YOU THINK, AHRIMAN.
IZZAT SO?
IT IS. YOU ALMOST GAVE IT AWAY BEFORE...
I MEAN, WHERE WOULD YOU LOOK IF YOU WANTED TO FIND A BUNCH OF UNICORNS?
HM?
RATHER NOT SAY?
THEN DON'T WORRY WHERE NICO'S AT RIGHT NOW. I THINK HE'LL FIND HIS WAY HERE BEFORE THIS IS OVER.
BUT WHEN HE DOES, I DOUBT YOU'LL BE AS EAGER TO SEE HIM.
OH YEAH? NOW WHO THINKS HE'S SMART? MAYBE THIS TIME IT'S YOUR TURN TO BE SURPRISED!

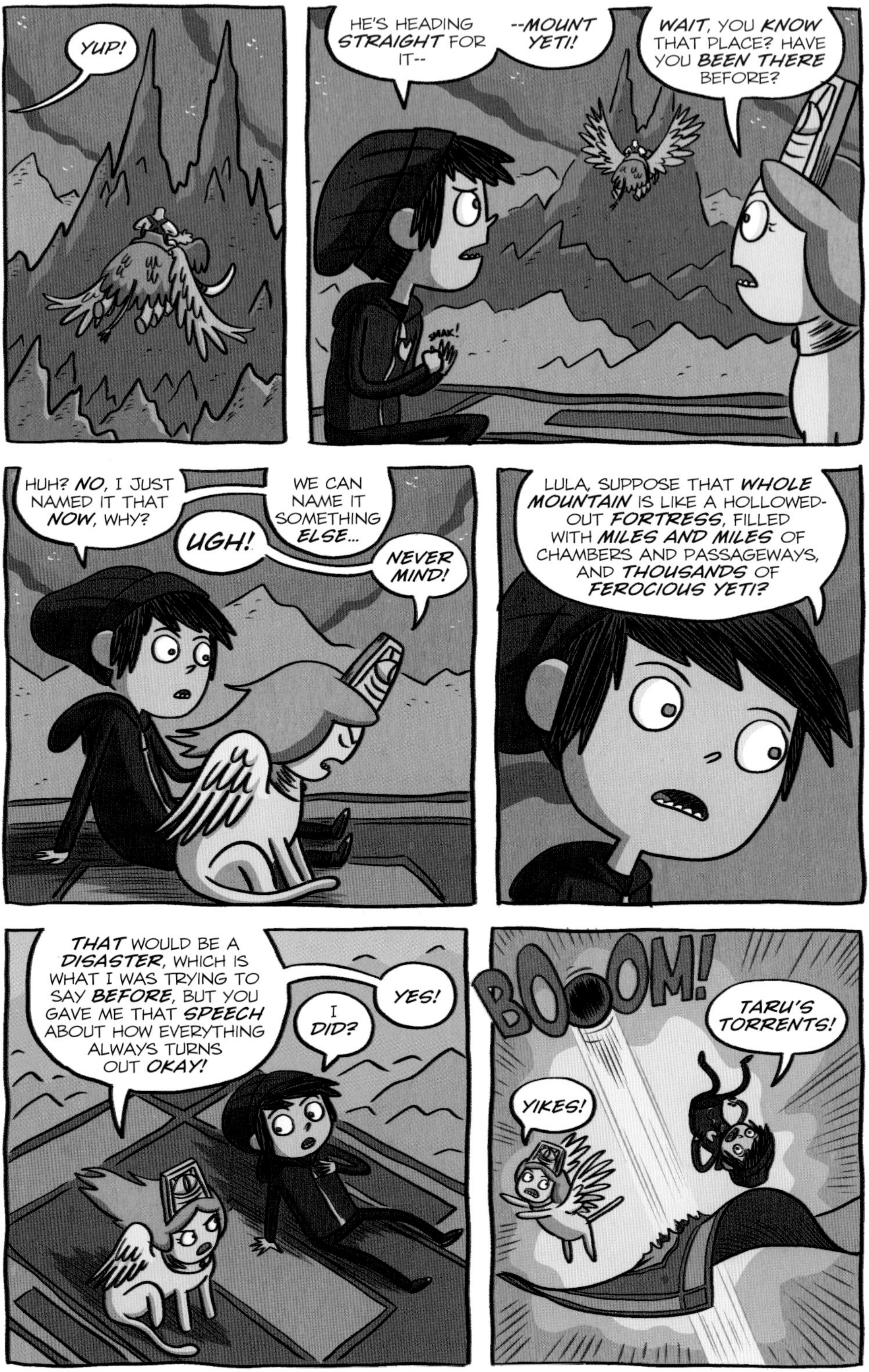
YUP!
HE'S HEADING STRAIGHT FOR IT--
--MOUNT YETI!
WAIT, YOU KNOW THAT PLACE? HAVE YOU BEEN THERE BEFORE?
HUH? NO, I JUST NAMED IT THAT NOW, WHY?
UGH!
WE CAN NAME IT SOMETHING ELSE...
NEVER MIND!
LULA, SUPPOSE THAT WHOLE MOUNTAIN IS LIKE A HOLLOWED-OUT FORTRESS, FILLED WITH MILES AND MILES OF CHAMBERS AND PASSAGEWAYS, AND THOUSANDS OF FEROCIOUS YETI?
THAT WOULD BE A DISASTER, WHICH IS WHAT I WAS TRYING TO SAY BEFORE, BUT YOU GAVE ME THAT SPEECH ABOUT HOW EVERYTHING ALWAYS TURNS OUT OKAY!
I DID?
YES!
BOOOM!
TARU'S TORRENTS!
YIKES!

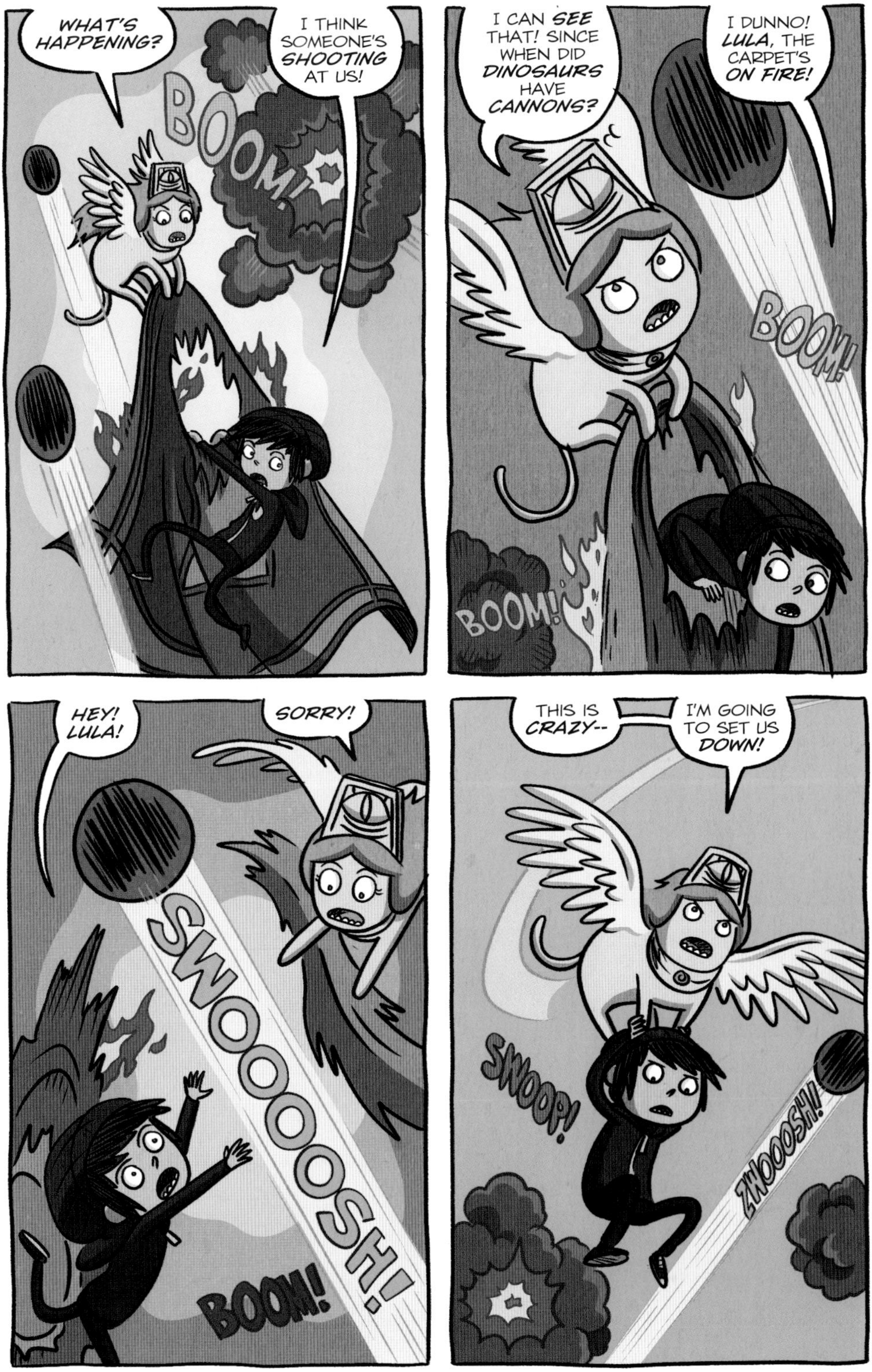
WHAT'S HAPPENING?
I THINK SOMEONE'S SHOOTING AT US!
BOOM!
I CAN SEE THAT! SINCE WHEN DID DINOSAURS HAVE CANNONS?
I DUNNO! LULA, THE CARPET'S ON FIRE!
BOOM!
BOOM!
HEY! LULA!
SORRY!
SWOOOOSH!
BOOM!
THIS IS CRAZY--
I'M GOING TO SET US DOWN!
SWOOP!
ZHOOOSH!

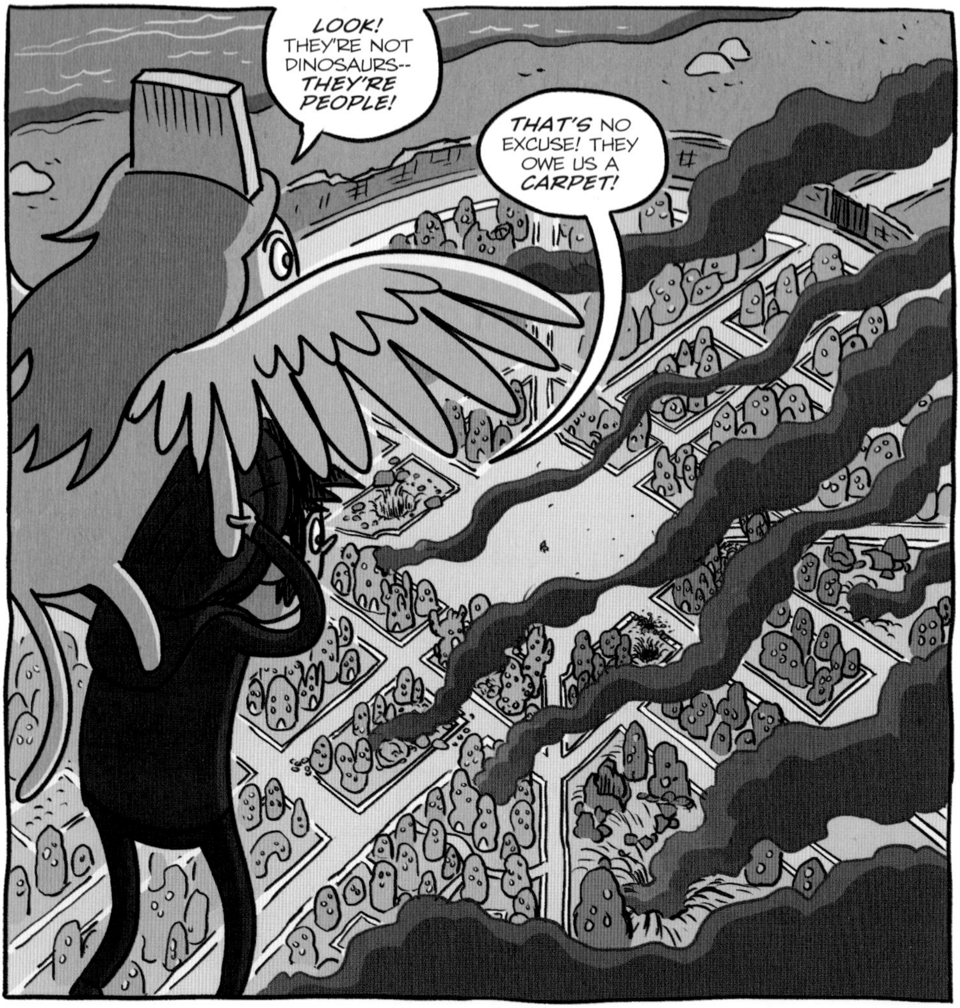
LOOK! THEY'RE NOT DINOSAURS-- THEY'RE PEOPLE!
THAT'S NO EXCUSE! THEY OWE US A CARPET!

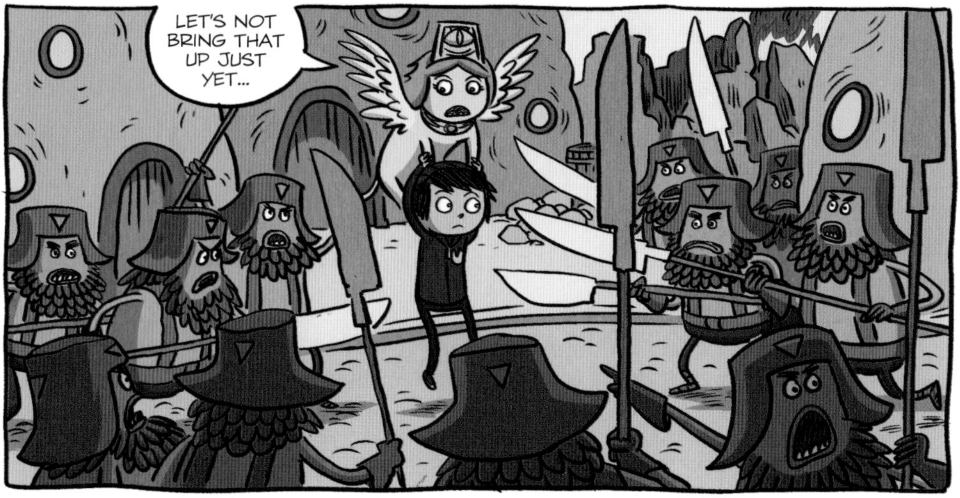
LET'S NOT BRING THAT UP JUST YET...

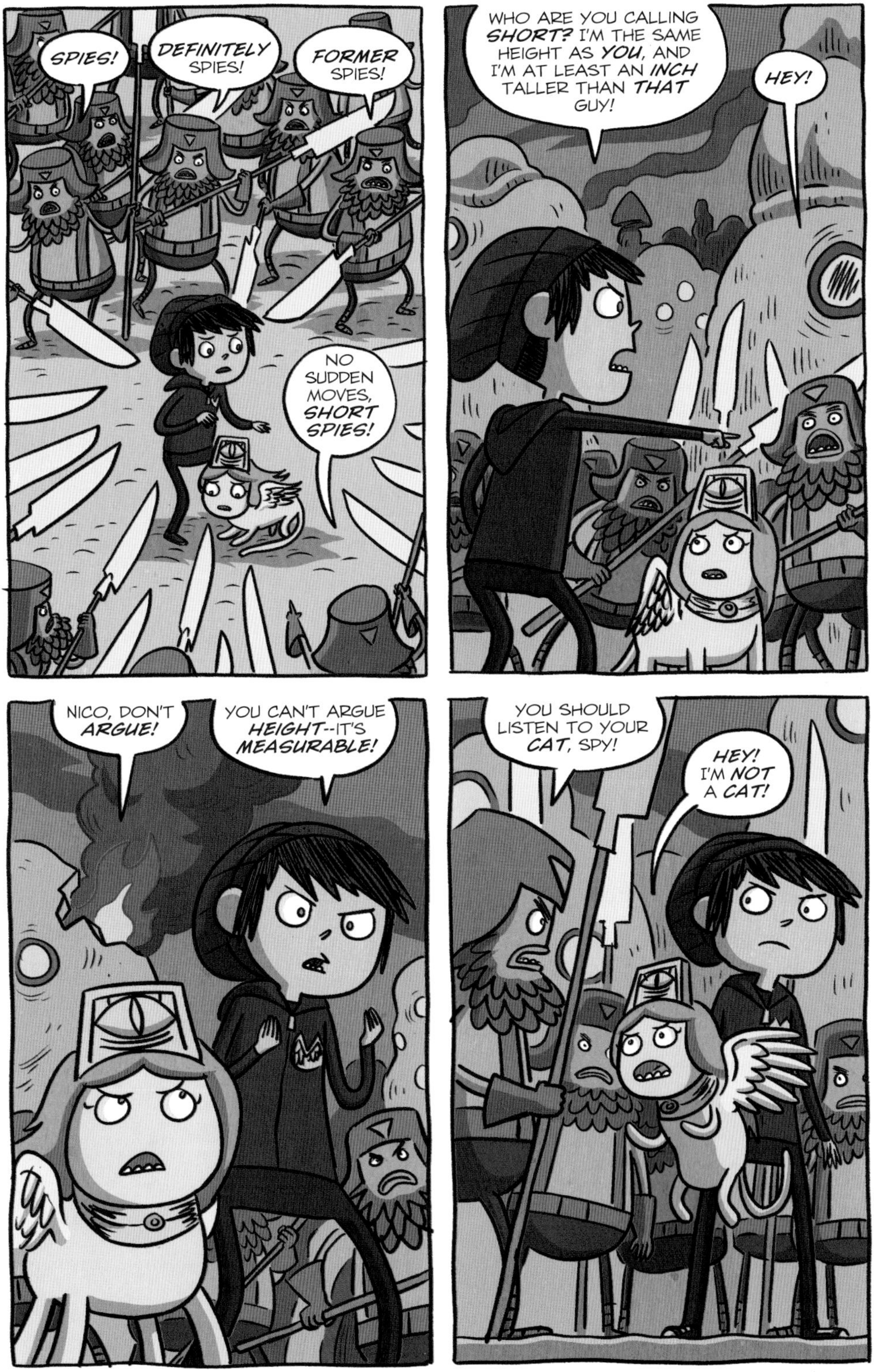
SPIES!
DEFINITELY SPIES!
FORMER SPIES!
NO SUDDEN MOVES, SHORT SPIES!
WHO ARE YOU CALLING SHORT? I'M THE SAME HEIGHT AS YOU, AND I'M AT LEAST AN INCH TALLER THAN THAT GUY!
HEY!
NICO, DON'T ARGUE!
YOU CAN'T ARGUE HEIGHT--IT'S MEASURABLE!
YOU SHOULD LISTEN TO YOUR CAT, SPY!
HEY! I'M NOT A CAT!

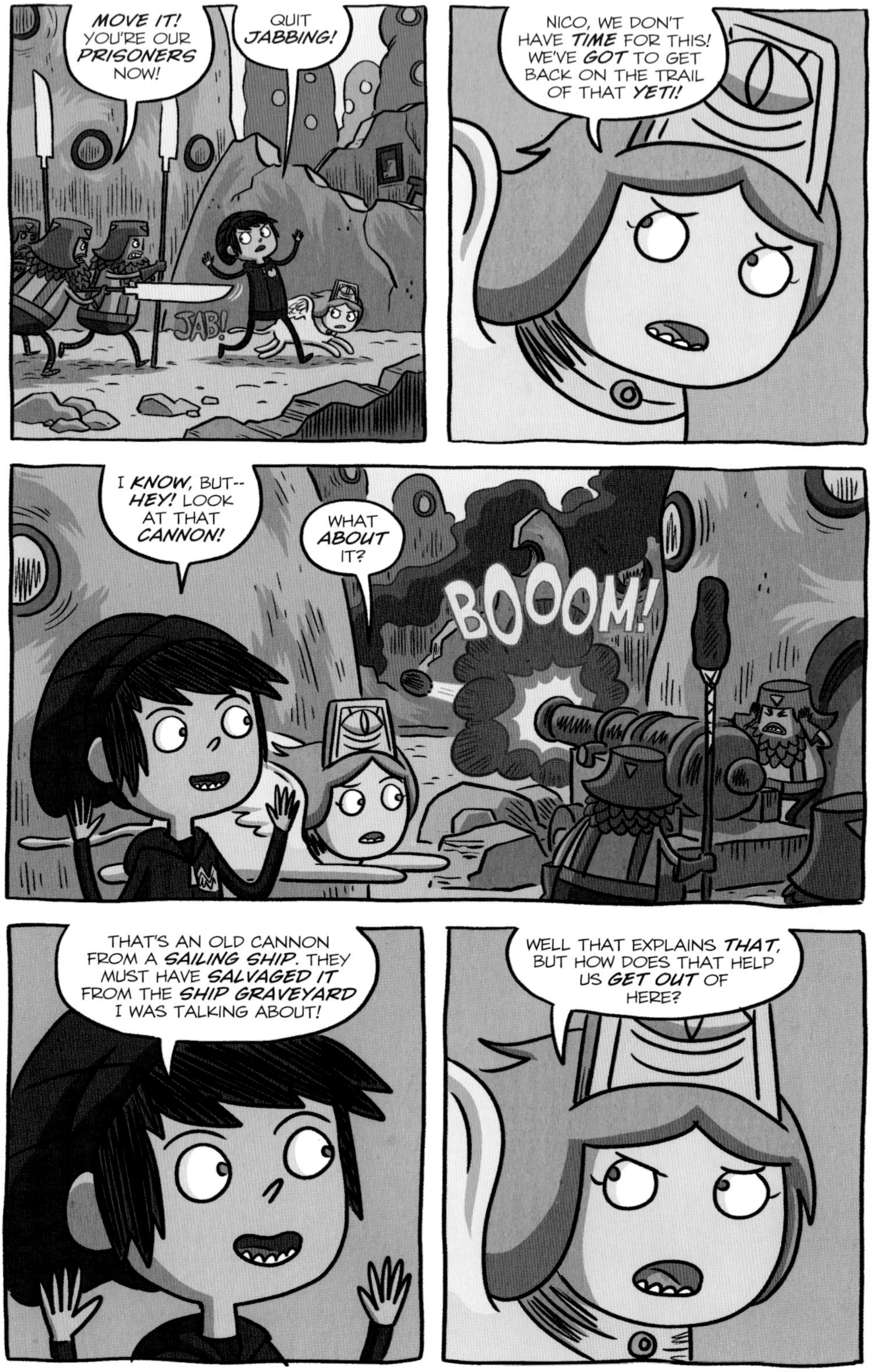
MOVE IT! YOU'RE OUR PRISONERS NOW!
QUIT JABBING!
JAB!
NICO, WE DON'T HAVE TIME FOR THIS! WE'VE GOT TO GET BACK ON THE TRAIL OF THAT YETI!
I KNOW, BUT-- HEY! LOOK AT THAT CANNON!
WHAT ABOUT IT?
BOOOM!
THAT'S AN OLD CANNON FROM A SAILING SHIP. THEY MUST HAVE SALVAGED IT FROM THE SHIP GRAVEYARD I WAS TALKING ABOUT!
WELL THAT EXPLAINS THAT, BUT HOW DOES THAT HELP US GET OUT OF HERE?

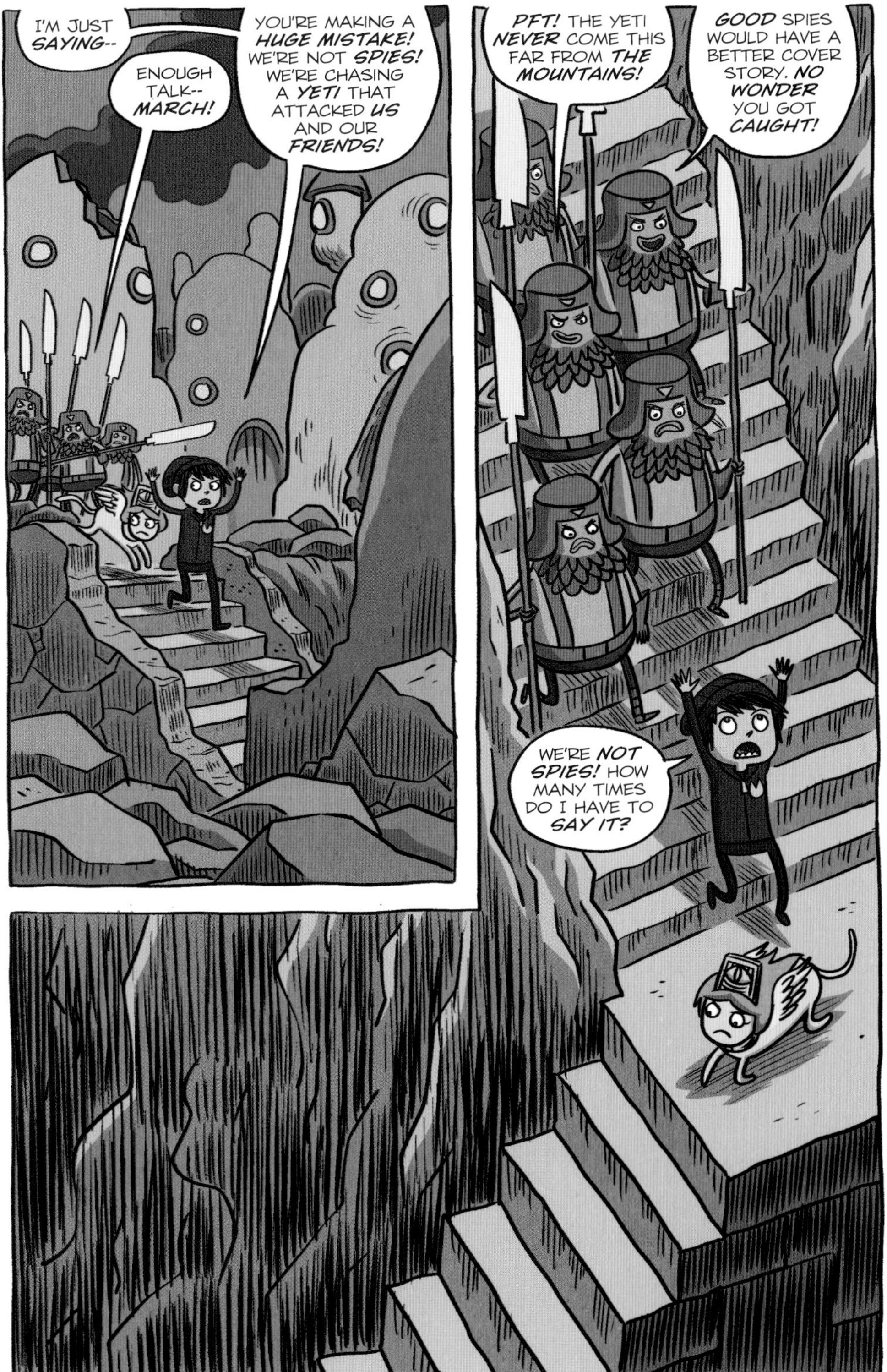
I'M JUST SAYING--
ENOUGH TALK-- MARCH!
YOU'RE MAKING A HUGE MISTAKE! WE'RE NOT SPIES! WE'RE CHASING A YETI THAT ATTACKED US AND OUR FRIENDS!
PFT! THE YETI NEVER COME THIS FAR FROM THE MOUNTAINS!
GOOD SPIES WOULD HAVE A BETTER COVER STORY. NO WONDER YOU GOT CAUGHT!
WE'RE NOT SPIES! HOW MANY TIMES DO I HAVE TO SAY IT?

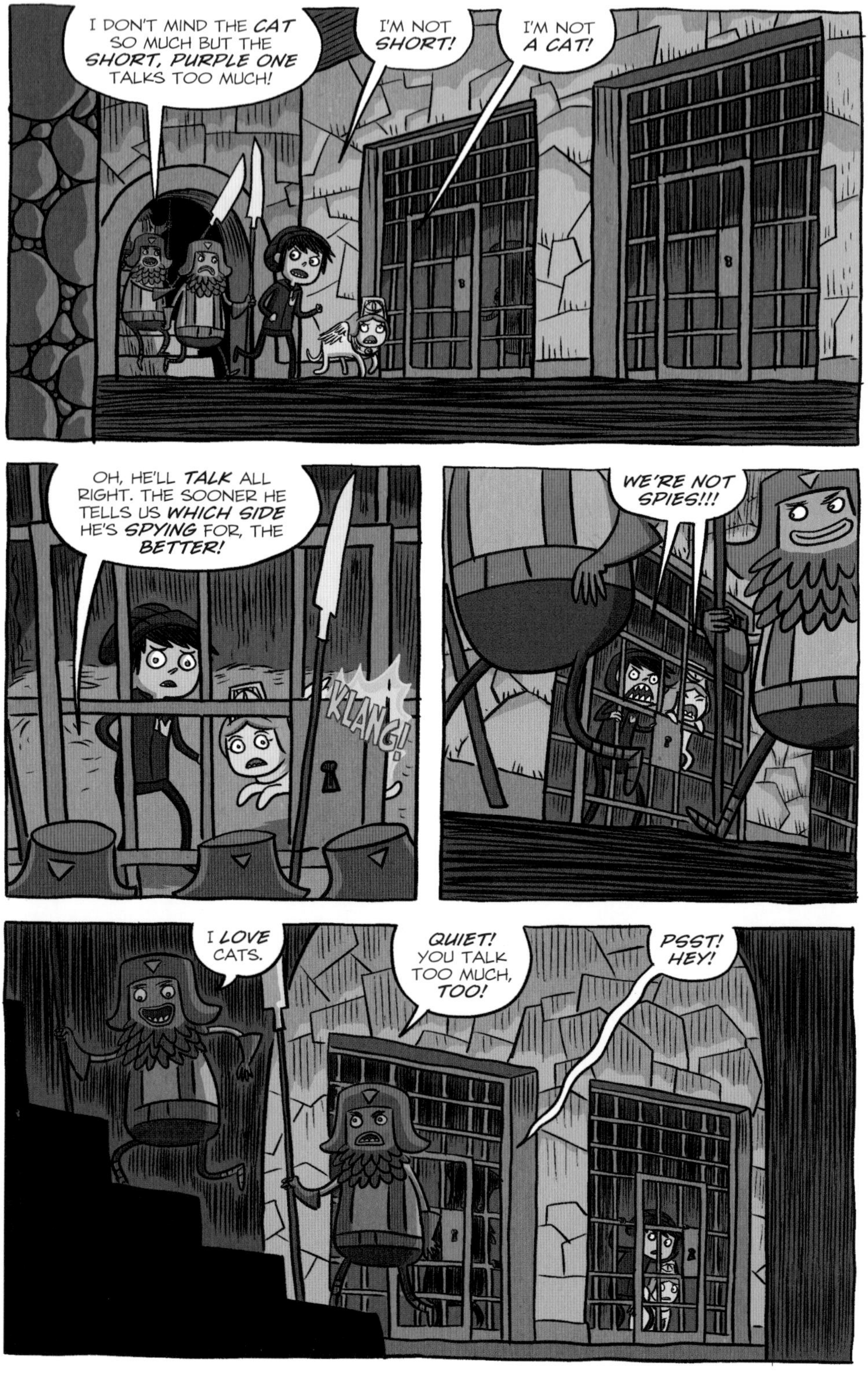
I DON'T MIND THE CAT SO MUCH BUT THE SHORT, PURPLE ONE TALKS TOO MUCH!
I'M NOT SHORT!
I'M NOT A CAT!
OH, HE'LL TALK ALL RIGHT. THE SOONER HE TELLS US WHICH SIDE HE'S SPYING FOR, THE BETTER!
KLANG!
WE'RE NOT SPIES!!!
I LOVE CATS.
QUIET! YOU TALK TOO MUCH, TOO!
PSST! HEY!

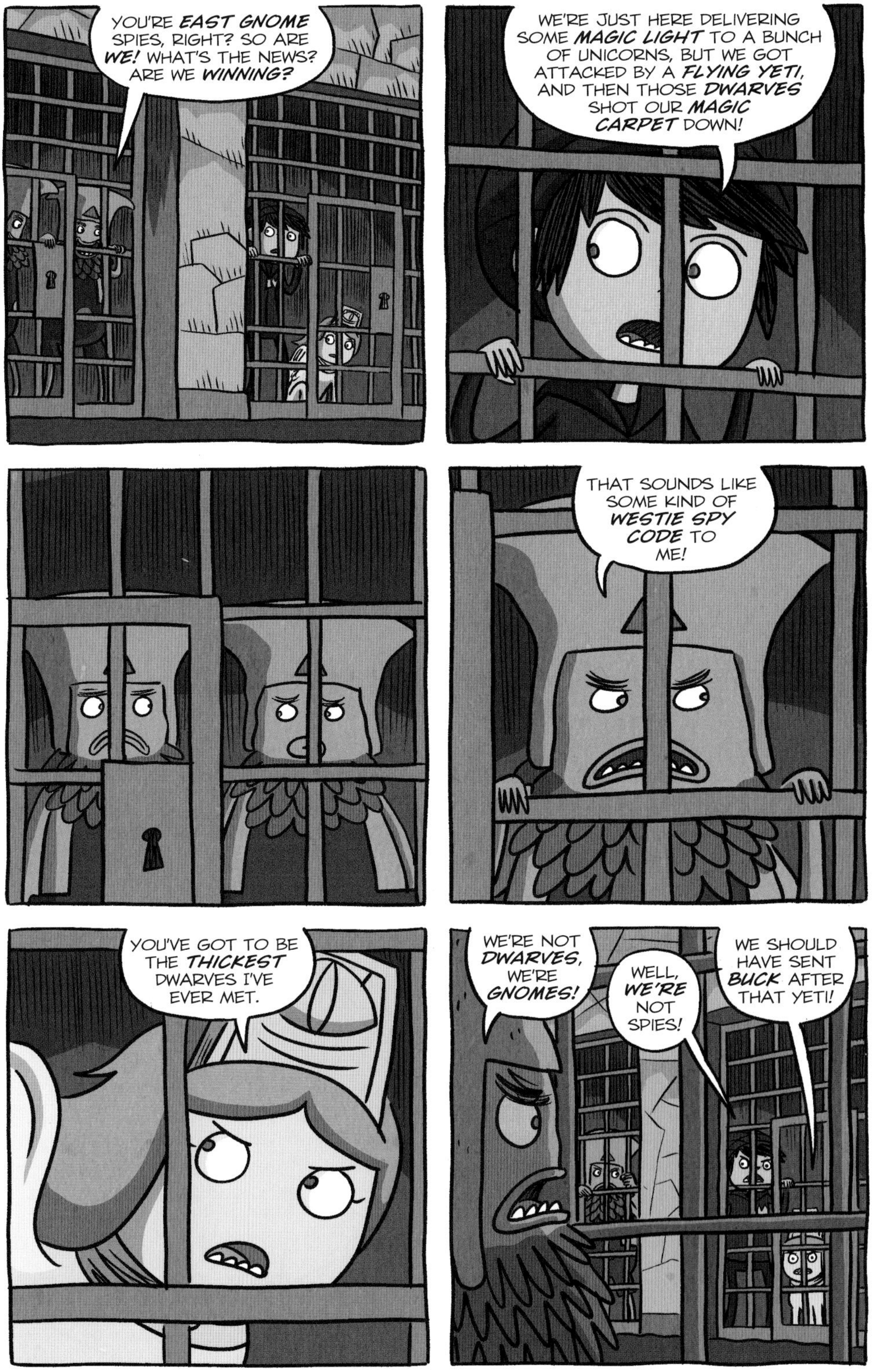
YOU'RE EAST GNOME SPIES, RIGHT? SO ARE WE! WHAT'S THE NEWS? ARE WE WINNING?
WE'RE JUST HERE DELIVERING SOME MAGIC LIGHT TO A BUNCH OF UNICORNS, BUT WE GOT ATTACKED BY A FLYING YETI, AND THEN THOSE DWARVES SHOT OUR MAGIC CARPET DOWN!
THAT SOUNDS LIKE SOME KIND OF WESTIE SPY CODE TO ME!
YOU'VE GOT TO BE THE THICKEST DWARVES I'VE EVER MET.
WE'RE NOT DWARVES, WE'RE GNOMES!
WELL, WE'RE NOT SPIES!
WE SHOULD HAVE SENT BUCK AFTER THAT YETI!

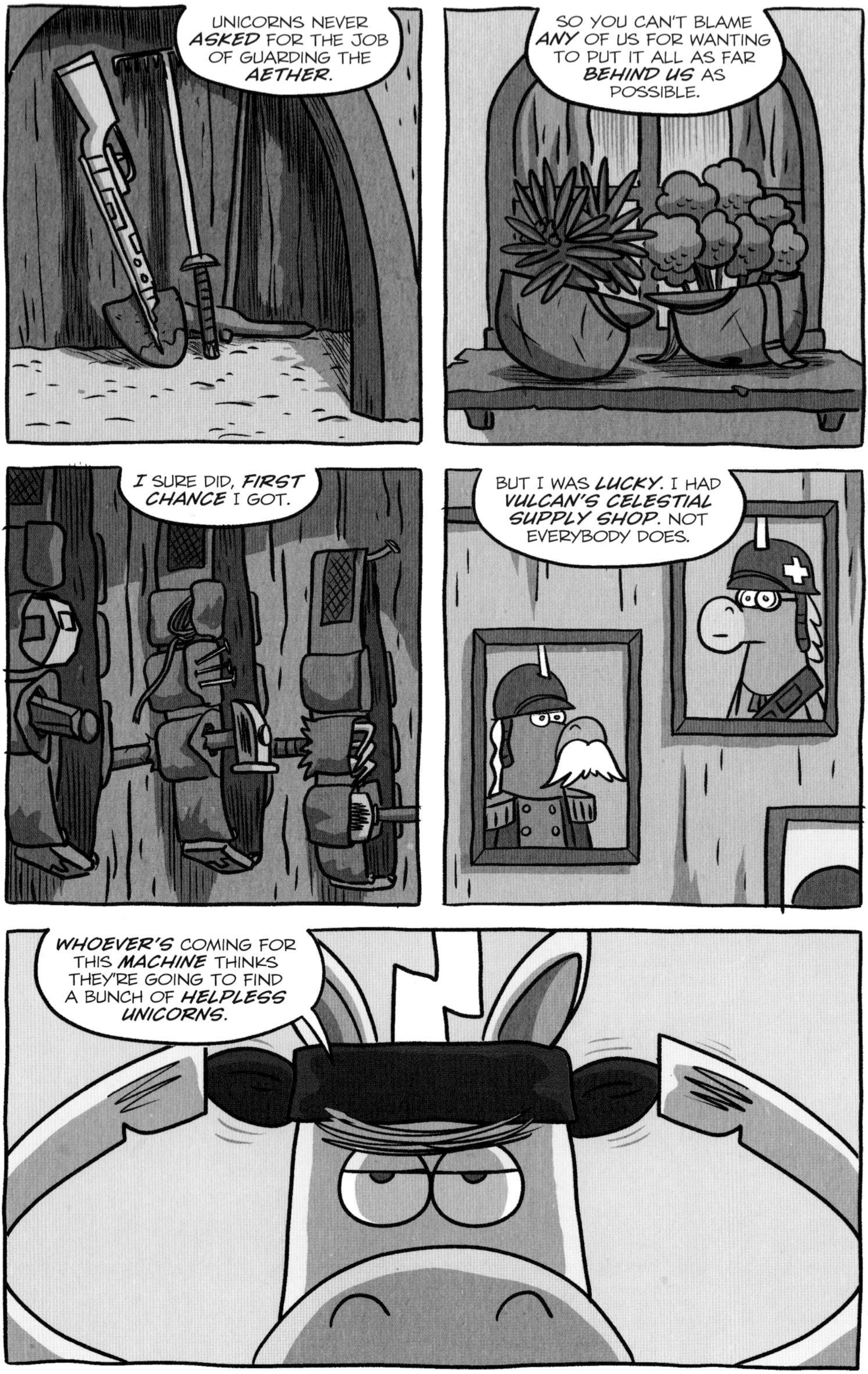
UNICORNS NEVER ASKED FOR THE JOB OF GUARDING THE AETHER.
SO YOU CAN'T BLAME ANY OF US FOR WANTING TO PUT IT ALL AS FAR BEHIND US AS POSSIBLE.
I SURE DID, FIRST CHANCE I GOT.
BUT I WAS LUCKY. I HAD VULCAN'S CELESTIAL SUPPLY SHOP. NOT EVERYBODY DOES.
WHOEVER'S COMING FOR THIS MACHINE THINKS THEY'RE GOING TO FIND A BUNCH OF HELPLESS UNICORNS.

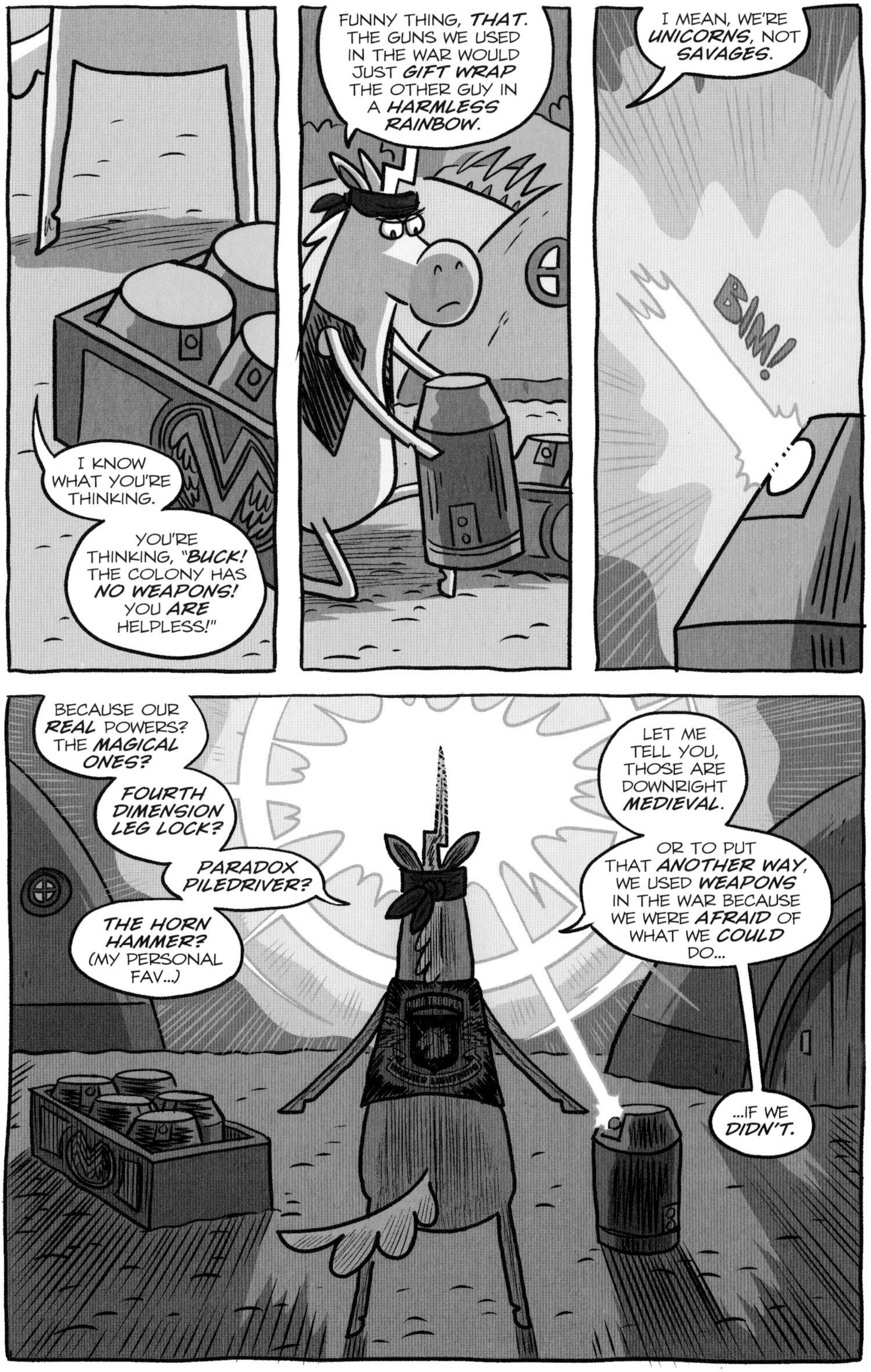
I KNOW WHAT YOU'RE THINKING.
YOU'RE THINKING, "BUCK! THE COLONY HAS NO WEAPONS! YOU ARE HELPLESS!"
FUNNY THING, THAT. THE GUNS WE USED IN THE WAR WOULD JUST GIFT WRAP THE OTHER GUY IN A HARMLESS RAINBOW.
I MEAN, WE'RE UNICORNS, NOT SAVAGES.
BIM!
BECAUSE OUR REAL POWERS? THE MAGICAL ONES?
FOURTH DIMENSION LEG LOCK?
PARADOX PILEDRIVER?
THE HORN HAMMER? (MY PERSONAL FAV...)
LET ME TELL YOU, THOSE ARE DOWNRIGHT MEDIEVAL.
OR TO PUT THAT ANOTHER WAY, WE USED WEAPONS IN THE WAR BECAUSE WE WERE AFRAID OF WHAT WE COULD DO...
...IF WE DIDN'T.

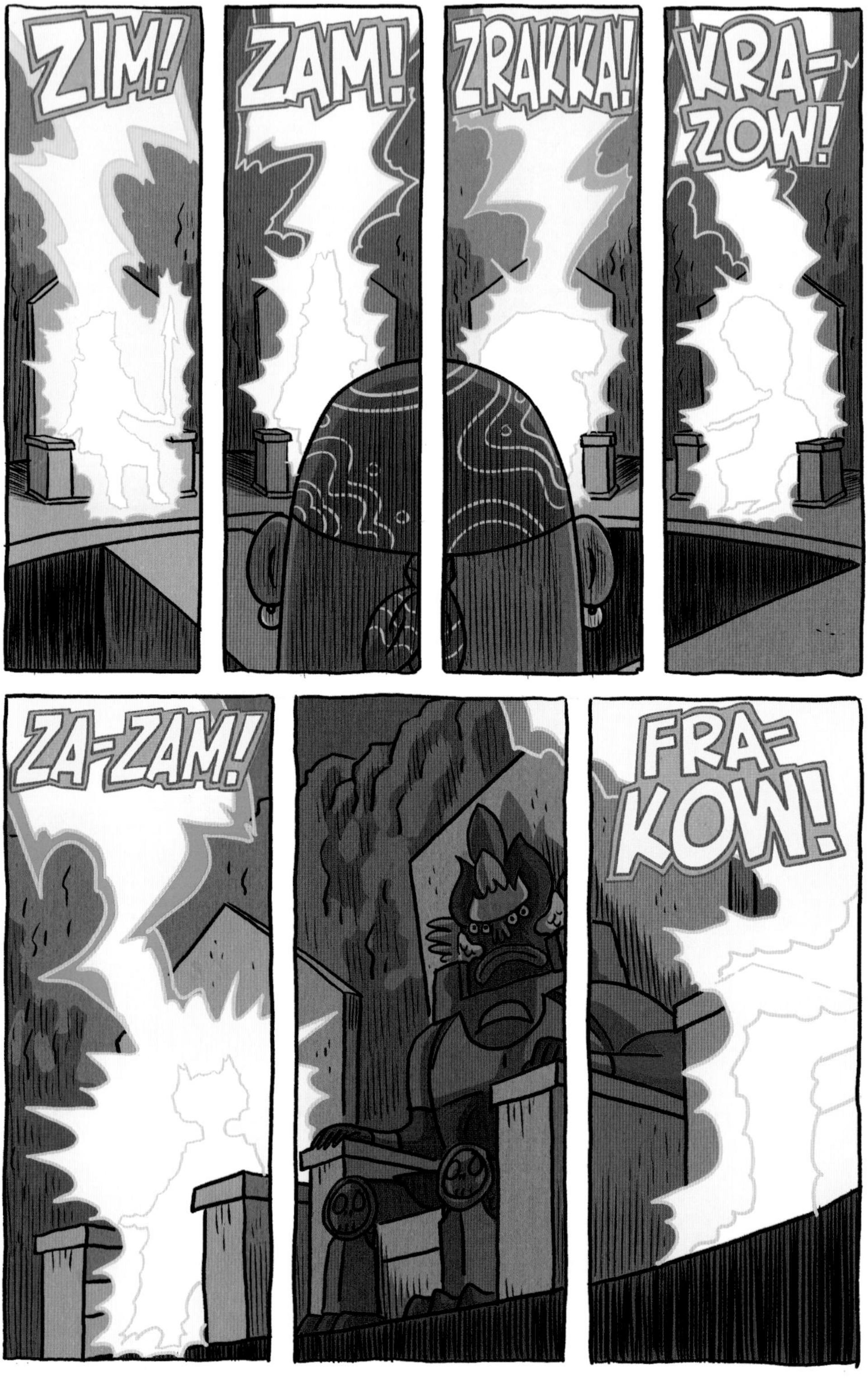
ZIM!
ZAM!
ZRAKKA!
KRA-ZOW!
ZA-ZAM!
FRA-KOW!

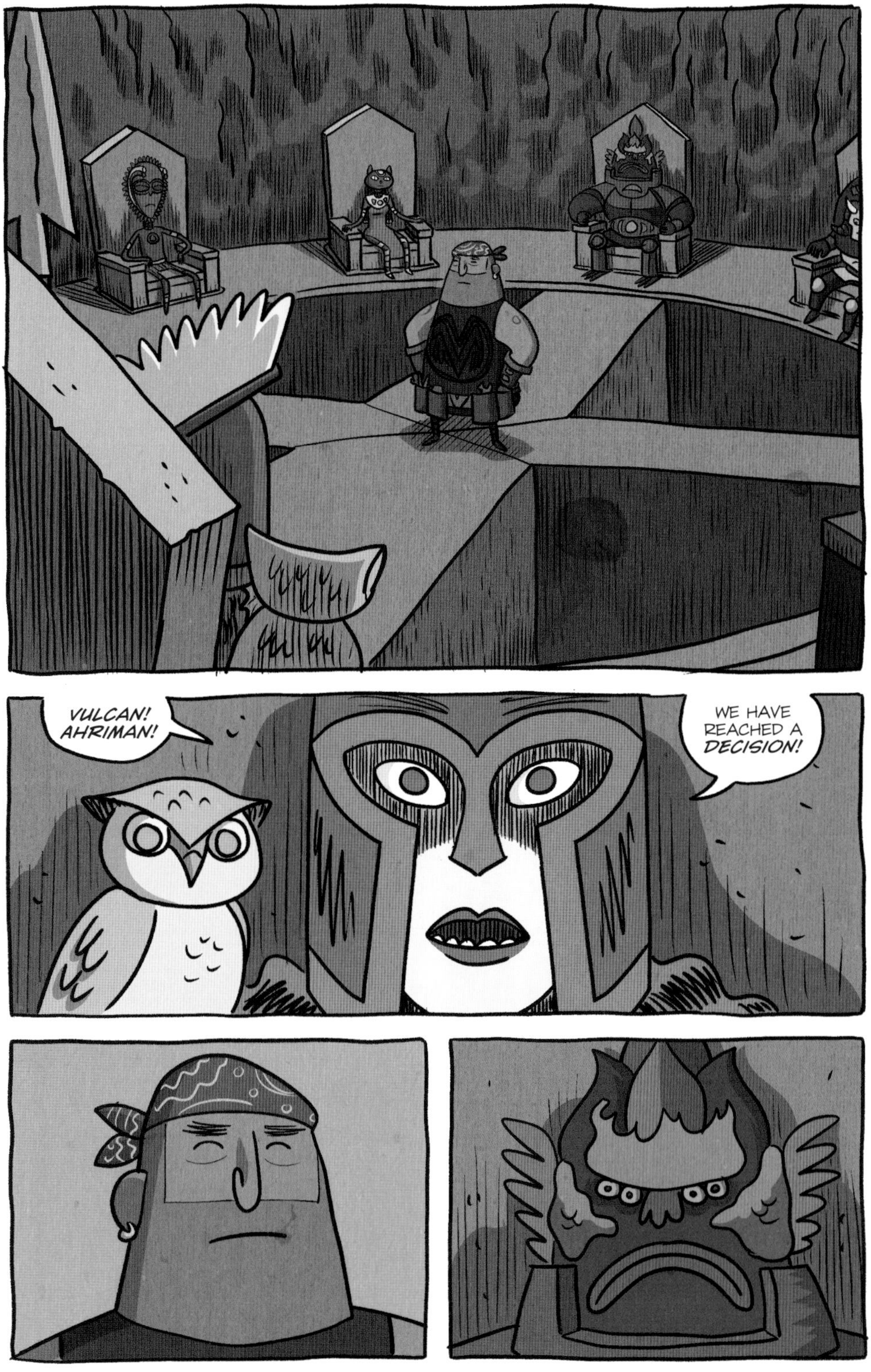
VULCAN! AHRIMAN!
WE HAVE REACHED A DECISION!

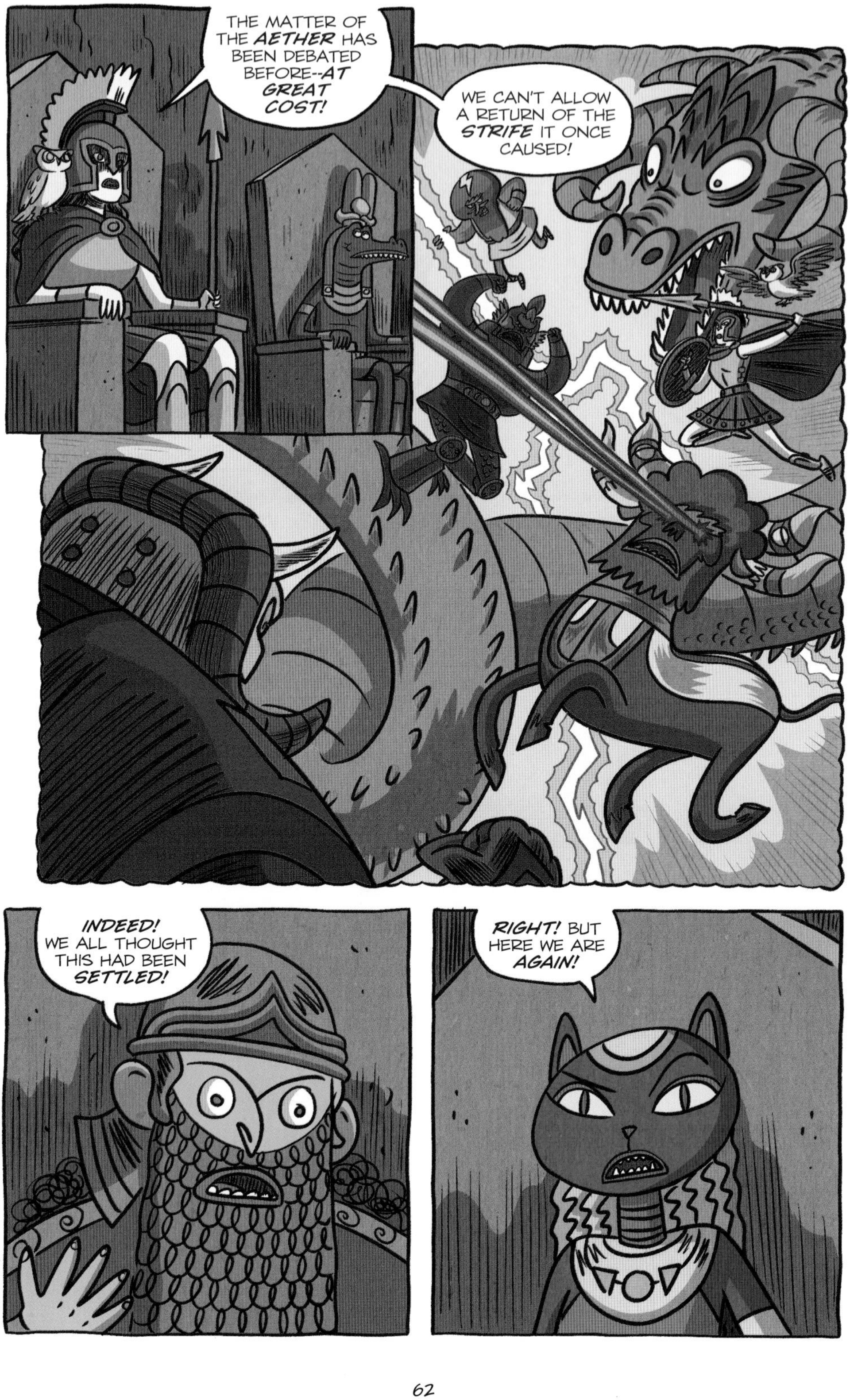
THE MATTER OF THE AETHER HAS BEEN DEBATED BEFORE--AT GREAT COST!
WE CAN'T ALLOW A RETURN OF THE STRIFE IT ONCE CAUSED!
INDEED! WE ALL THOUGHT THIS HAD BEEN SETTLED!
RIGHT! BUT HERE WE ARE AGAIN!

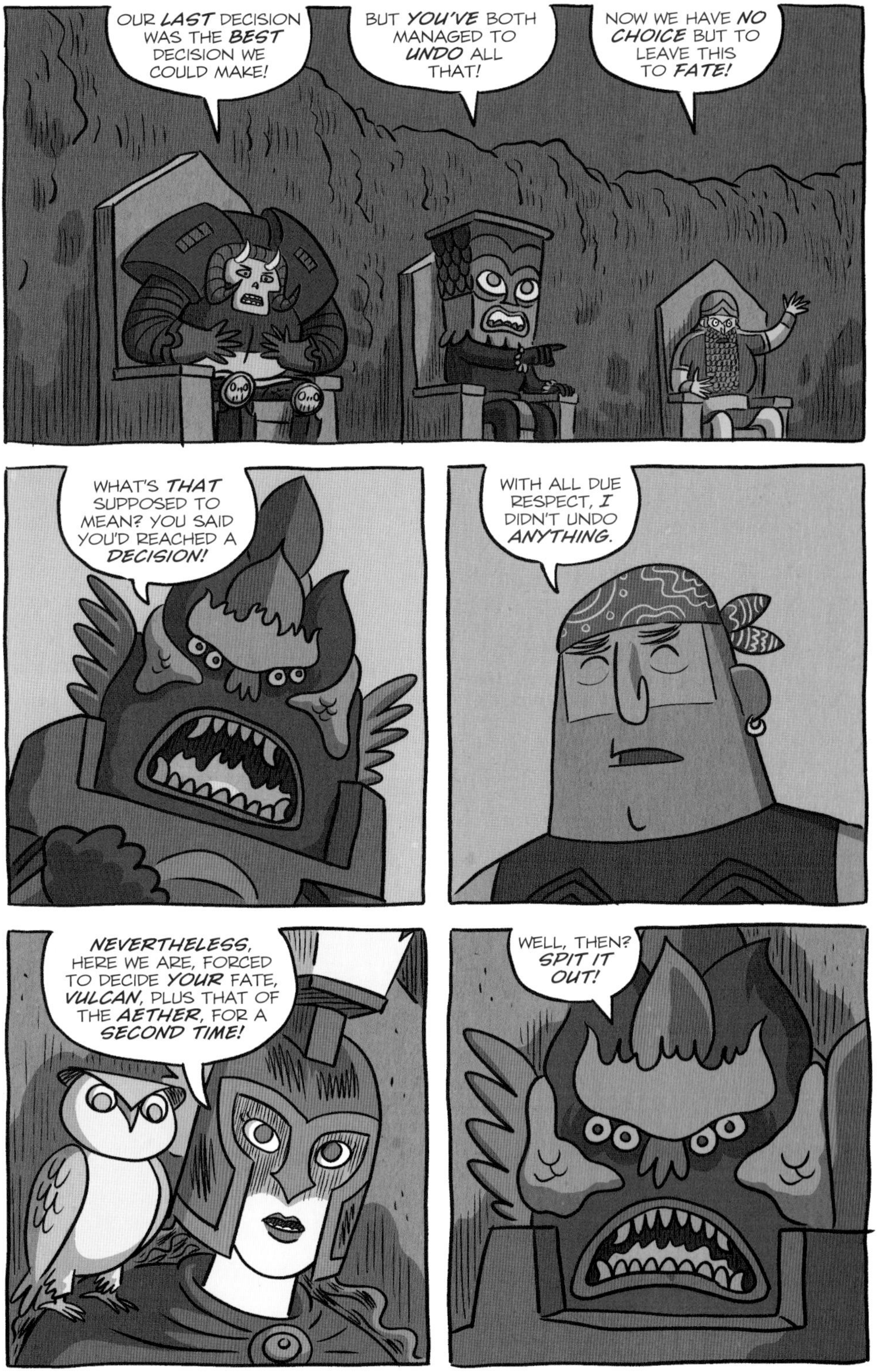
OUR LAST DECISION WAS THE BEST DECISION WE COULD MAKE!
BUT YOU'VE BOTH MANAGED TO UNDO ALL THAT!
NOW WE HAVE NO CHOICE BUT TO LEAVE THIS TO FATE!
WHAT'S THAT SUPPOSED TO MEAN? YOU SAID YOU'D REACHED A DECISION!
WITH ALL DUE RESPECT, I DIDN'T UNDO ANYTHING.
NEVERTHELESS, HERE WE ARE, FORCED TO DECIDE YOUR FATE, VULCAN, PLUS THAT OF THE AETHER, FOR A SECOND TIME!
WELL, THEN? SPIT IT OUT!

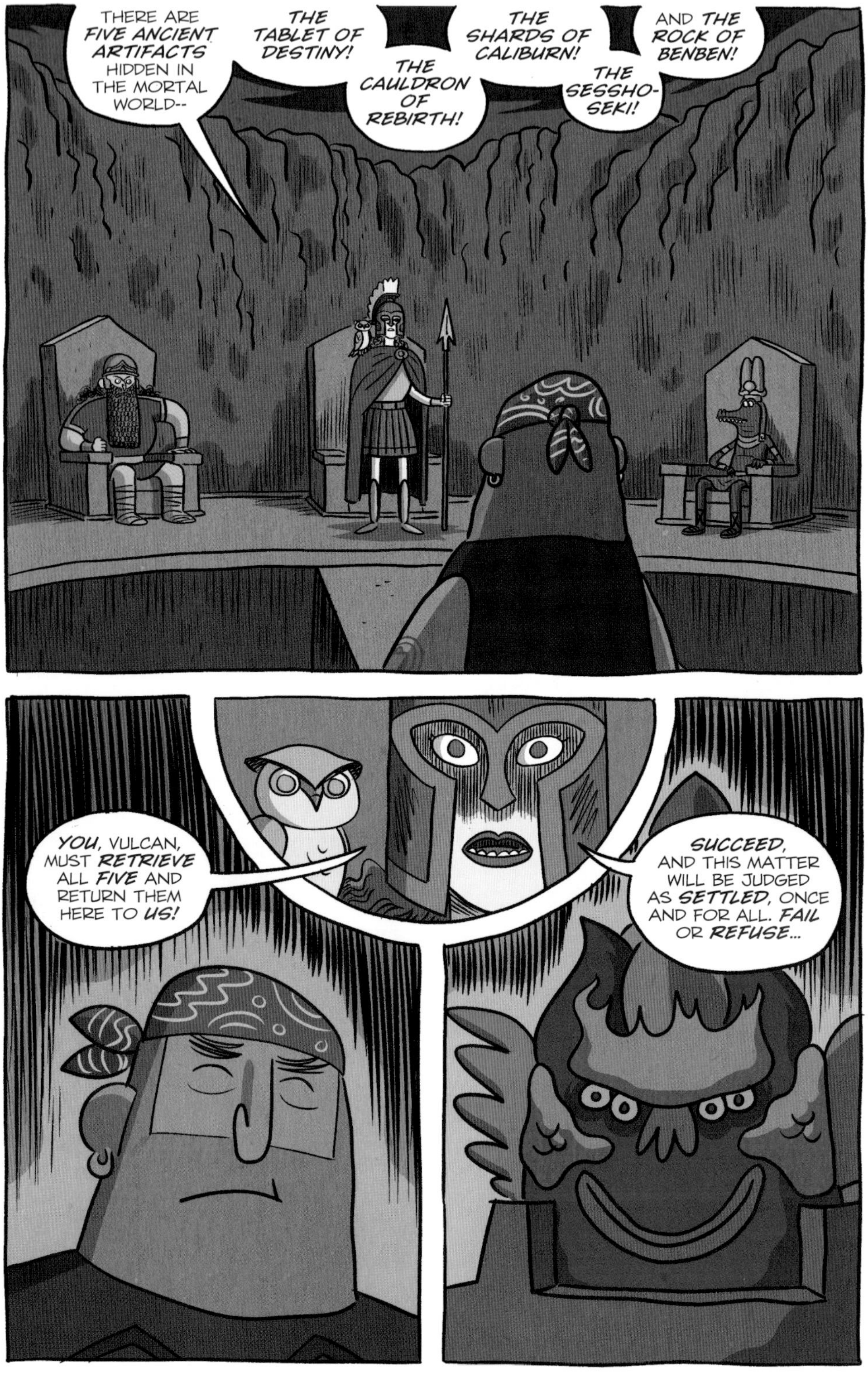
THERE ARE FIVE ANCIENT ARTIFACTS HIDDEN IN THE MORTAL WORLD--
THE TABLET OF DESTINY!
THE CAULDRON OF REBIRTH!
THE SHARDS OF CALIBURN!
THE SESSHO-SEKI!
AND THE ROCK OF BENBEN!
YOU, VULCAN, MUST RETRIEVE ALL FIVE AND RETURN THEM HERE TO US!
SUCCEED, AND THIS MATTER WILL BE JUDGED AS SETTLED, ONCE AND FOR ALL. FAIL OR REFUSE...

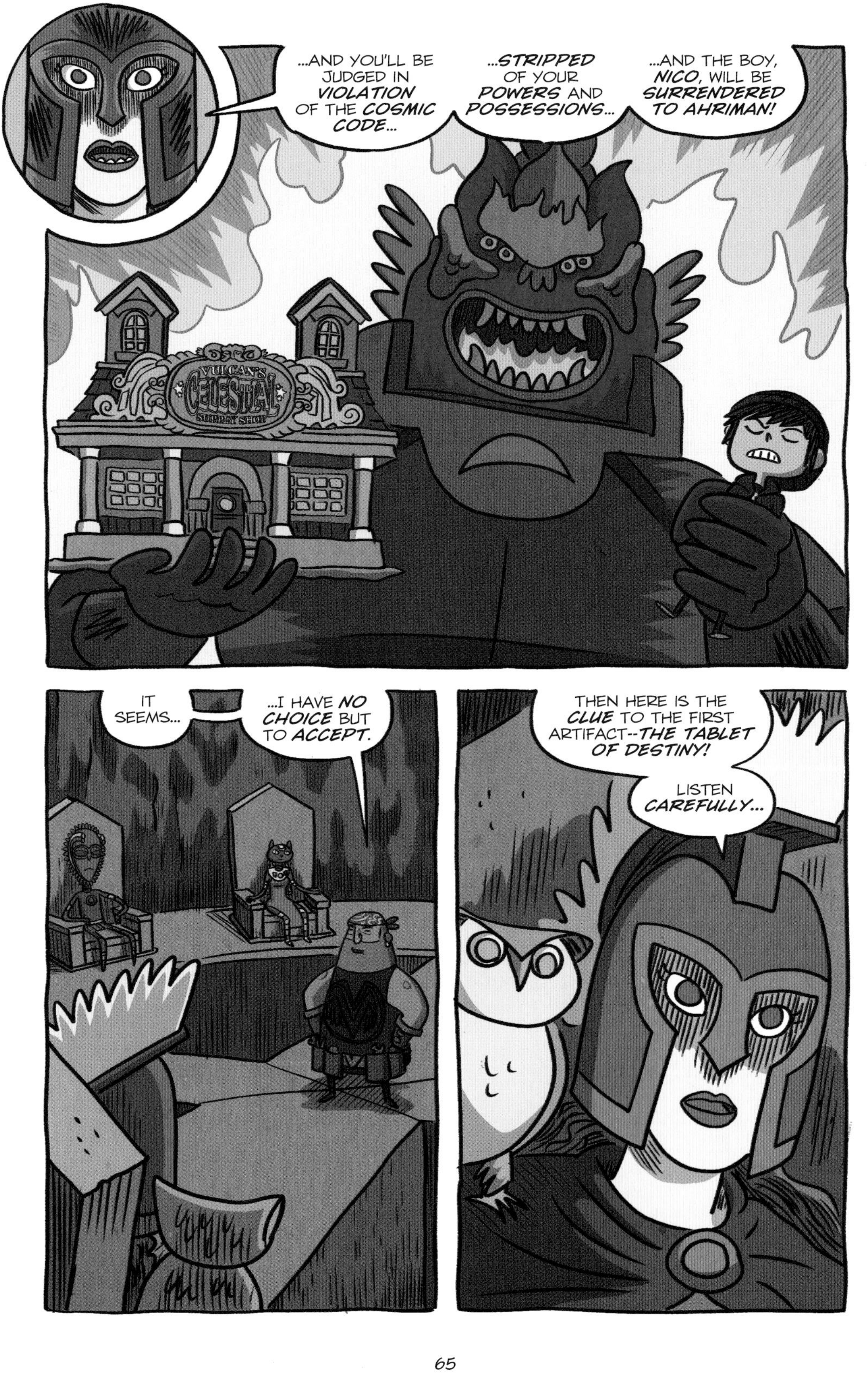
...AND YOU'LL BE JUDGED IN VIOLATION OF THE COSMIC CODE...
...STRIPPED OF YOUR POWERS AND POSSESSIONS...
...AND THE BOY, NICO, WILL BE SURRENDERED TO AHRIMAN!
VULCAN'S CELESTIAL SUPPLY SHOP
IT SEEMS...
...I HAVE NO CHOICE BUT TO ACCEPT.
THEN HERE IS THE CLUE TO THE FIRST ARTIFACT--THE TABLET OF DESTINY!
LISTEN CAREFULLY...

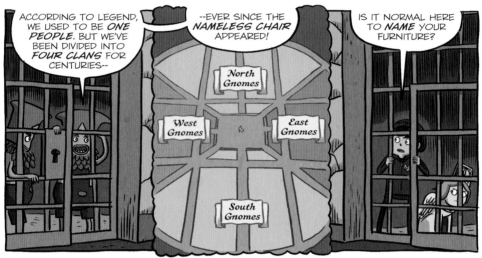

ACCORDING TO LEGEND, WE USED TO BE *ONE PEOPLE*. BUT WE'VE BEEN DIVIDED INTO *FOUR CLANS* FOR CENTURIES--

--EVER SINCE THE *NAMELESS CHAIR* APPEARED!

IS IT NORMAL HERE TO *NAME* YOUR FURNITURE?

North Gnomes

West Gnomes

East Gnomes

South Gnomes

OF COURSE NOT! IT'S *NAMELESS* BECAUSE IT BELONGS TO THE *NAMELESS GOD!* HE WHO WILL *RETURN* TO *DESTROY* THE ENEMIES OF HIS PEOPLE!

OH, I SEE. WELL, THAT'S PRETTY *STANDARD* STUFF AS *LEGENDS* GO. WHO ARE THE *ENEMIES?*

WHICHEVER CLAN THE CHAIR'S *FACING* WHEN THE *NAMELESS GOD* APPEARS IN IT! *DUH!*

ARE YOU SAYING ALL THIS *FIGHTING'S* OVER WHICH DIRECTION THAT CHAIR IS *FACING?*

BOOOOOMM!!!

TARU'S TORRENTS! IT SOUNDS LIKE WE JUST TOOK A *DIRECT HIT!*

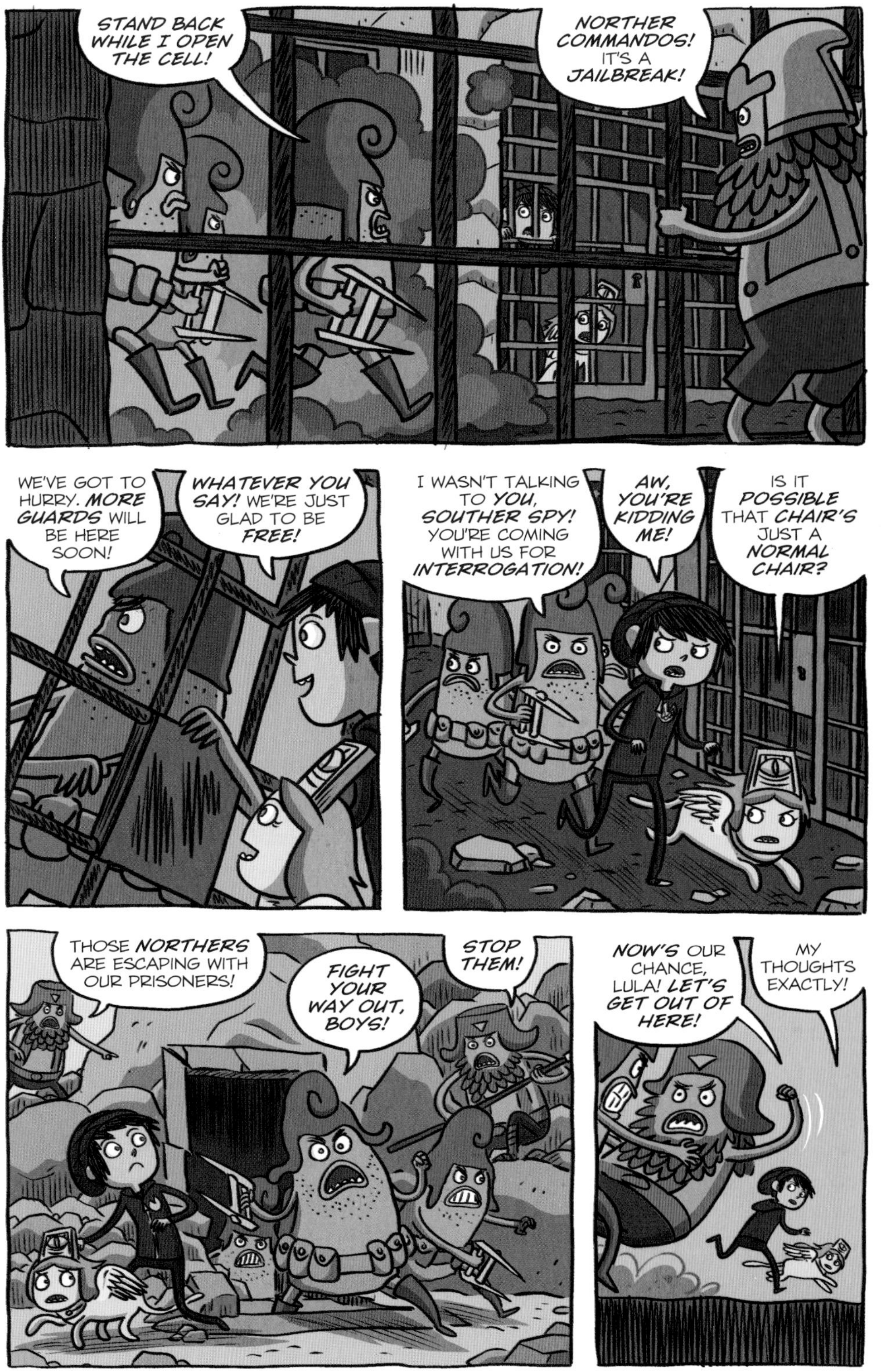
STAND BACK WHILE I OPEN THE CELL!
NORTHER COMMANDOS! IT'S A JAILBREAK!
WE'VE GOT TO HURRY. MORE GUARDS WILL BE HERE SOON!
WHATEVER YOU SAY! WE'RE JUST GLAD TO BE FREE!
I WASN'T TALKING TO YOU, SOUTHER SPY! YOU'RE COMING WITH US FOR INTERROGATION!
AW, YOU'RE KIDDING ME!
IS IT POSSIBLE THAT CHAIR'S JUST A NORMAL CHAIR?
THOSE NORTHERS ARE ESCAPING WITH OUR PRISONERS!
FIGHT YOUR WAY OUT, BOYS!
STOP THEM!
NOW'S OUR CHANCE, LULA! LET'S GET OUT OF HERE!
MY THOUGHTS EXACTLY!

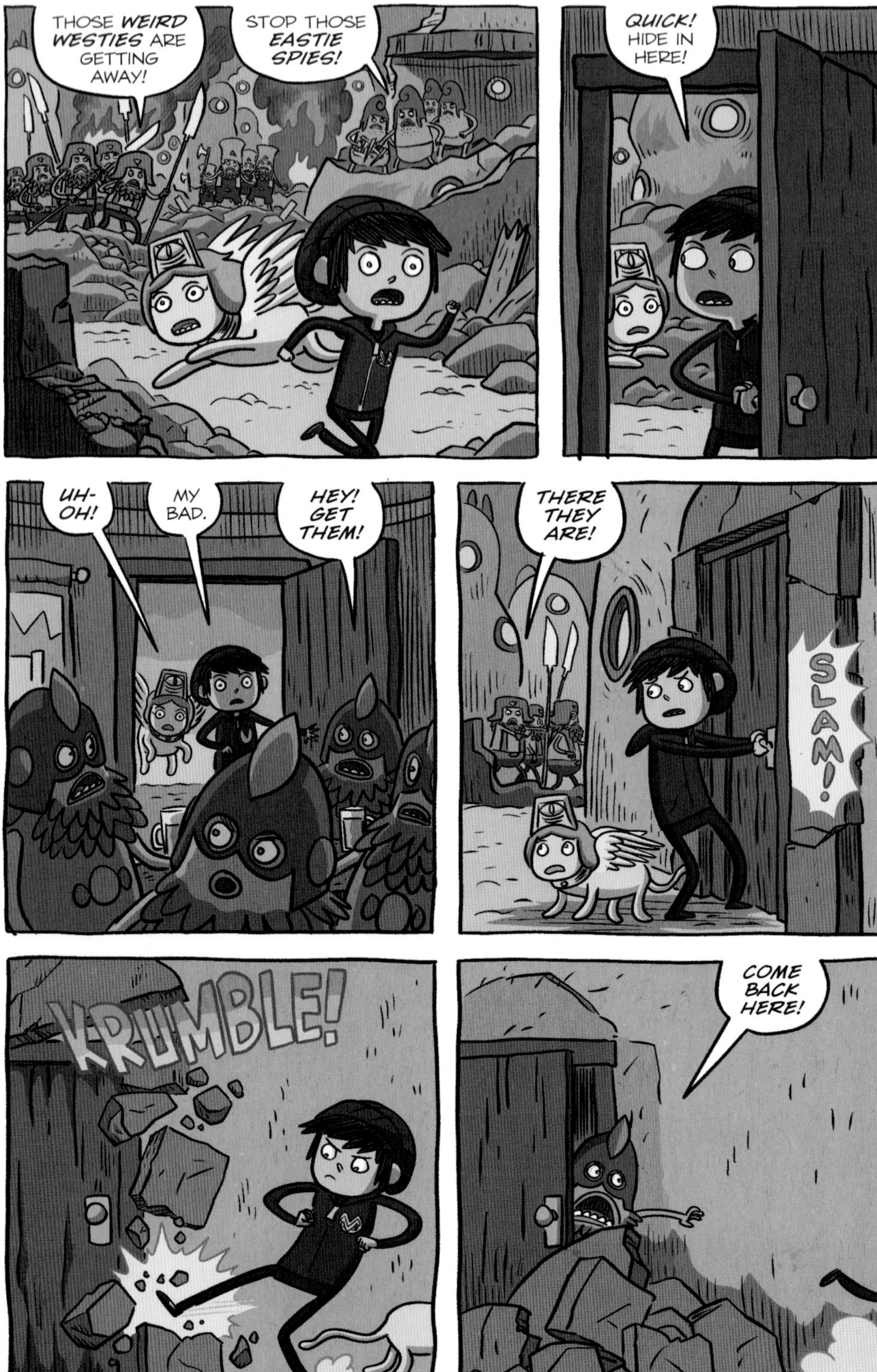
THOSE WEIRD WESTIES ARE GETTING AWAY!
STOP THOSE EASTIE SPIES!
QUICK! HIDE IN HERE!
UH-OH!
MY BAD.
HEY! GET THEM!
THERE THEY ARE!
SLAM!
KRUMBLE!
COME BACK HERE!

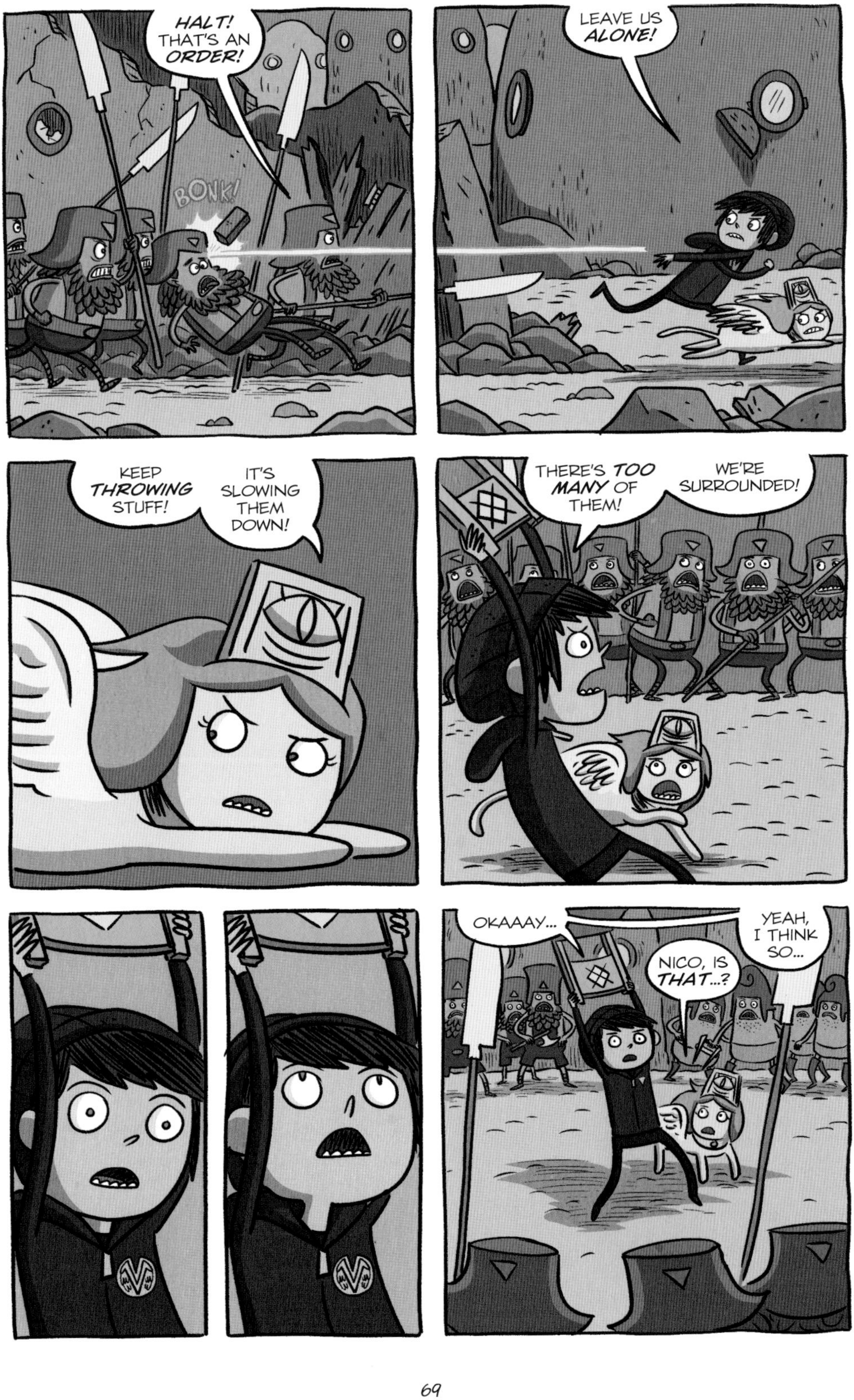
HALT! THAT'S AN ORDER!
BONK!
LEAVE US ALONE!
KEEP THROWING STUFF!
IT'S SLOWING THEM DOWN!
THERE'S TOO MANY OF THEM!
WE'RE SURROUNDED!
OKAAAY...
NICO, IS THAT...?
YEAH, I THINK SO...

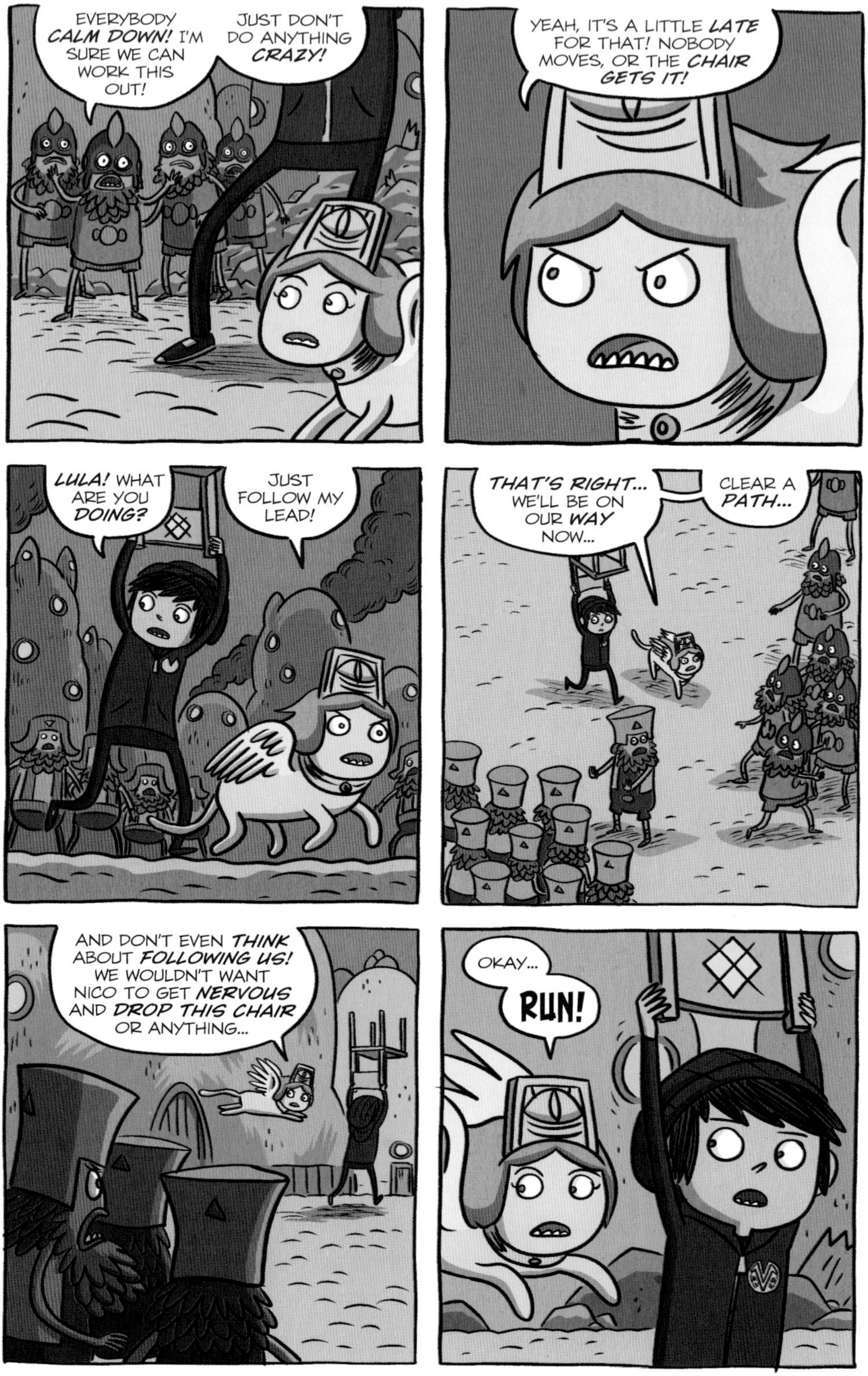
EVERYBODY CALM DOWN! I'M SURE WE CAN WORK THIS OUT!
JUST DON'T DO ANYTHING CRAZY!
YEAH, IT'S A LITTLE LATE FOR THAT! NOBODY MOVES, OR THE CHAIR GETS IT!
LULA! WHAT ARE YOU DOING?
JUST FOLLOW MY LEAD!
THAT'S RIGHT... WE'LL BE ON OUR WAY NOW...
CLEAR A PATH...
AND DON'T EVEN THINK ABOUT FOLLOWING US! WE WOULDN'T WANT NICO TO GET NERVOUS AND DROP THIS CHAIR OR ANYTHING...
OKAY...
RUN!

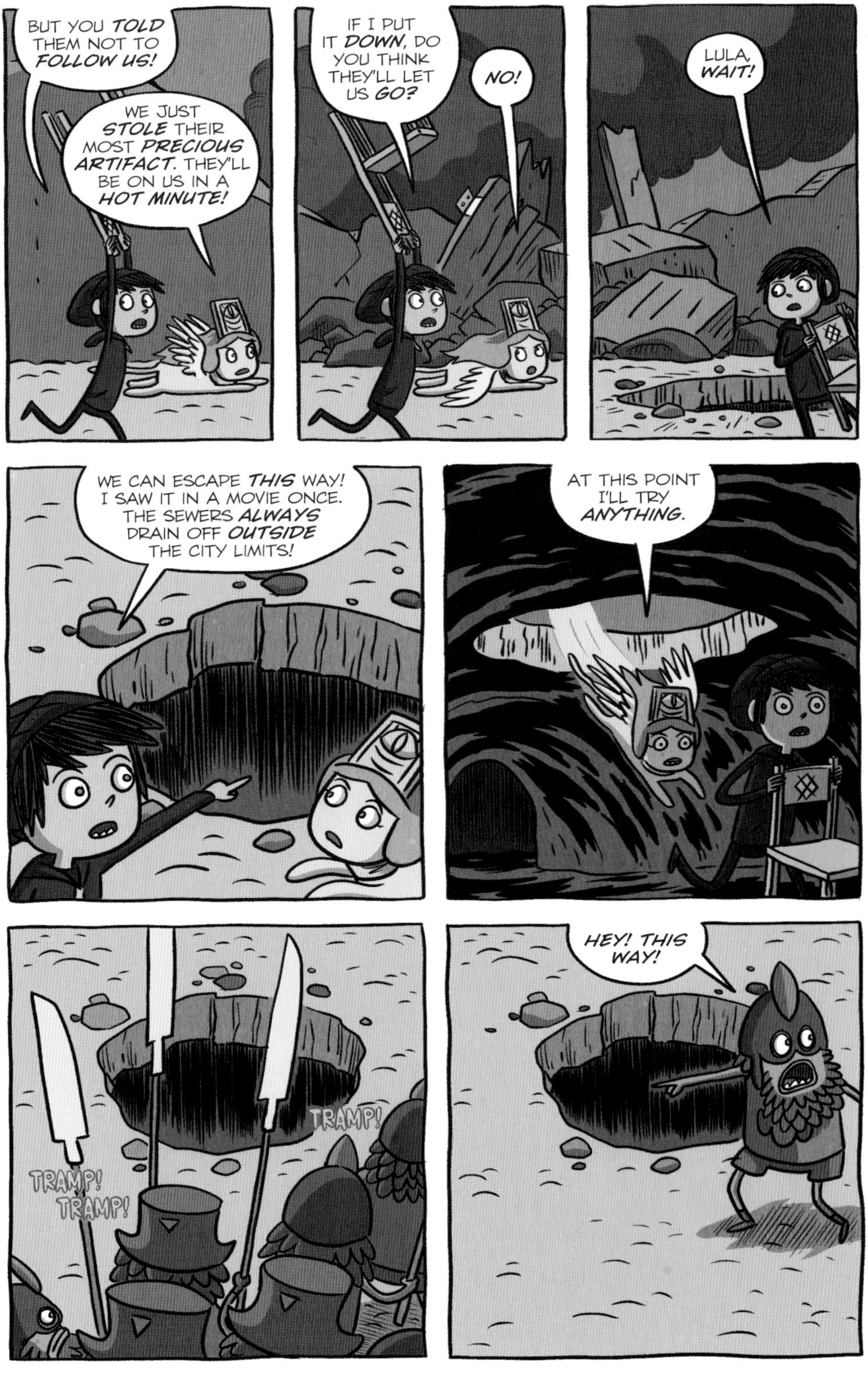
BUT YOU TOLD THEM NOT TO FOLLOW US!
WE JUST STOLE THEIR MOST PRECIOUS ARTIFACT. THEY'LL BE ON US IN A HOT MINUTE!
IF I PUT IT DOWN, DO YOU THINK THEY'LL LET US GO?
NO!
LULA, WAIT!
WE CAN ESCAPE THIS WAY! I SAW IT IN A MOVIE ONCE. THE SEWERS ALWAYS DRAIN OFF OUTSIDE THE CITY LIMITS!
AT THIS POINT I'LL TRY ANYTHING.
TRAMP!
TRAMP!
TRAMP!
HEY! THIS WAY!

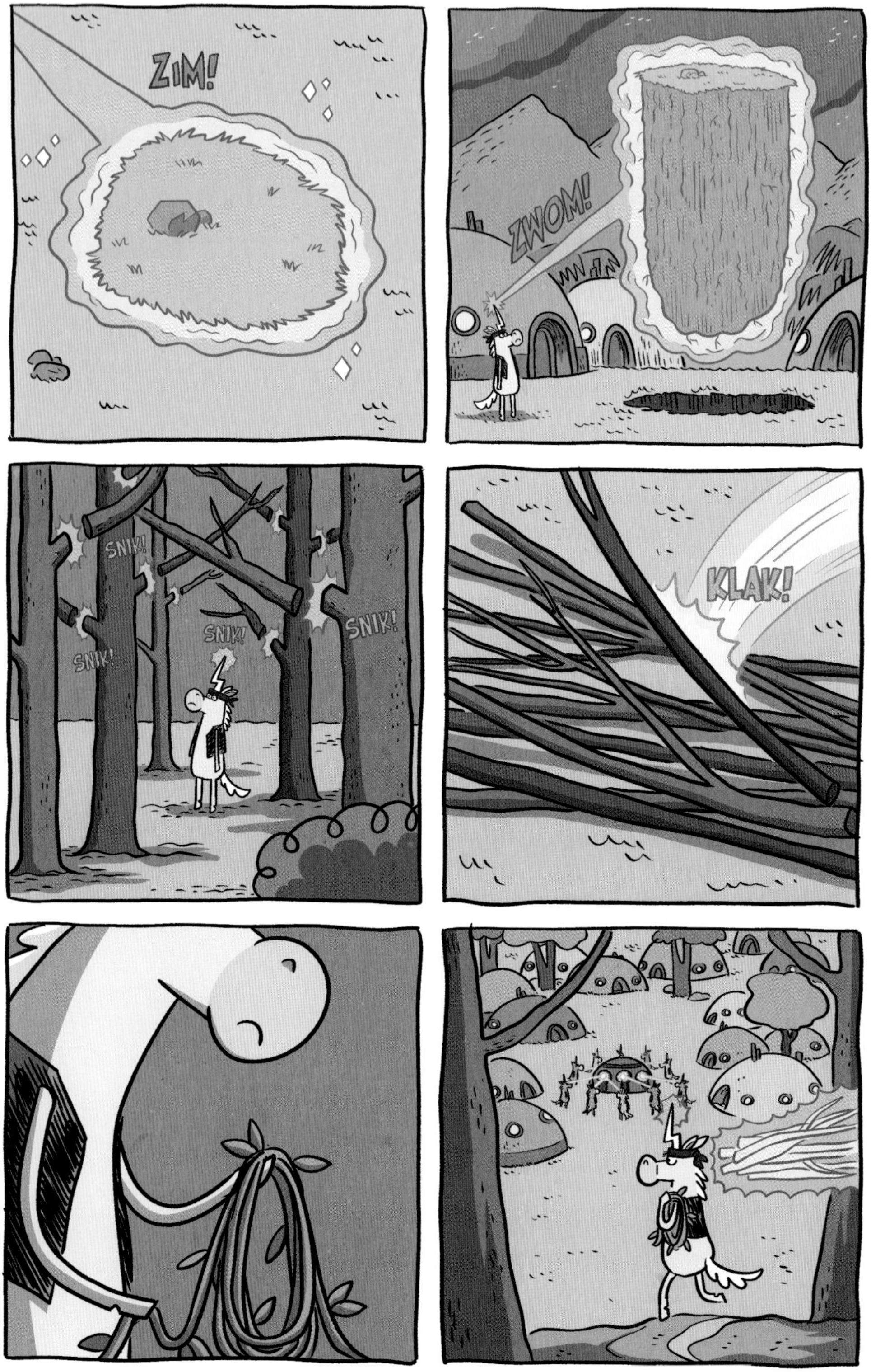
ZIM!
ZWOM!
SNIK!
SNIK!
SNIK!
SNIK!
KLAK!

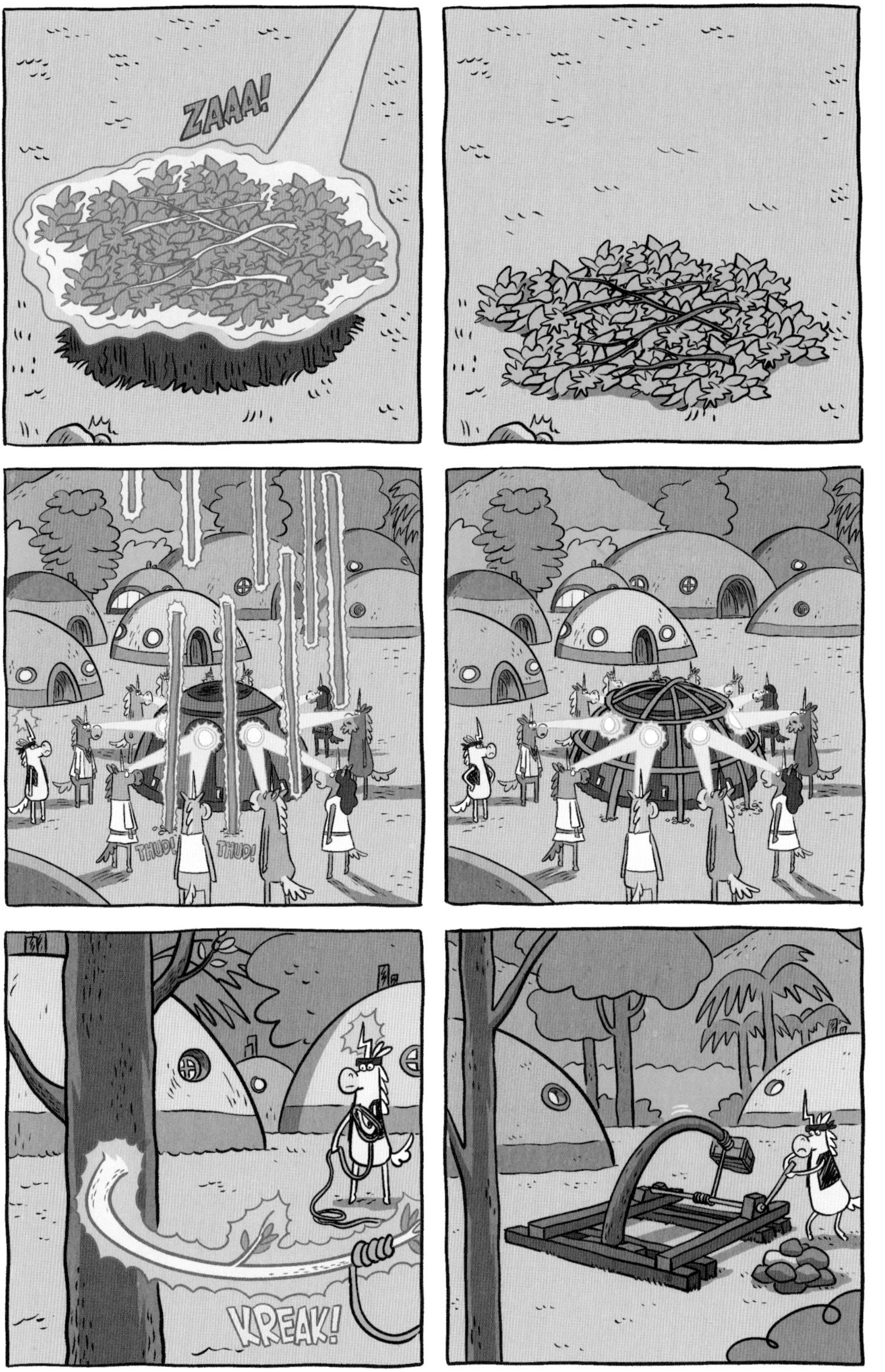
ZAAA!
THUD!
THUD!
KREAK!

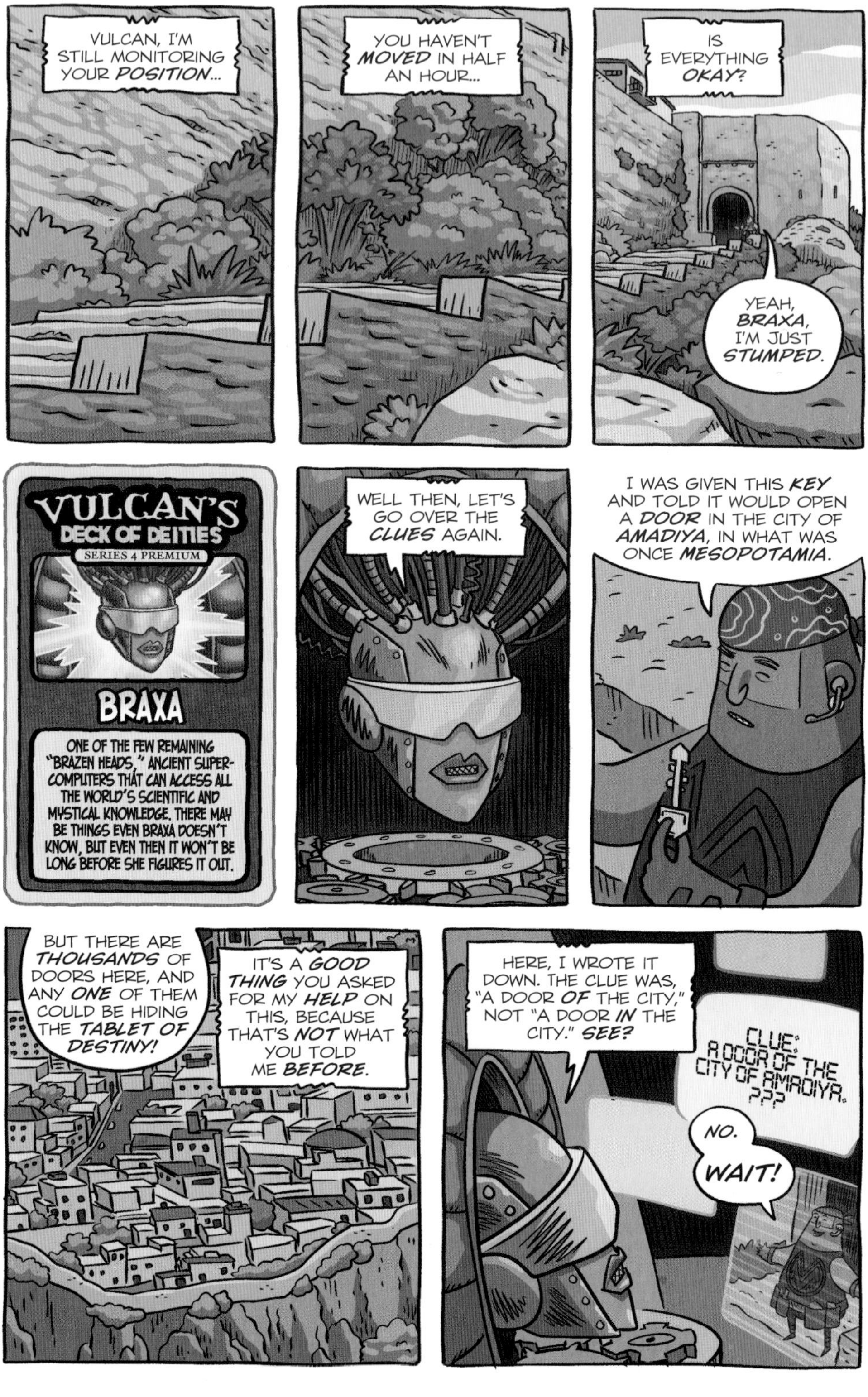
VULCAN, I'M STILL MONITORING YOUR POSITION...
YOU HAVEN'T MOVED IN HALF AN HOUR...
IS EVERYTHING OKAY?
YEAH, BRAXA, I'M JUST STUMPED.
VULCAN'S DECK OF DEITIES
SERIES 4 PREMIUM
BRAXA
ONE OF THE FEW REMAINING "BRAZEN HEADS," ANCIENT SUPER-COMPUTERS THAT CAN ACCESS ALL THE WORLD'S SCIENTIFIC AND MYSTICAL KNOWLEDGE. THERE MAY BE THINGS EVEN BRAXA DOESN'T KNOW, BUT EVEN THEN IT WON'T BE LONG BEFORE SHE FIGURES IT OUT.
WELL THEN, LET'S GO OVER THE CLUES AGAIN.
I WAS GIVEN THIS KEY AND TOLD IT WOULD OPEN A DOOR IN THE CITY OF AMADIYA, IN WHAT WAS ONCE MESOPOTAMIA.
BUT THERE ARE THOUSANDS OF DOORS HERE, AND ANY ONE OF THEM COULD BE HIDING THE TABLET OF DESTINY!
IT'S A GOOD THING YOU ASKED FOR MY HELP ON THIS, BECAUSE THAT'S NOT WHAT YOU TOLD ME BEFORE.
HERE, I WROTE IT DOWN. THE CLUE WAS, "A DOOR OF THE CITY," NOT "A DOOR IN THE CITY." SEE?
CLUE: A DOOR OF THE CITY OF AMADIYA. ???
NO.
WAIT!

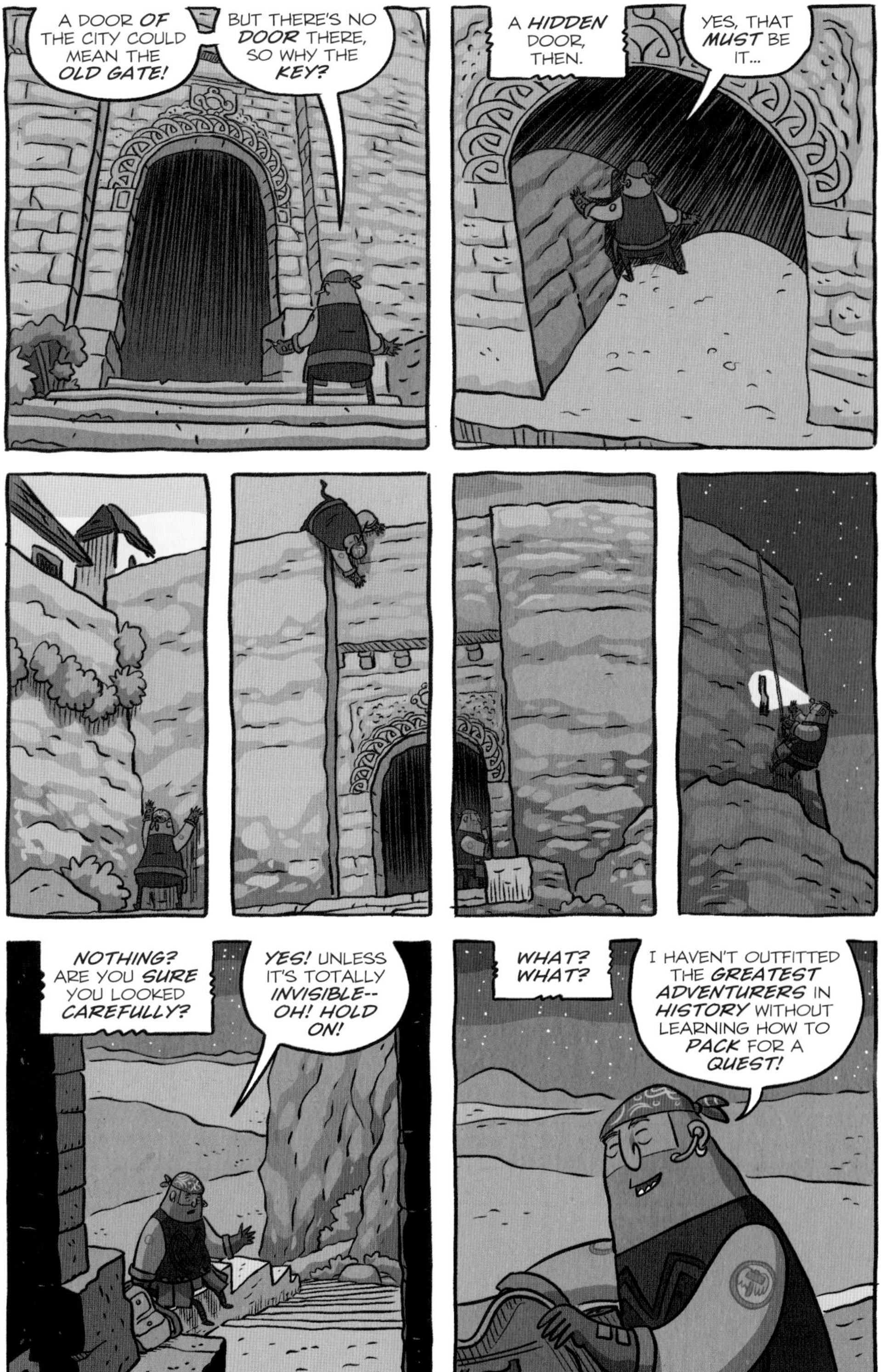
A DOOR OF THE CITY COULD MEAN THE OLD GATE!
BUT THERE'S NO DOOR THERE, SO WHY THE KEY?
A HIDDEN DOOR, THEN.
YES, THAT MUST BE IT...
NOTHING? ARE YOU SURE YOU LOOKED CAREFULLY?
YES! UNLESS IT'S TOTALLY INVISIBLE-- OH! HOLD ON!
WHAT? WHAT?
I HAVEN'T OUTFITTED THE GREATEST ADVENTURERS IN HISTORY WITHOUT LEARNING HOW TO PACK FOR A QUEST!

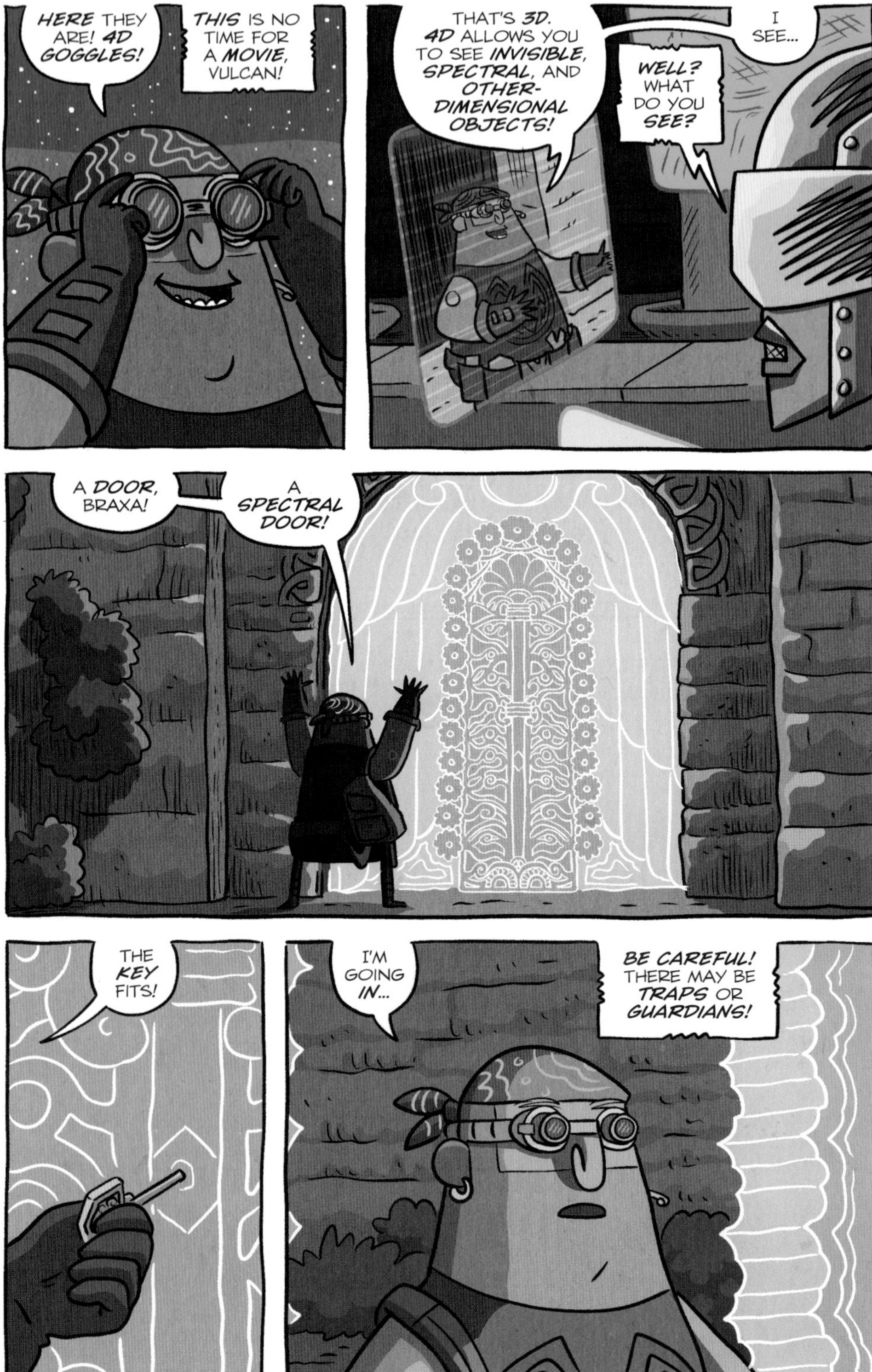
HERE THEY ARE! 4D GOGGLES!
THIS IS NO TIME FOR A MOVIE, VULCAN!
THAT'S 3D. 4D ALLOWS YOU TO SEE INVISIBLE, SPECTRAL, AND OTHER-DIMENSIONAL OBJECTS!
I SEE...
WELL? WHAT DO YOU SEE?
A DOOR, BRAXA!
A SPECTRAL DOOR!
THE KEY FITS!
I'M GOING IN...
BE CAREFUL! THERE MAY BE TRAPS OR GUARDIANS!

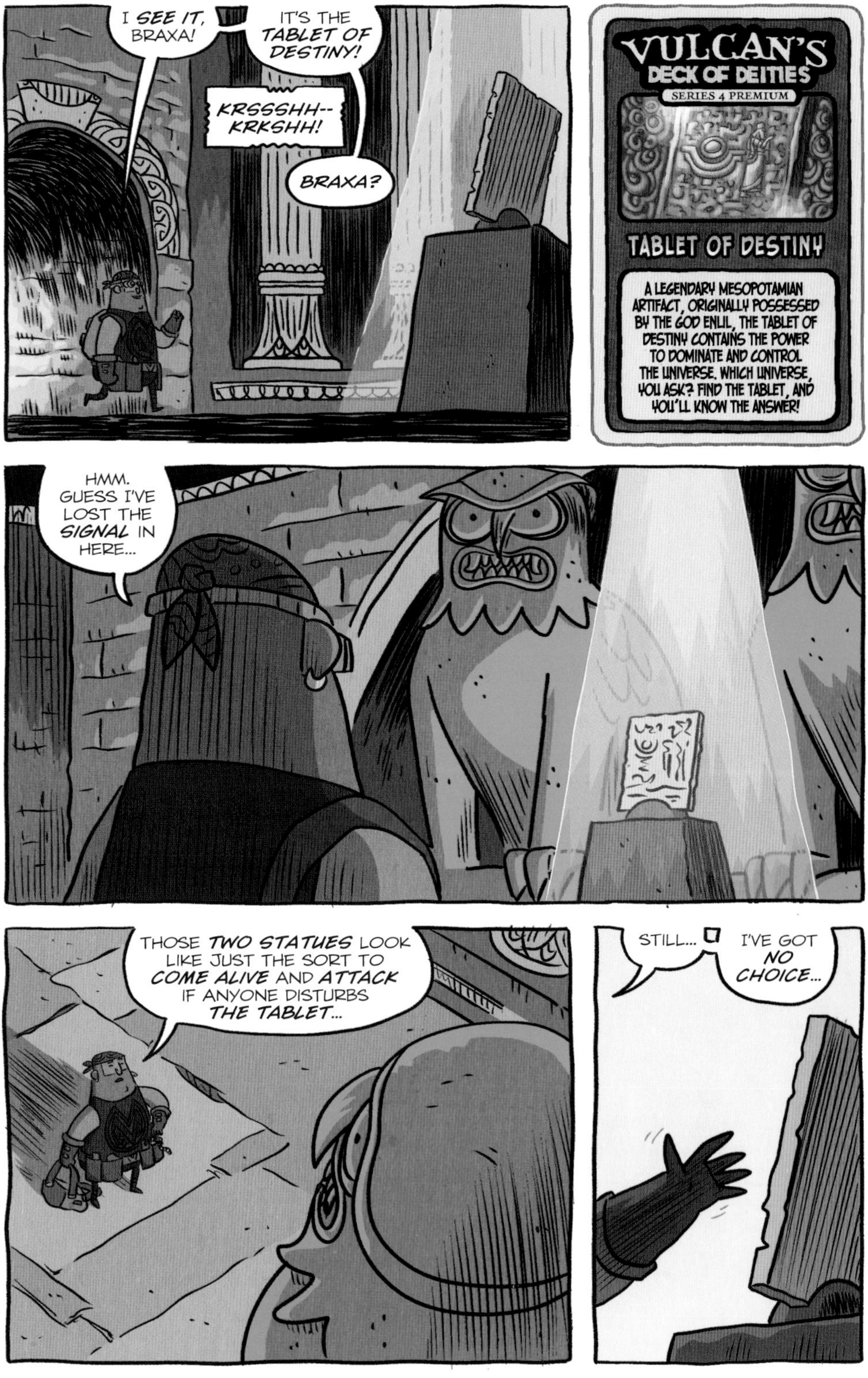

I SEE IT, BRAXA!
IT'S THE TABLET OF DESTINY!
KRSSSHH-- KRKSHH!
BRAXA?
VULCAN'S DECK OF DEITIES
SERIES 4 PREMIUM
TABLET OF DESTINY
A LEGENDARY MESOPOTAMIAN ARTIFACT, ORIGINALLY POSSESSED BY THE GOD ENLIL, THE TABLET OF DESTINY CONTAINS THE POWER TO DOMINATE AND CONTROL THE UNIVERSE. WHICH UNIVERSE, YOU ASK? FIND THE TABLET, AND YOU'LL KNOW THE ANSWER!
HMM. GUESS I'VE LOST THE SIGNAL IN HERE...
THOSE TWO STATUES LOOK LIKE JUST THE SORT TO COME ALIVE AND ATTACK IF ANYONE DISTURBS THE TABLET...
STILL...
I'VE GOT NO CHOICE...

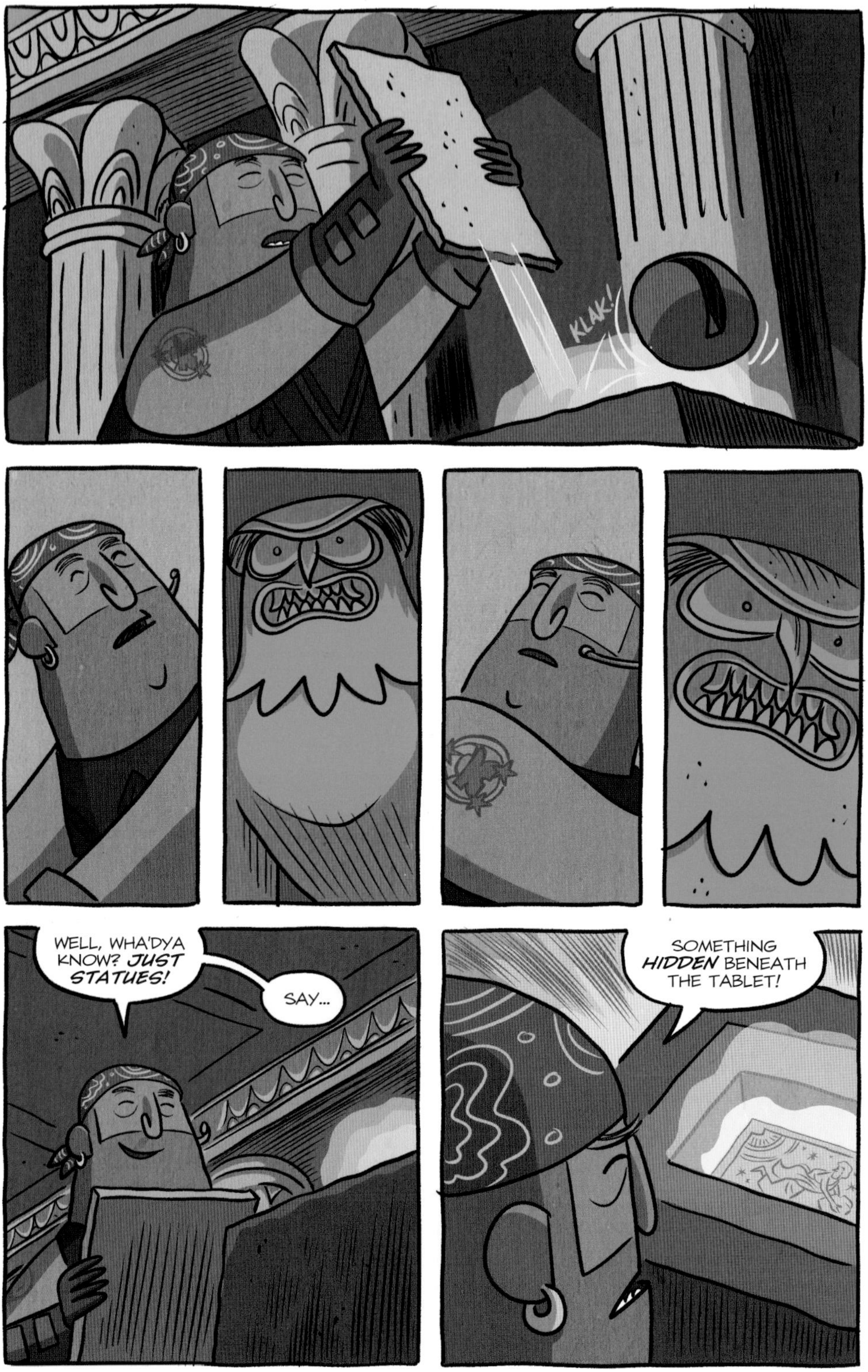
KLAK!
WELL, WHA'DYA KNOW? **JUST STATUES!**
SAY...
SOMETHING **HIDDEN** BENEATH THE TABLET!

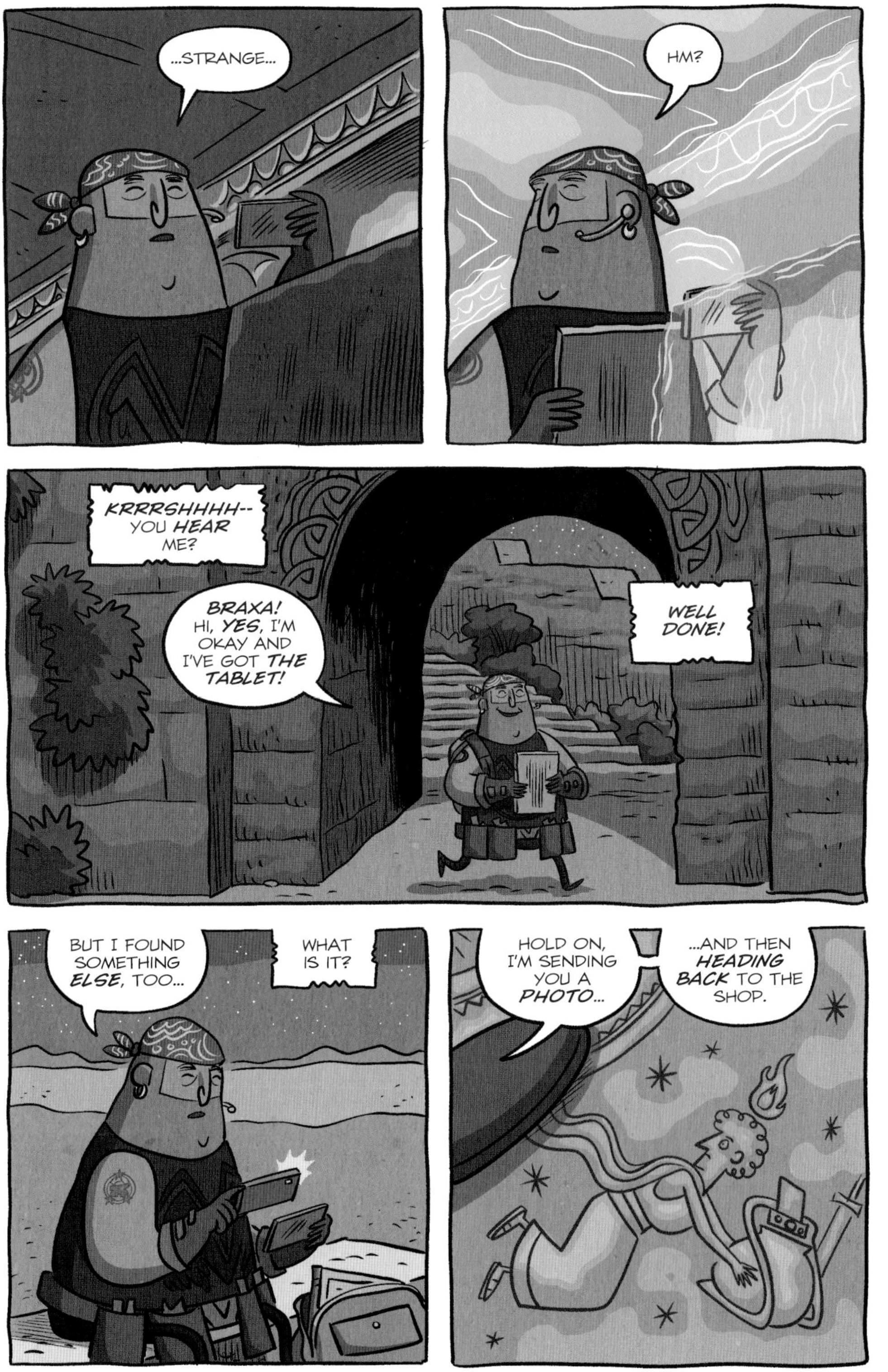
...STRANGE...
HM?
KRRRSHHHH-- YOU HEAR ME?
BRAXA! HI, YES, I'M OKAY AND I'VE GOT THE TABLET!
WELL DONE!
BUT I FOUND SOMETHING ELSE, TOO...
WHAT IS IT?
HOLD ON, I'M SENDING YOU A PHOTO...
...AND THEN HEADING BACK TO THE SHOP.

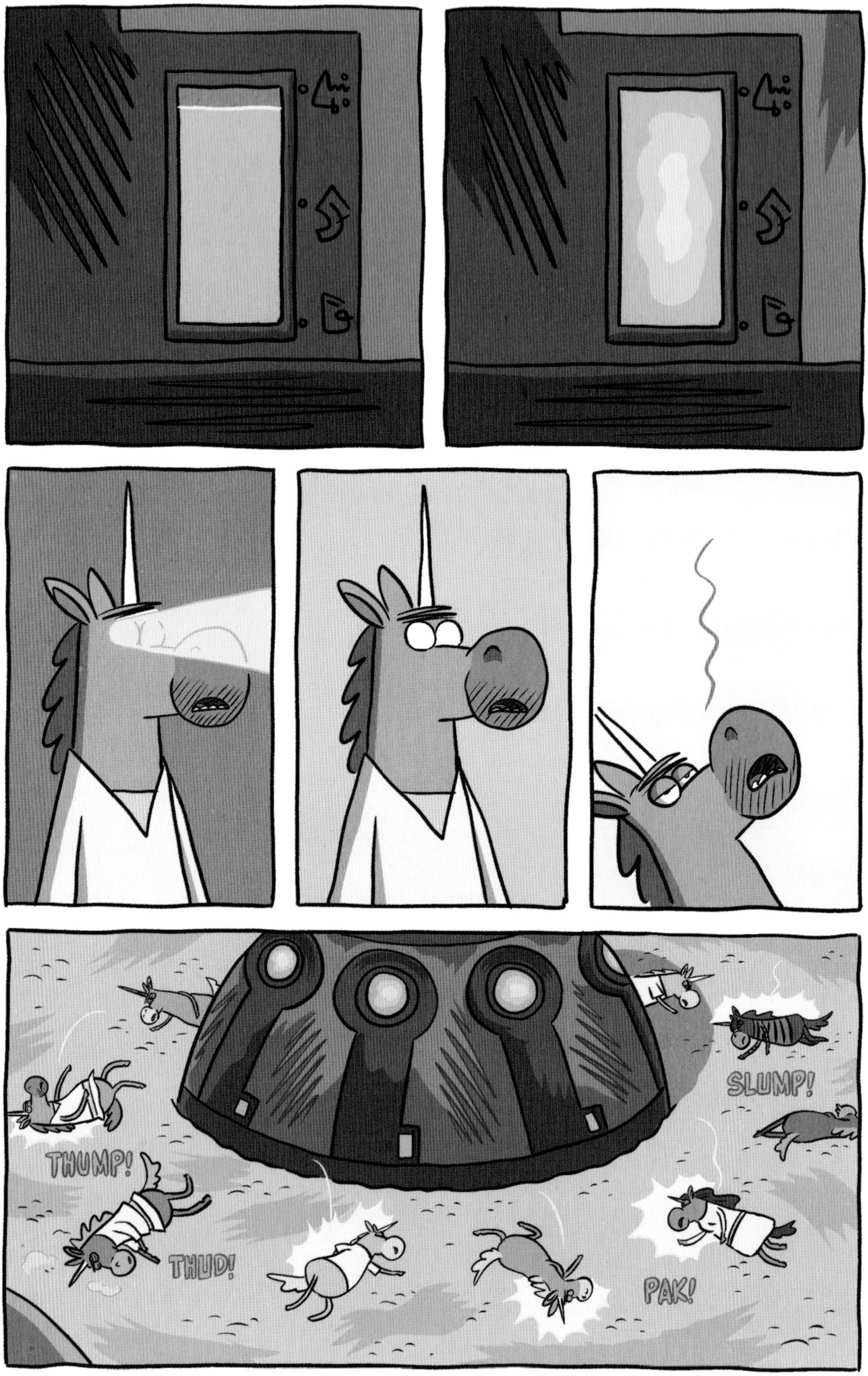
SLUMP!
THUMP!
THUD!
PAK!

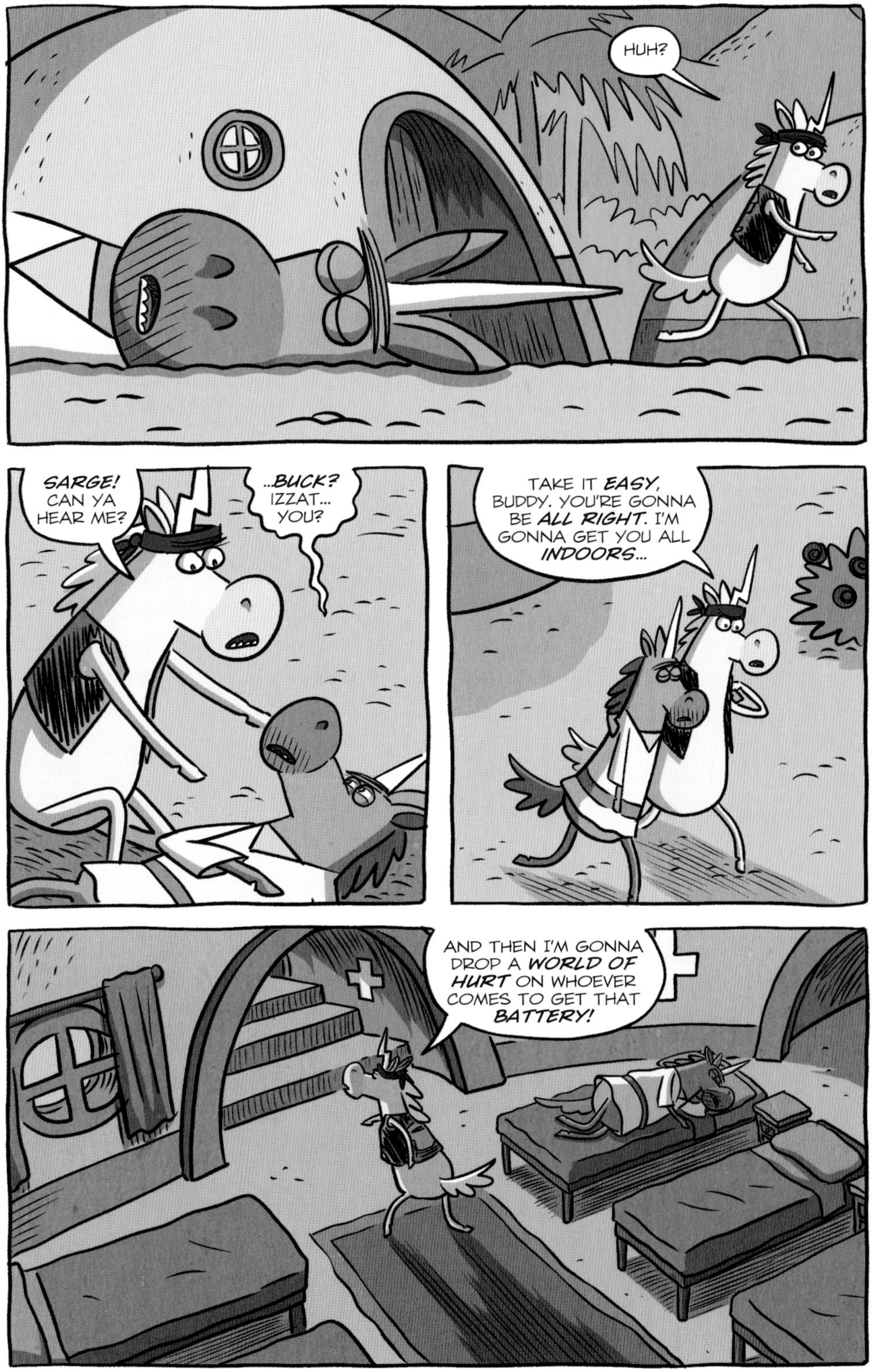
HUH?
SARGE! CAN YA HEAR ME?
...BUCK? IZZAT... YOU?
TAKE IT EASY, BUDDY. YOU'RE GONNA BE ALL RIGHT. I'M GONNA GET YOU ALL INDOORS...
AND THEN I'M GONNA DROP A WORLD OF HURT ON WHOEVER COMES TO GET THAT BATTERY!

SLAP! SPLISH! SPLASH!

SPLISH! SPLASH! SPLAP!

NICO, IN THAT *MOVIE* YOU SAW, DID THE *GOOD GUYS* GET AWAY?

FLAP! FLAP! FLAP!

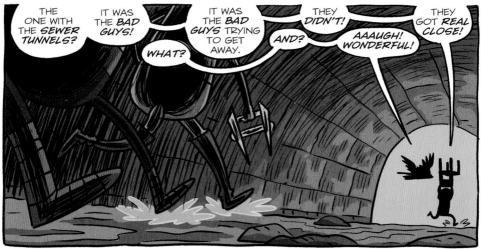

THE ONE WITH THE *SEWER TUNNELS?*

IT WAS THE *BAD GUYS!*

WHAT?

IT WAS THE *BAD GUYS* TRYING TO GET AWAY.

AND?

THEY *DIDN'T!*

AAAUGH! WONDERFUL!

THEY GOT *REAL CLOSE!*

WAIT, LULA! *IN HERE!*

THE SIGN SAYS *"DO NOT ENTER!"*

EXACTLY! THEY WON'T *FOLLOW* US!

DO NOT ENTER!

LOST CAVERNS

DANGER!

DO NOT ENTER

WHY *NOT?*

BECAUSE THE *SIGN!* COME ON!

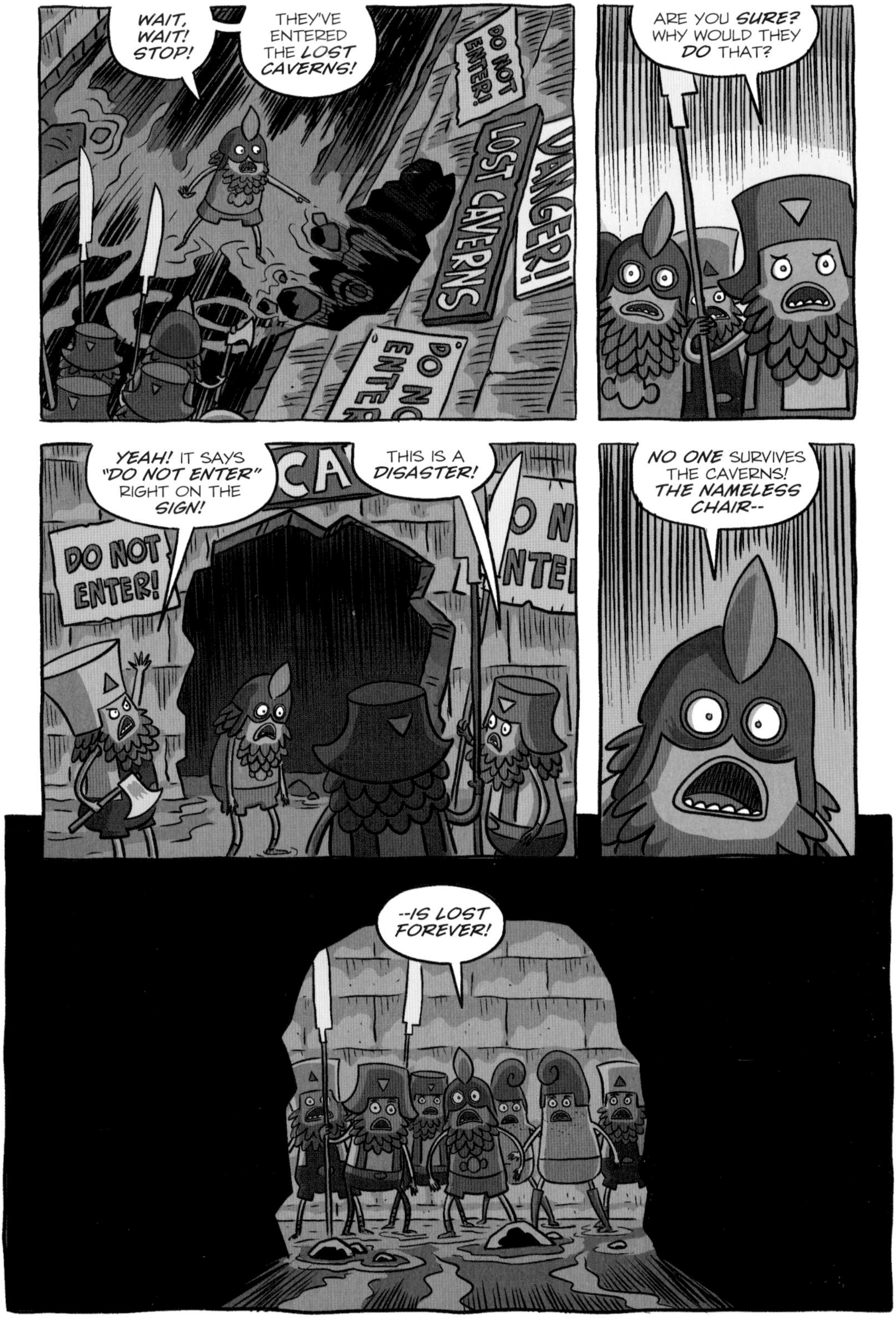

WAIT, WAIT! STOP!
THEY'VE ENTERED THE LOST CAVERNS!
DO NOT ENTER!
LOST CAVERNS
DANGER!
DO NOT ENTER
ARE YOU SURE? WHY WOULD THEY DO THAT?
YEAH! IT SAYS "DO NOT ENTER" RIGHT ON THE SIGN!
THIS IS A DISASTER!
DO NOT ENTER!
NO ONE SURVIVES THE CAVERNS! THE NAMELESS CHAIR--
--IS LOST FOREVER!

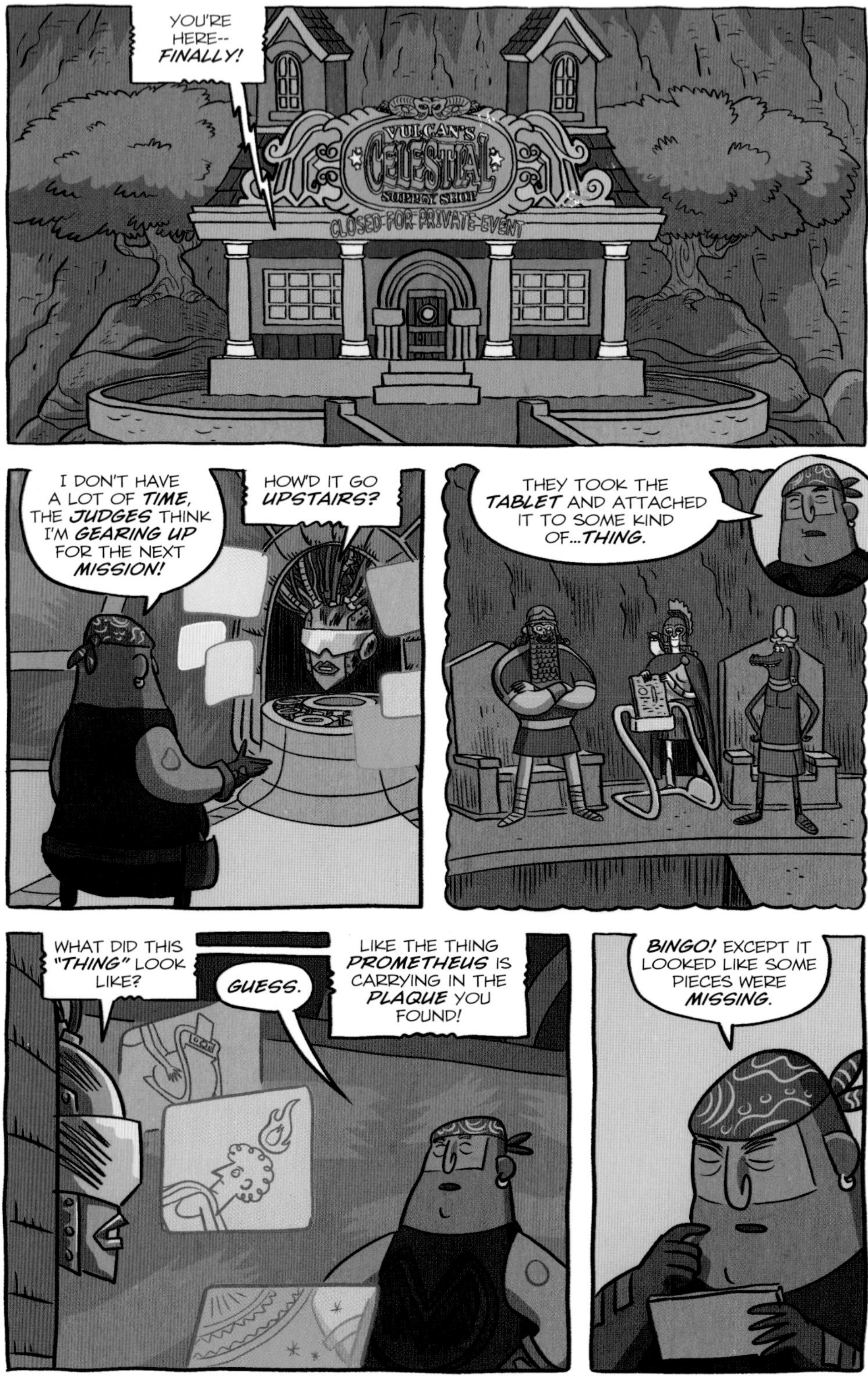

YOU'RE HERE-- FINALLY!
VULCAN'S CELESTIAL SUPPLY SHOP
CLOSED-FOR-PRIVATE-EVENT
I DON'T HAVE A LOT OF TIME, THE JUDGES THINK I'M GEARING UP FOR THE NEXT MISSION!
HOW'D IT GO UPSTAIRS?
THEY TOOK THE TABLET AND ATTACHED IT TO SOME KIND OF...THING.
WHAT DID THIS "THING" LOOK LIKE?
GUESS.
LIKE THE THING PROMETHEUS IS CARRYING IN THE PLAQUE YOU FOUND!
BINGO! EXCEPT IT LOOKED LIKE SOME PIECES WERE MISSING.

A-HA! NO DOUBT THE **SAME PIECES** YOU'RE COLLECTING!

DID YOU TELL THEM ABOUT **THE PLAQUE?**

OF COURSE NOT. AND THEY **DIDN'T** ASK.

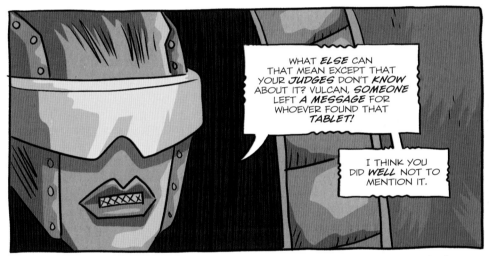

WHAT **ELSE** CAN THAT MEAN EXCEPT THAT YOUR **JUDGES** DON'T **KNOW** ABOUT IT? VULCAN, **SOMEONE** LEFT **A MESSAGE** FOR WHOEVER FOUND THAT **TABLET!**

I THINK YOU DID **WELL** NOT TO MENTION IT.

THE **QUESTION** IS WHAT DOES IT **MEAN?**

WAIT!

YOU CALLED HIM **PROMETHEUS!** HOW'D YOU FIGURE **THAT?**

THE *FLAME*, ESCAPING A *CELESTIAL REALM*, BRINGING SOME OBJECT TO *EARTH*. I THOUGHT IT WAS PRETTY *OBVIOUS*.

PROMETHEUS WASN'T CAUGHT STEALING SOME *CONTRAPTION*. HE STOLE *FIRE* FROM THE GODS AND GAVE IT TO *MORTALS*.

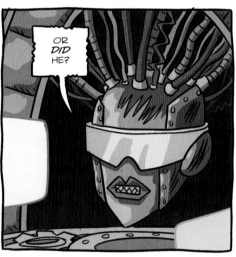

OR *DID* HE?

I DON'T FOLLOW. WE *ALL KNOW* THE MYTH.

EXACTLY. VOLCANOES WERE *GOING OFF* LEFT AND RIGHT, *LIGHTNING* STRUCK TREES *ALL OVER THE PLANET*, ANY NUMBER OF *FIRE-BASED CREATURES* ROAMED THE EARTH! MORTALS DIDN'T *NEED* PROMETHEUS, THEY HAD *PLENTY OF FIRE!*

I'VE *ALWAYS* THOUGHT THAT *PARTICULAR* MYTH WAS *RUBBISH*.

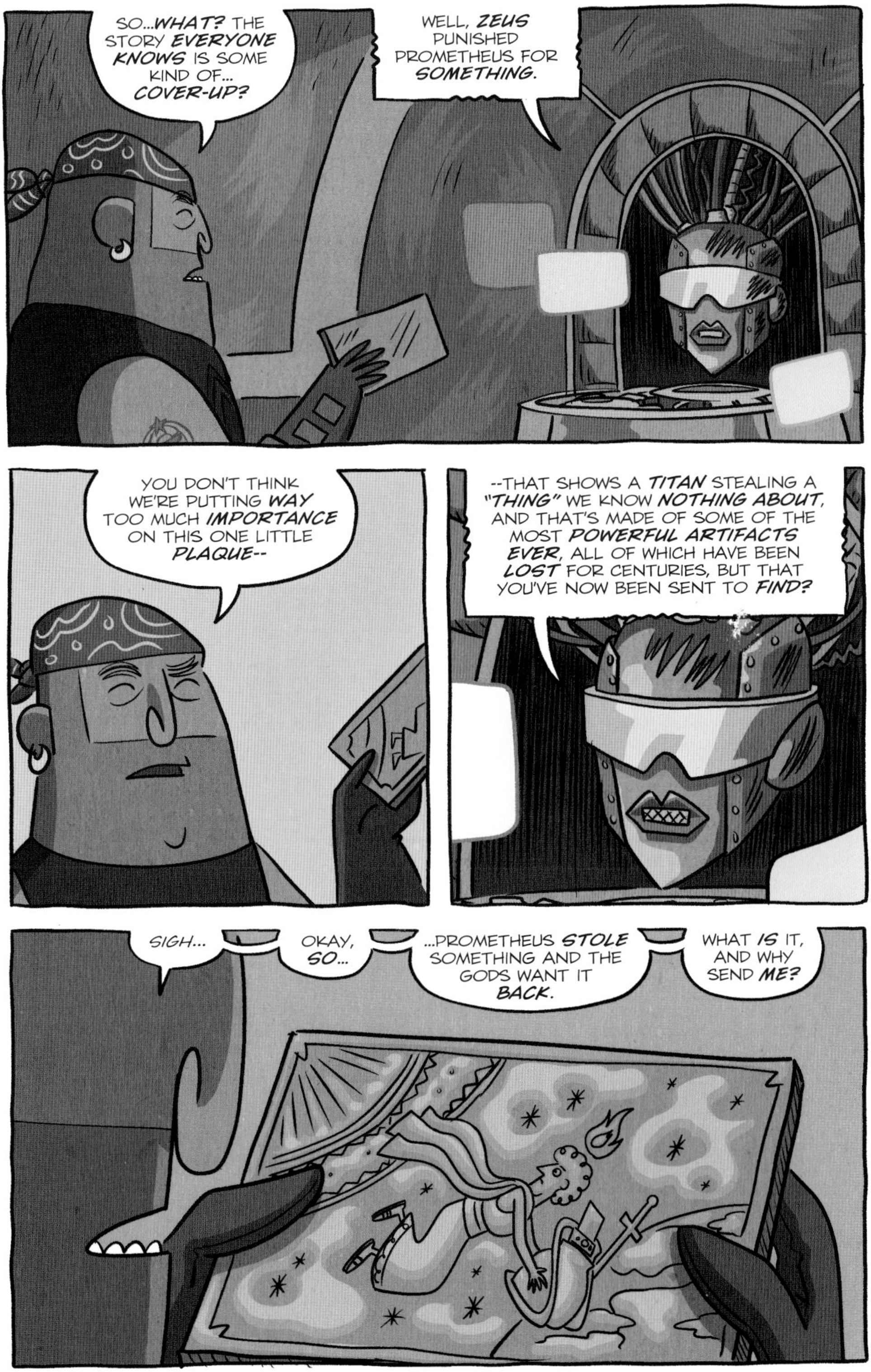
SO...WHAT? THE STORY EVERYONE KNOWS IS SOME KIND OF... COVER-UP?
WELL, ZEUS PUNISHED PROMETHEUS FOR SOMETHING.
YOU DON'T THINK WE'RE PUTTING WAY TOO MUCH IMPORTANCE ON THIS ONE LITTLE PLAQUE--
--THAT SHOWS A TITAN STEALING A "THING" WE KNOW NOTHING ABOUT, AND THAT'S MADE OF SOME OF THE MOST POWERFUL ARTIFACTS EVER, ALL OF WHICH HAVE BEEN LOST FOR CENTURIES, BUT THAT YOU'VE NOW BEEN SENT TO FIND?
SIGH...
OKAY, SO...
...PROMETHEUS STOLE SOMETHING AND THE GODS WANT IT BACK.
WHAT IS IT, AND WHY SEND ME?

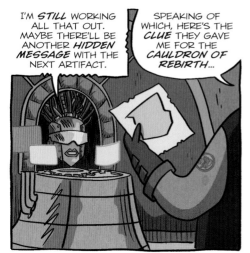

I'M **STILL** WORKING ALL THAT OUT. MAYBE THERE'LL BE ANOTHER **HIDDEN MESSAGE** WITH THE NEXT ARTIFACT.

SPEAKING OF WHICH, HERE'S THE **CLUE** THEY GAVE ME FOR THE **CAULDRON OF REBIRTH**...

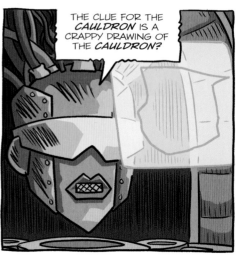

THE CLUE FOR THE **CAULDRON** IS A CRAPPY DRAWING OF THE **CAULDRON**?

IT'S NOT VERY **HELPFUL**, IS IT? ANYWAY, ASSUMING YOU'RE **RIGHT** ABOUT **ANY** OF THIS--

I'M **ALWAYS** RIGHT.

THEN I THINK A **QUICK STOP** TO ASK **PROMETHEUS** WHAT HE KNOWS ABOUT THIS, IF **ANYTHING**, IS IN ORDER!

GOOD! MEANWHILE, I'LL SEE IF I CAN MAKE HEADS OR TAILS OF THIS **CAULDRON CLUE!**

GOOD LUCK TO US **BOTH!**

YOU DON'T **NEED** LUCK, VULCAN-- YOU'VE GOT **ME.**

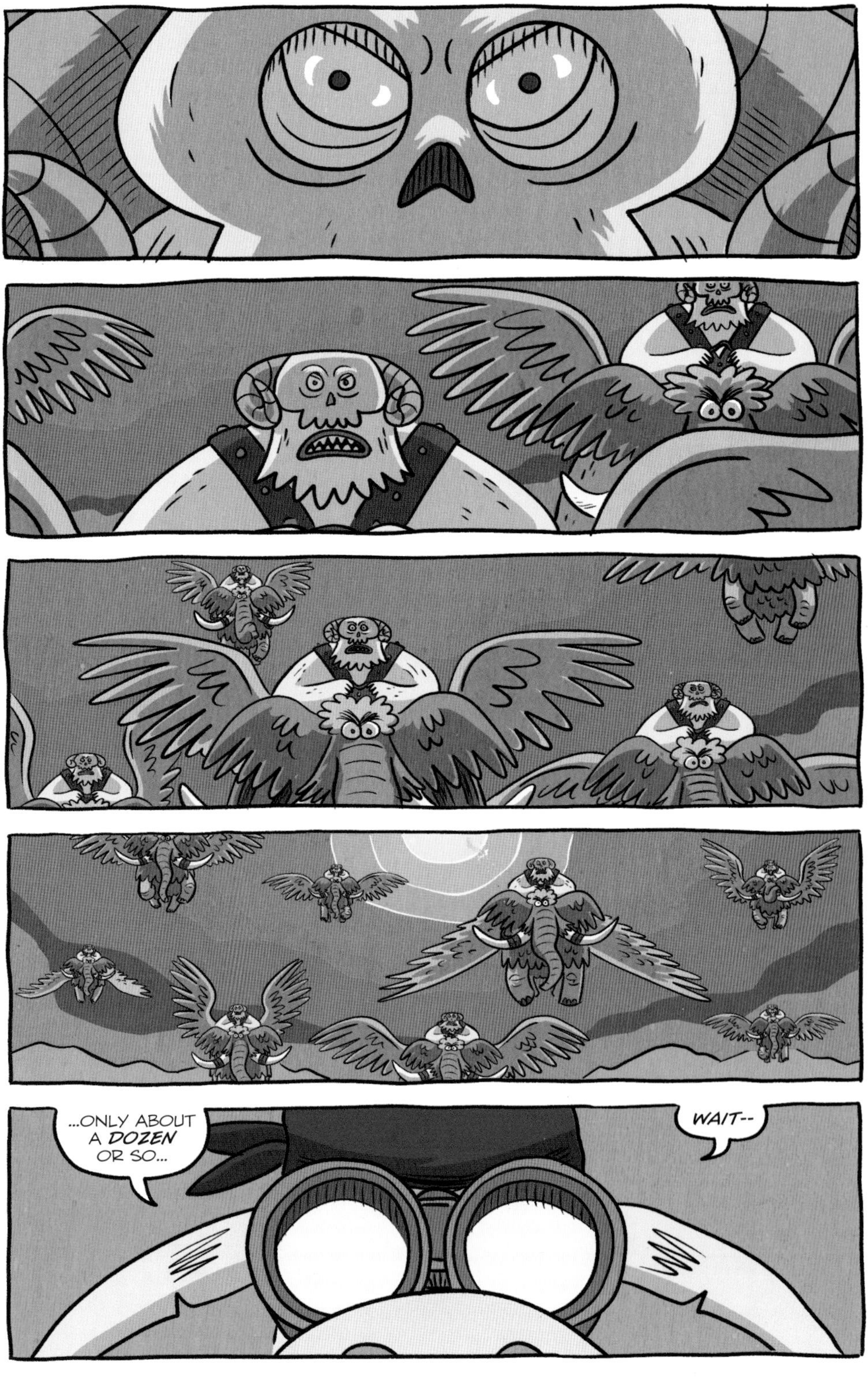
...ONLY ABOUT A DOZEN OR SO...
WAIT--

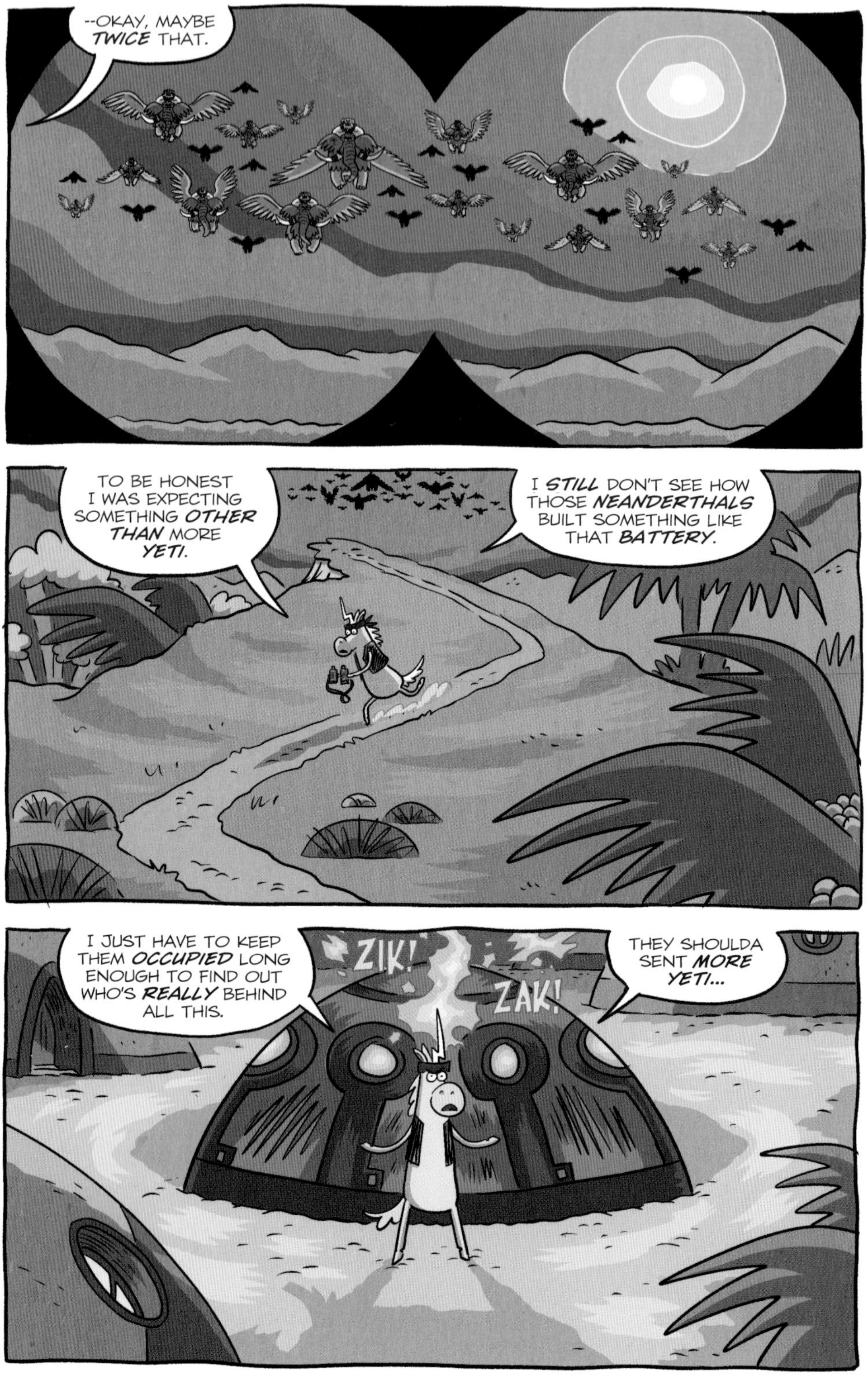
--OKAY, MAYBE TWICE THAT.
TO BE HONEST I WAS EXPECTING SOMETHING OTHER THAN MORE YETI.
I STILL DON'T SEE HOW THOSE NEANDERTHALS BUILT SOMETHING LIKE THAT BATTERY.
I JUST HAVE TO KEEP THEM OCCUPIED LONG ENOUGH TO FIND OUT WHO'S REALLY BEHIND ALL THIS.
ZIK!
ZAK!
THEY SHOULDA SENT MORE YETI...

PART 2:
THE END OF THE BEGINNING.

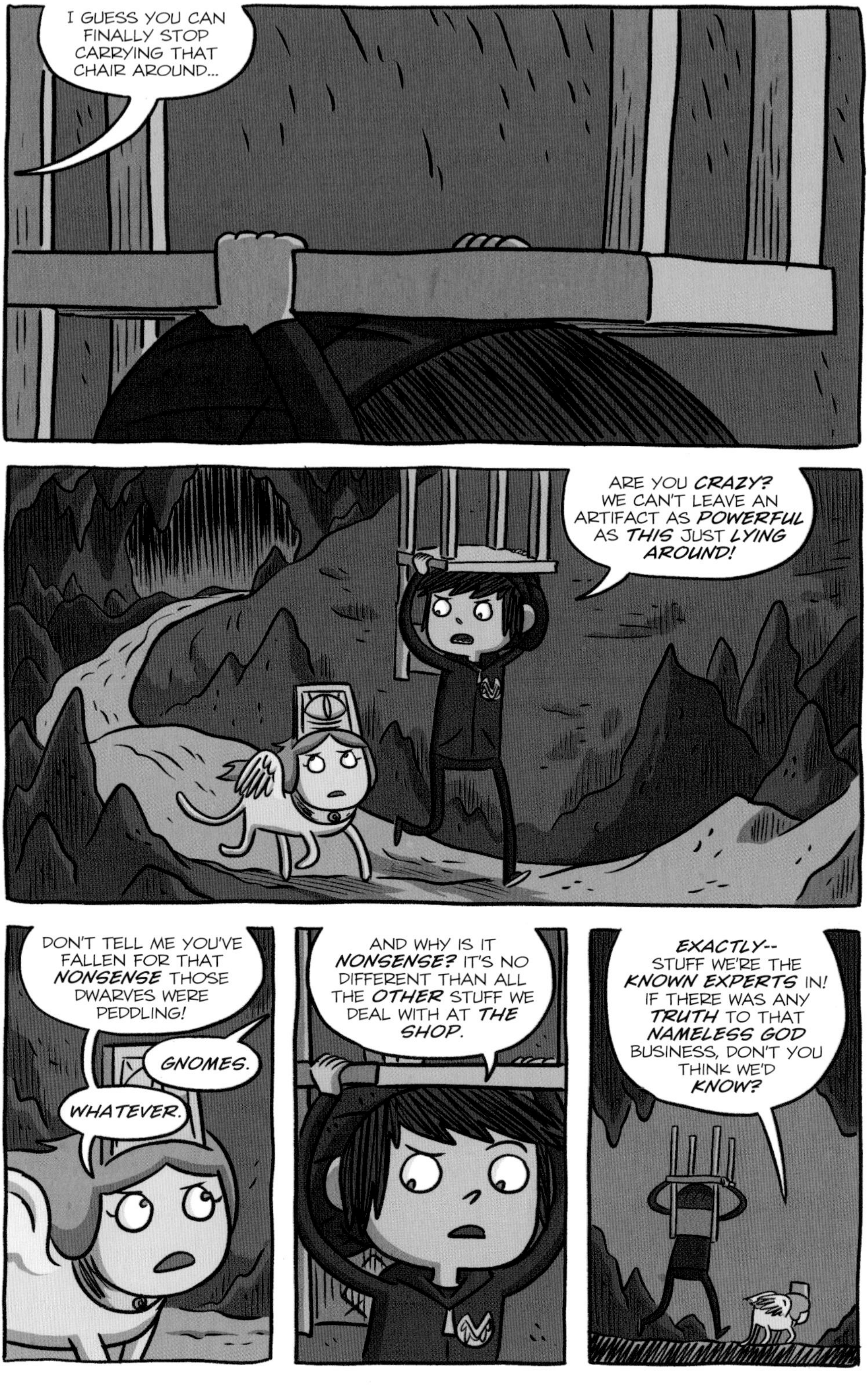
I GUESS YOU CAN FINALLY STOP CARRYING THAT CHAIR AROUND...
ARE YOU *CRAZY?* WE CAN'T LEAVE AN ARTIFACT AS *POWERFUL* AS *THIS* JUST *LYING AROUND!*
DON'T TELL ME YOU'VE FALLEN FOR THAT *NONSENSE* THOSE DWARVES WERE PEDDLING!
GNOMES.
WHATEVER.
AND WHY IS IT *NONSENSE?* IT'S NO DIFFERENT THAN ALL THE *OTHER* STUFF WE DEAL WITH AT *THE SHOP*.
EXACTLY-- STUFF WE'RE THE *KNOWN EXPERTS* IN! IF THERE WAS ANY *TRUTH* TO THAT *NAMELESS GOD* BUSINESS, DON'T YOU THINK WE'D *KNOW?*

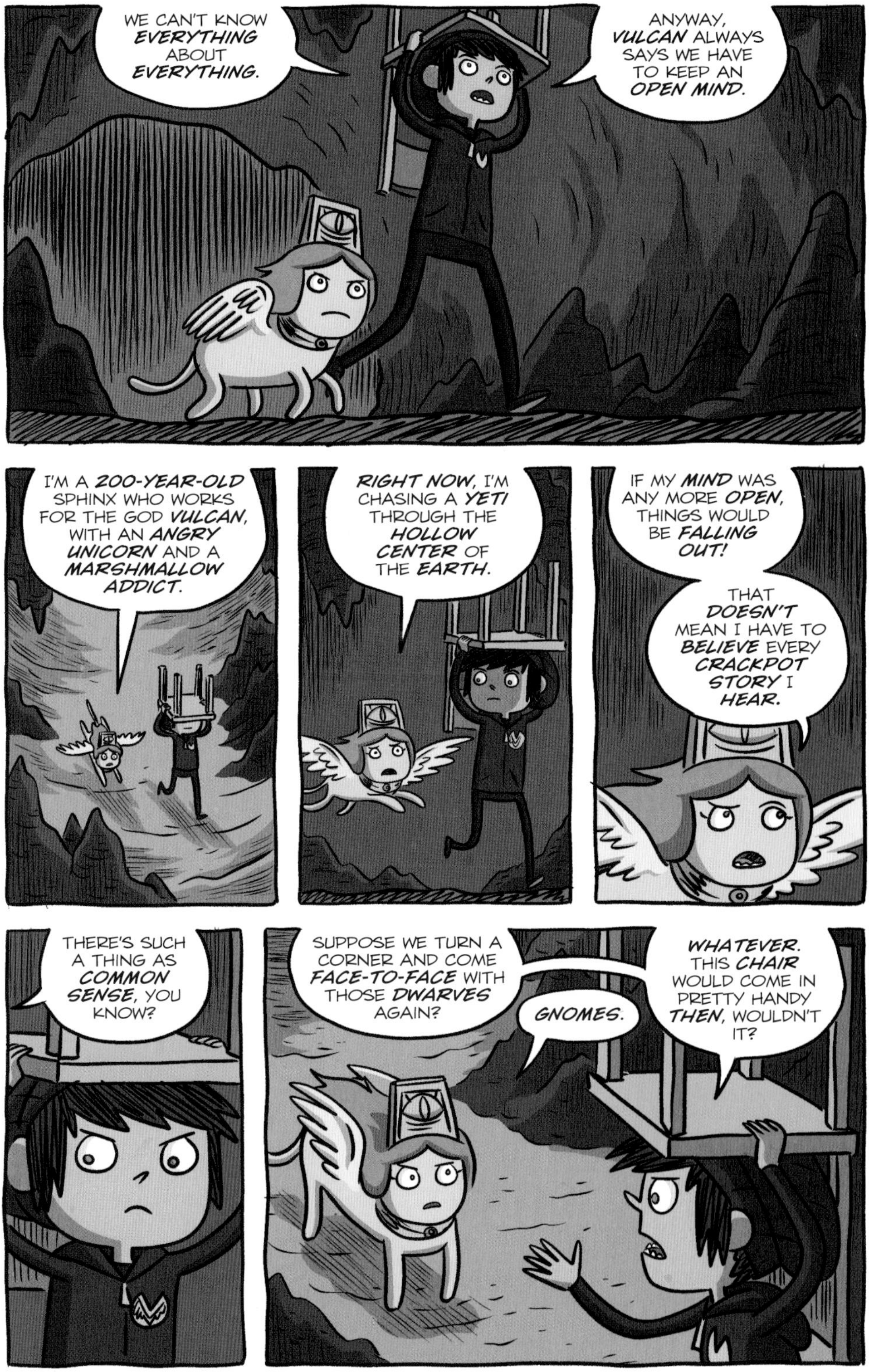

WE CAN'T KNOW EVERYTHING ABOUT EVERYTHING.
ANYWAY, VULCAN ALWAYS SAYS WE HAVE TO KEEP AN OPEN MIND.
I'M A 200-YEAR-OLD SPHINX WHO WORKS FOR THE GOD VULCAN, WITH AN ANGRY UNICORN AND A MARSHMALLOW ADDICT.
RIGHT NOW, I'M CHASING A YETI THROUGH THE HOLLOW CENTER OF THE EARTH.
IF MY MIND WAS ANY MORE OPEN, THINGS WOULD BE FALLING OUT!
THAT DOESN'T MEAN I HAVE TO BELIEVE EVERY CRACKPOT STORY I HEAR.
THERE'S SUCH A THING AS COMMON SENSE, YOU KNOW?
SUPPOSE WE TURN A CORNER AND COME FACE-TO-FACE WITH THOSE DWARVES AGAIN?
GNOMES.
WHATEVER. THIS CHAIR WOULD COME IN PRETTY HANDY THEN, WOULDN'T IT?

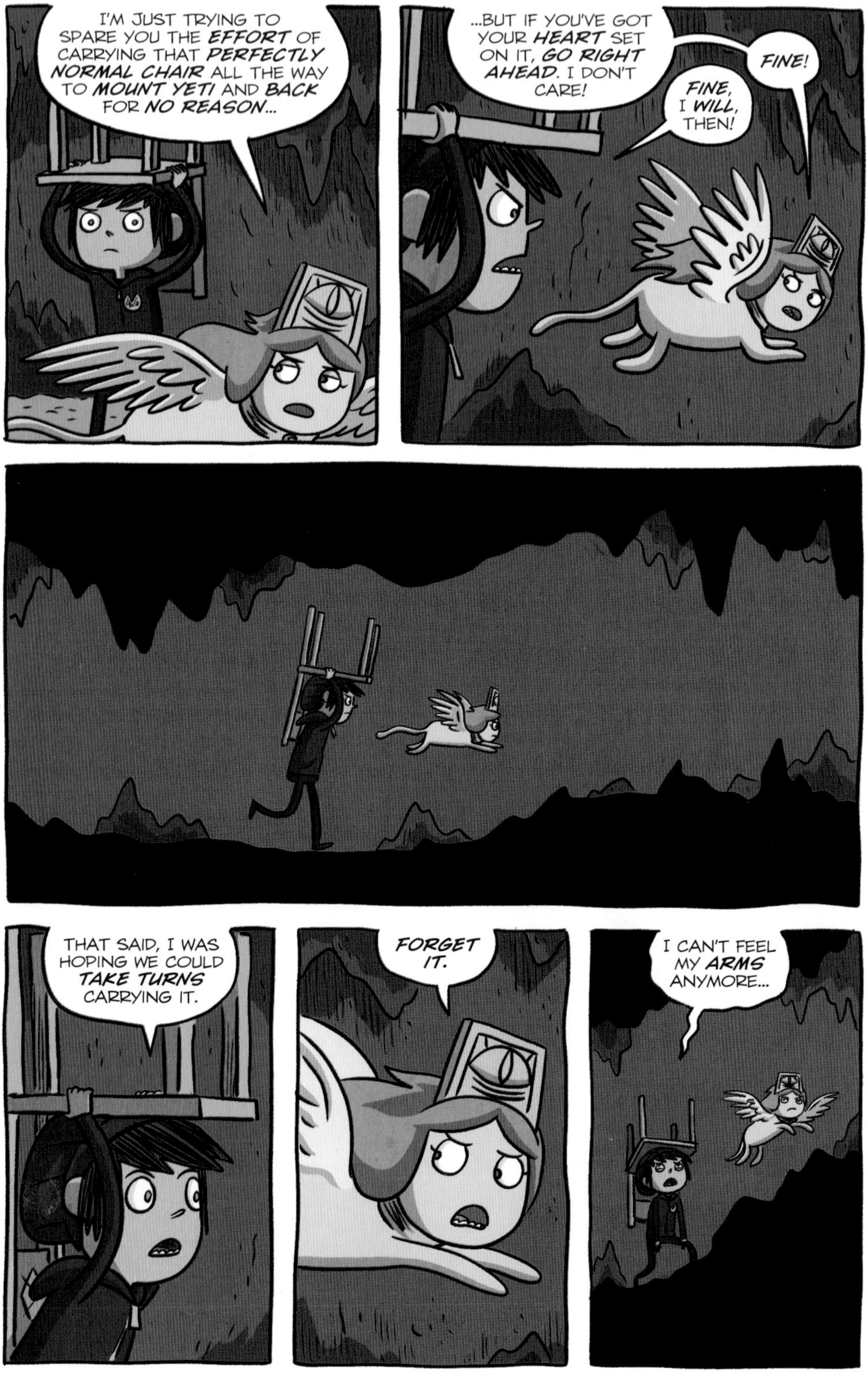
I'M JUST TRYING TO SPARE YOU THE EFFORT OF CARRYING THAT PERFECTLY NORMAL CHAIR ALL THE WAY TO MOUNT YETI AND BACK FOR NO REASON...
...BUT IF YOU'VE GOT YOUR HEART SET ON IT, GO RIGHT AHEAD. I DON'T CARE!
FINE, I WILL, THEN!
FINE!
THAT SAID, I WAS HOPING WE COULD TAKE TURNS CARRYING IT.
FORGET IT.
I CAN'T FEEL MY ARMS ANYMORE...

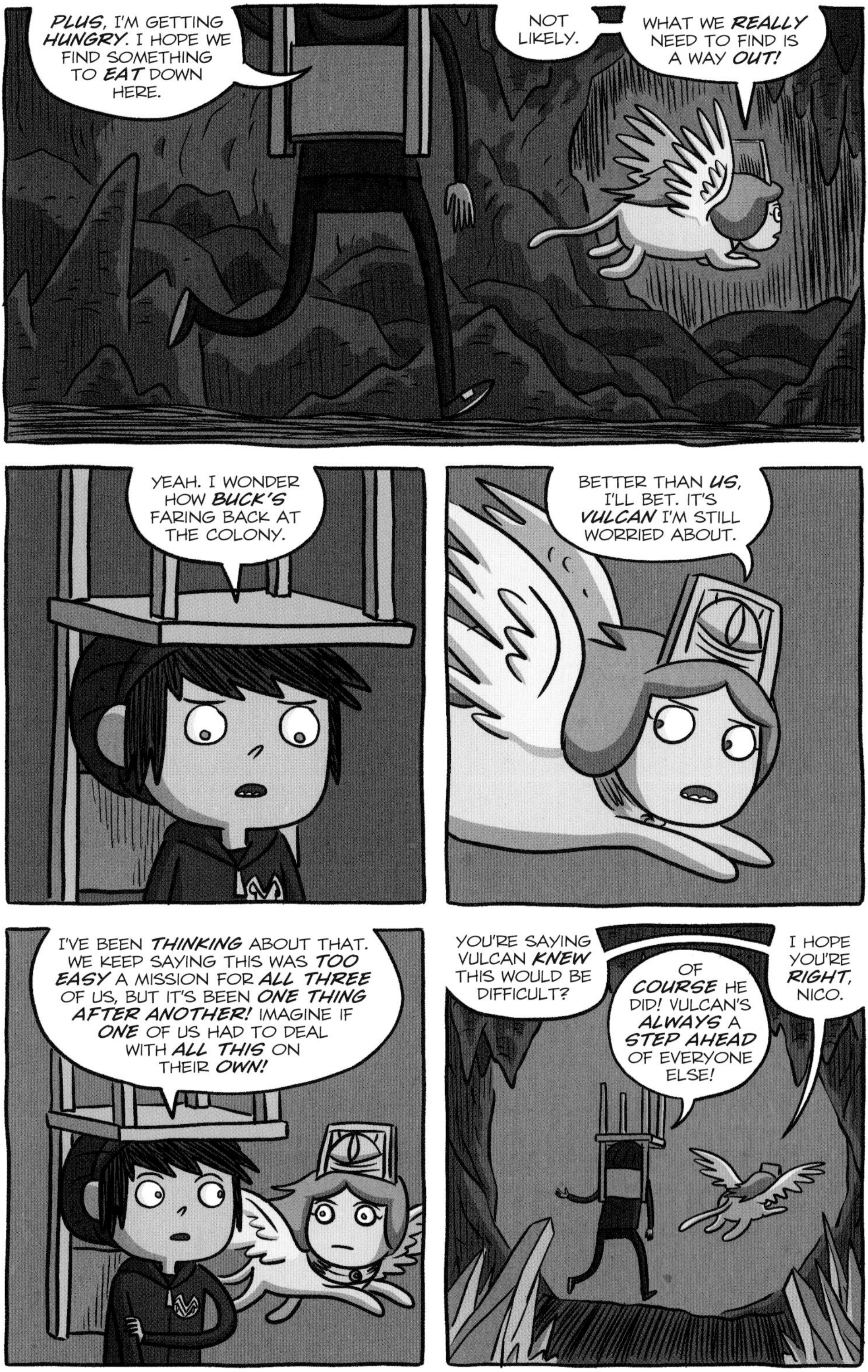
PLUS, I'M GETTING HUNGRY. I HOPE WE FIND SOMETHING TO EAT DOWN HERE.
NOT LIKELY.
WHAT WE REALLY NEED TO FIND IS A WAY OUT!
YEAH. I WONDER HOW BUCK'S FARING BACK AT THE COLONY.
BETTER THAN US, I'LL BET. IT'S VULCAN I'M STILL WORRIED ABOUT.
I'VE BEEN THINKING ABOUT THAT. WE KEEP SAYING THIS WAS TOO EASY A MISSION FOR ALL THREE OF US, BUT IT'S BEEN ONE THING AFTER ANOTHER! IMAGINE IF ONE OF US HAD TO DEAL WITH ALL THIS ON THEIR OWN!
YOU'RE SAYING VULCAN KNEW THIS WOULD BE DIFFICULT?
OF COURSE HE DID! VULCAN'S ALWAYS A STEP AHEAD OF EVERYONE ELSE!
I HOPE YOU'RE RIGHT, NICO.

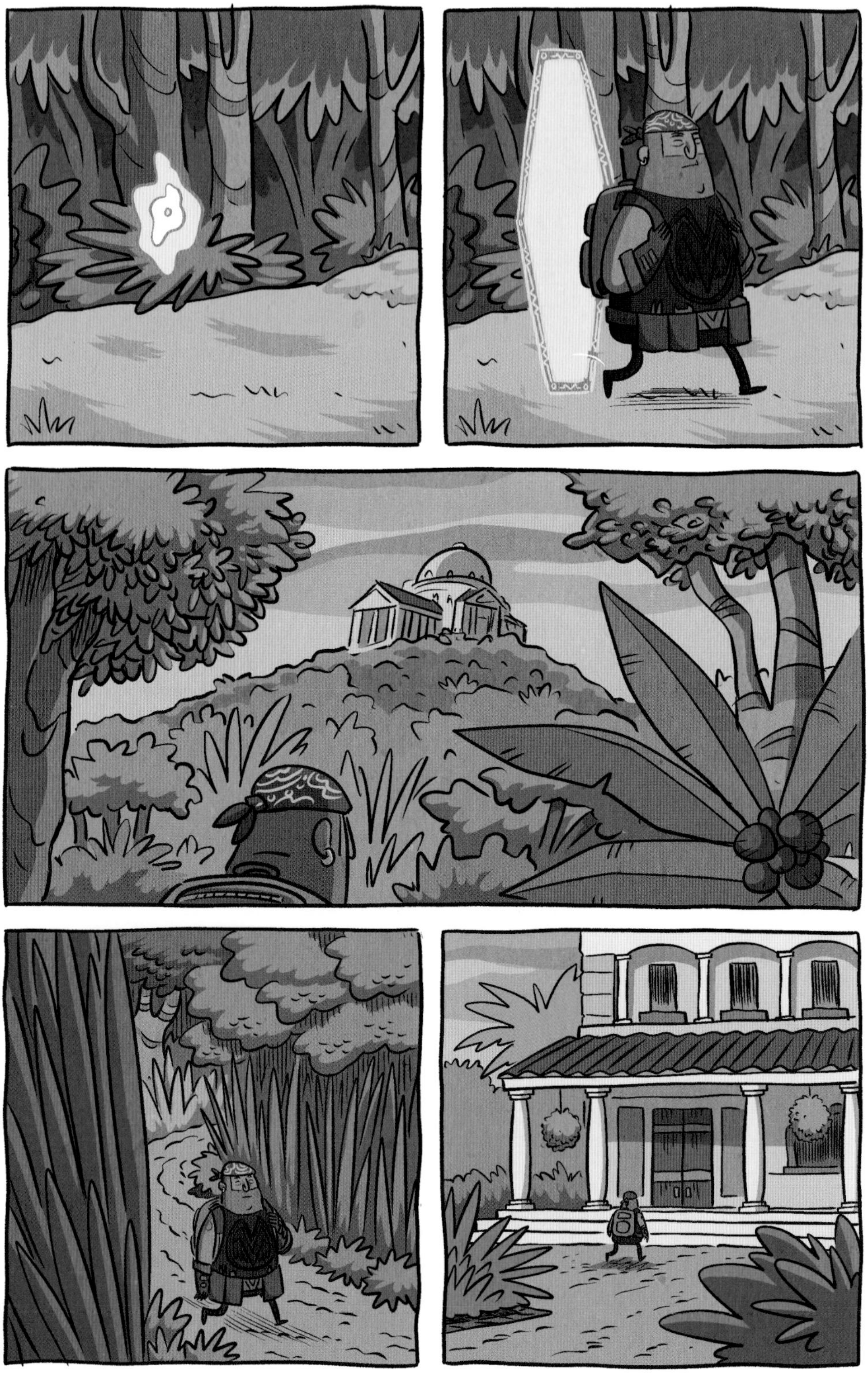

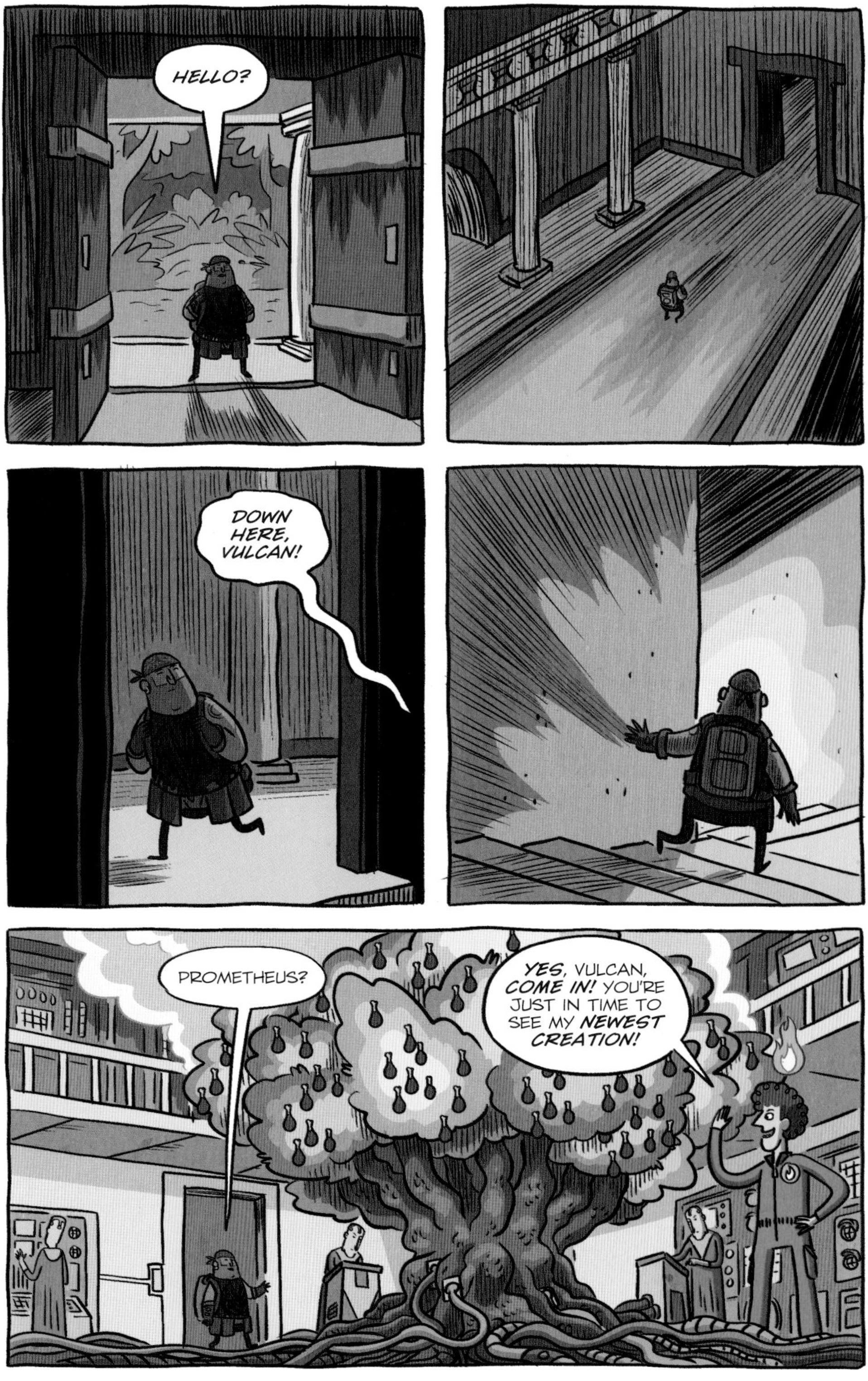
HELLO?
DOWN HERE, VULCAN!
PROMETHEUS?
YES, VULCAN, COME IN! YOU'RE JUST IN TIME TO SEE MY NEWEST CREATION!

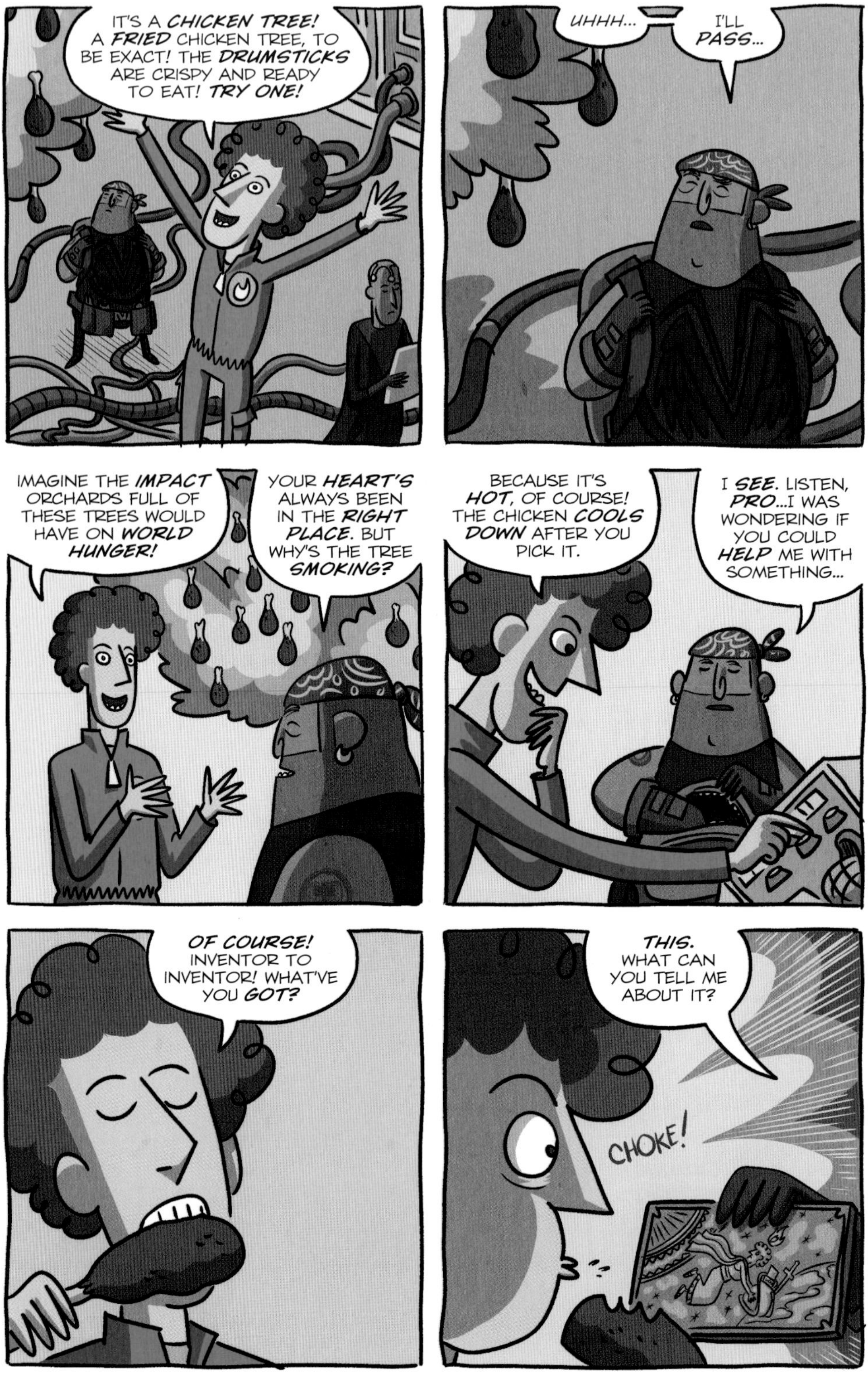
IT'S A CHICKEN TREE! A FRIED CHICKEN TREE, TO BE EXACT! THE DRUMSTICKS ARE CRISPY AND READY TO EAT! TRY ONE!
UHHH...
I'LL PASS...
IMAGINE THE IMPACT ORCHARDS FULL OF THESE TREES WOULD HAVE ON WORLD HUNGER!
YOUR HEART'S ALWAYS BEEN IN THE RIGHT PLACE. BUT WHY'S THE TREE SMOKING?
BECAUSE IT'S HOT, OF COURSE! THE CHICKEN COOLS DOWN AFTER YOU PICK IT.
I SEE. LISTEN, PRO...I WAS WONDERING IF YOU COULD HELP ME WITH SOMETHING...
OF COURSE! INVENTOR TO INVENTOR! WHAT'VE YOU GOT?
THIS. WHAT CAN YOU TELL ME ABOUT IT?
CHOKE!

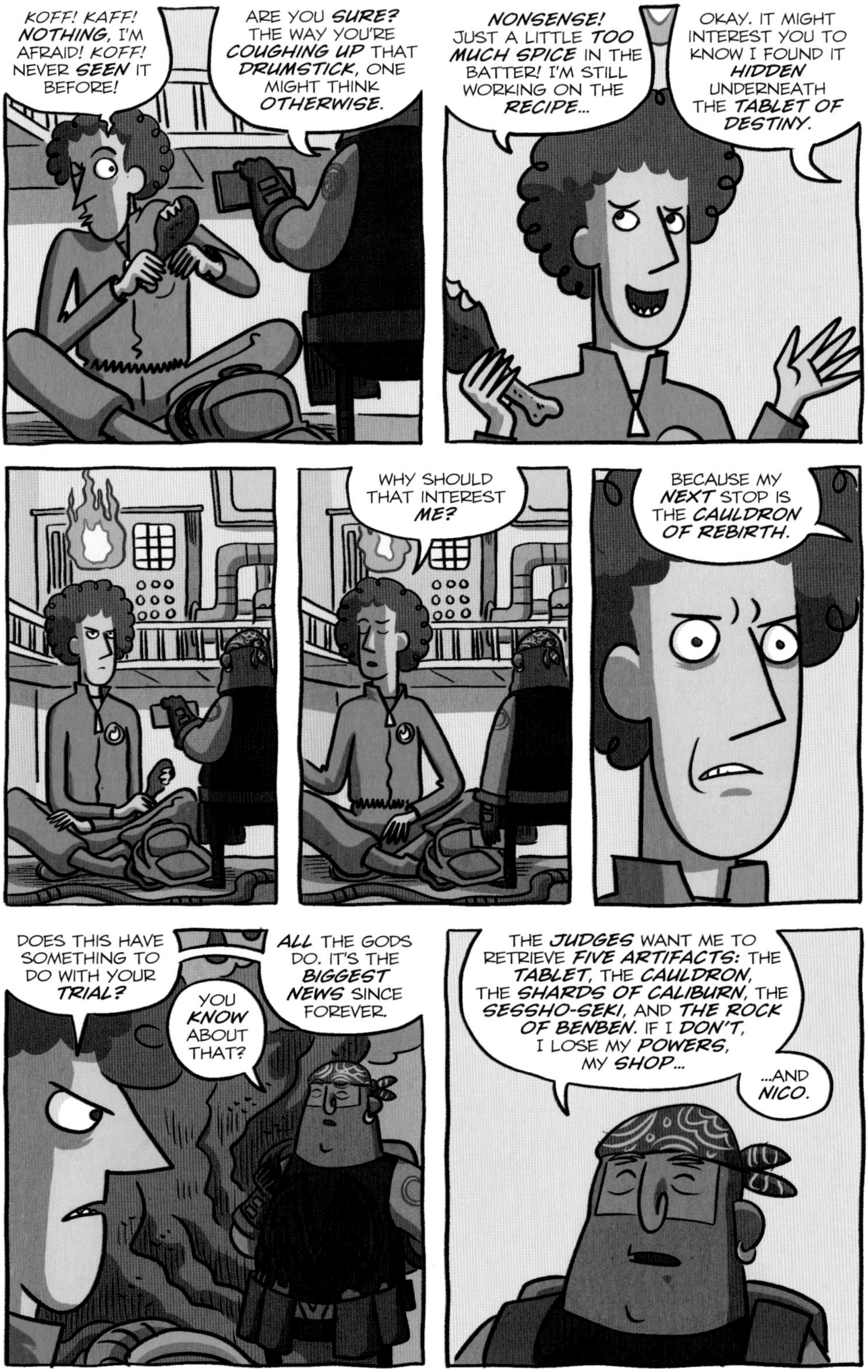
KOFF! KAFF! NOTHING, I'M AFRAID! KOFF! NEVER SEEN IT BEFORE!
ARE YOU SURE? THE WAY YOU'RE COUGHING UP THAT DRUMSTICK, ONE MIGHT THINK OTHERWISE.
NONSENSE! JUST A LITTLE TOO MUCH SPICE IN THE BATTER! I'M STILL WORKING ON THE RECIPE...
OKAY. IT MIGHT INTEREST YOU TO KNOW I FOUND IT HIDDEN UNDERNEATH THE TABLET OF DESTINY.
WHY SHOULD THAT INTEREST ME?
BECAUSE MY NEXT STOP IS THE CAULDRON OF REBIRTH.
DOES THIS HAVE SOMETHING TO DO WITH YOUR TRIAL?
YOU KNOW ABOUT THAT?
ALL THE GODS DO. IT'S THE BIGGEST NEWS SINCE FOREVER.
THE JUDGES WANT ME TO RETRIEVE FIVE ARTIFACTS: THE TABLET, THE CAULDRON, THE SHARDS OF CALIBURN, THE SESSHO-SEKI, AND THE ROCK OF BENBEN. IF I DON'T, I LOSE MY POWERS, MY SHOP...
...AND NICO.

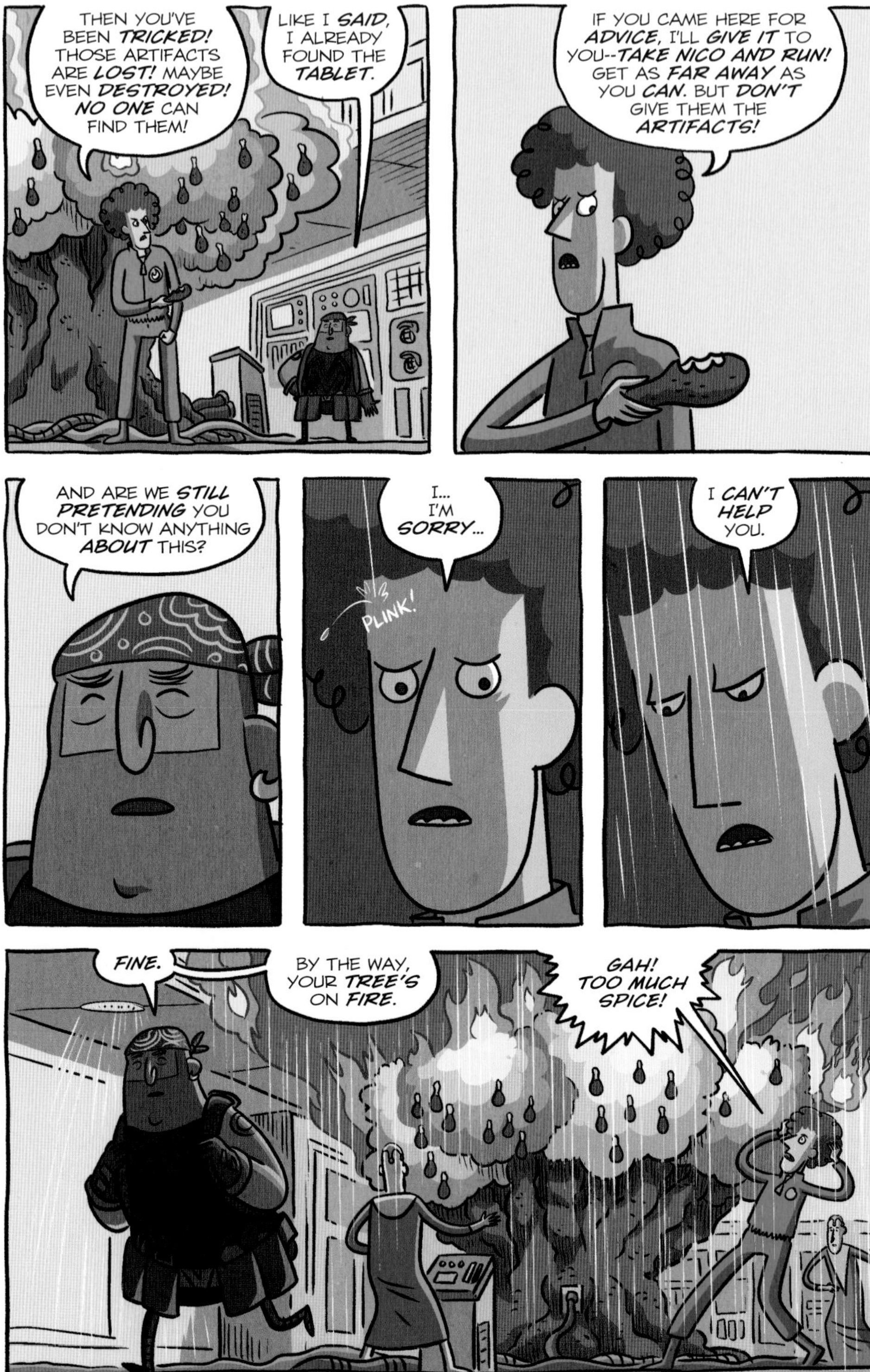
THEN YOU'VE BEEN TRICKED! THOSE ARTIFACTS ARE LOST! MAYBE EVEN DESTROYED! NO ONE CAN FIND THEM!
LIKE I SAID, I ALREADY FOUND THE TABLET.
IF YOU CAME HERE FOR ADVICE, I'LL GIVE IT TO YOU--TAKE NICO AND RUN! GET AS FAR AWAY AS YOU CAN. BUT DON'T GIVE THEM THE ARTIFACTS!
AND ARE WE STILL PRETENDING YOU DON'T KNOW ANYTHING ABOUT THIS?
I... I'M SORRY...
PLINK!
I CAN'T HELP YOU.
FINE.
BY THE WAY, YOUR TREE'S ON FIRE.
GAH! TOO MUCH SPICE!

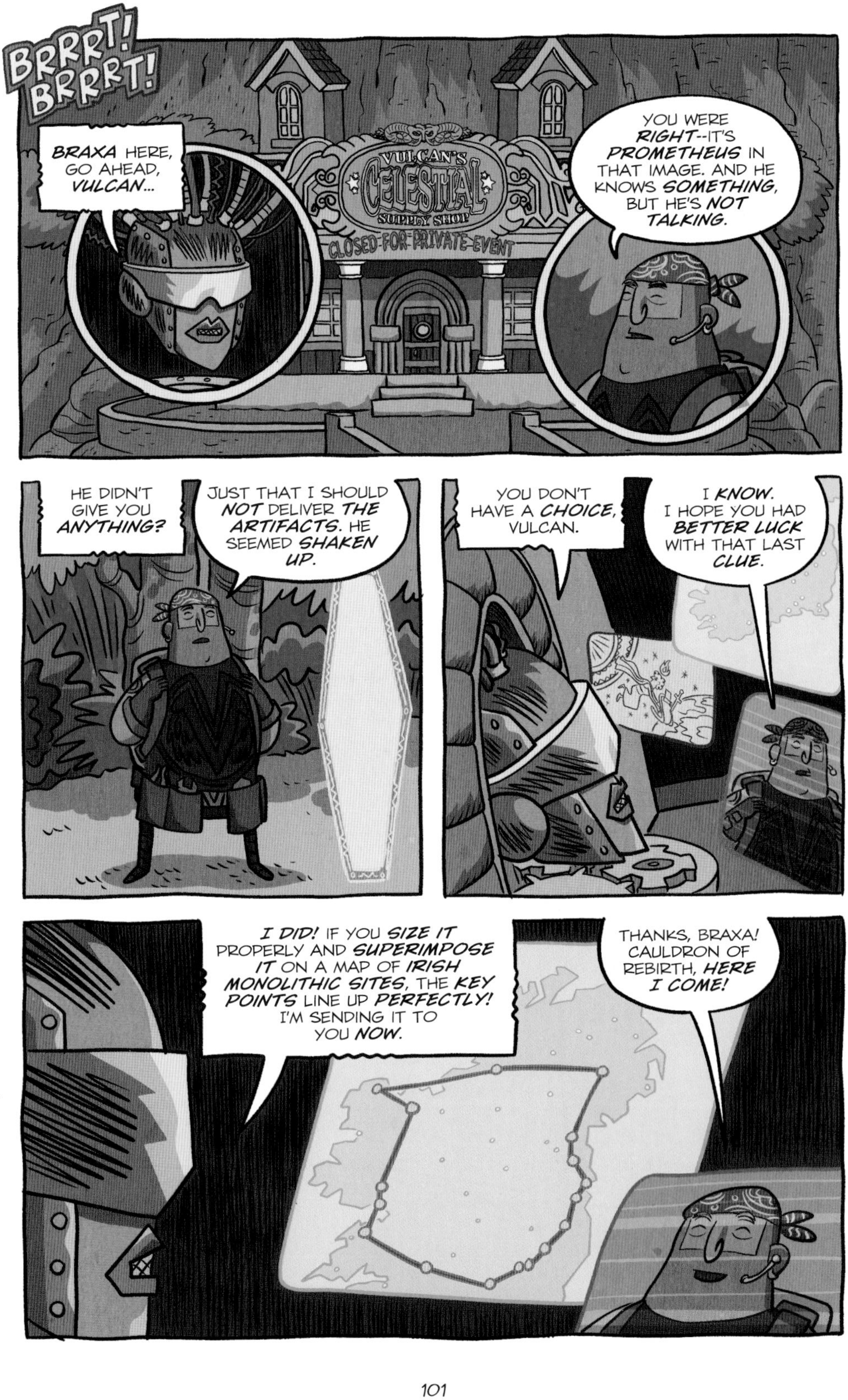
BRRRT! BRRRT!
BRAXA HERE, GO AHEAD, VULCAN...
VULCAN'S CELESTIAL SUPPLY SHOP
CLOSED-FOR-PRIVATE-EVENT
YOU WERE RIGHT--IT'S PROMETHEUS IN THAT IMAGE. AND HE KNOWS SOMETHING, BUT HE'S NOT TALKING.
HE DIDN'T GIVE YOU ANYTHING?
JUST THAT I SHOULD NOT DELIVER THE ARTIFACTS. HE SEEMED SHAKEN UP.
YOU DON'T HAVE A CHOICE, VULCAN.
I KNOW. I HOPE YOU HAD BETTER LUCK WITH THAT LAST CLUE.
I DID! IF YOU SIZE IT PROPERLY AND SUPERIMPOSE IT ON A MAP OF IRISH MONOLITHIC SITES, THE KEY POINTS LINE UP PERFECTLY! I'M SENDING IT TO YOU NOW.
THANKS, BRAXA! CAULDRON OF REBIRTH, HERE I COME!

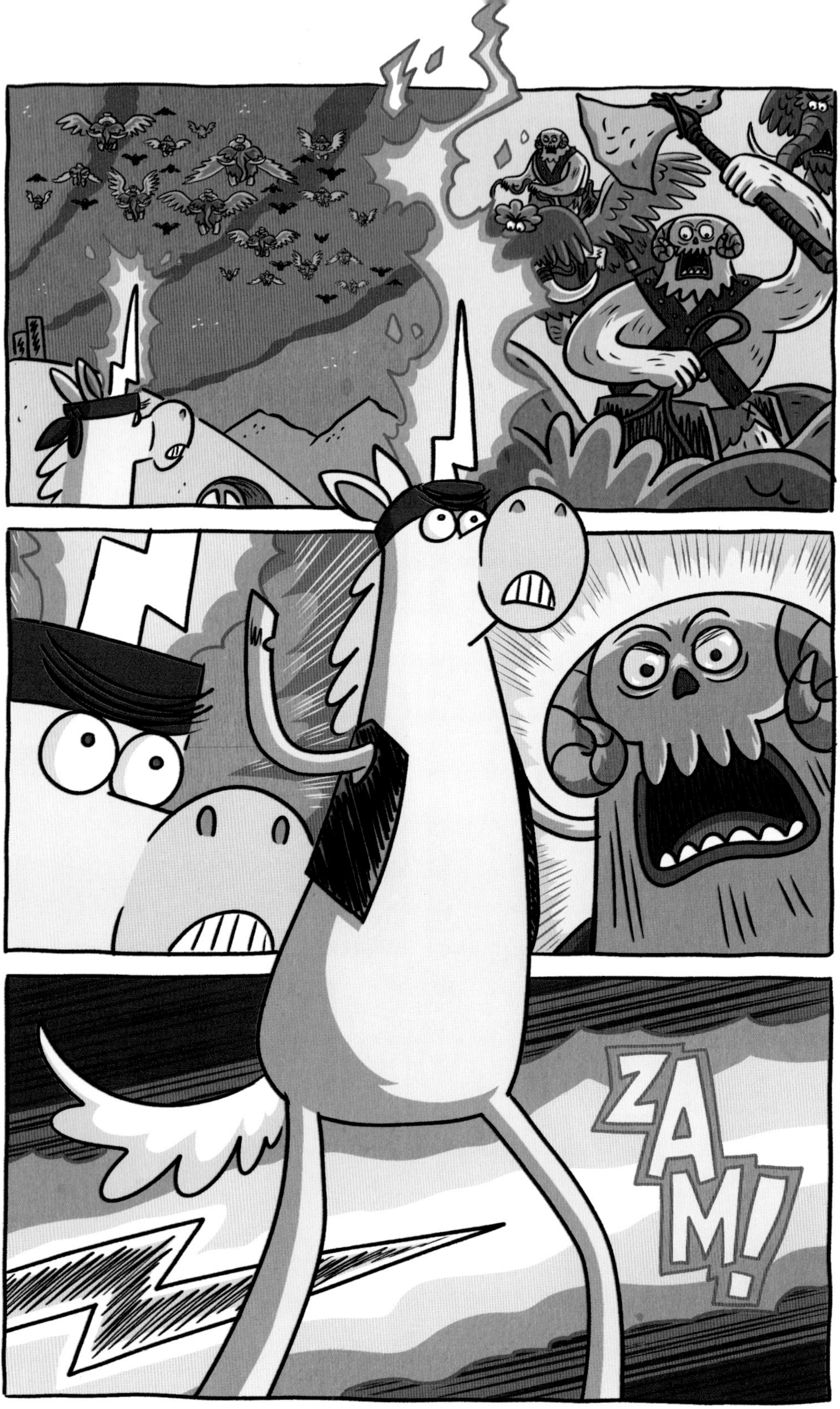
ZAM!

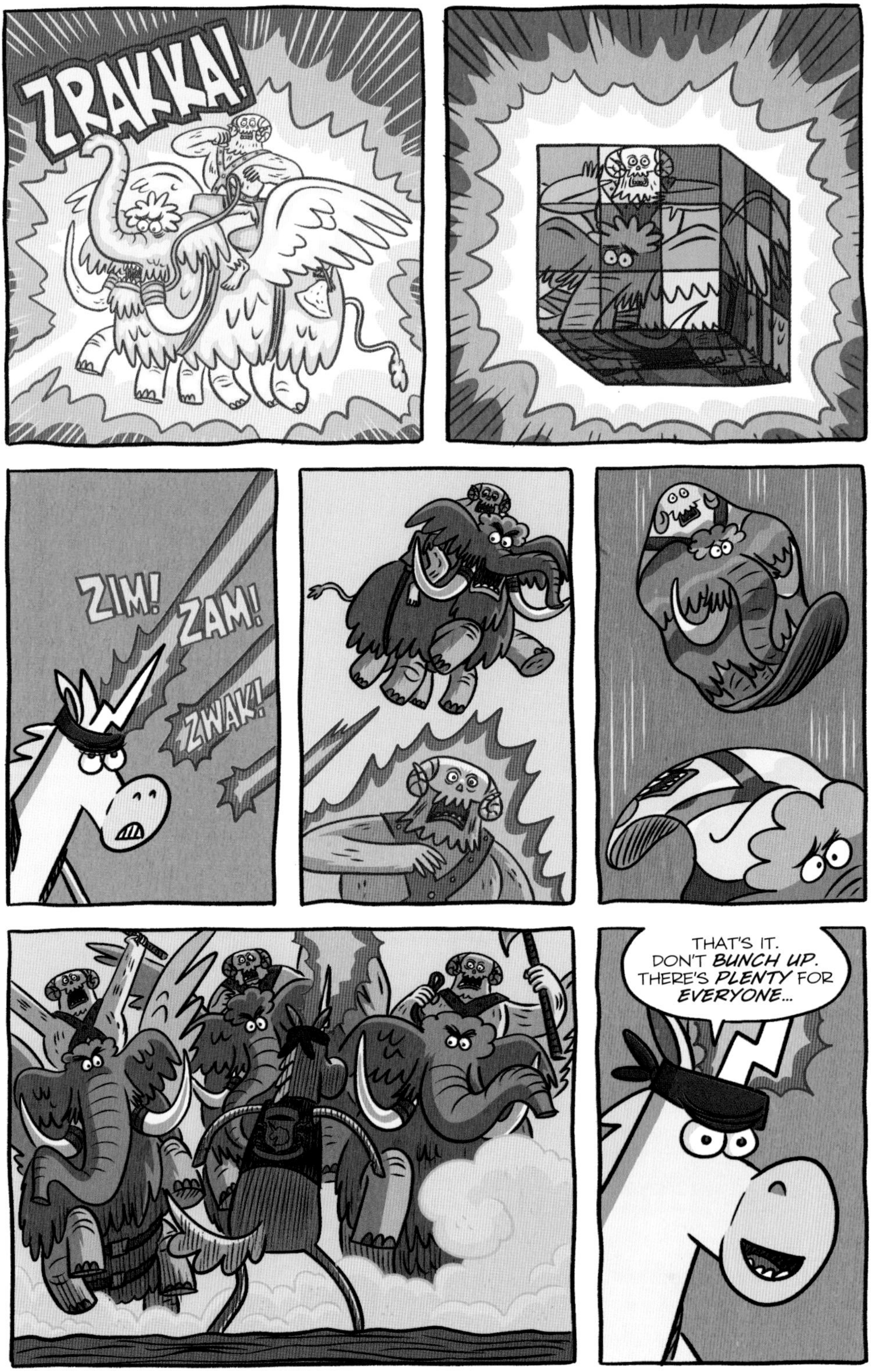
ZRAKKA!
ZIM!
ZAM!
ZWAK!
THAT'S IT. DON'T BUNCH UP. THERE'S PLENTY FOR EVERYONE...

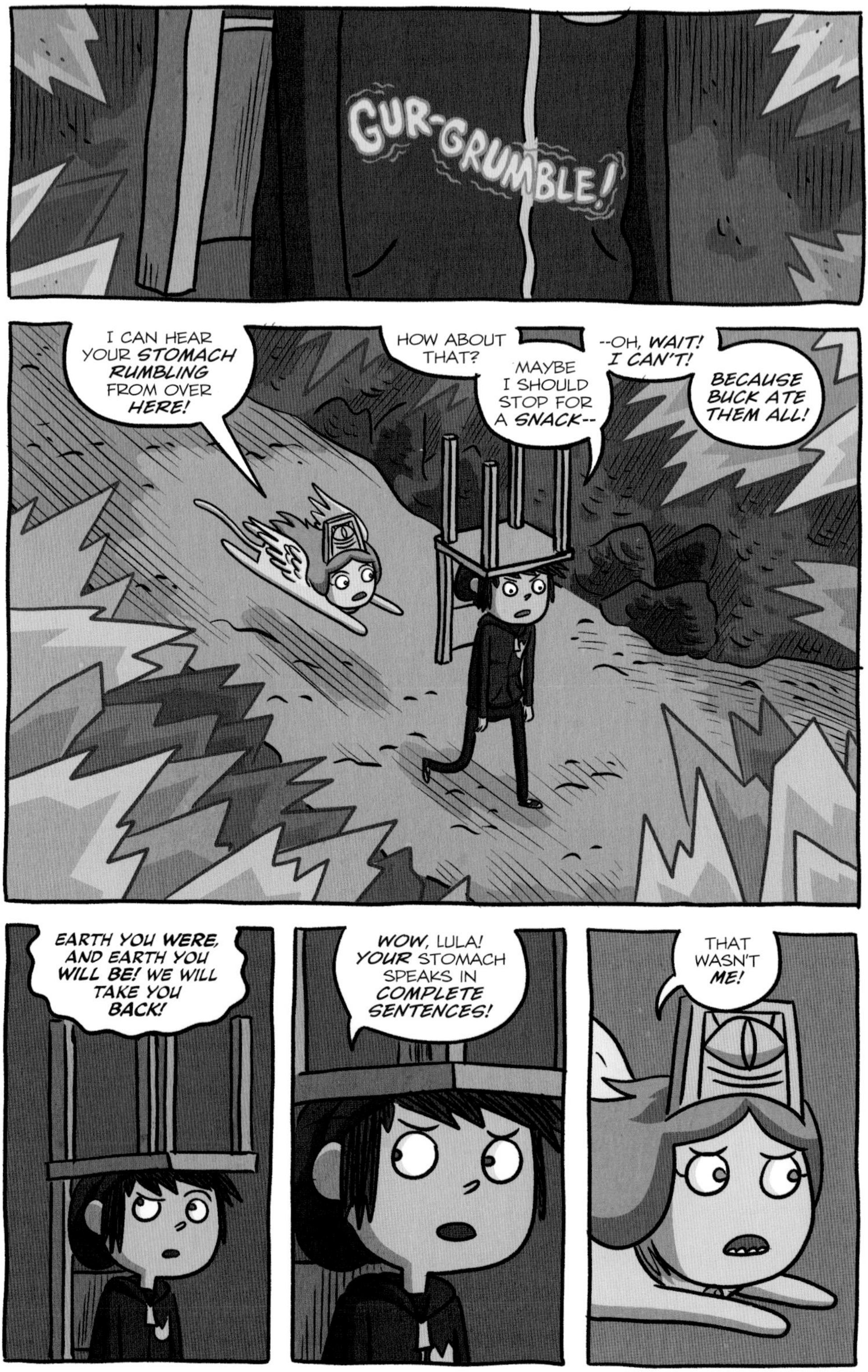
GUR-GRUMBLE!
I CAN HEAR YOUR STOMACH RUMBLING FROM OVER HERE!
HOW ABOUT THAT?
MAYBE I SHOULD STOP FOR A SNACK--
--OH, WAIT! I CAN'T!
BECAUSE BUCK ATE THEM ALL!
EARTH YOU WERE, AND EARTH YOU WILL BE! WE WILL TAKE YOU BACK!
WOW, LULA! YOUR STOMACH SPEAKS IN COMPLETE SENTENCES!
THAT WASN'T ME!

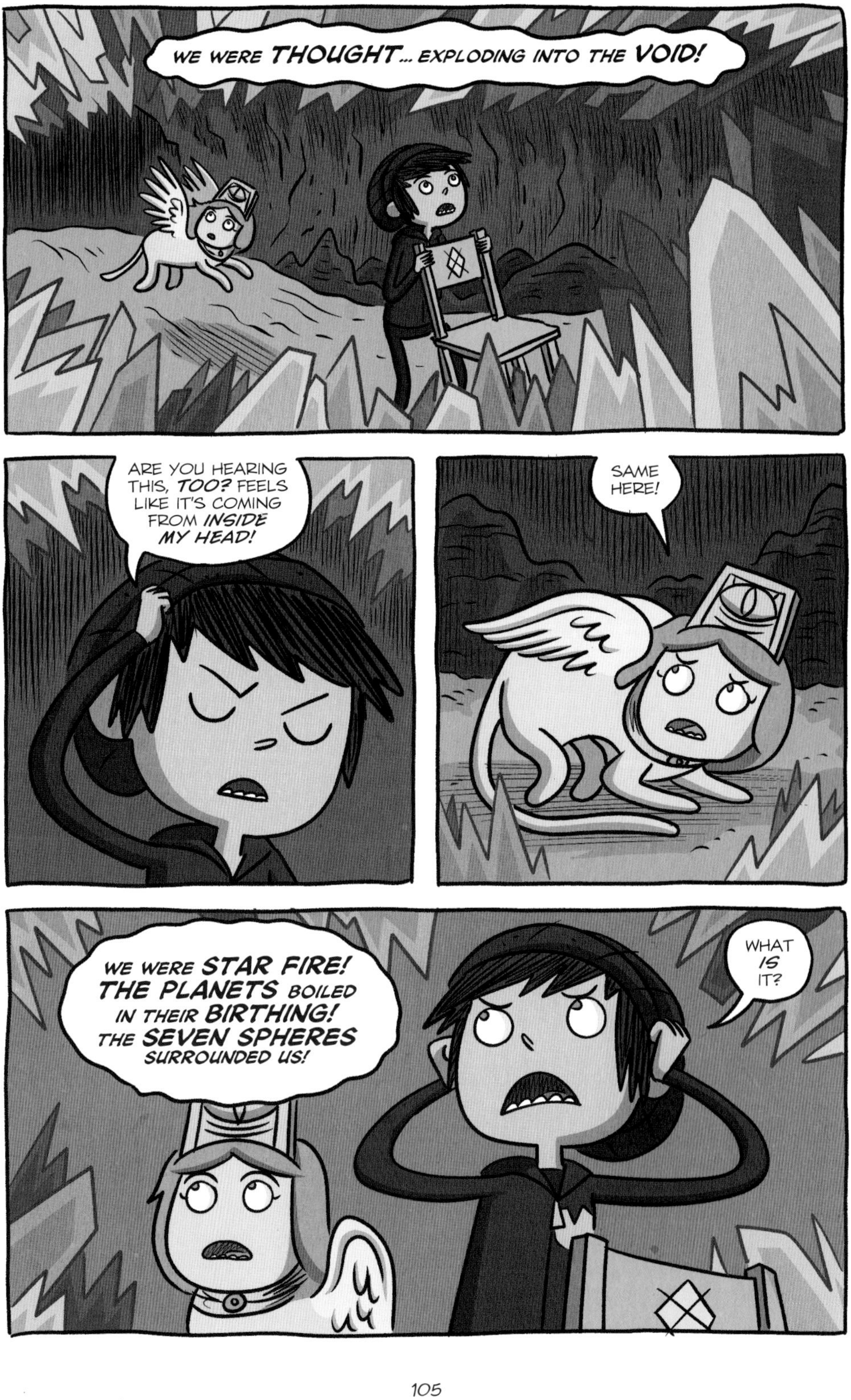
WE WERE THOUGHT... EXPLODING INTO THE VOID!
ARE YOU HEARING THIS, TOO? FEELS LIKE IT'S COMING FROM INSIDE MY HEAD!
SAME HERE!
WE WERE STAR FIRE! THE PLANETS BOILED IN THEIR BIRTHING! THE SEVEN SPHERES SURROUNDED US!
WHAT IS IT?

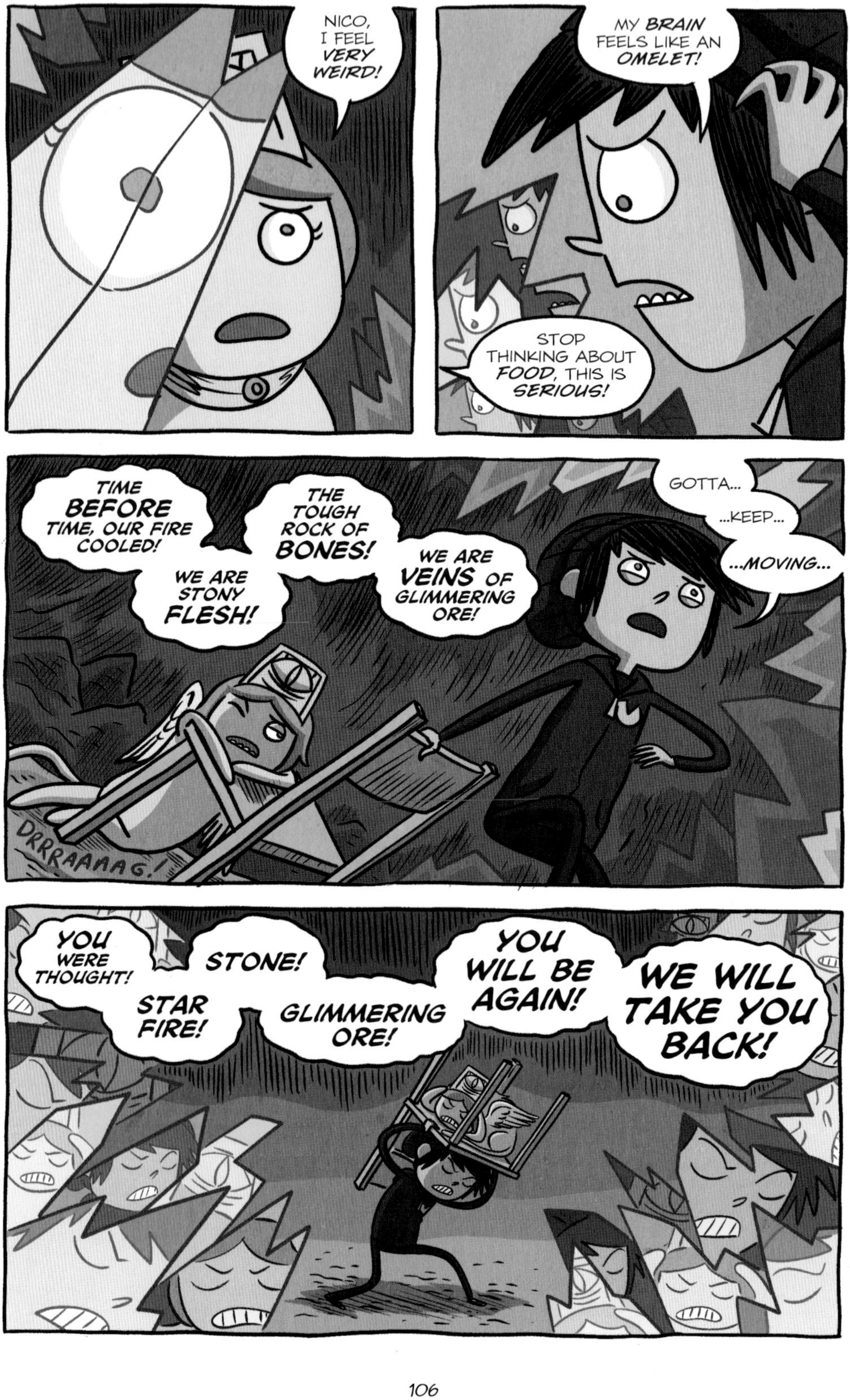
NICO, I FEEL VERY WEIRD!
MY BRAIN FEELS LIKE AN OMELET!
STOP THINKING ABOUT FOOD, THIS IS SERIOUS!
TIME BEFORE TIME, OUR FIRE COOLED!
WE ARE STONY FLESH!
THE TOUGH ROCK OF BONES!
WE ARE VEINS OF GLIMMERING ORE!
GOTTA...
...KEEP...
...MOVING...
DRRRAAMAG!
YOU WERE THOUGHT!
STAR FIRE!
STONE!
GLIMMERING ORE!
YOU WILL BE AGAIN!
WE WILL TAKE YOU BACK!

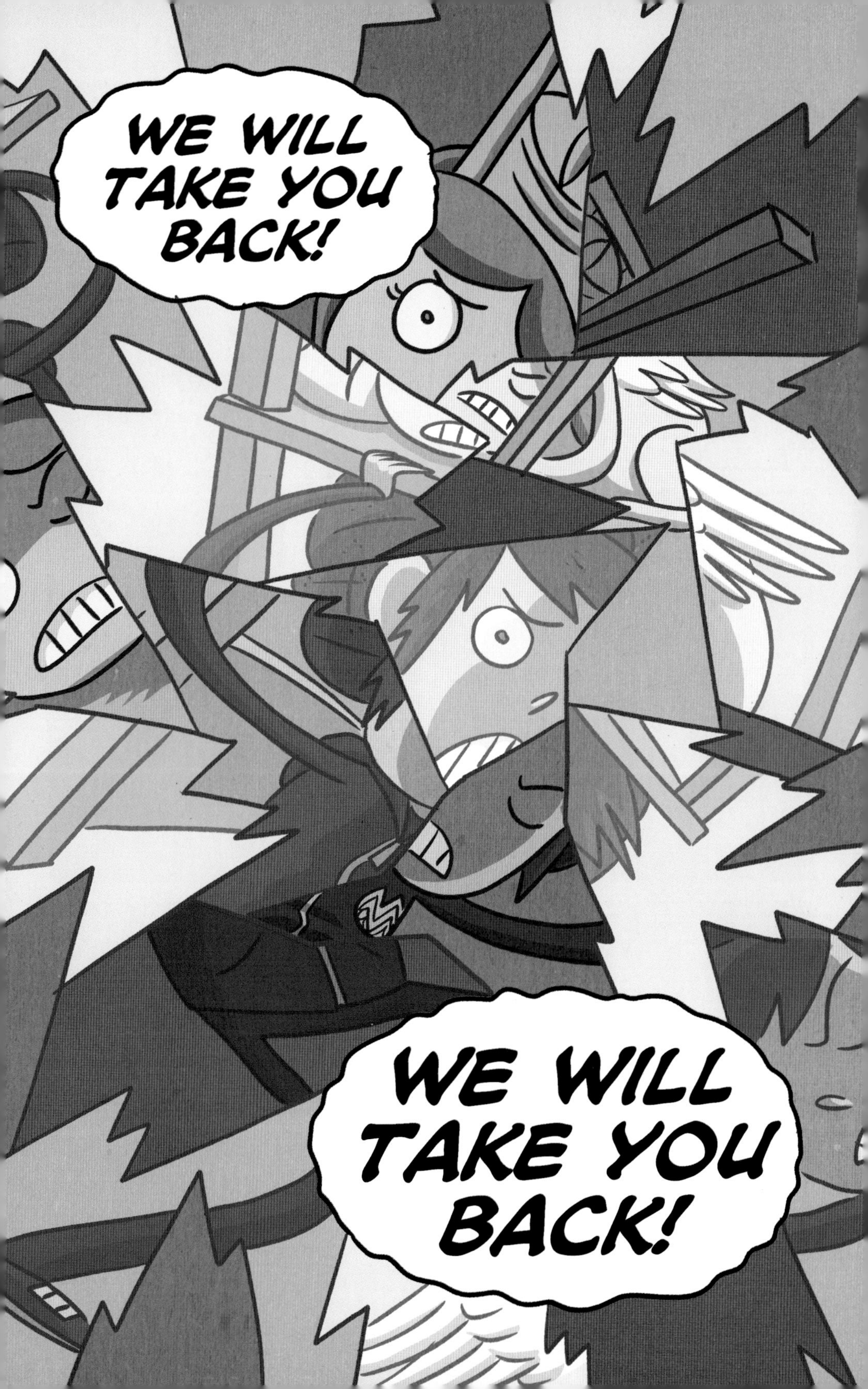
WE WILL TAKE YOU BACK!
WE WILL TAKE YOU BACK!

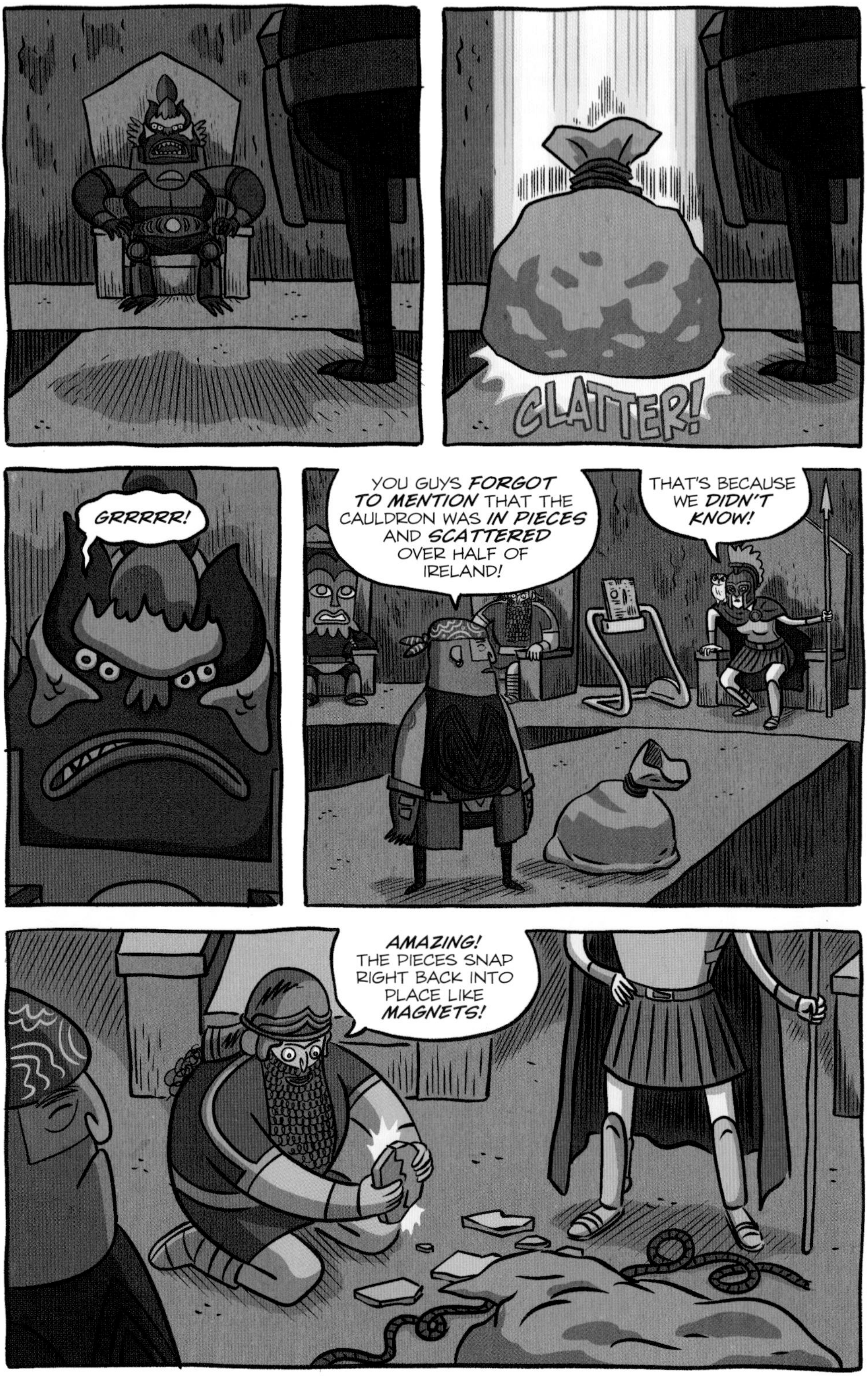
CLATTER!
GRRRRR!
YOU GUYS FORGOT TO MENTION THAT THE CAULDRON WAS IN PIECES AND SCATTERED OVER HALF OF IRELAND!
THAT'S BECAUSE WE DIDN'T KNOW!
AMAZING! THE PIECES SNAP RIGHT BACK INTO PLACE LIKE MAGNETS!

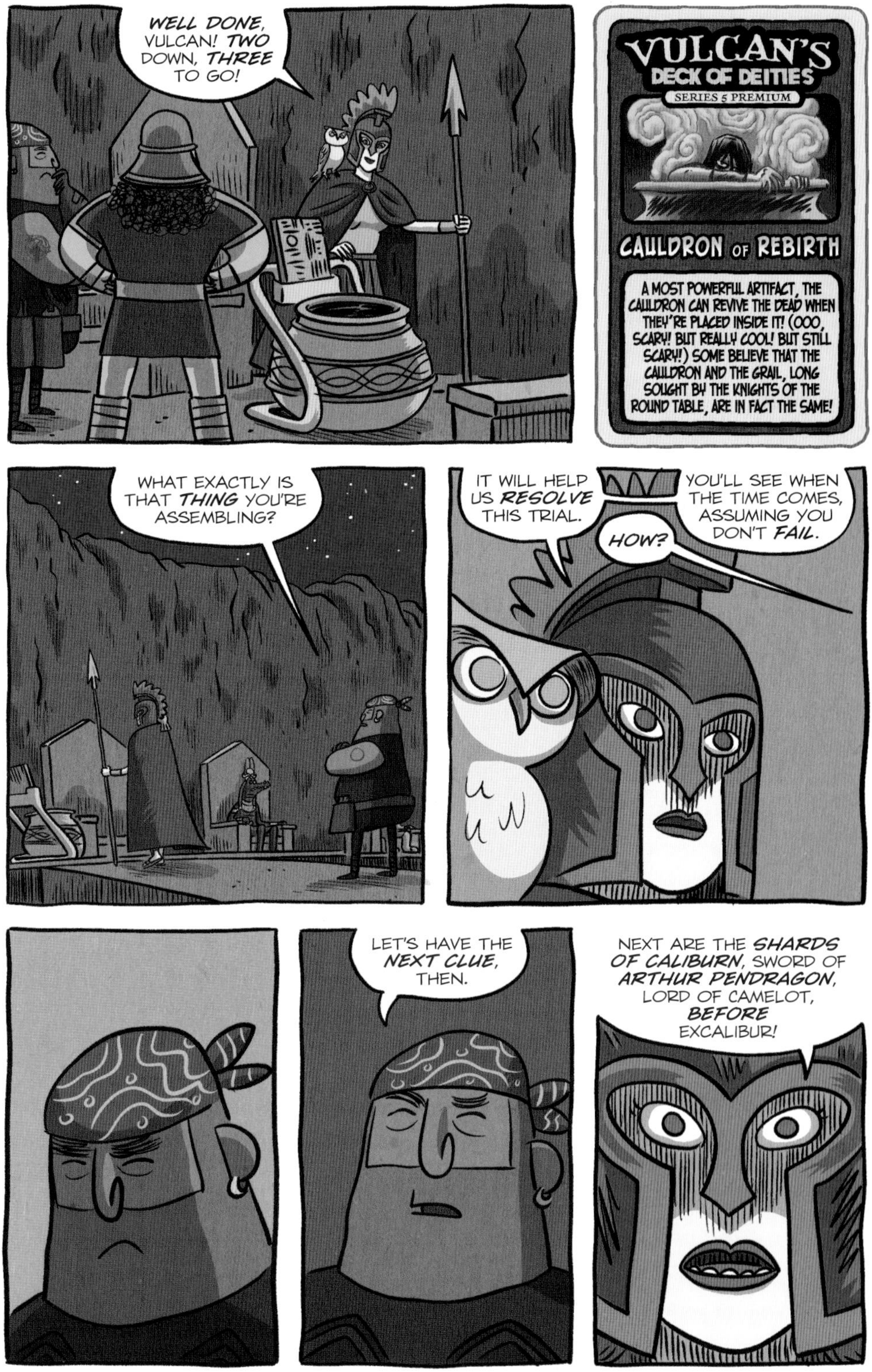
WELL DONE, VULCAN! TWO DOWN, THREE TO GO!
VULCAN'S DECK OF DEITIES
SERIES 5 PREMIUM
CAULDRON OF REBIRTH
A MOST POWERFUL ARTIFACT, THE CAULDRON CAN REVIVE THE DEAD WHEN THEY'RE PLACED INSIDE IT! (OOO, SCARY! BUT REALLY COOL! BUT STILL SCARY!) SOME BELIEVE THAT THE CAULDRON AND THE GRAIL, LONG SOUGHT BY THE KNIGHTS OF THE ROUND TABLE, ARE IN FACT THE SAME!
WHAT EXACTLY IS THAT THING YOU'RE ASSEMBLING?
IT WILL HELP US RESOLVE THIS TRIAL.
HOW?
YOU'LL SEE WHEN THE TIME COMES, ASSUMING YOU DON'T FAIL.
LET'S HAVE THE NEXT CLUE, THEN.
NEXT ARE THE SHARDS OF CALIBURN, SWORD OF ARTHUR PENDRAGON, LORD OF CAMELOT, BEFORE EXCALIBUR!

LATER, *DOWNSTAIRS* IN THE *SUPPLY SHOP*...

FASCINATING! A *SECOND* PLAQUE HIDDEN WITH THE *CAULDRON OF REBIRTH!*

YUP. HERE, PROMETHEUS ARRIVES WITH *THE OBJECT* AND IS MET BY A GROUP OF *PEOPLE*...

NOT *JUST* PEOPLE, VULCAN, *LOOK CLOSELY!* *DIFFERENT* PEOPLE, OF *DIFFERENT* NATIONS!

THESE PLAQUES ARE TELLING *A STORY,* ONE IMAGE AT A TIME!

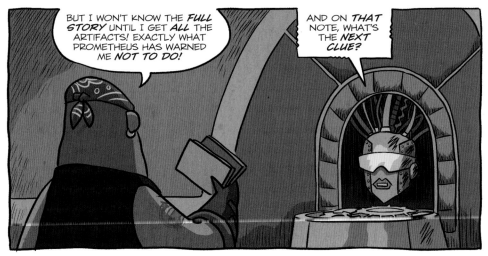

BUT I WON'T KNOW THE *FULL STORY* UNTIL I GET *ALL* THE ARTIFACTS! EXACTLY WHAT PROMETHEUS HAS WARNED ME *NOT TO DO!*

AND ON *THAT* NOTE, WHAT'S THE *NEXT CLUE?*

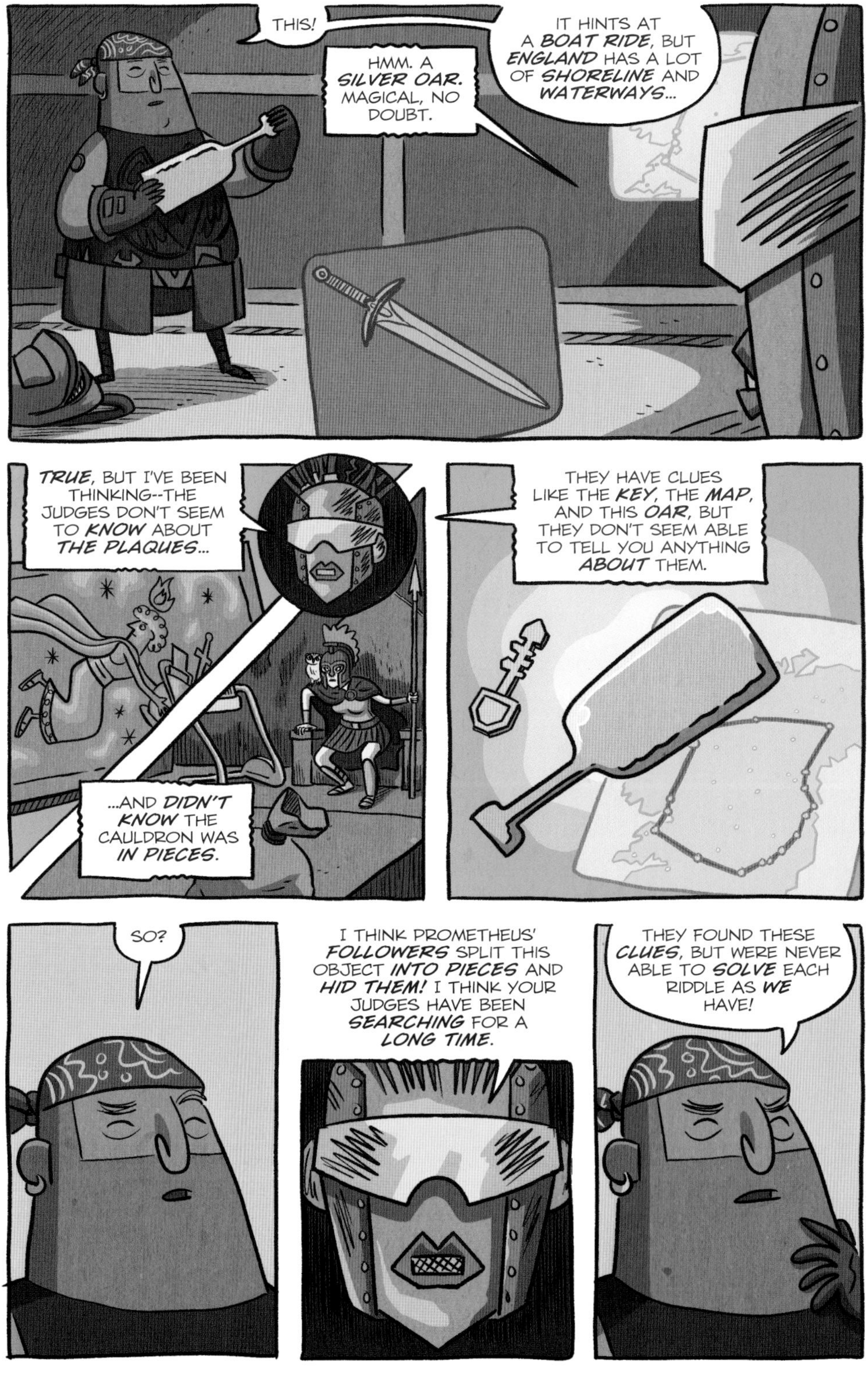
THIS!
HMM. A SILVER OAR. MAGICAL, NO DOUBT.
IT HINTS AT A BOAT RIDE, BUT ENGLAND HAS A LOT OF SHORELINE AND WATERWAYS...
TRUE, BUT I'VE BEEN THINKING--THE JUDGES DON'T SEEM TO KNOW ABOUT THE PLAQUES...
...AND DIDN'T KNOW THE CAULDRON WAS IN PIECES.
THEY HAVE CLUES LIKE THE KEY, THE MAP, AND THIS OAR, BUT THEY DON'T SEEM ABLE TO TELL YOU ANYTHING ABOUT THEM.
SO?
I THINK PROMETHEUS' FOLLOWERS SPLIT THIS OBJECT INTO PIECES AND HID THEM! I THINK YOUR JUDGES HAVE BEEN SEARCHING FOR A LONG TIME.
THEY FOUND THESE CLUES, BUT WERE NEVER ABLE TO SOLVE EACH RIDDLE AS WE HAVE!

WELL, THEY DIDN'T HAVE *YOU*!

TRUE, BUT YOU *MADE* ME! LET'S FACE IT--YOU'RE A PROBLEM *SOLVER* BY NATURE, WHEREAS MOST OF THE *OTHER* GODS ARE PROBLEM *MAKERS*, AND THEY *KNOW IT*!

I'LL AGREE WITH THAT *LAST PART*! BUT WHAT'S YOUR *POINT* HERE?

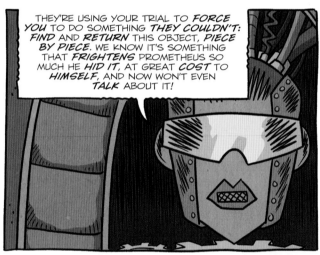

THEY'RE USING YOUR TRIAL TO *FORCE YOU* TO DO SOMETHING *THEY COULDN'T*: FIND AND *RETURN* THIS OBJECT, *PIECE BY PIECE*. WE KNOW IT'S SOMETHING THAT *FRIGHTENS* PROMETHEUS SO MUCH HE *HID IT*, AT GREAT *COST* TO *HIMSELF*, AND NOW WON'T EVEN *TALK* ABOUT IT!

THAT SOUNDS *PLAUSIBLE*, BUT WE BOTH KNOW WHAT HAPPENS IF I *DON'T* DO THIS. AND IT *DOESN'T* SHED ANY LIGHT ON *THIS* CLUE!

YES, IT DOES! I'M GETTING TO THAT!

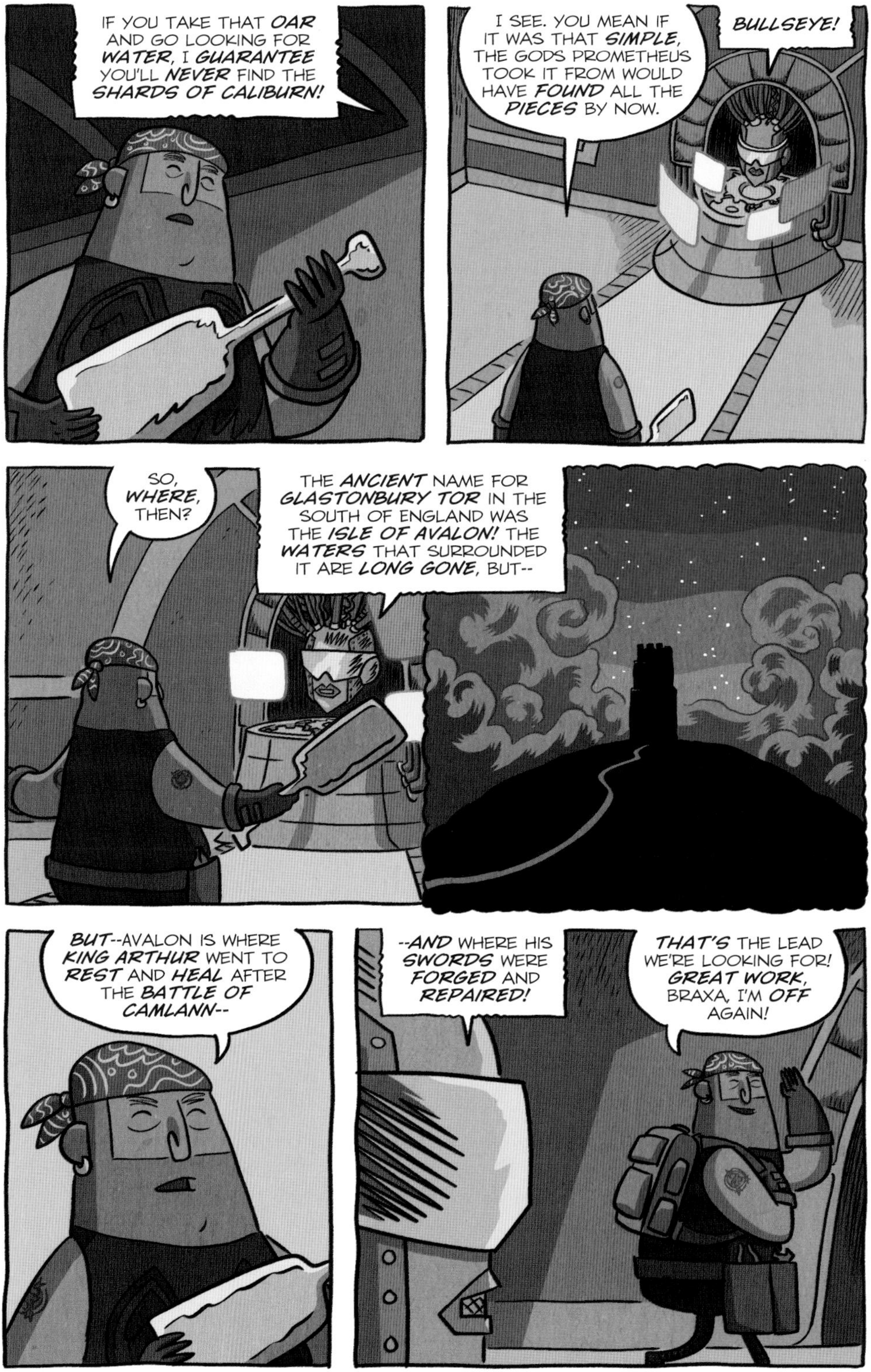
IF YOU TAKE THAT OAR AND GO LOOKING FOR WATER, I GUARANTEE YOU'LL NEVER FIND THE SHARDS OF CALIBURN!
I SEE. YOU MEAN IF IT WAS THAT SIMPLE, THE GODS PROMETHEUS TOOK IT FROM WOULD HAVE FOUND ALL THE PIECES BY NOW.
BULLSEYE!
SO, WHERE, THEN?
THE ANCIENT NAME FOR GLASTONBURY TOR IN THE SOUTH OF ENGLAND WAS THE ISLE OF AVALON! THE WATERS THAT SURROUNDED IT ARE LONG GONE, BUT--
BUT--AVALON IS WHERE KING ARTHUR WENT TO REST AND HEAL AFTER THE BATTLE OF CAMLANN--
--AND WHERE HIS SWORDS WERE FORGED AND REPAIRED!
THAT'S THE LEAD WE'RE LOOKING FOR! GREAT WORK, BRAXA, I'M OFF AGAIN!

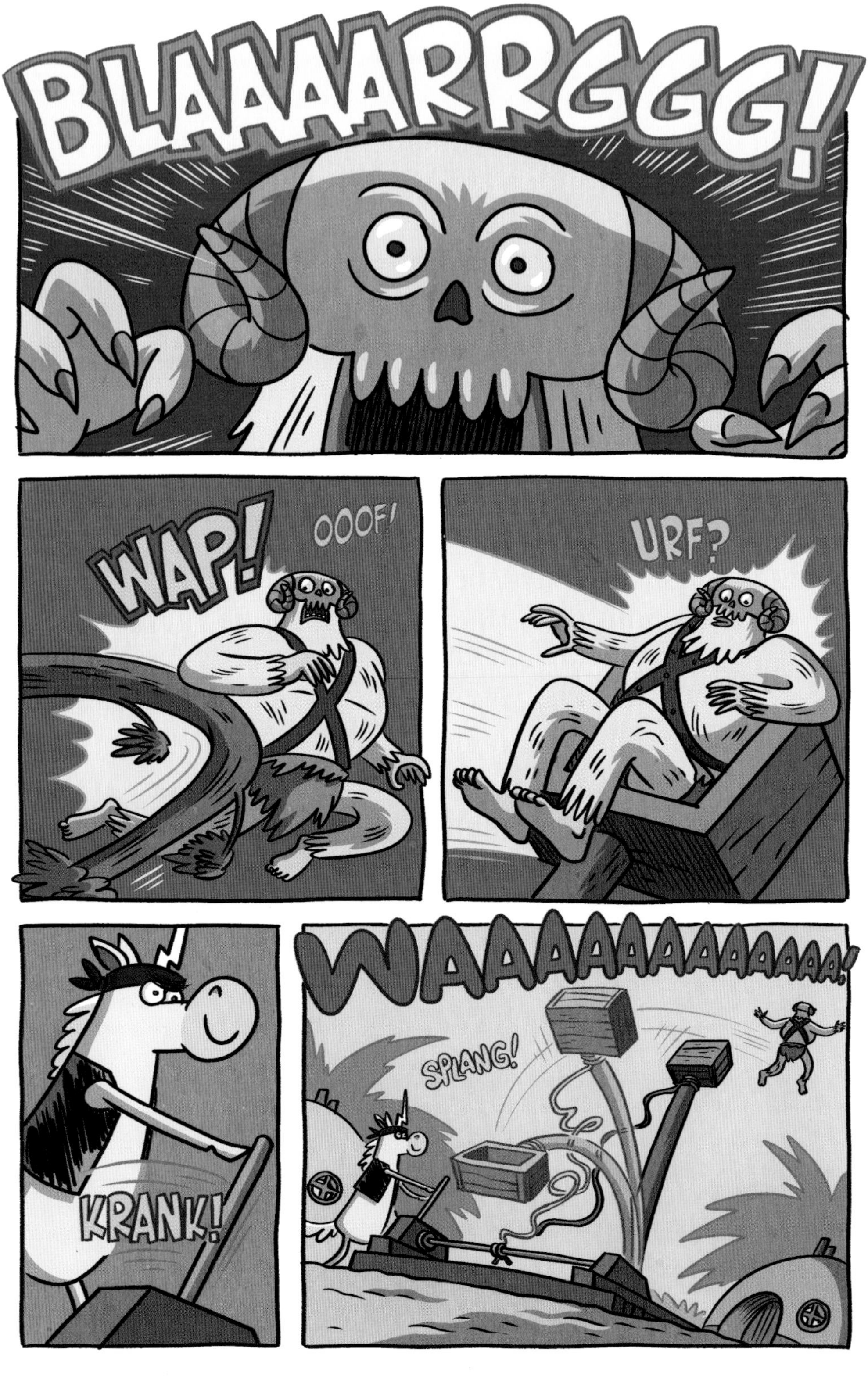
BLAAAARRGGG!
WAP!
OOOF!
URF?
KRANK!
WAAAAAAAAAAAA!
SPLANG!

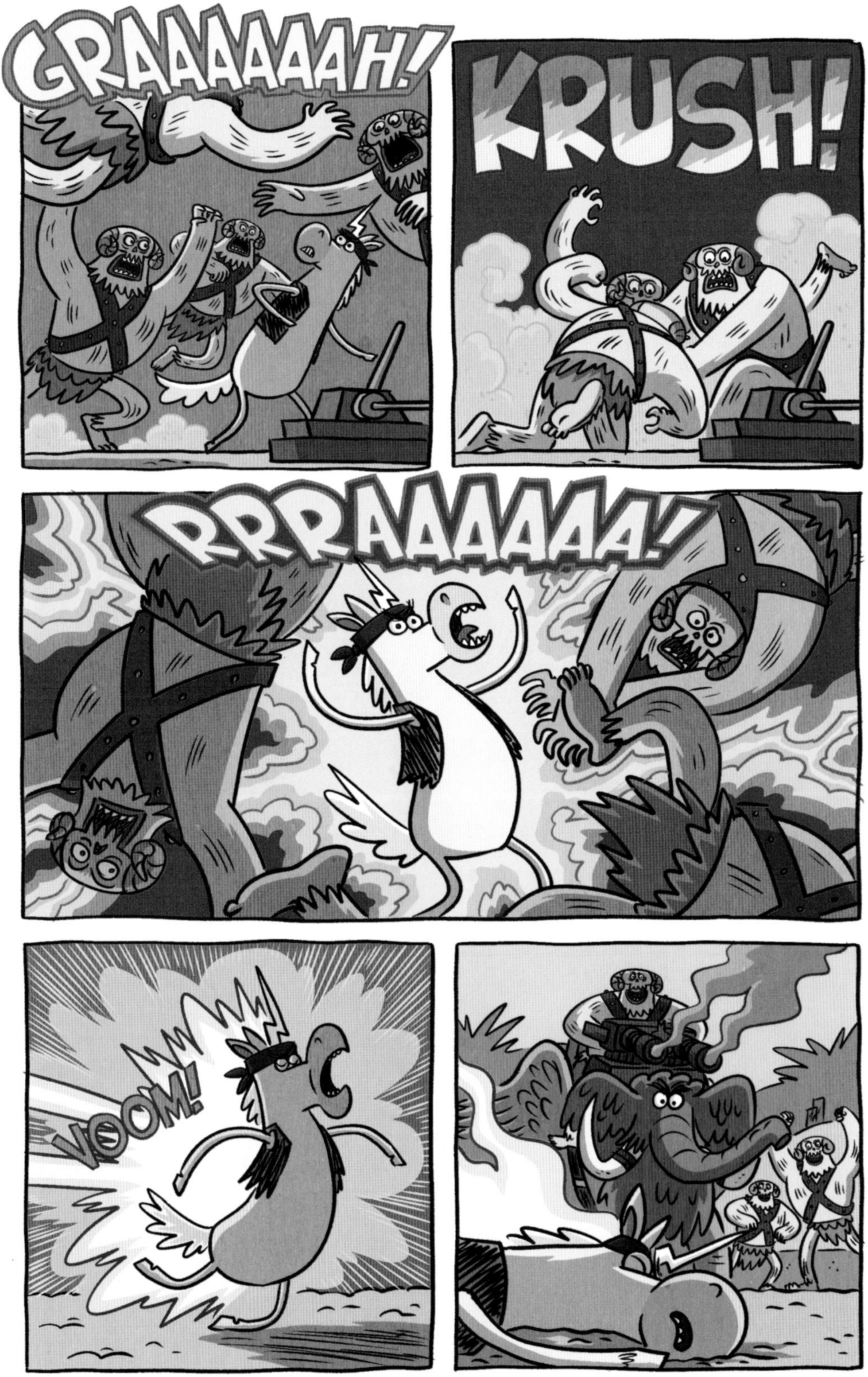
GRAAAAAAH!
KRUSH!
RRRAAAAAA!
VOOM!

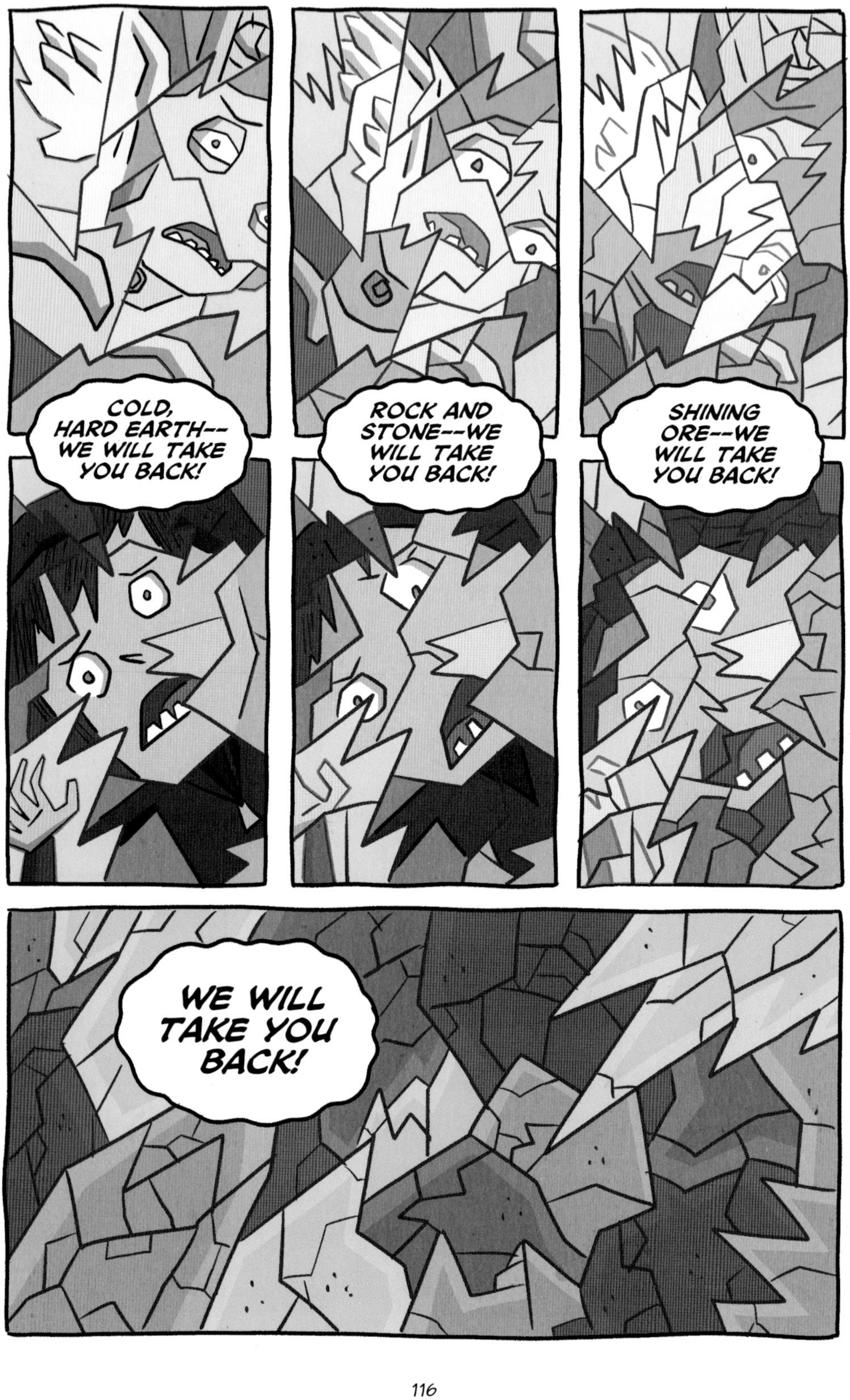
COLD, HARD EARTH-- WE WILL TAKE YOU BACK!
ROCK AND STONE--WE WILL TAKE YOU BACK!
SHINING ORE--WE WILL TAKE YOU BACK!
WE WILL TAKE YOU BACK!

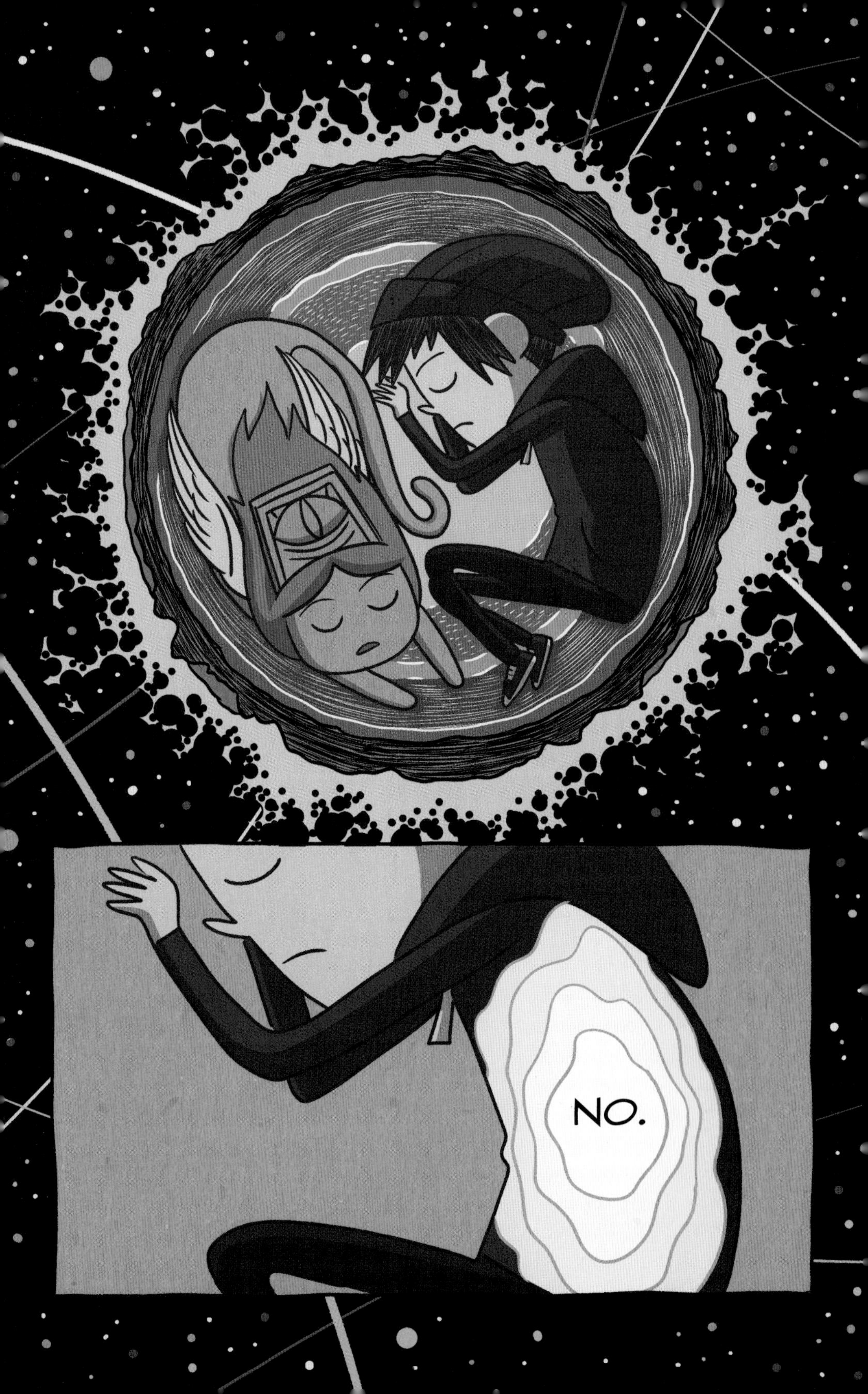
NO.

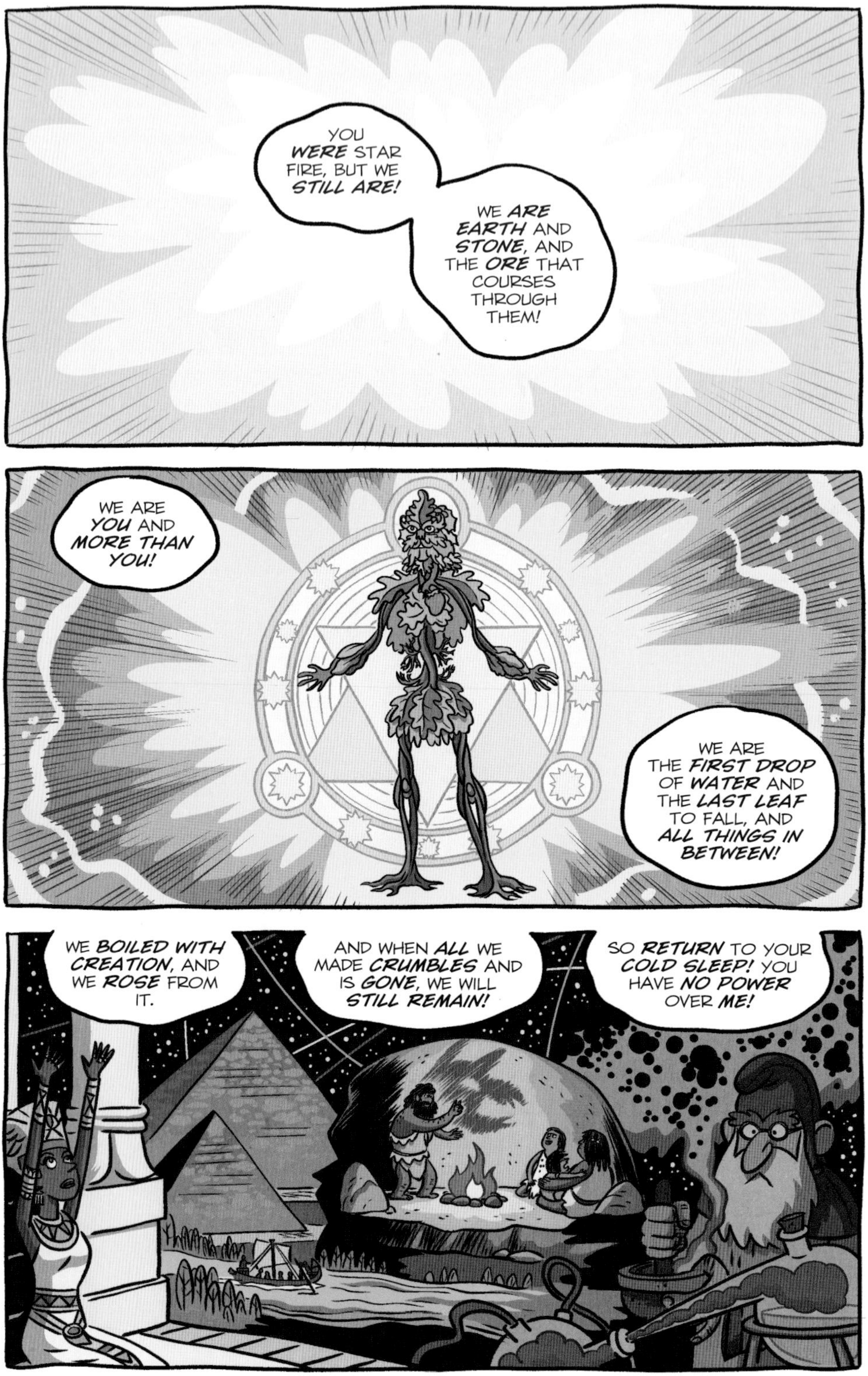
YOU WERE STAR FIRE, BUT WE STILL ARE!
WE ARE EARTH AND STONE, AND THE ORE THAT COURSES THROUGH THEM!
WE ARE YOU AND MORE THAN YOU!
WE ARE THE FIRST DROP OF WATER AND THE LAST LEAF TO FALL, AND ALL THINGS IN BETWEEN!
WE BOILED WITH CREATION, AND WE ROSE FROM IT.
AND WHEN ALL WE MADE CRUMBLES AND IS GONE, WE WILL STILL REMAIN!
SO RETURN TO YOUR COLD SLEEP! YOU HAVE NO POWER OVER ME!

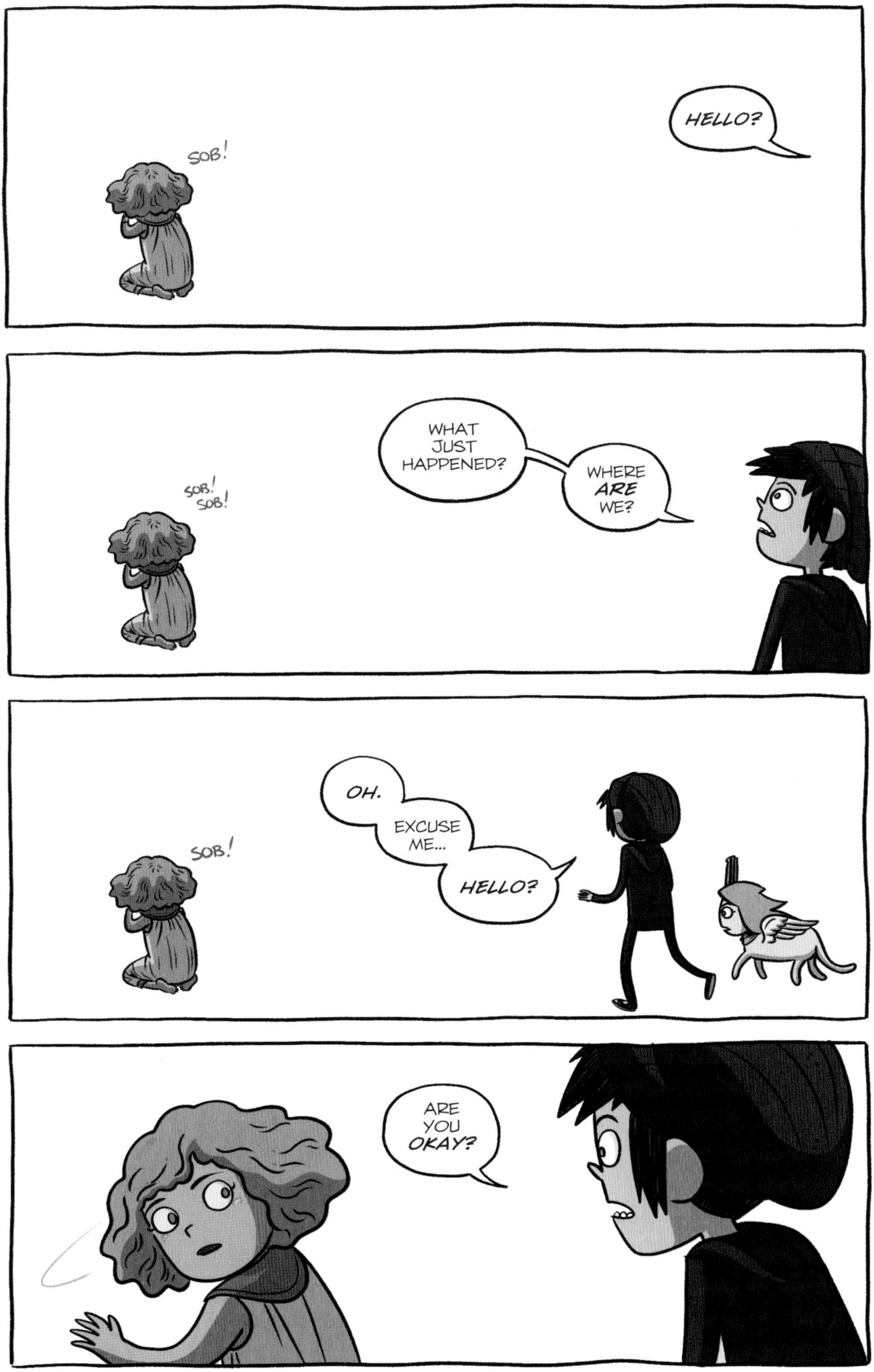
HELLO?
SOB!
SOB! SOB!
WHAT JUST HAPPENED?
WHERE ARE WE?
SOB!
OH.
EXCUSE ME...
HELLO?
ARE YOU OKAY?

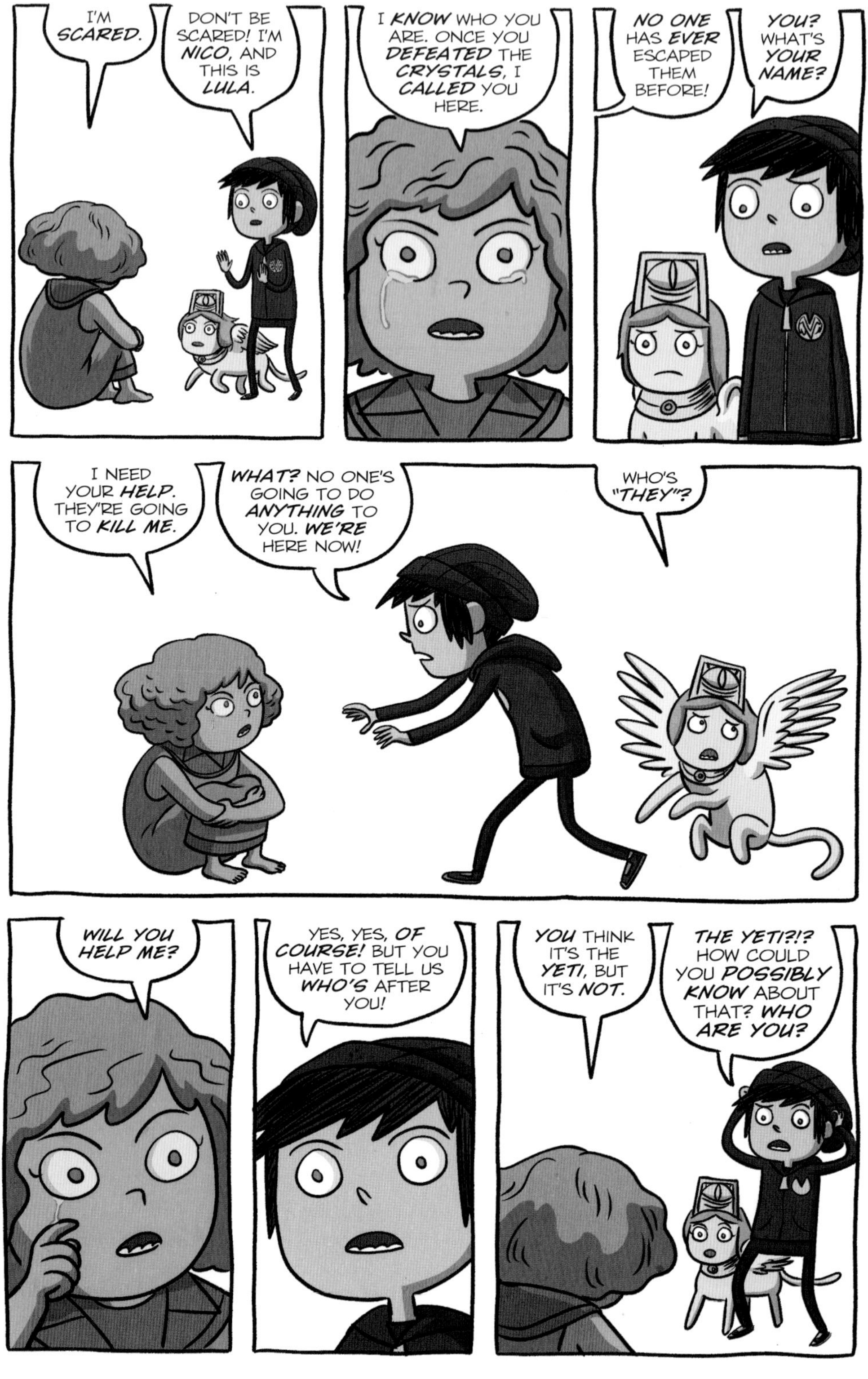
I'M SCARED.
DON'T BE SCARED! I'M NICO, AND THIS IS LULA.
I KNOW WHO YOU ARE. ONCE YOU DEFEATED THE CRYSTALS, I CALLED YOU HERE.
NO ONE HAS EVER ESCAPED THEM BEFORE!
YOU? WHAT'S YOUR NAME?
I NEED YOUR HELP. THEY'RE GOING TO KILL ME.
WHAT? NO ONE'S GOING TO DO ANYTHING TO YOU. WE'RE HERE NOW!
WHO'S "THEY"?
WILL YOU HELP ME?
YES, YES, OF COURSE! BUT YOU HAVE TO TELL US WHO'S AFTER YOU!
YOU THINK IT'S THE YETI, BUT IT'S NOT.
THE YETI?!? HOW COULD YOU POSSIBLY KNOW ABOUT THAT? WHO ARE YOU?

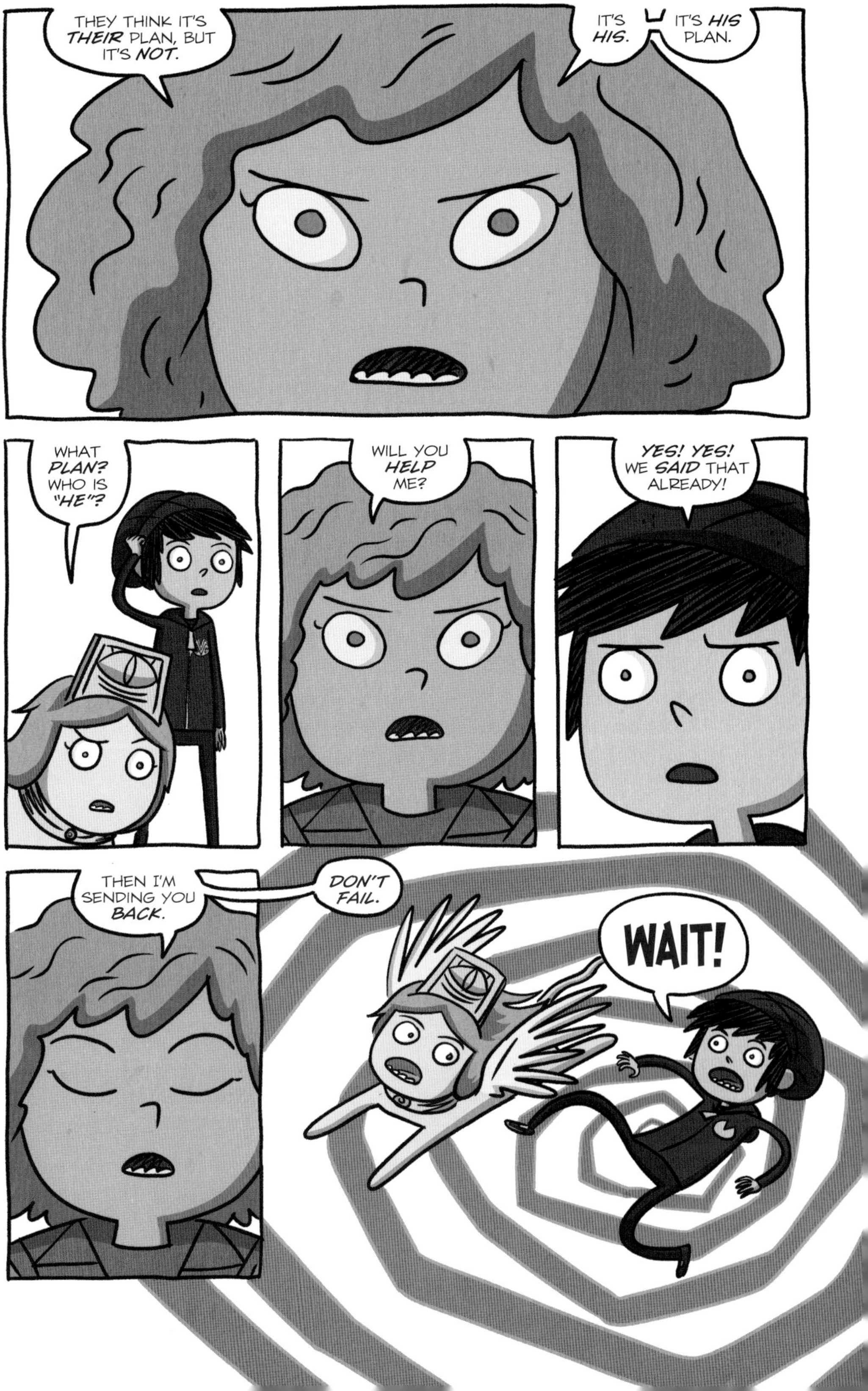
THEY THINK IT'S THEIR PLAN, BUT IT'S NOT.
IT'S HIS.
IT'S HIS PLAN.
WHAT PLAN? WHO IS "HE"?
WILL YOU HELP ME?
YES! YES! WE SAID THAT ALREADY!
THEN I'M SENDING YOU BACK.
DON'T FAIL.
WAIT!

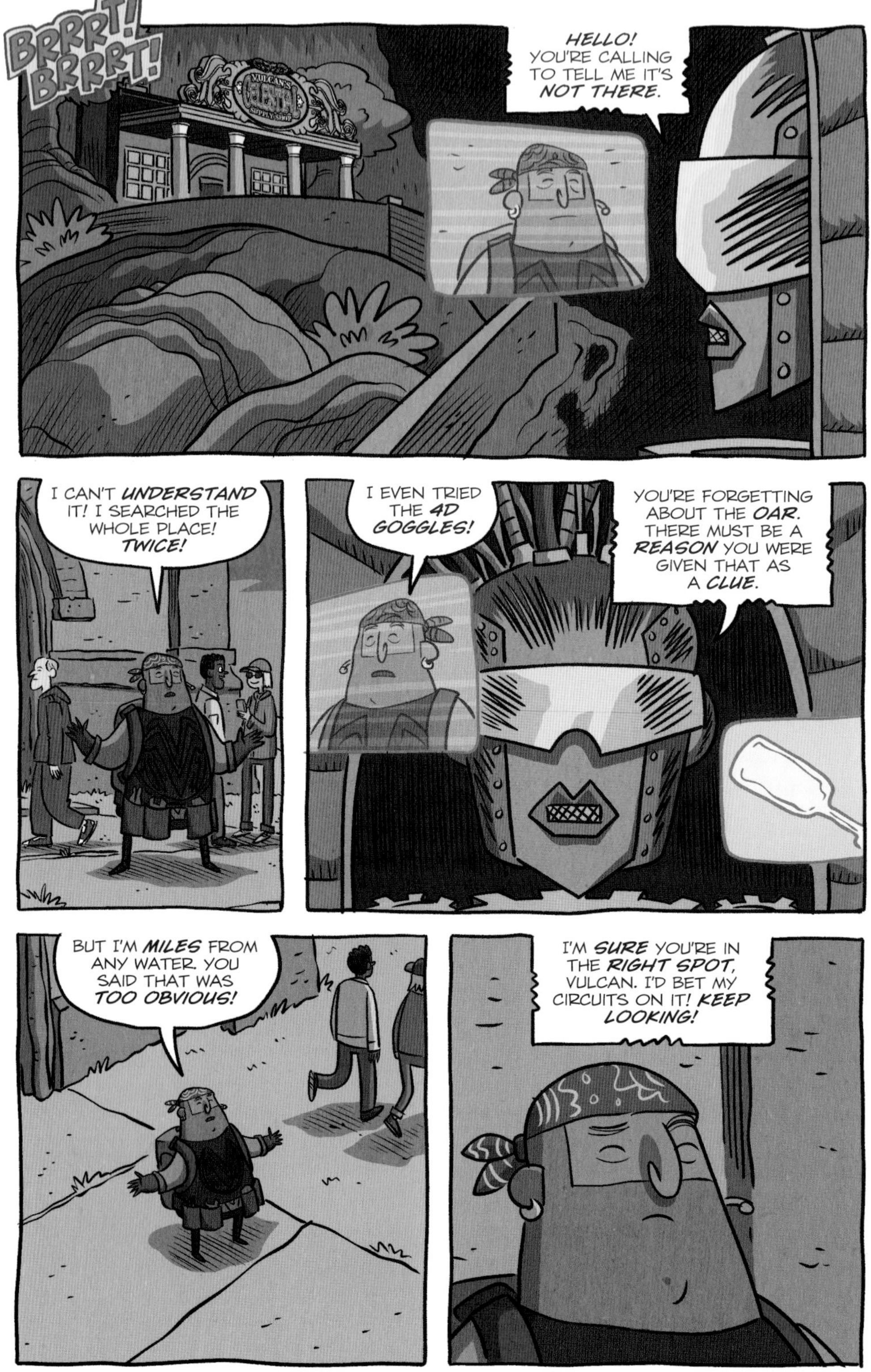
BRRRT! BRRRT!
HELLO! YOU'RE CALLING TO TELL ME IT'S NOT THERE.
I CAN'T UNDERSTAND IT! I SEARCHED THE WHOLE PLACE! TWICE!
I EVEN TRIED THE 4D GOGGLES!
YOU'RE FORGETTING ABOUT THE OAR. THERE MUST BE A REASON YOU WERE GIVEN THAT AS A CLUE.
BUT I'M MILES FROM ANY WATER. YOU SAID THAT WAS TOO OBVIOUS!
I'M SURE YOU'RE IN THE RIGHT SPOT, VULCAN. I'D BET MY CIRCUITS ON IT! KEEP LOOKING!

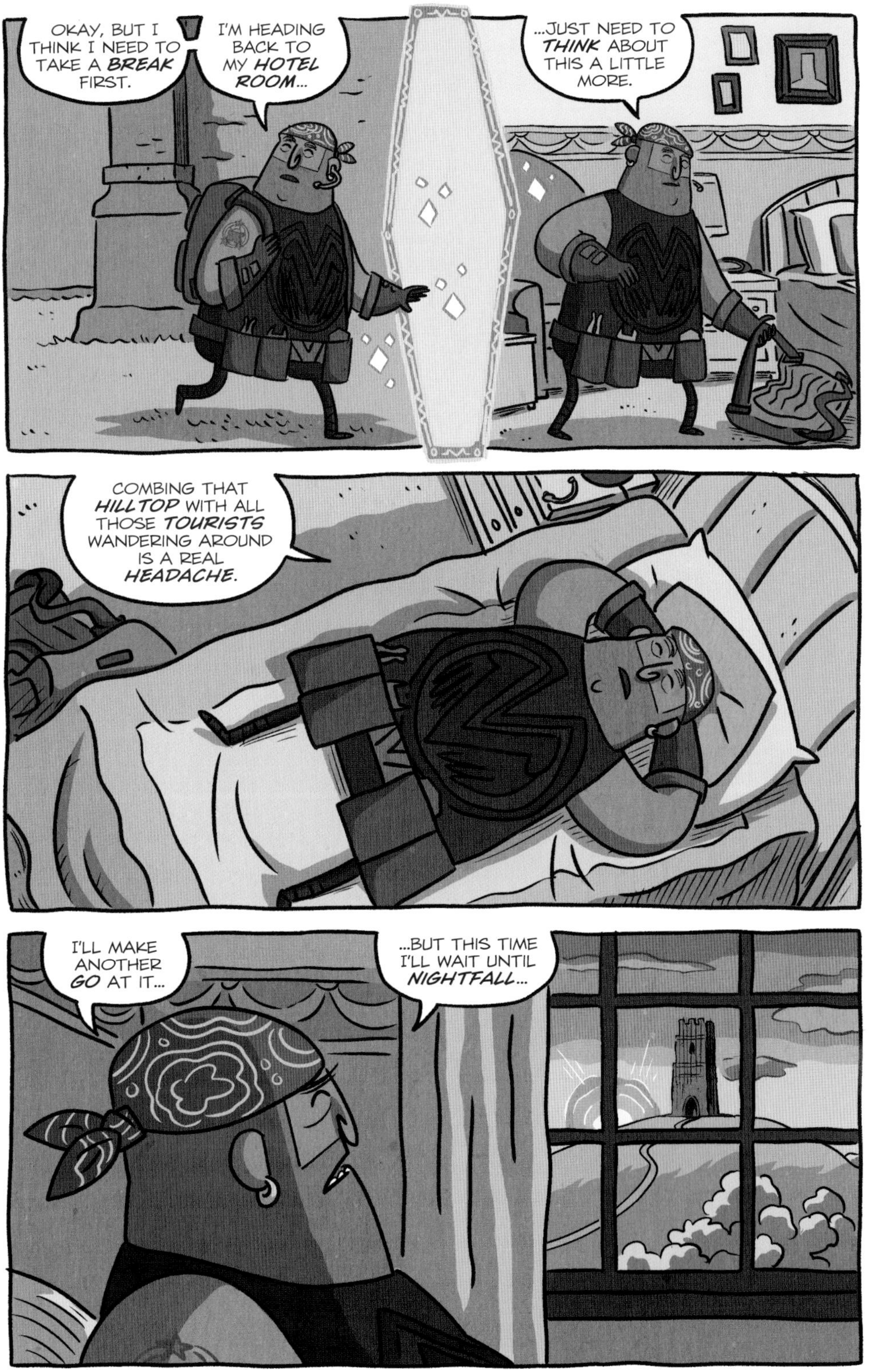
OKAY, BUT I THINK I NEED TO TAKE A BREAK FIRST.
I'M HEADING BACK TO MY HOTEL ROOM...
...JUST NEED TO THINK ABOUT THIS A LITTLE MORE.
COMBING THAT HILLTOP WITH ALL THOSE TOURISTS WANDERING AROUND IS A REAL HEADACHE.
I'LL MAKE ANOTHER GO AT IT...
...BUT THIS TIME I'LL WAIT UNTIL NIGHTFALL...

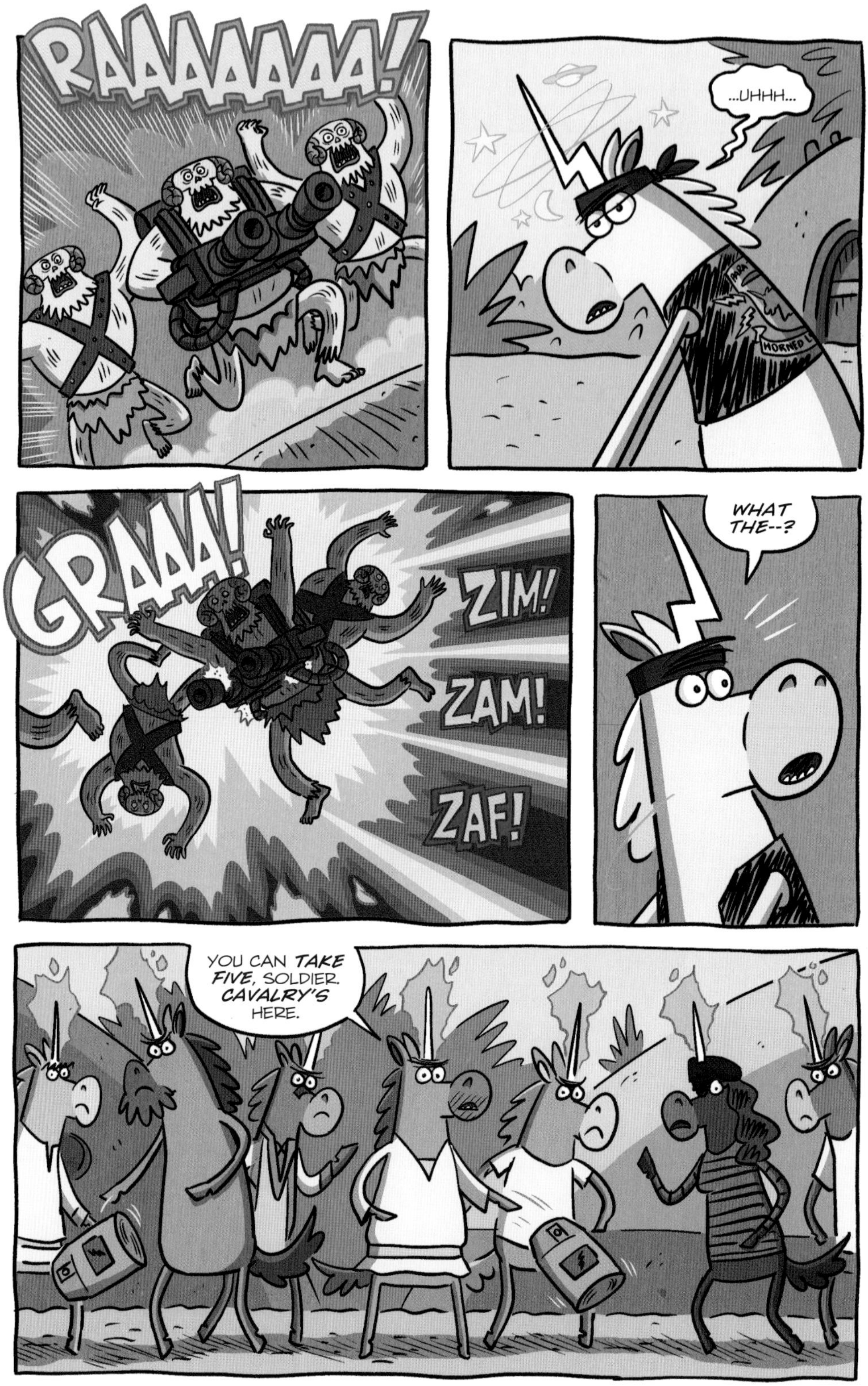
RAAAAAAA!
...UHHH...
PARA
HORNED
GRAAA!
ZIM!
ZAM!
ZAF!
WHAT THE--?
YOU CAN *TAKE FIVE*, SOLDIER. *CAVALRY'S* HERE.

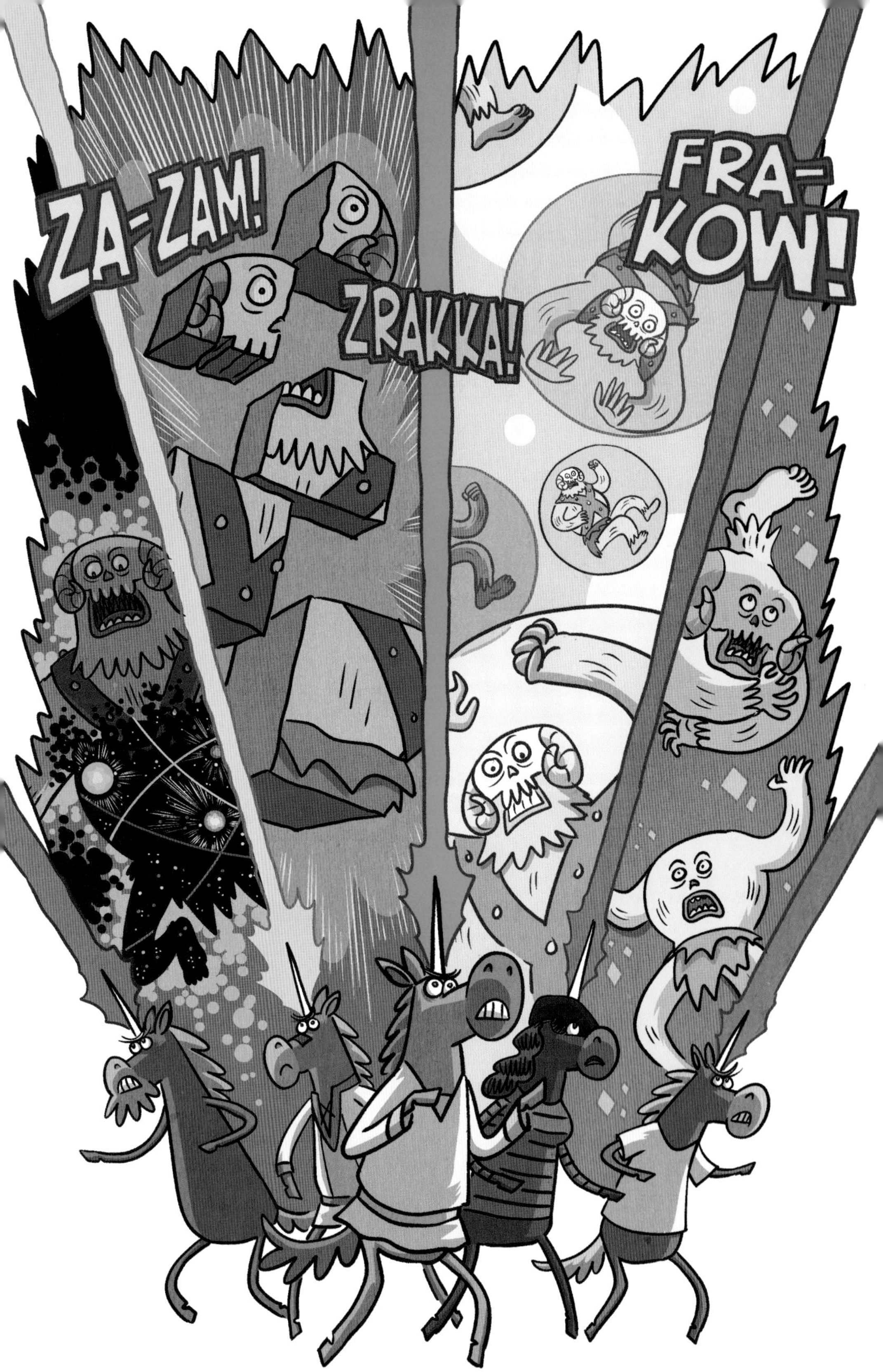
ZA-ZAM!
ZRAKKA!
FRA-
KOW!

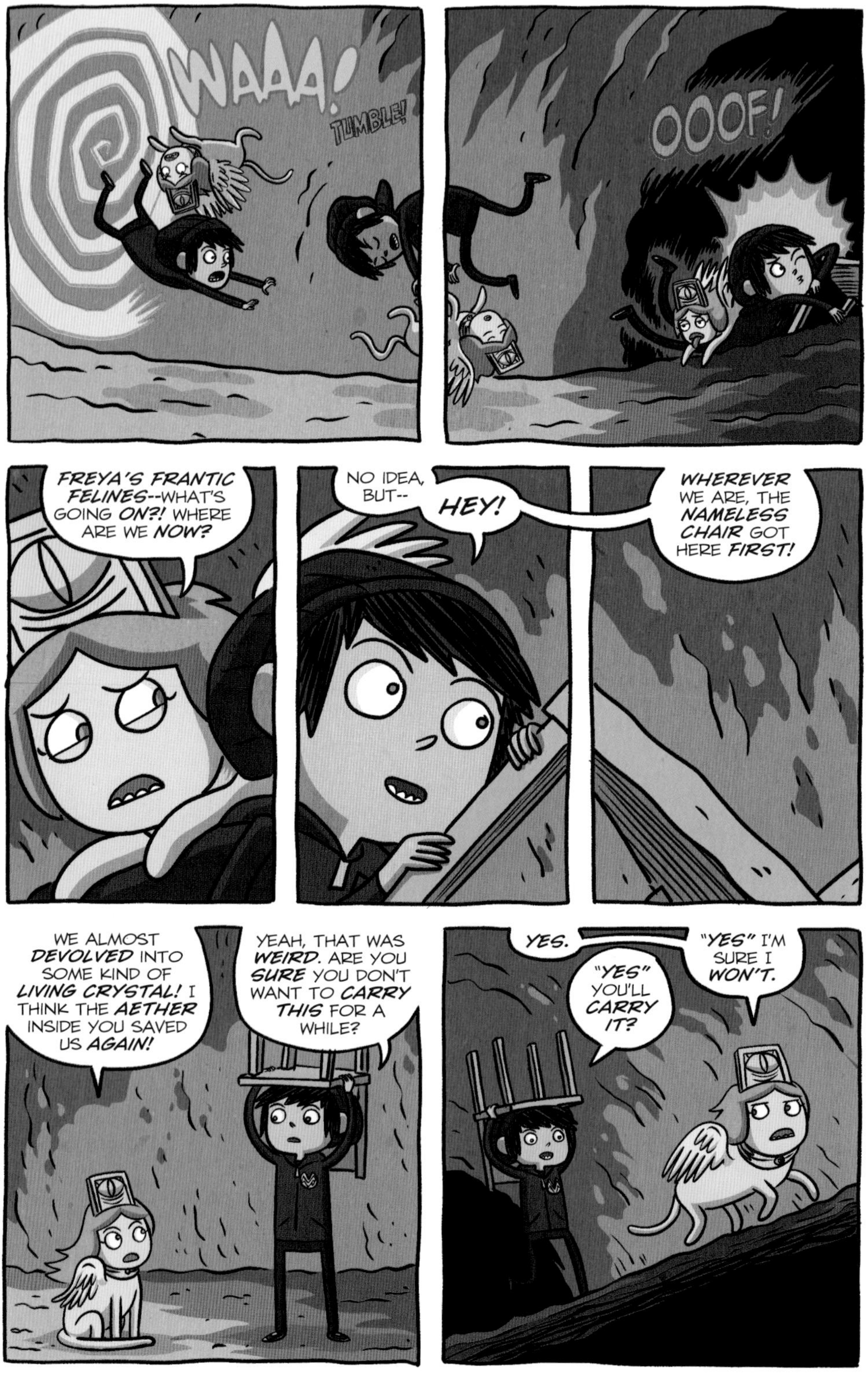
WAAA!
TUMBLE!
OOOF!
FREYA'S FRANTIC FELINES--WHAT'S GOING ON?! WHERE ARE WE NOW?
NO IDEA, BUT--
HEY!
WHEREVER WE ARE, THE NAMELESS CHAIR GOT HERE FIRST!
WE ALMOST DEVOLVED INTO SOME KIND OF LIVING CRYSTAL! I THINK THE AETHER INSIDE YOU SAVED US AGAIN!
YEAH, THAT WAS WEIRD. ARE YOU SURE YOU DON'T WANT TO CARRY THIS FOR A WHILE?
YES.
"YES" YOU'LL CARRY IT?
"YES" I'M SURE I WON'T.

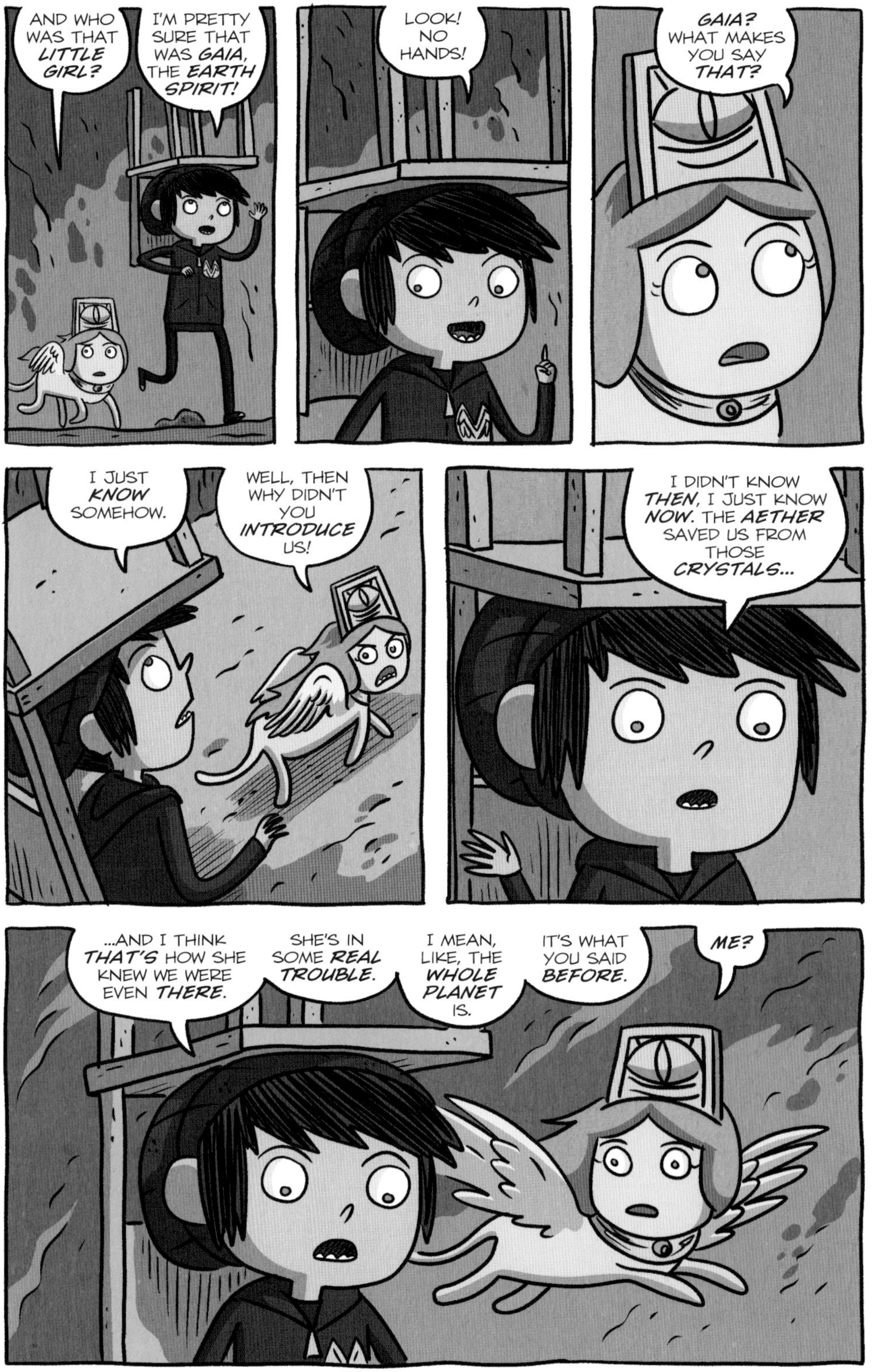
AND WHO WAS THAT *LITTLE GIRL?*
I'M PRETTY SURE THAT WAS *GAIA*, THE *EARTH SPIRIT!*
LOOK! NO HANDS!
GAIA? WHAT MAKES YOU SAY *THAT?*
I JUST *KNOW* SOMEHOW.
WELL, THEN WHY DIDN'T YOU *INTRODUCE* US!
I DIDN'T KNOW *THEN*, I JUST KNOW *NOW*. THE *AETHER* SAVED US FROM THOSE *CRYSTALS...*
...AND I THINK *THAT'S* HOW SHE KNEW WE WERE EVEN *THERE*.
SHE'S IN SOME *REAL TROUBLE*.
I MEAN, LIKE, THE *WHOLE PLANET* IS.
IT'S WHAT YOU SAID *BEFORE*.
ME?

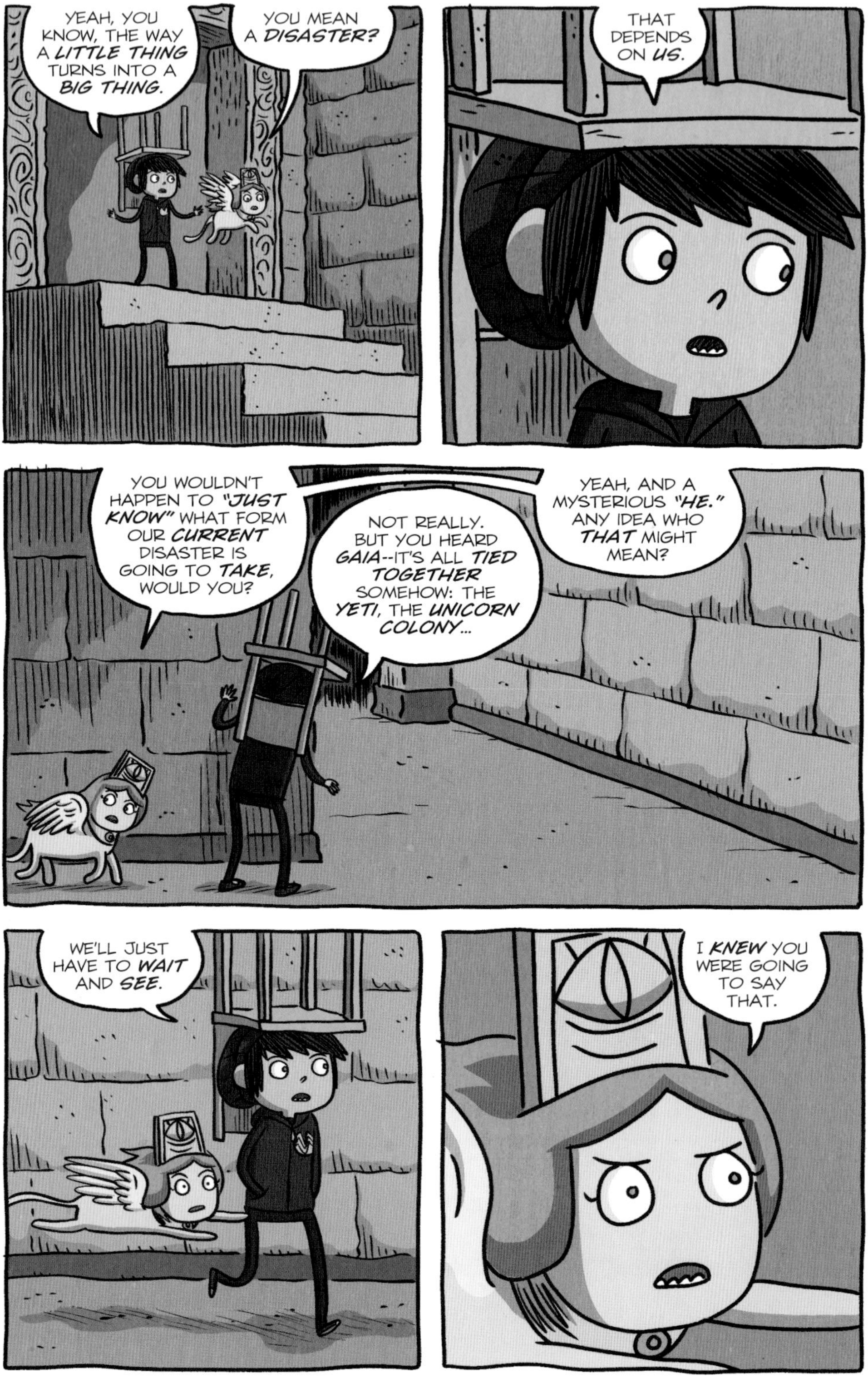
YEAH, YOU KNOW, THE WAY A LITTLE THING TURNS INTO A BIG THING.
YOU MEAN A DISASTER?
THAT DEPENDS ON US.
YOU WOULDN'T HAPPEN TO "JUST KNOW" WHAT FORM OUR CURRENT DISASTER IS GOING TO TAKE, WOULD YOU?
NOT REALLY. BUT YOU HEARD GAIA--IT'S ALL TIED TOGETHER SOMEHOW: THE YETI, THE UNICORN COLONY...
YEAH, AND A MYSTERIOUS "HE." ANY IDEA WHO THAT MIGHT MEAN?
WE'LL JUST HAVE TO WAIT AND SEE.
I KNEW YOU WERE GOING TO SAY THAT.

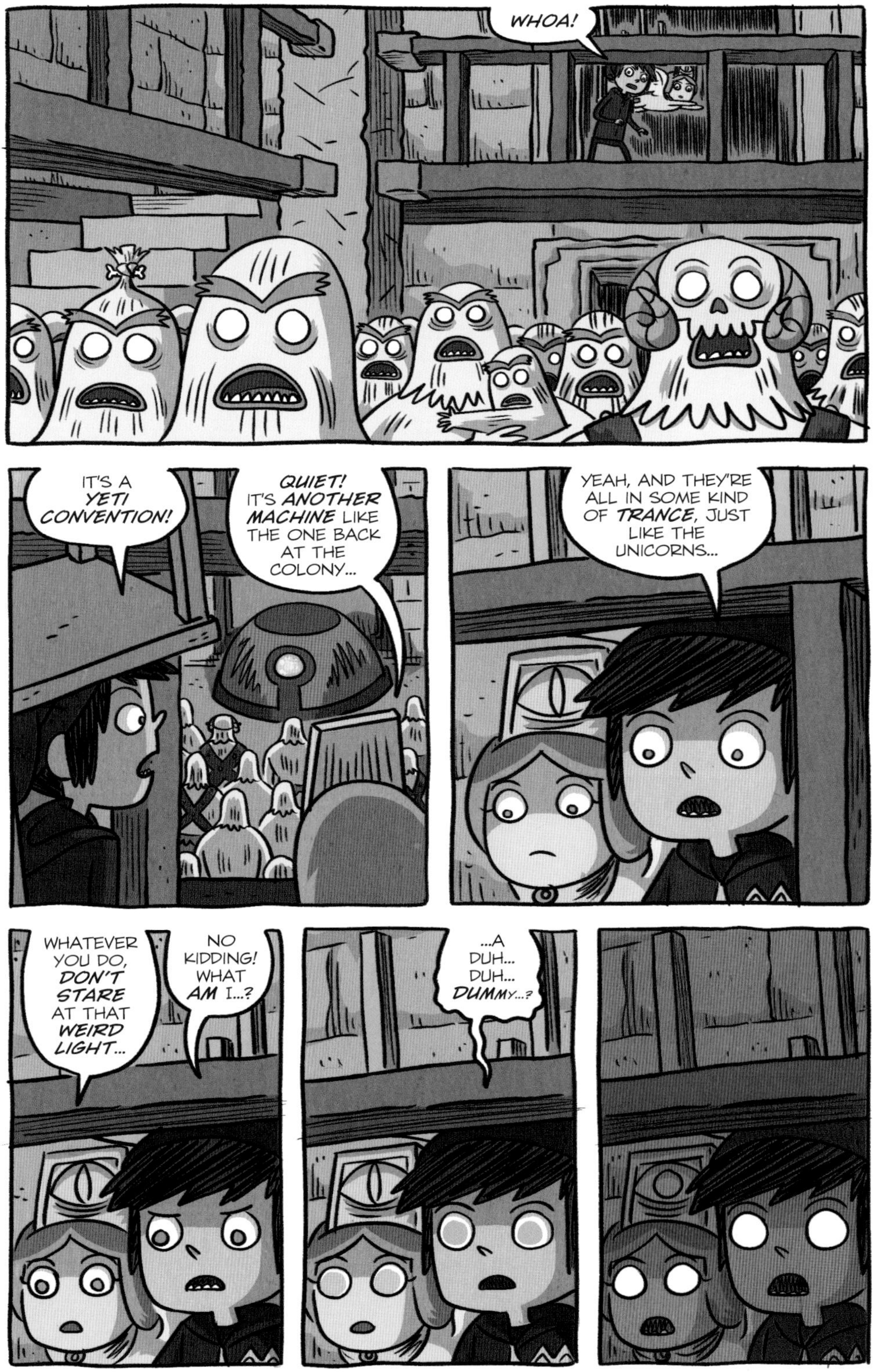

WHOA!
IT'S A YETI CONVENTION!
QUIET! IT'S ANOTHER MACHINE LIKE THE ONE BACK AT THE COLONY...
YEAH, AND THEY'RE ALL IN SOME KIND OF TRANCE, JUST LIKE THE UNICORNS...
WHATEVER YOU DO, DON'T STARE AT THAT WEIRD LIGHT...
NO KIDDING! WHAT AM I...?
...A DUH... DUH... DUMMY...?

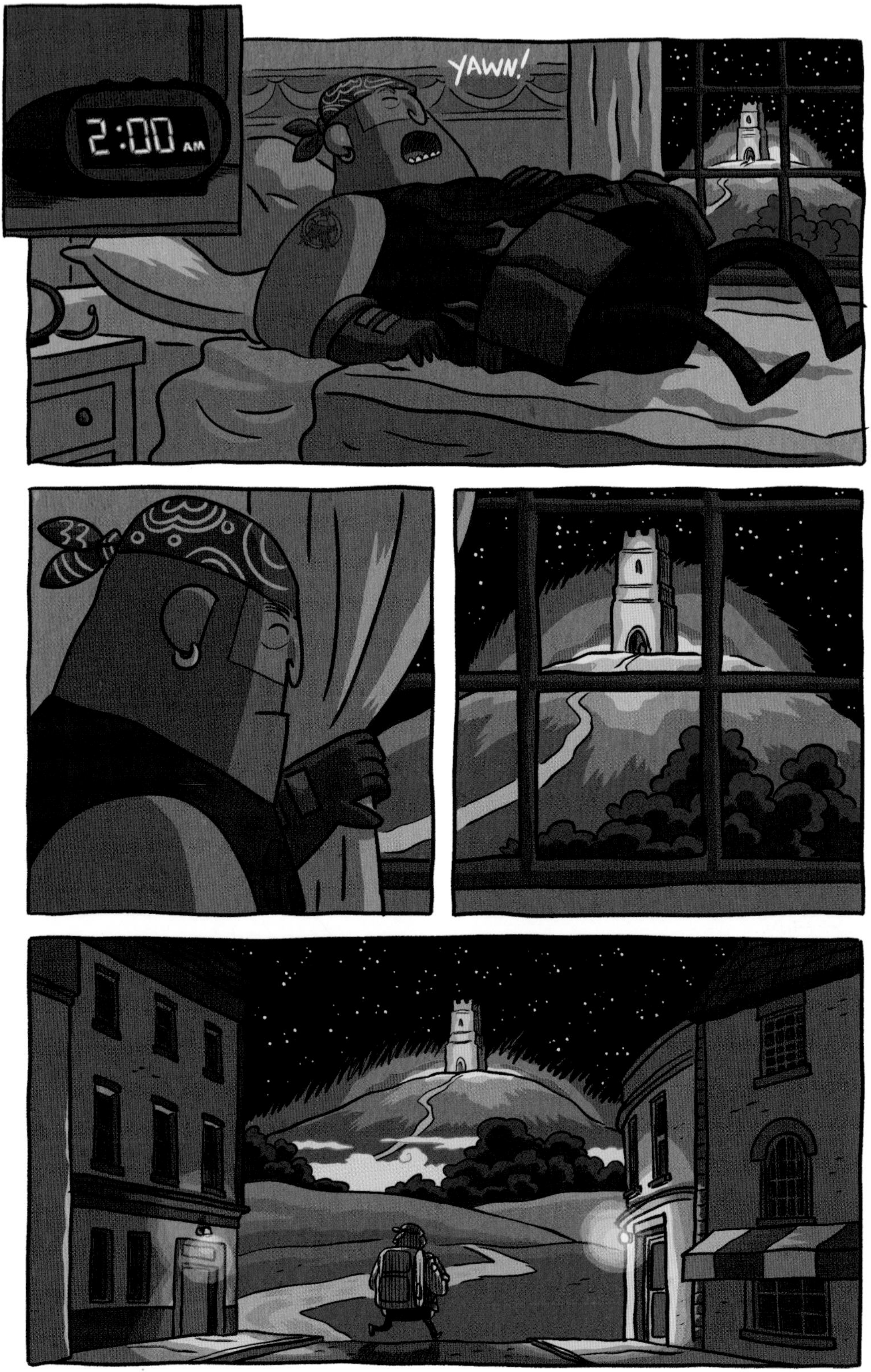
2:00 AM
YAWN!

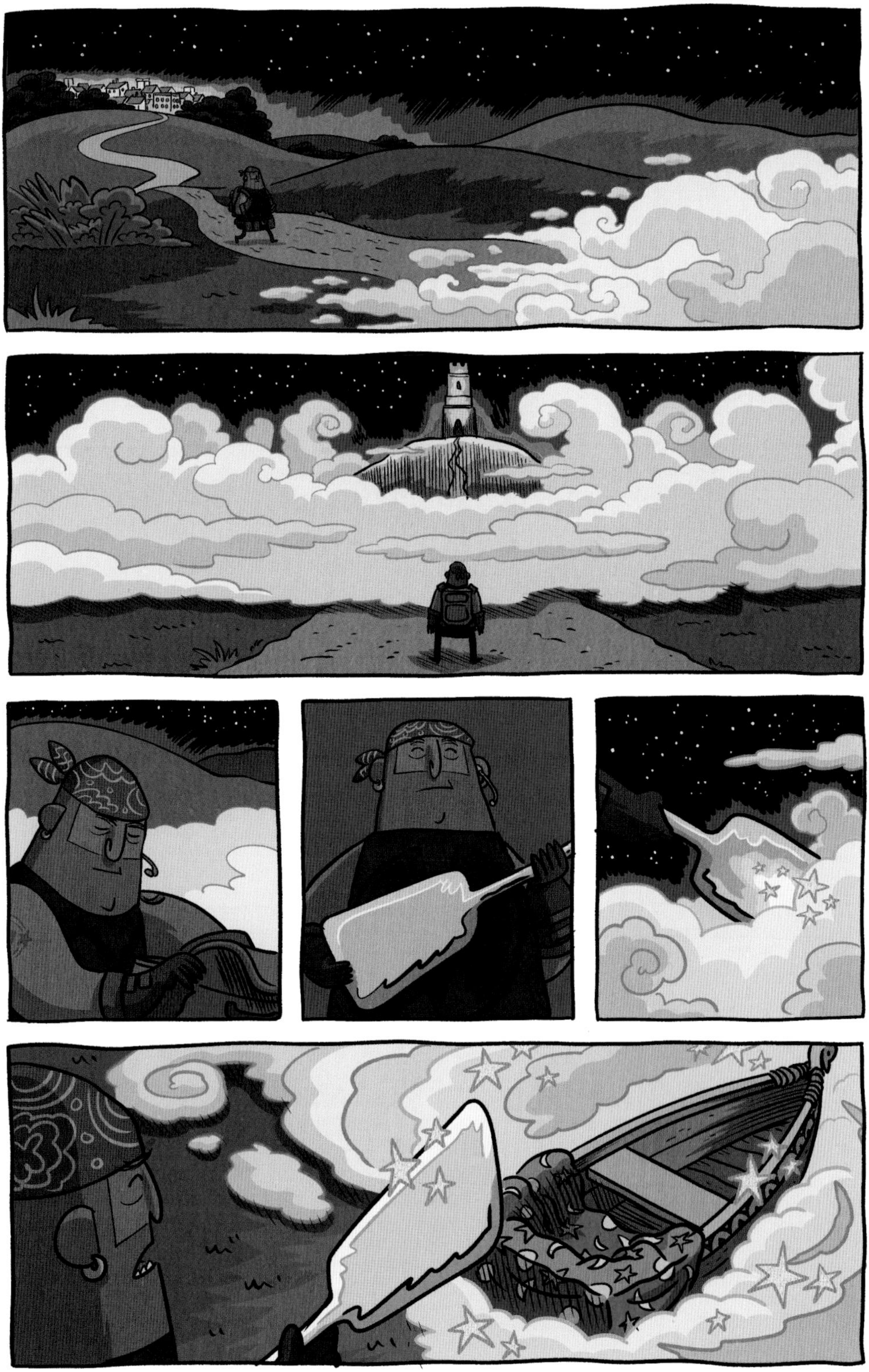

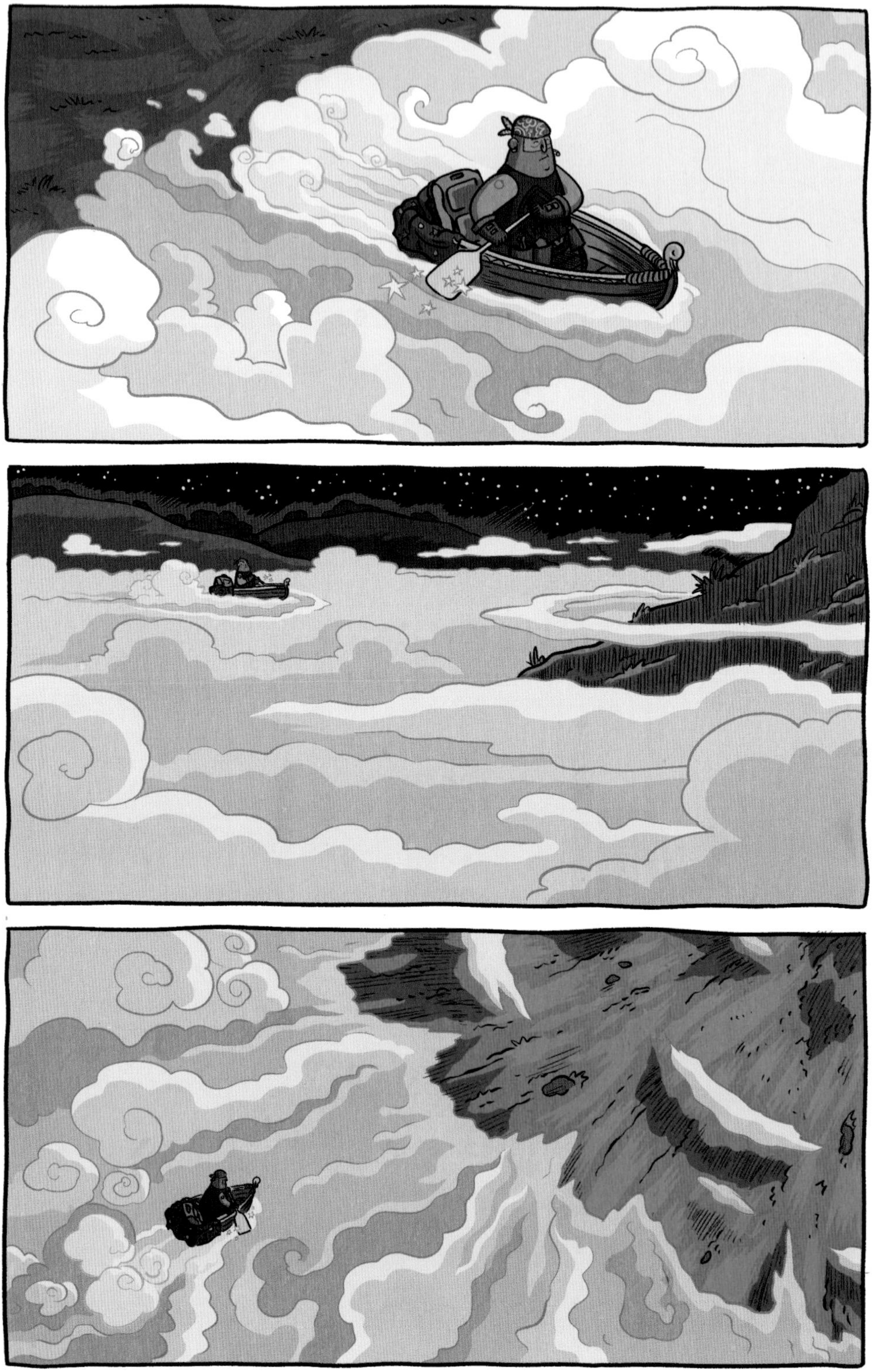

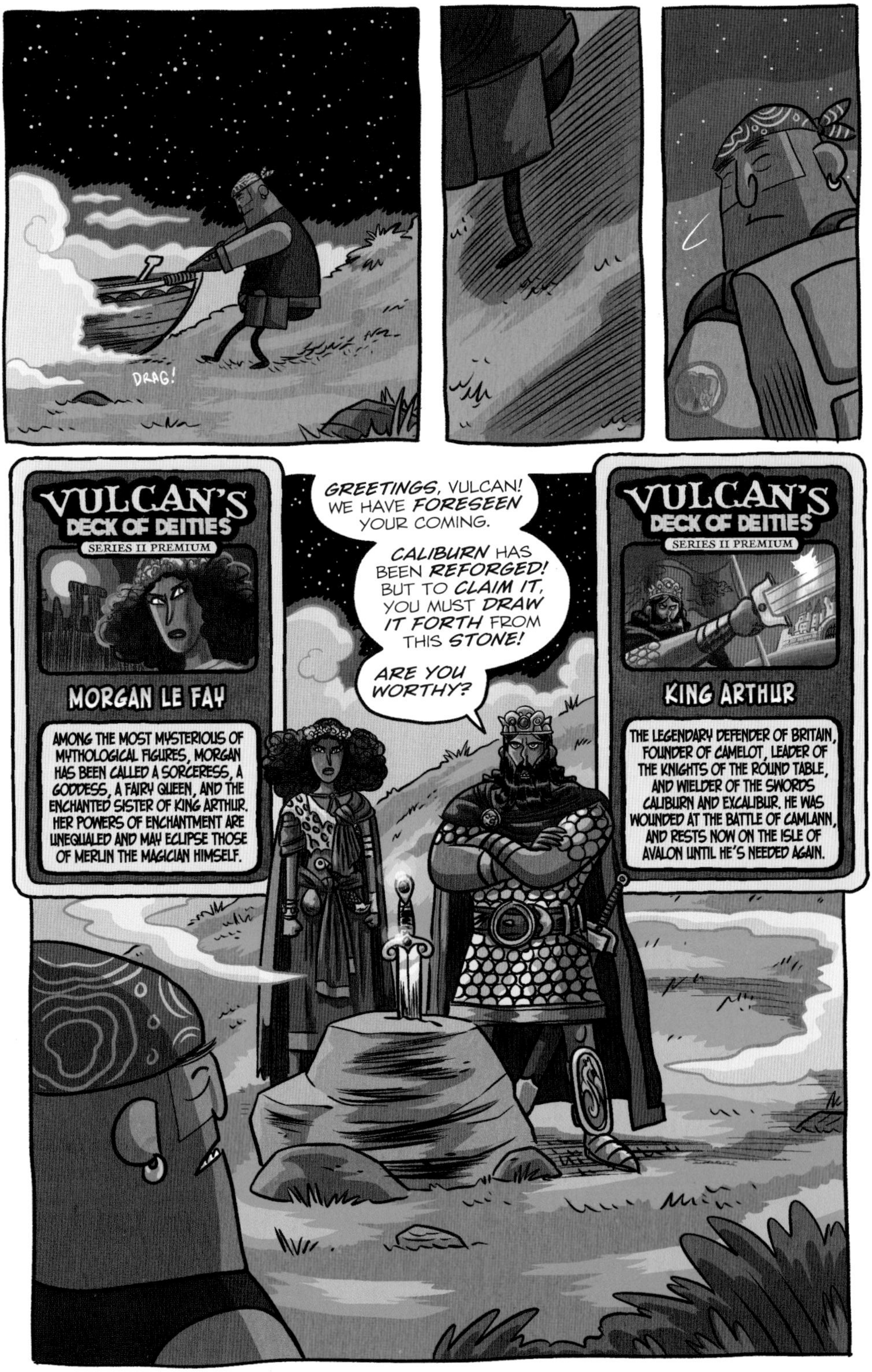
DRAG!
VULCAN'S DECK OF DEITIES
SERIES II PREMIUM
MORGAN LE FAY
AMONG THE MOST MYSTERIOUS OF MYTHOLOGICAL FIGURES, MORGAN HAS BEEN CALLED A SORCERESS, A GODDESS, A FAIRY QUEEN, AND THE ENCHANTED SISTER OF KING ARTHUR. HER POWERS OF ENCHANTMENT ARE UNEQUALED AND MAY ECLIPSE THOSE OF MERLIN THE MAGICIAN HIMSELF.
GREETINGS, VULCAN! WE HAVE FORESEEN YOUR COMING.
CALIBURN HAS BEEN REFORGED! BUT TO CLAIM IT, YOU MUST DRAW IT FORTH FROM THIS STONE!
ARE YOU WORTHY?
VULCAN'S DECK OF DEITIES
SERIES II PREMIUM
KING ARTHUR
THE LEGENDARY DEFENDER OF BRITAIN, FOUNDER OF CAMELOT, LEADER OF THE KNIGHTS OF THE ROUND TABLE, AND WIELDER OF THE SWORDS CALIBURN AND EXCALIBUR. HE WAS WOUNDED AT THE BATTLE OF CAMLANN, AND RESTS NOW ON THE ISLE OF AVALON UNTIL HE'S NEEDED AGAIN.

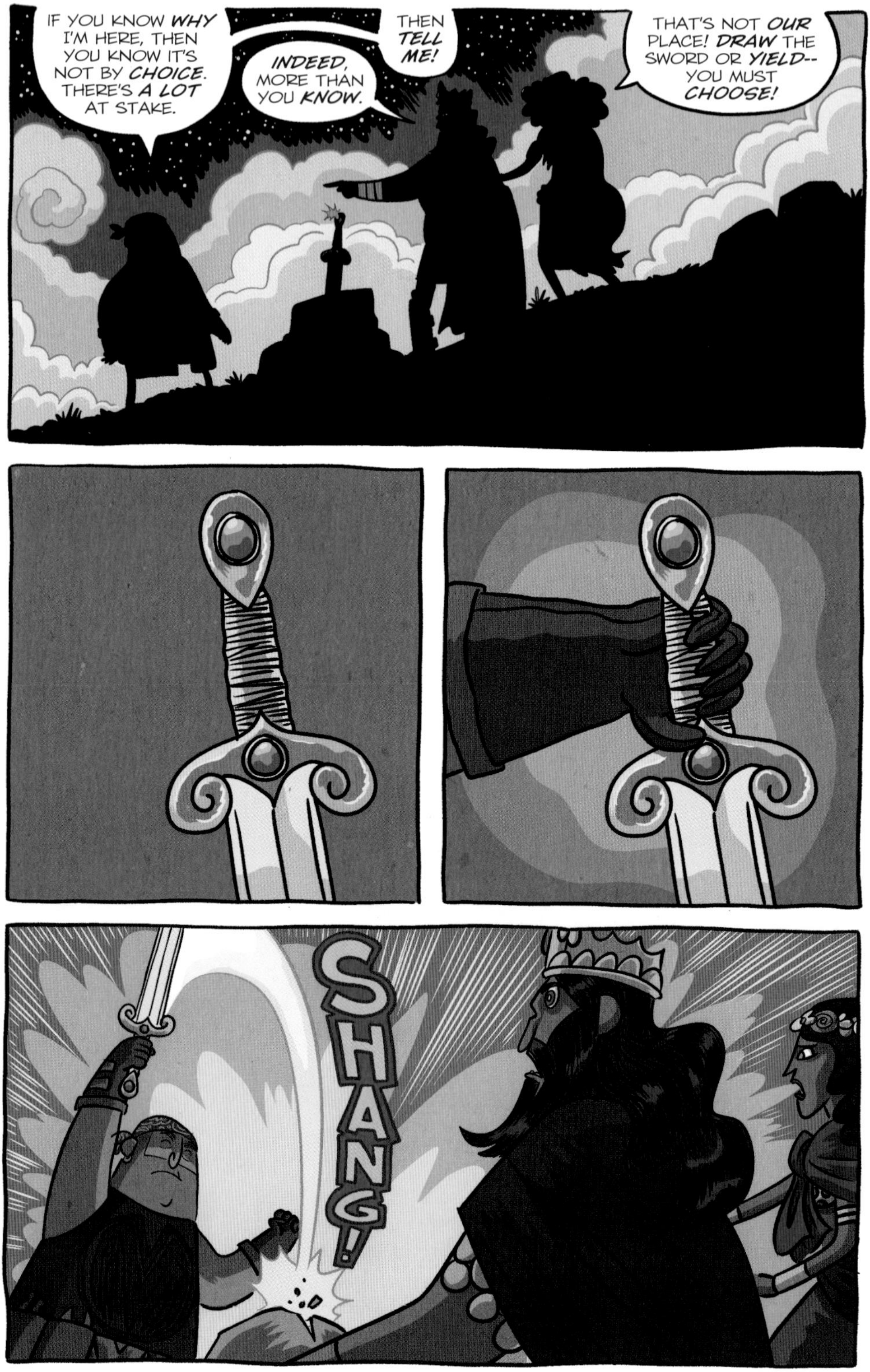
IF YOU KNOW WHY I'M HERE, THEN YOU KNOW IT'S NOT BY CHOICE. THERE'S A LOT AT STAKE.
INDEED, MORE THAN YOU KNOW.
THEN TELL ME!
THAT'S NOT OUR PLACE! DRAW THE SWORD OR YIELD-- YOU MUST CHOOSE!
SHANG!

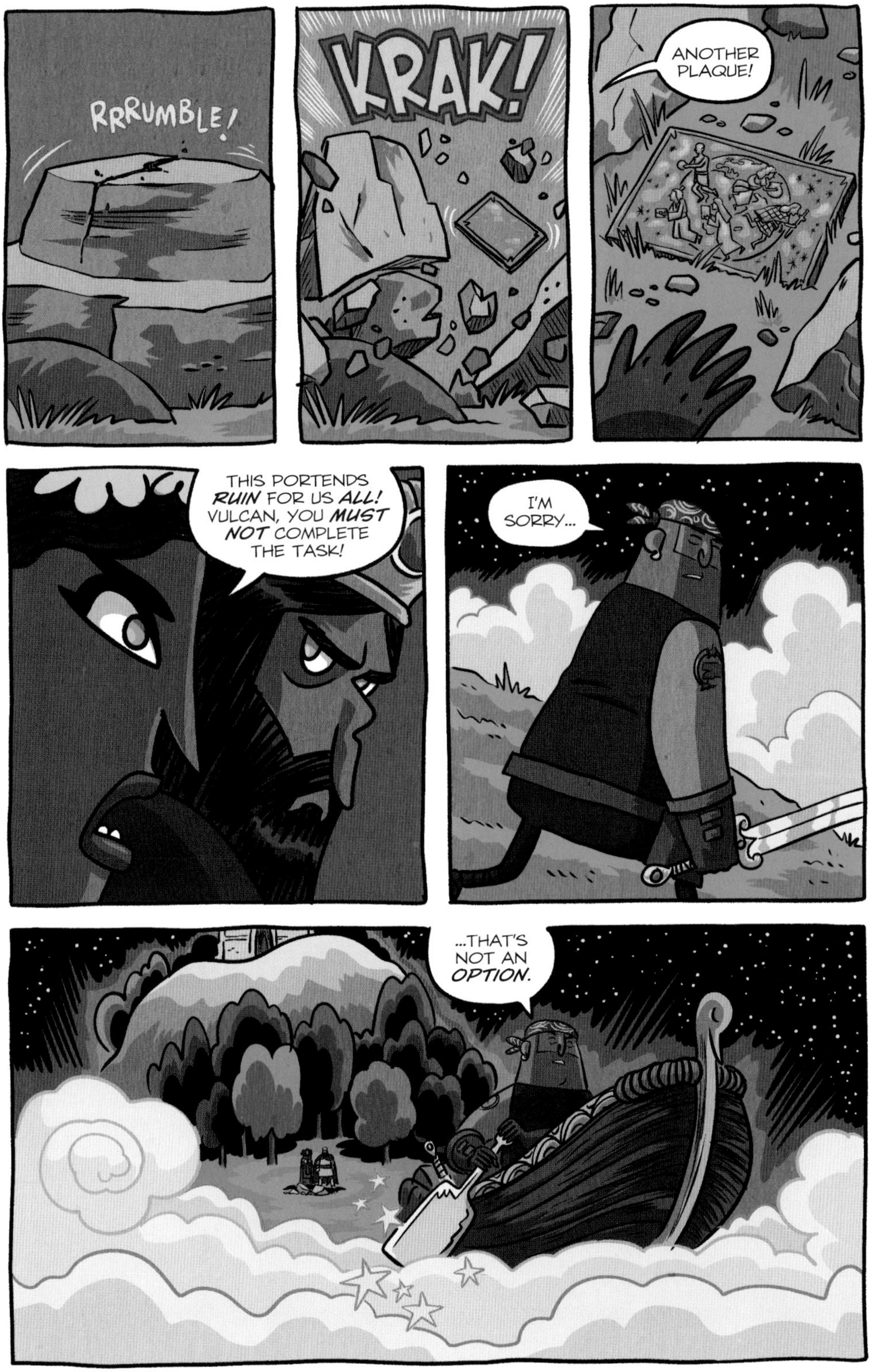
RRRUMBLE!
KRAK!
ANOTHER PLAQUE!
THIS PORTENDS **RUIN** FOR US **ALL!** VULCAN, YOU **MUST NOT** COMPLETE THE TASK!
I'M SORRY...
...THAT'S NOT AN **OPTION**.

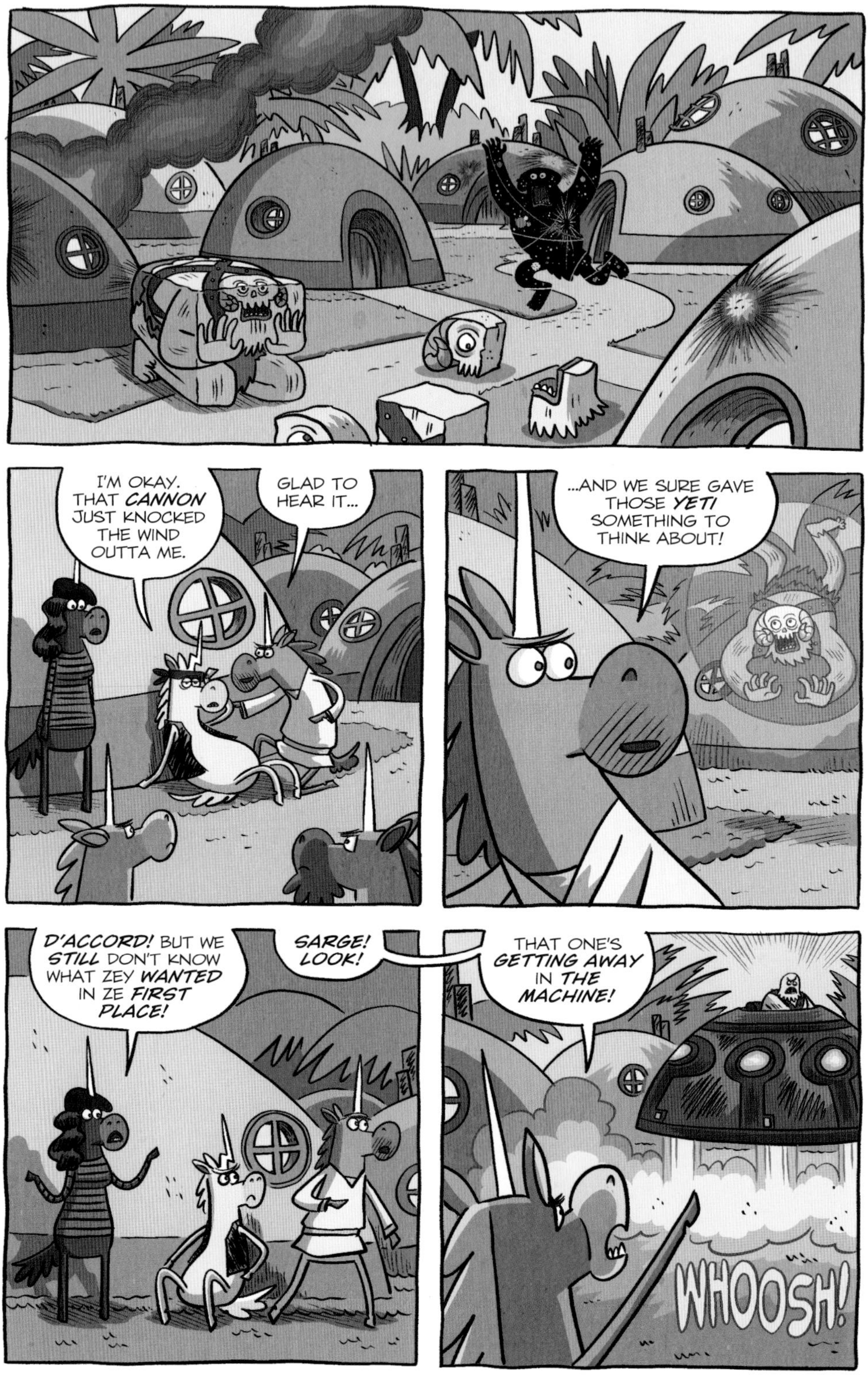
I'M OKAY. THAT CANNON JUST KNOCKED THE WIND OUTTA ME.
GLAD TO HEAR IT...
...AND WE SURE GAVE THOSE YETI SOMETHING TO THINK ABOUT!
D'ACCORD! BUT WE STILL DON'T KNOW WHAT ZEY WANTED IN ZE FIRST PLACE!
SARGE! LOOK!
THAT ONE'S GETTING AWAY IN THE MACHINE!
WHOOSH!

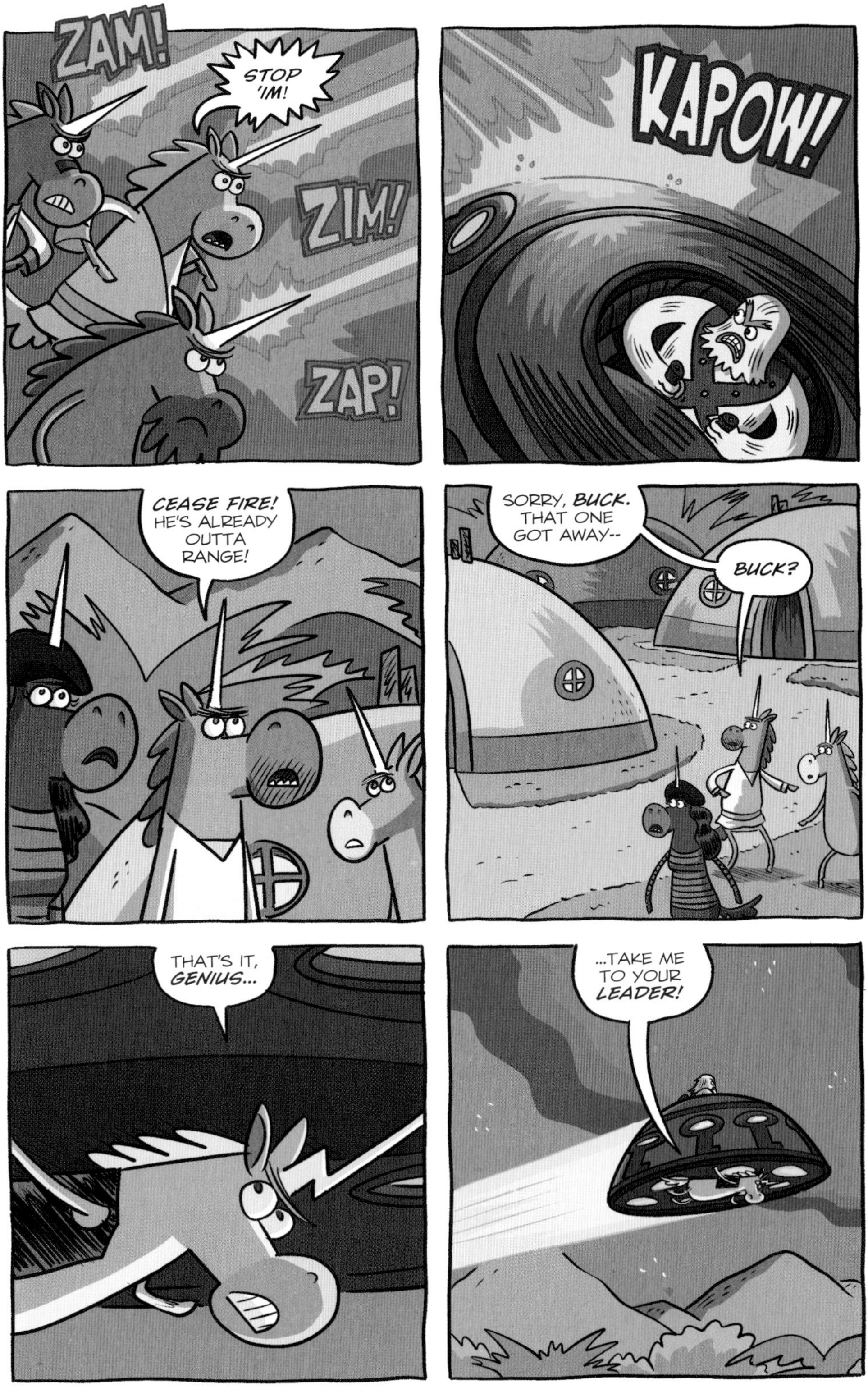
ZAM!
STOP 'IM!
ZIM!
ZAP!
KAPOW!
CEASE FIRE! HE'S ALREADY OUTTA RANGE!
SORRY, BUCK. THAT ONE GOT AWAY--
BUCK?
THAT'S IT, GENIUS...
...TAKE ME TO YOUR LEADER!

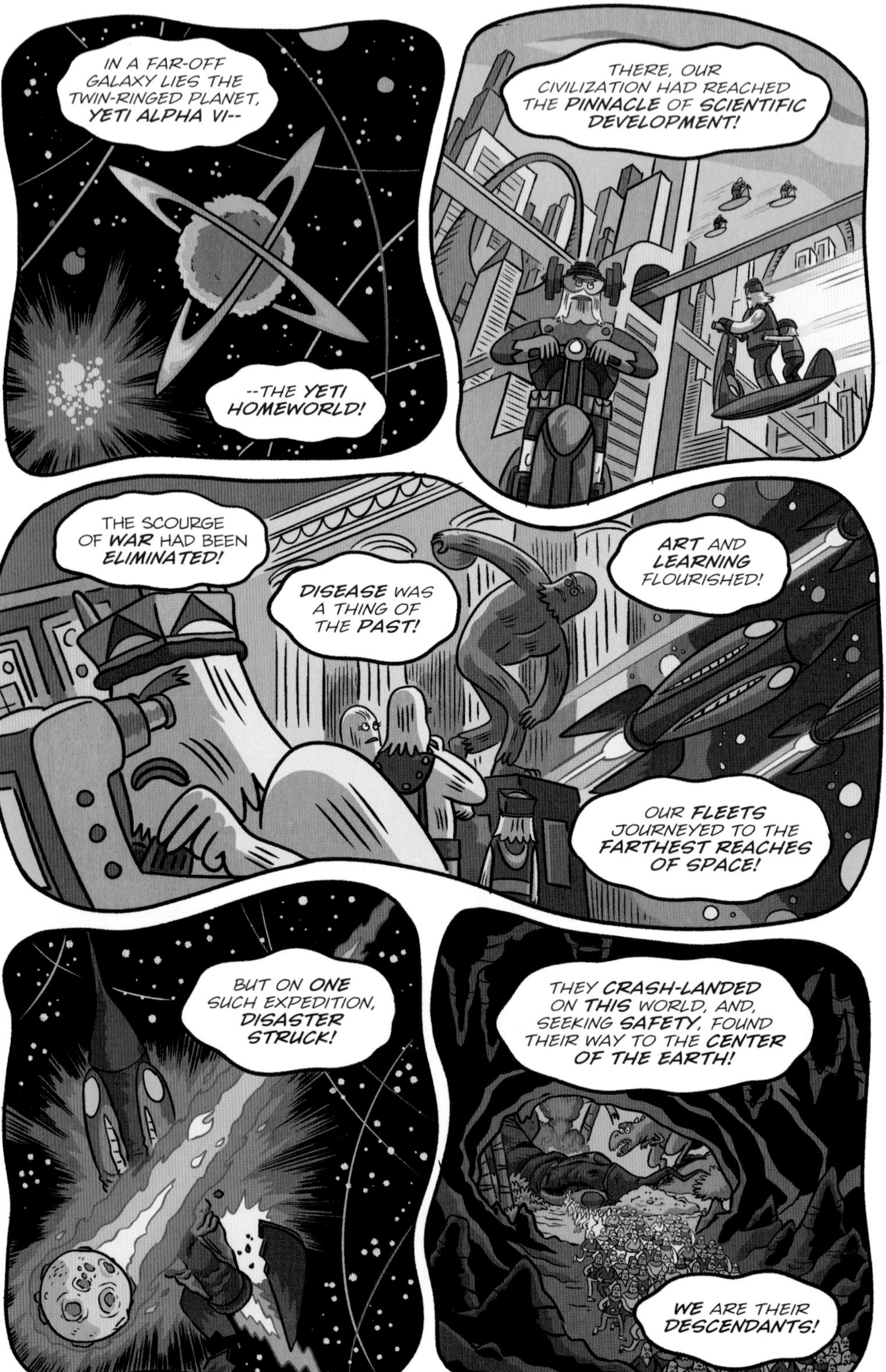
IN A FAR-OFF GALAXY LIES THE TWIN-RINGED PLANET, YETI ALPHA VI--
--THE YETI HOMEWORLD!
THERE, OUR CIVILIZATION HAD REACHED THE PINNACLE OF SCIENTIFIC DEVELOPMENT!
THE SCOURGE OF WAR HAD BEEN ELIMINATED!
DISEASE WAS A THING OF THE PAST!
ART AND LEARNING FLOURISHED!
OUR FLEETS JOURNEYED TO THE FARTHEST REACHES OF SPACE!
BUT ON ONE SUCH EXPEDITION, DISASTER STRUCK!
THEY CRASH-LANDED ON THIS WORLD, AND, SEEKING SAFETY, FOUND THEIR WAY TO THE CENTER OF THE EARTH!
WE ARE THEIR DESCENDANTS!

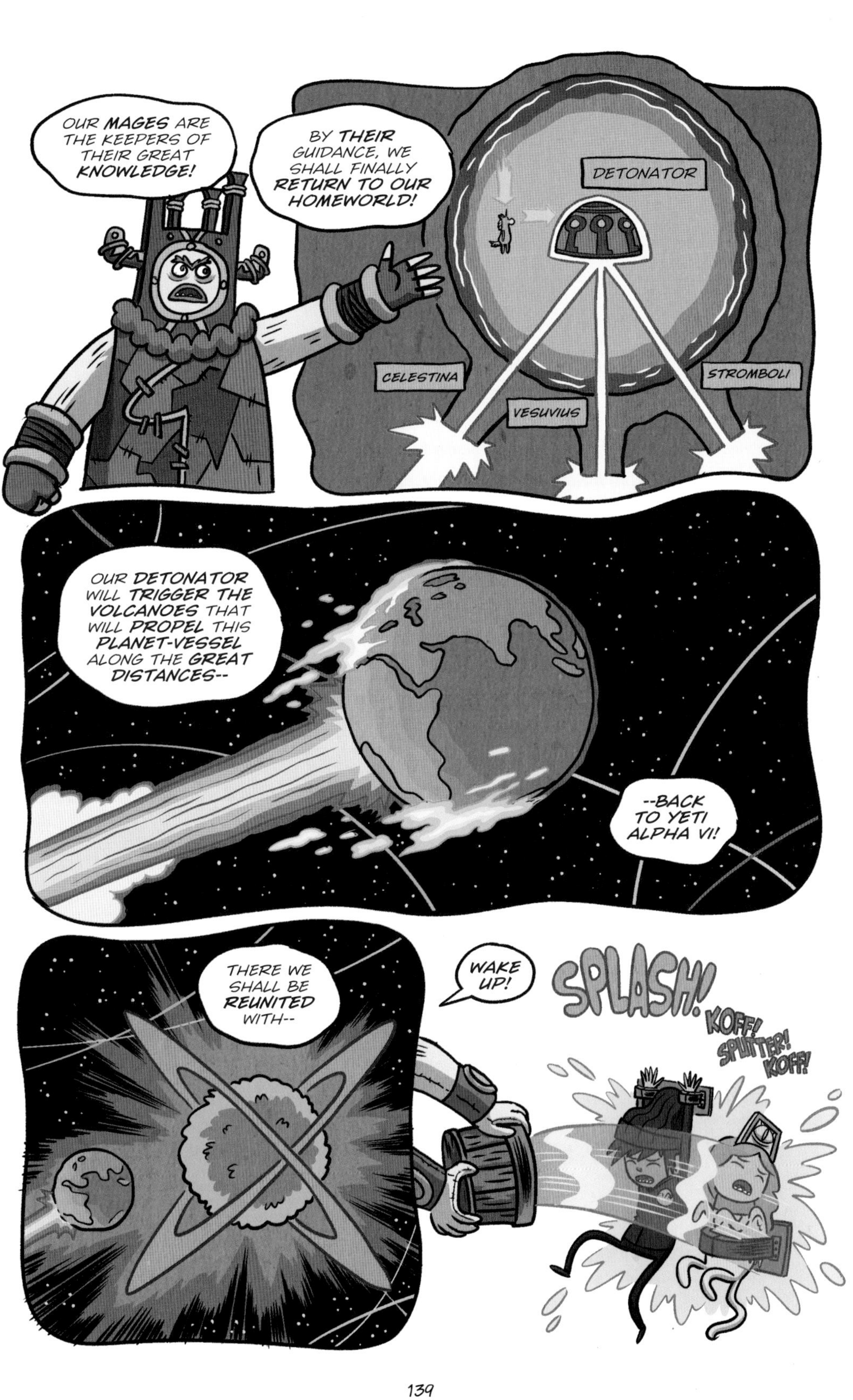
OUR MAGES ARE THE KEEPERS OF THEIR GREAT KNOWLEDGE!
BY THEIR GUIDANCE, WE SHALL FINALLY RETURN TO OUR HOMEWORLD!
DETONATOR
CELESTINA
VESUVIUS
STROMBOLI
OUR DETONATOR WILL TRIGGER THE VOLCANOES THAT WILL PROPEL THIS PLANET-VESSEL ALONG THE GREAT DISTANCES--
--BACK TO YETI ALPHA VI!
THERE WE SHALL BE REUNITED WITH--
WAKE UP!
SPLASH!
KOFF! SPLUTTER! KOFF!

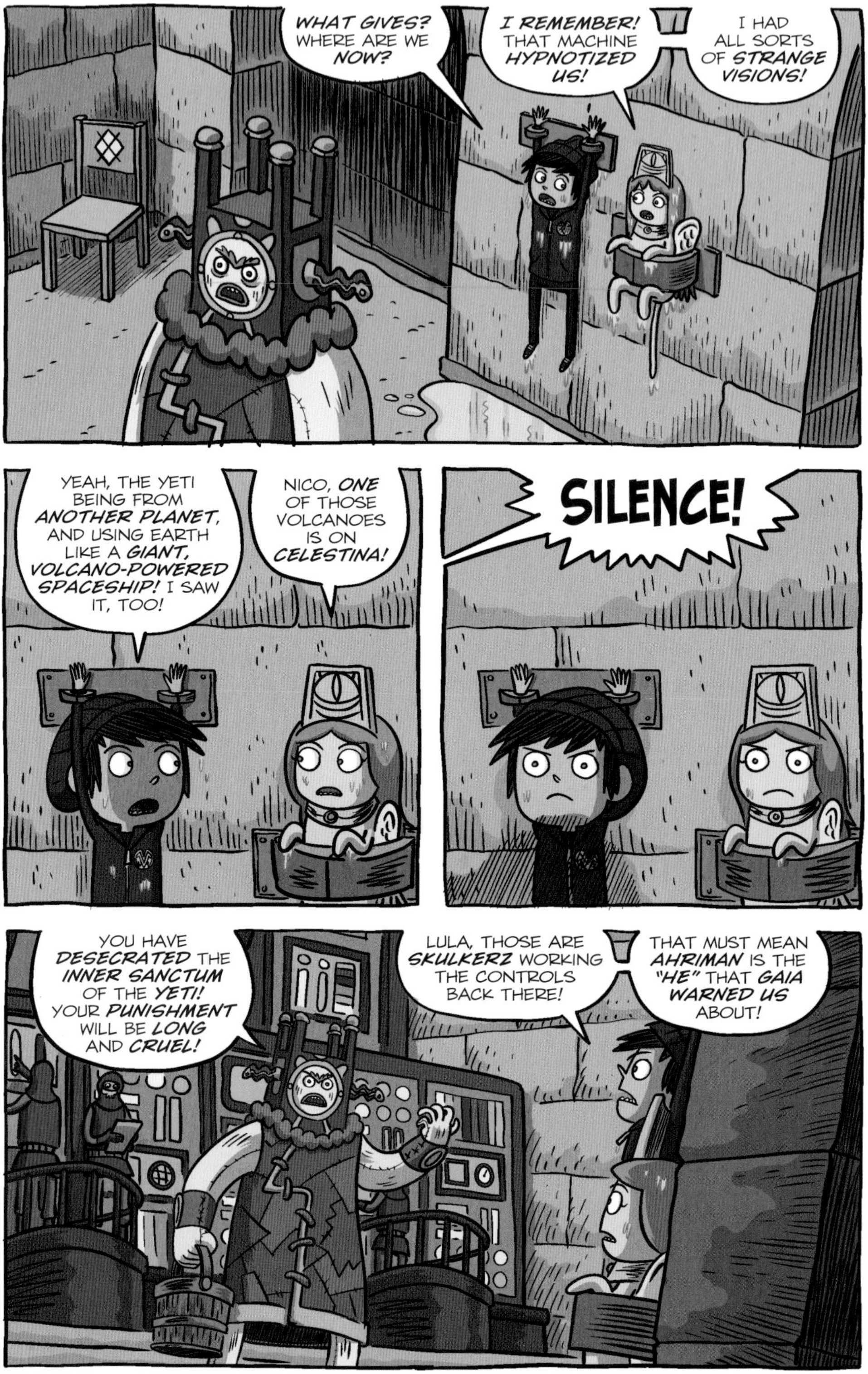
WHAT GIVES? WHERE ARE WE NOW?
I REMEMBER! THAT MACHINE HYPNOTIZED US!
I HAD ALL SORTS OF STRANGE VISIONS!
YEAH, THE YETI BEING FROM ANOTHER PLANET, AND USING EARTH LIKE A GIANT, VOLCANO-POWERED SPACESHIP! I SAW IT, TOO!
NICO, ONE OF THOSE VOLCANOES IS ON CELESTINA!
SILENCE!
YOU HAVE DESECRATED THE INNER SANCTUM OF THE YETI! YOUR PUNISHMENT WILL BE LONG AND CRUEL!
LULA, THOSE ARE SKULKERZ WORKING THE CONTROLS BACK THERE!
THAT MUST MEAN AHRIMAN IS THE "HE" THAT GAIA WARNED US ABOUT!

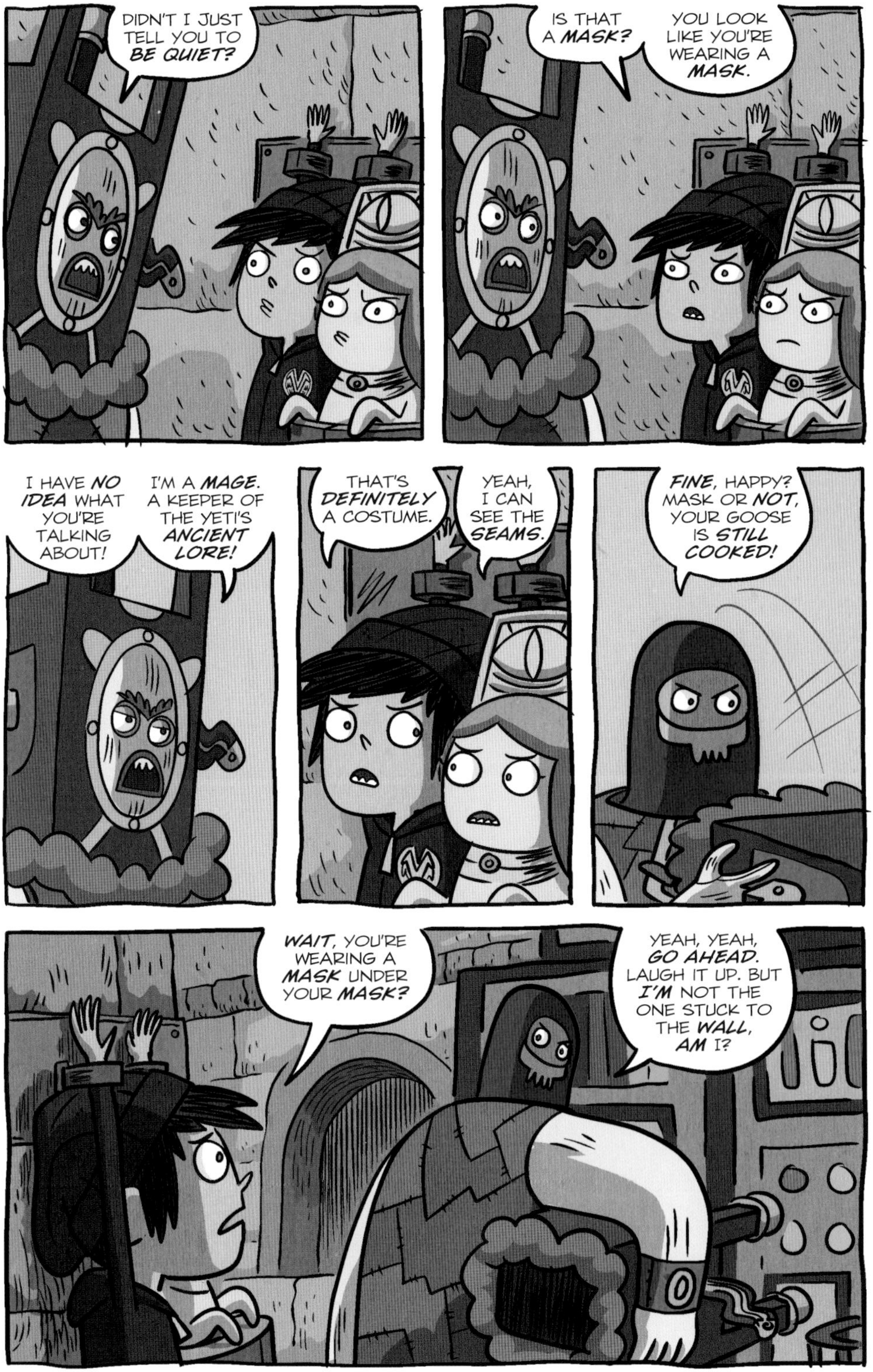
DIDN'T I JUST TELL YOU TO BE QUIET?
IS THAT A MASK?
YOU LOOK LIKE YOU'RE WEARING A MASK.
I HAVE NO IDEA WHAT YOU'RE TALKING ABOUT!
I'M A MAGE. A KEEPER OF THE YETI'S ANCIENT LORE!
THAT'S DEFINITELY A COSTUME.
YEAH, I CAN SEE THE SEAMS.
FINE, HAPPY? MASK OR NOT, YOUR GOOSE IS STILL COOKED!
WAIT, YOU'RE WEARING A MASK UNDER YOUR MASK?
YEAH, YEAH, GO AHEAD. LAUGH IT UP. BUT I'M NOT THE ONE STUCK TO THE WALL, AM I?

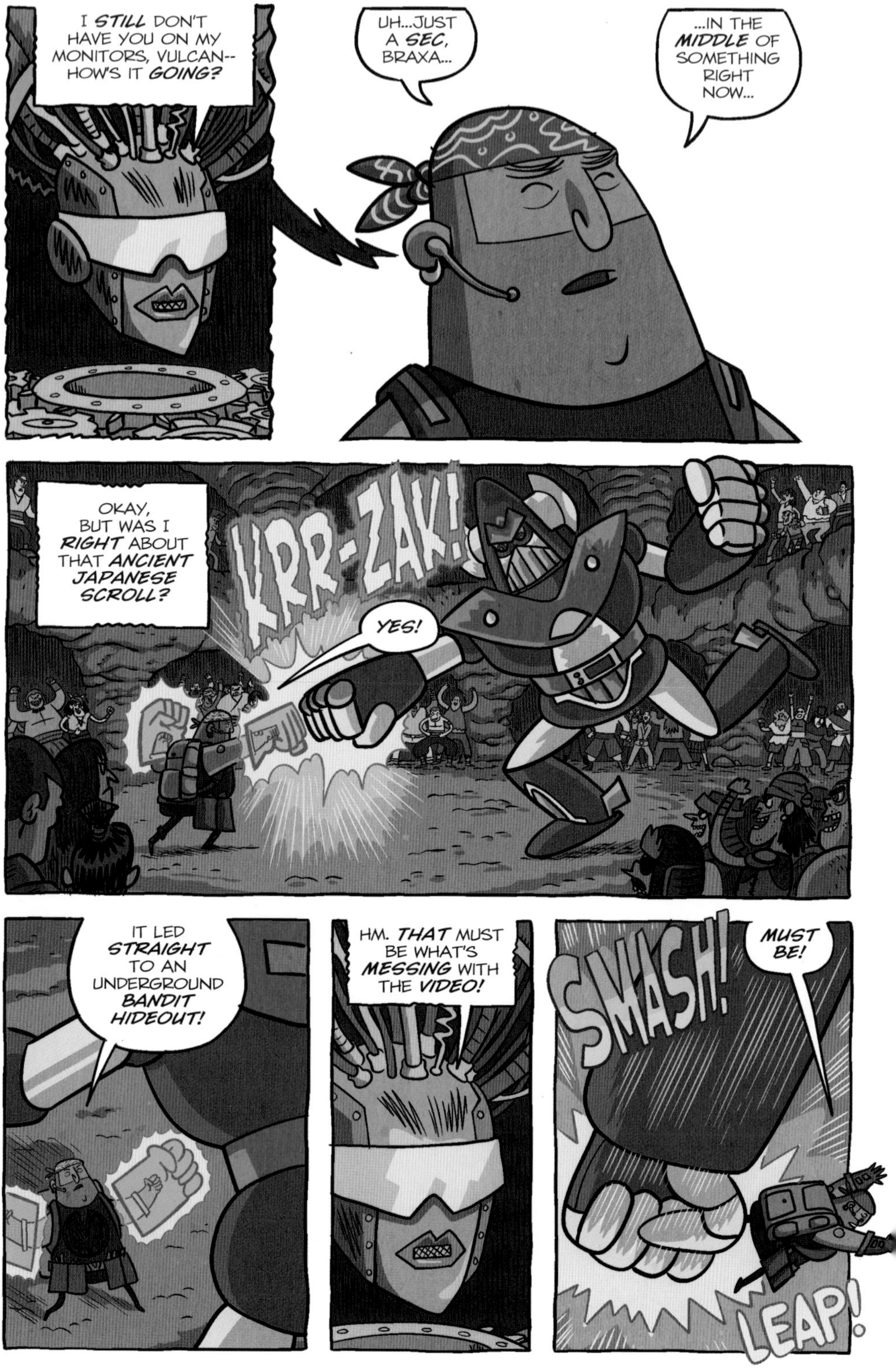
I STILL DON'T HAVE YOU ON MY MONITORS, VULCAN-- HOW'S IT GOING?
UH...JUST A SEC, BRAXA...
...IN THE MIDDLE OF SOMETHING RIGHT NOW...
OKAY, BUT WAS I RIGHT ABOUT THAT ANCIENT JAPANESE SCROLL?
KRR-ZAK!
YES!
IT LED STRAIGHT TO AN UNDERGROUND BANDIT HIDEOUT!
HM. THAT MUST BE WHAT'S MESSING WITH THE VIDEO!
SMASH!
MUST BE!
LEAP!

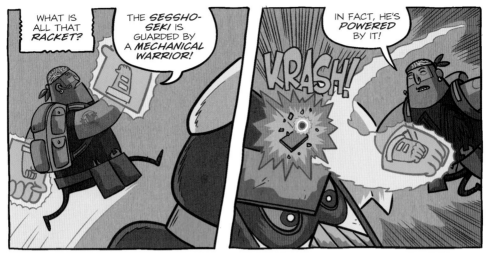

WHAT IS ALL THAT *RACKET?*

THE *SESSHO-SEKI* IS GUARDED BY A *MECHANICAL WARRIOR!*

IN FACT, HE'S *POWERED* BY IT!

KRASH!

AT LEAST...

...HE *WAS!*

TOOOM!

OKAY, I'VE GOT THE *STONE...*

...*AND* ANOTHER PLAQUE!

GREAT! SEE YOU *SOON!*

UH... YEAH. I HOPE SO...

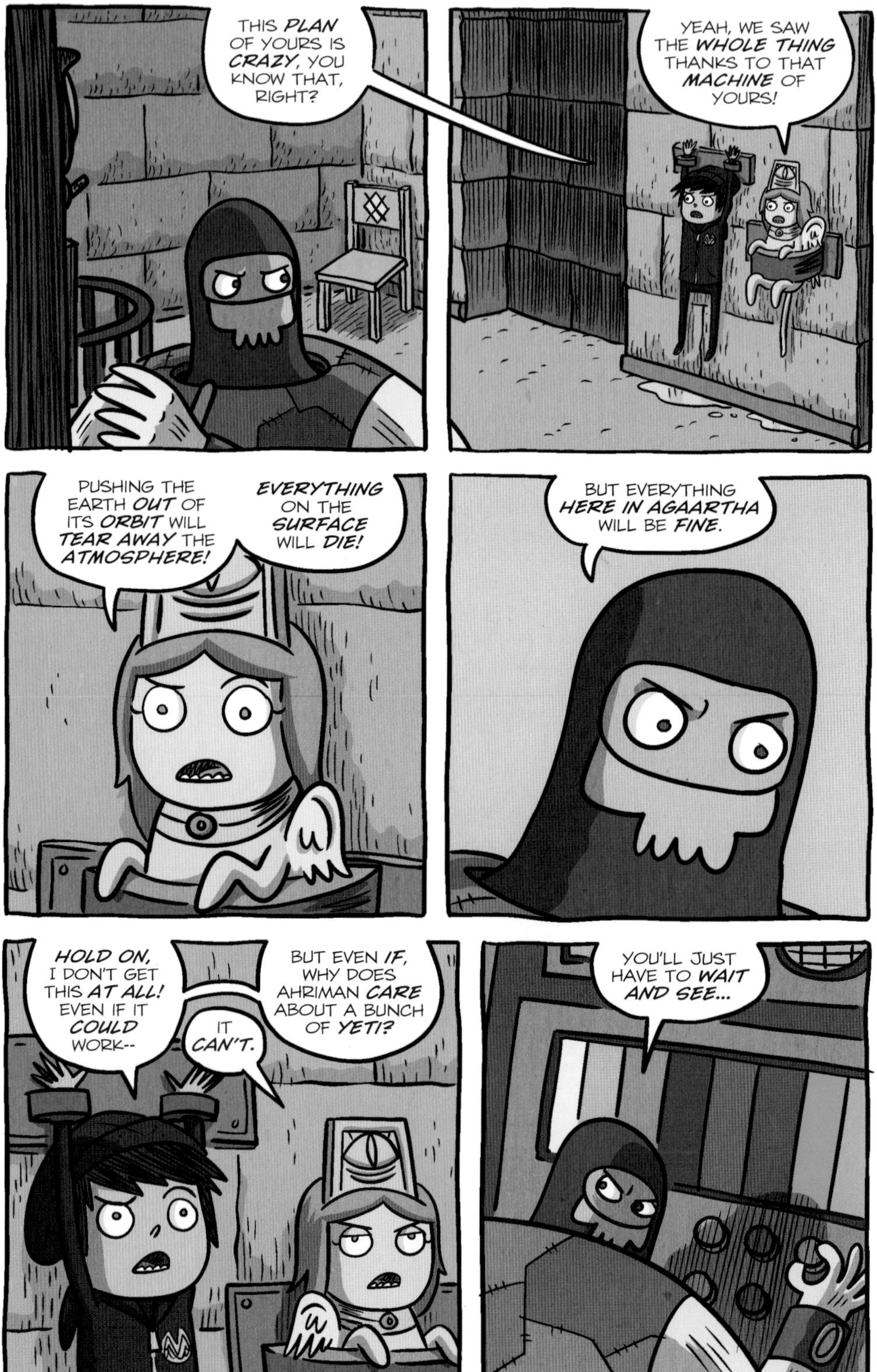
THIS PLAN OF YOURS IS CRAZY, YOU KNOW THAT, RIGHT?
YEAH, WE SAW THE WHOLE THING THANKS TO THAT MACHINE OF YOURS!
PUSHING THE EARTH OUT OF ITS ORBIT WILL TEAR AWAY THE ATMOSPHERE!
EVERYTHING ON THE SURFACE WILL DIE!
BUT EVERYTHING HERE IN AGAARTHA WILL BE FINE.
HOLD ON, I DON'T GET THIS AT ALL! EVEN IF IT COULD WORK--
IT CAN'T.
BUT EVEN IF, WHY DOES AHRIMAN CARE ABOUT A BUNCH OF YETI?
YOU'LL JUST HAVE TO WAIT AND SEE...

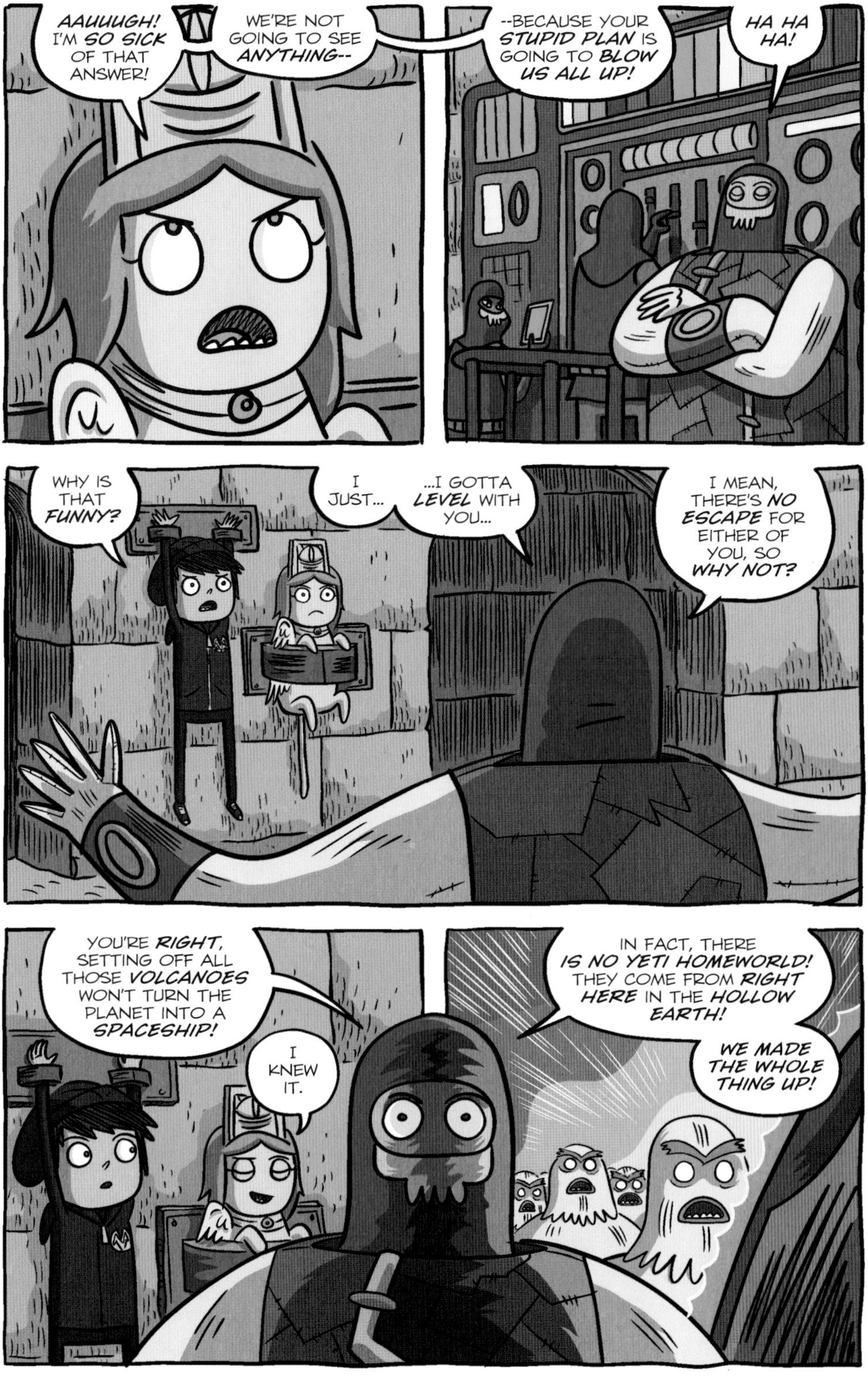
AAUUUGH! I'M SO SICK OF THAT ANSWER!
WE'RE NOT GOING TO SEE ANYTHING--
--BECAUSE YOUR STUPID PLAN IS GOING TO BLOW US ALL UP!
HA HA HA!
WHY IS THAT FUNNY?
I JUST...
...I GOTTA LEVEL WITH YOU...
I MEAN, THERE'S NO ESCAPE FOR EITHER OF YOU, SO WHY NOT?
YOU'RE RIGHT, SETTING OFF ALL THOSE VOLCANOES WON'T TURN THE PLANET INTO A SPACESHIP!
I KNEW IT.
IN FACT, THERE IS NO YETI HOMEWORLD! THEY COME FROM RIGHT HERE IN THE HOLLOW EARTH!
WE MADE THE WHOLE THING UP!

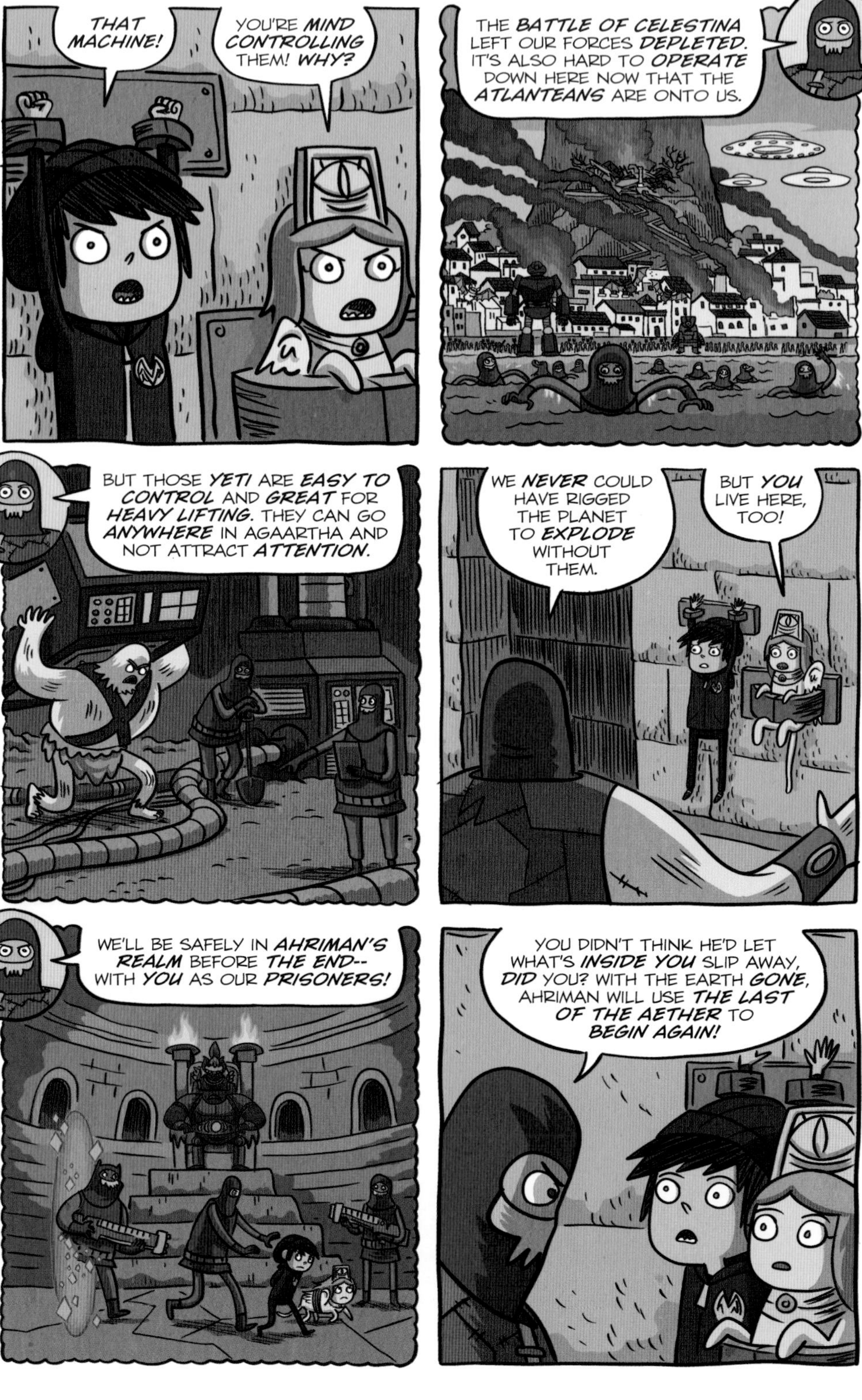
THAT MACHINE!
YOU'RE MIND CONTROLLING THEM! WHY?
THE BATTLE OF CELESTINA LEFT OUR FORCES DEPLETED. IT'S ALSO HARD TO OPERATE DOWN HERE NOW THAT THE ATLANTEANS ARE ONTO US.
BUT THOSE YETI ARE EASY TO CONTROL AND GREAT FOR HEAVY LIFTING. THEY CAN GO ANYWHERE IN AGAARTHA AND NOT ATTRACT ATTENTION.
WE NEVER COULD HAVE RIGGED THE PLANET TO EXPLODE WITHOUT THEM.
BUT YOU LIVE HERE, TOO!
WE'LL BE SAFELY IN AHRIMAN'S REALM BEFORE THE END-- WITH YOU AS OUR PRISONERS!
YOU DIDN'T THINK HE'D LET WHAT'S INSIDE YOU SLIP AWAY, DID YOU? WITH THE EARTH GONE, AHRIMAN WILL USE THE LAST OF THE AETHER TO BEGIN AGAIN!

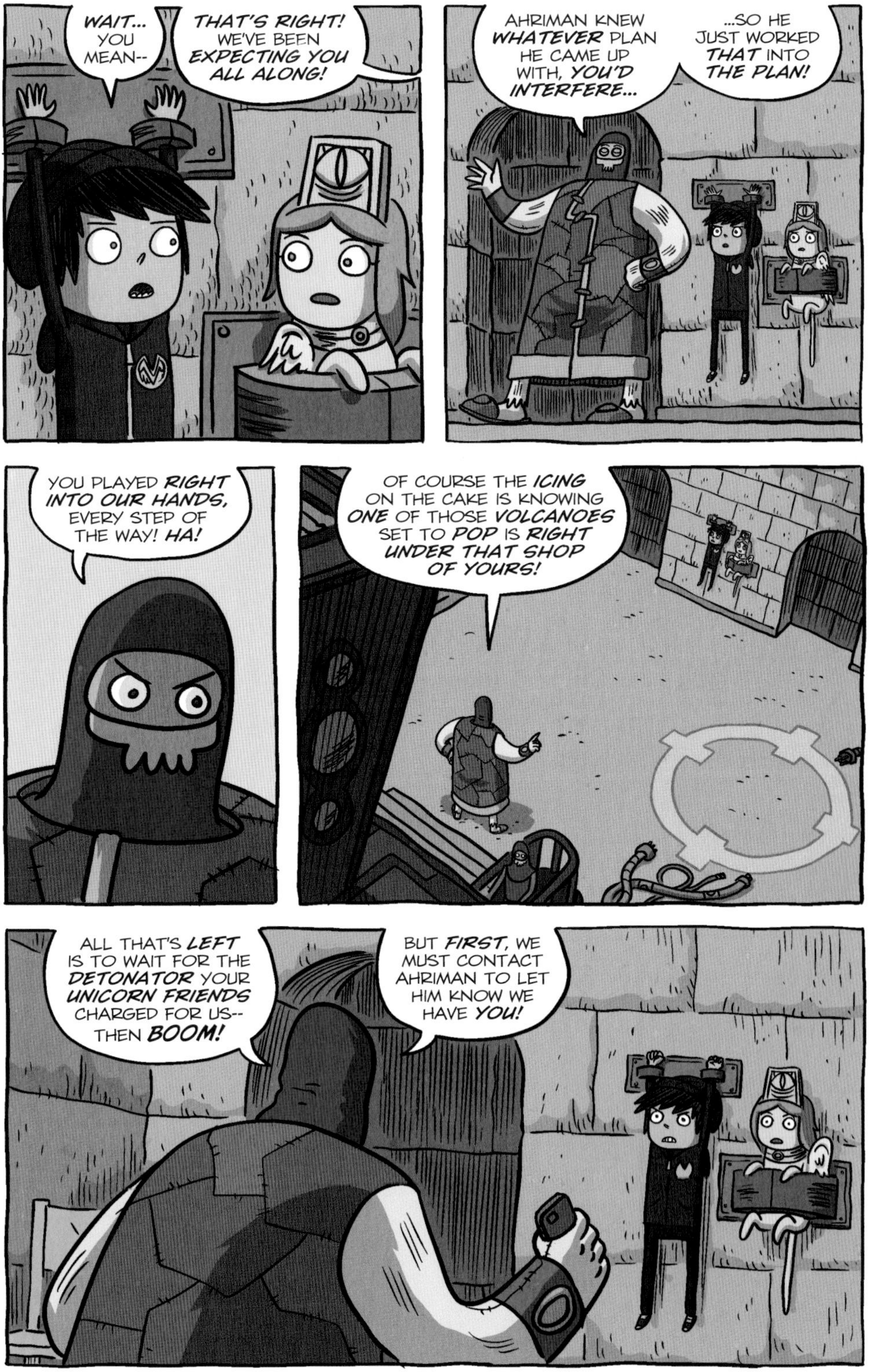
WAIT... YOU MEAN--
THAT'S RIGHT! WE'VE BEEN EXPECTING YOU ALL ALONG!
AHRIMAN KNEW WHATEVER PLAN HE CAME UP WITH, YOU'D INTERFERE...
...SO HE JUST WORKED THAT INTO THE PLAN!
YOU PLAYED RIGHT INTO OUR HANDS, EVERY STEP OF THE WAY! HA!
OF COURSE THE ICING ON THE CAKE IS KNOWING ONE OF THOSE VOLCANOES SET TO POP IS RIGHT UNDER THAT SHOP OF YOURS!
ALL THAT'S LEFT IS TO WAIT FOR THE DETONATOR YOUR UNICORN FRIENDS CHARGED FOR US-- THEN BOOM!
BUT FIRST, WE MUST CONTACT AHRIMAN TO LET HIM KNOW WE HAVE YOU!

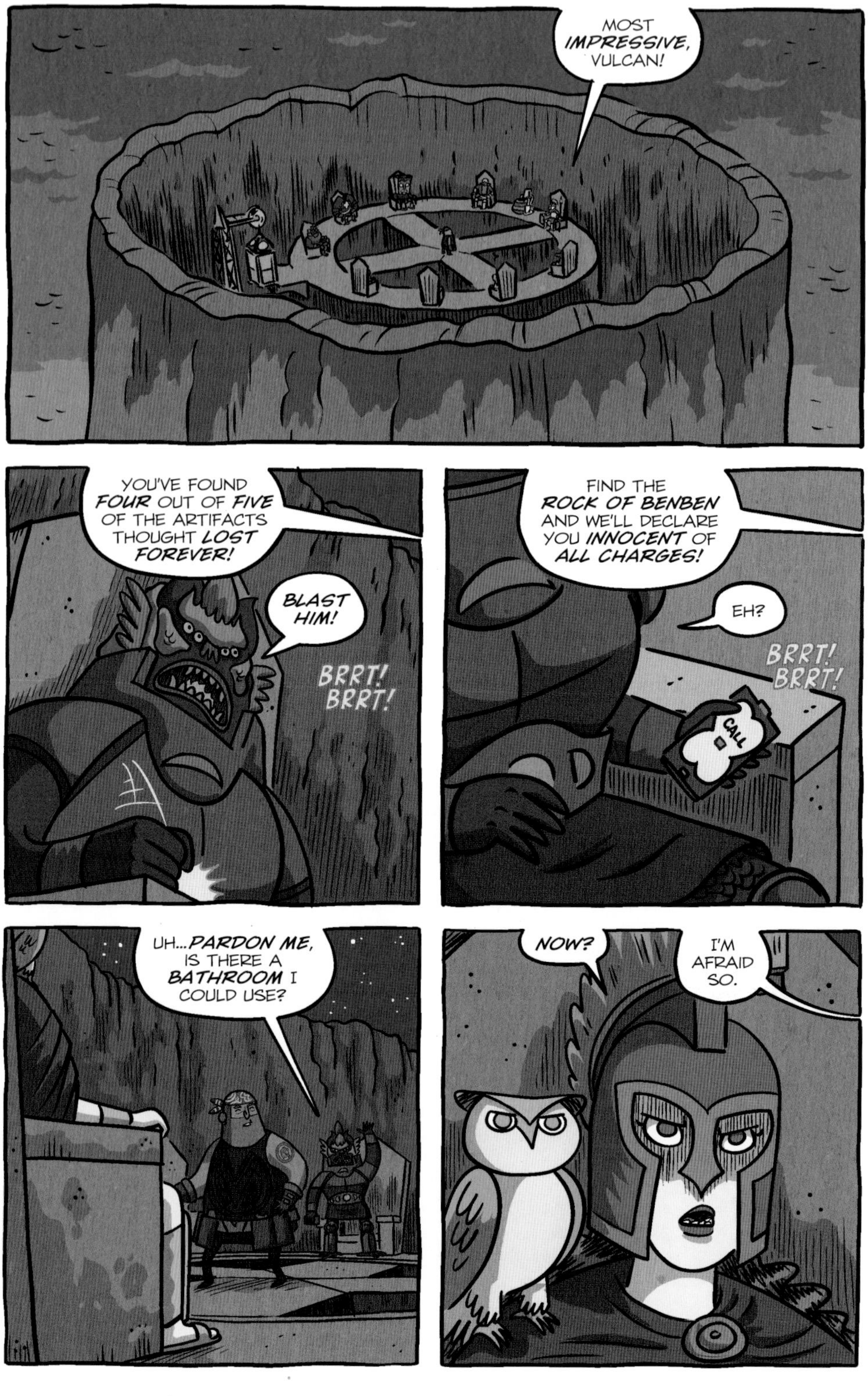
MOST IMPRESSIVE, VULCAN!
YOU'VE FOUND FOUR OUT OF FIVE OF THE ARTIFACTS THOUGHT LOST FOREVER!
BLAST HIM!
BRRT! BRRT!
FIND THE ROCK OF BENBEN AND WE'LL DECLARE YOU INNOCENT OF ALL CHARGES!
EH?
BRRT! BRRT!
CALL
UH...PARDON ME, IS THERE A BATHROOM I COULD USE?
NOW?
I'M AFRAID SO.

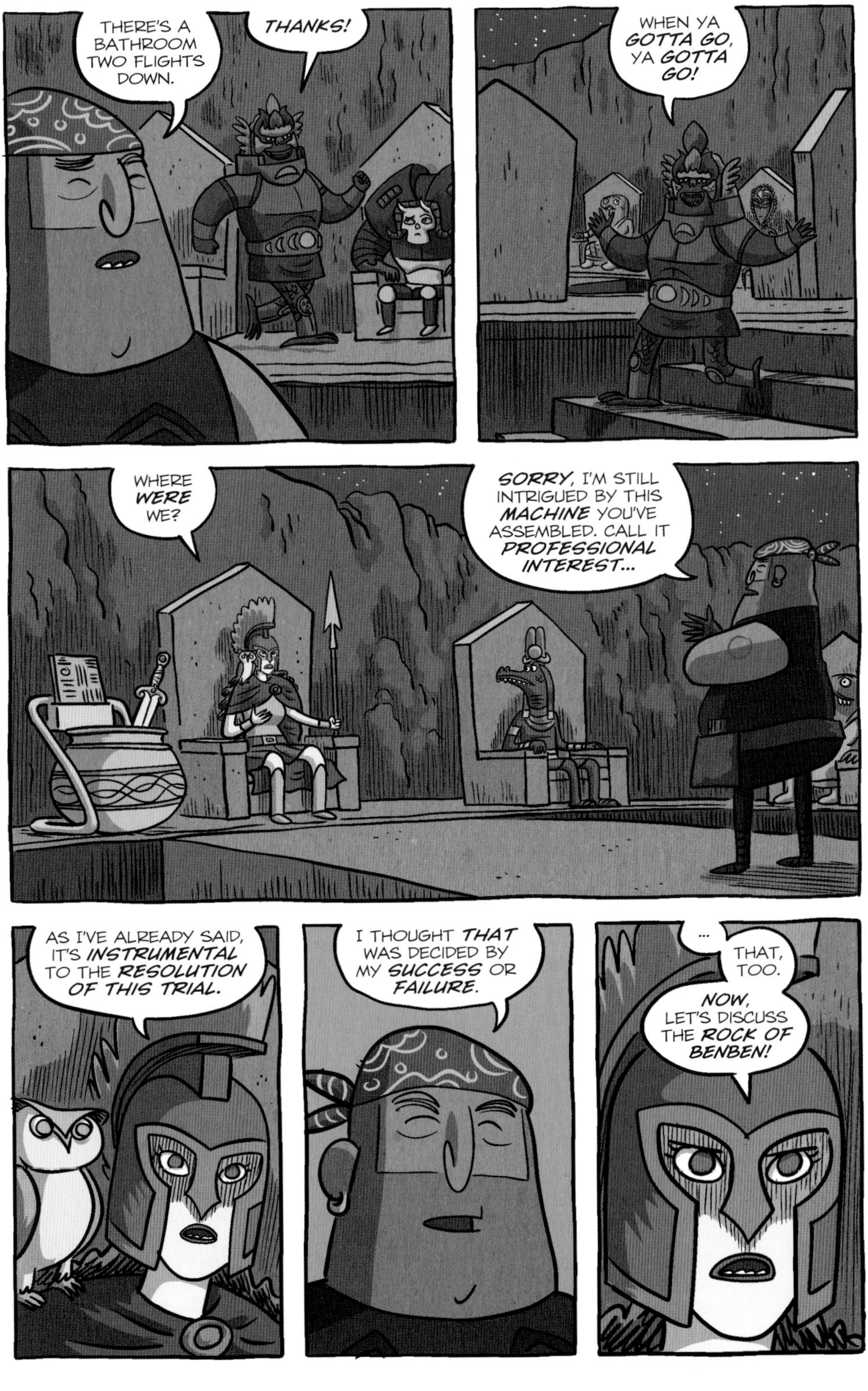
THERE'S A BATHROOM TWO FLIGHTS DOWN.
THANKS!
WHEN YA GOTTA GO, YA GOTTA GO!
WHERE WERE WE?
SORRY, I'M STILL INTRIGUED BY THIS MACHINE YOU'VE ASSEMBLED. CALL IT PROFESSIONAL INTEREST...
AS I'VE ALREADY SAID, IT'S INSTRUMENTAL TO THE RESOLUTION OF THIS TRIAL.
I THOUGHT THAT WAS DECIDED BY MY SUCCESS OR FAILURE.
...
THAT, TOO.
NOW, LET'S DISCUSS THE ROCK OF BENBEN!

THAT'S *IT?* ANOTHER *KEY?*

YUP.

THAT'S NOT MUCH TO *GO ON.* ARE YOU *SURE* THERE WASN'T *ANY MORE* TO THE CLUE?

WELL... *YES* AND *NO.*

HONESTLY, VULCAN, WHAT DOES *THAT* MEAN?

I NOTICED IT BACK ON THE *SECOND PLAQUE* BUT I *WASN'T SURE.*

THE ONE WITH ALL THE *DIFFERENT PEOPLE?*

YEAH.

BUT HERE'S THE *FOURTH ONE.* PROMETHEUS AND HIS *HELPERS* CAPTURED BY *ZEUS.*

THIS ONE ON THE BOTTOM RIGHT? *I'VE MET HER!*

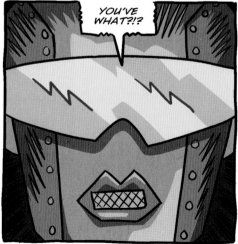

YOU'VE WHAT?!?

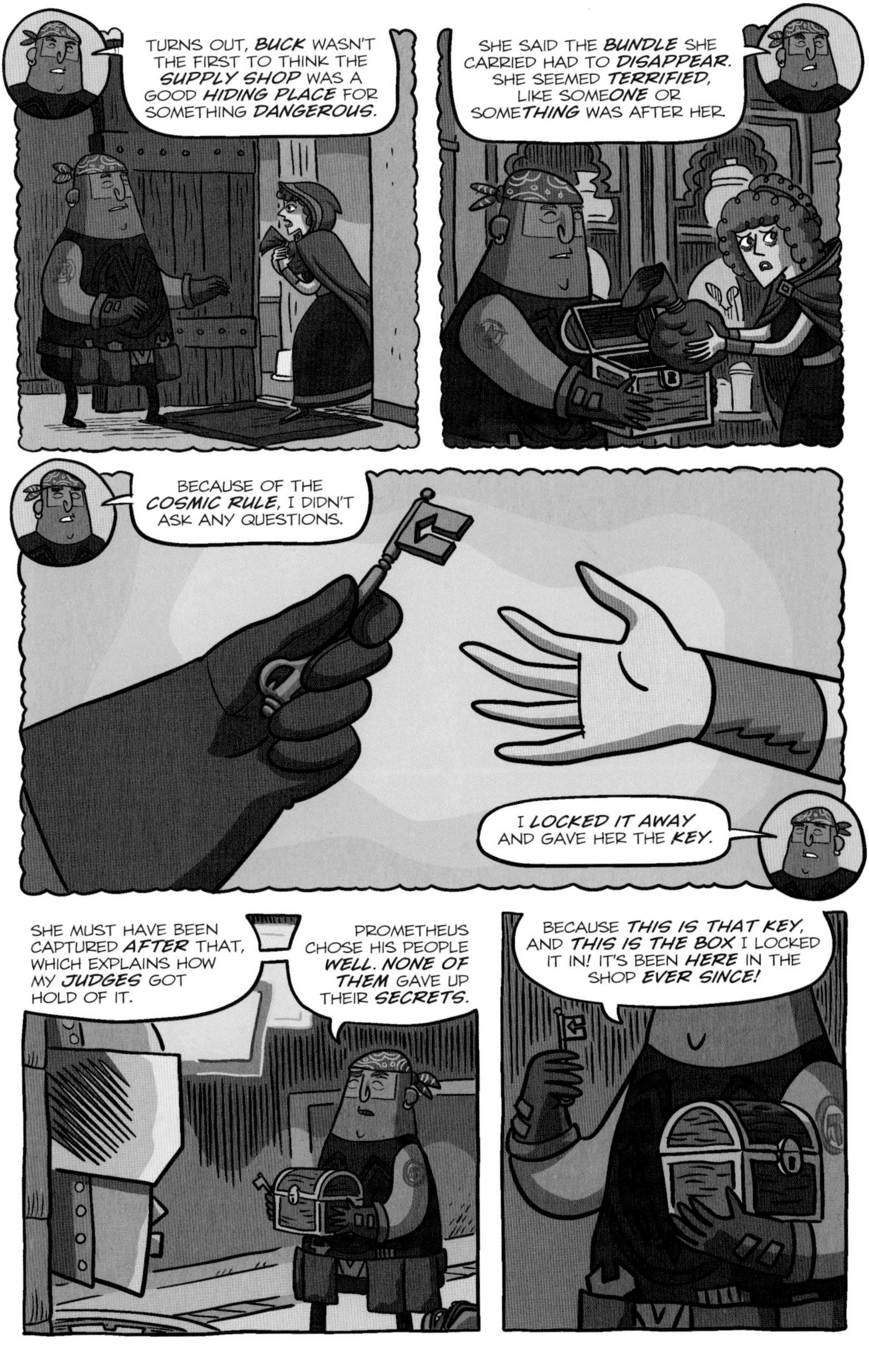
TURNS OUT, BUCK WASN'T THE FIRST TO THINK THE SUPPLY SHOP WAS A GOOD HIDING PLACE FOR SOMETHING DANGEROUS.
SHE SAID THE BUNDLE SHE CARRIED HAD TO DISAPPEAR. SHE SEEMED TERRIFIED, LIKE SOMEONE OR SOMETHING WAS AFTER HER.
BECAUSE OF THE COSMIC RULE, I DIDN'T ASK ANY QUESTIONS.
I LOCKED IT AWAY AND GAVE HER THE KEY.
SHE MUST HAVE BEEN CAPTURED AFTER THAT, WHICH EXPLAINS HOW MY JUDGES GOT HOLD OF IT.
PROMETHEUS CHOSE HIS PEOPLE WELL. NONE OF THEM GAVE UP THEIR SECRETS.
BECAUSE THIS IS THAT KEY, AND THIS IS THE BOX I LOCKED IT IN! IT'S BEEN HERE IN THE SHOP EVER SINCE!

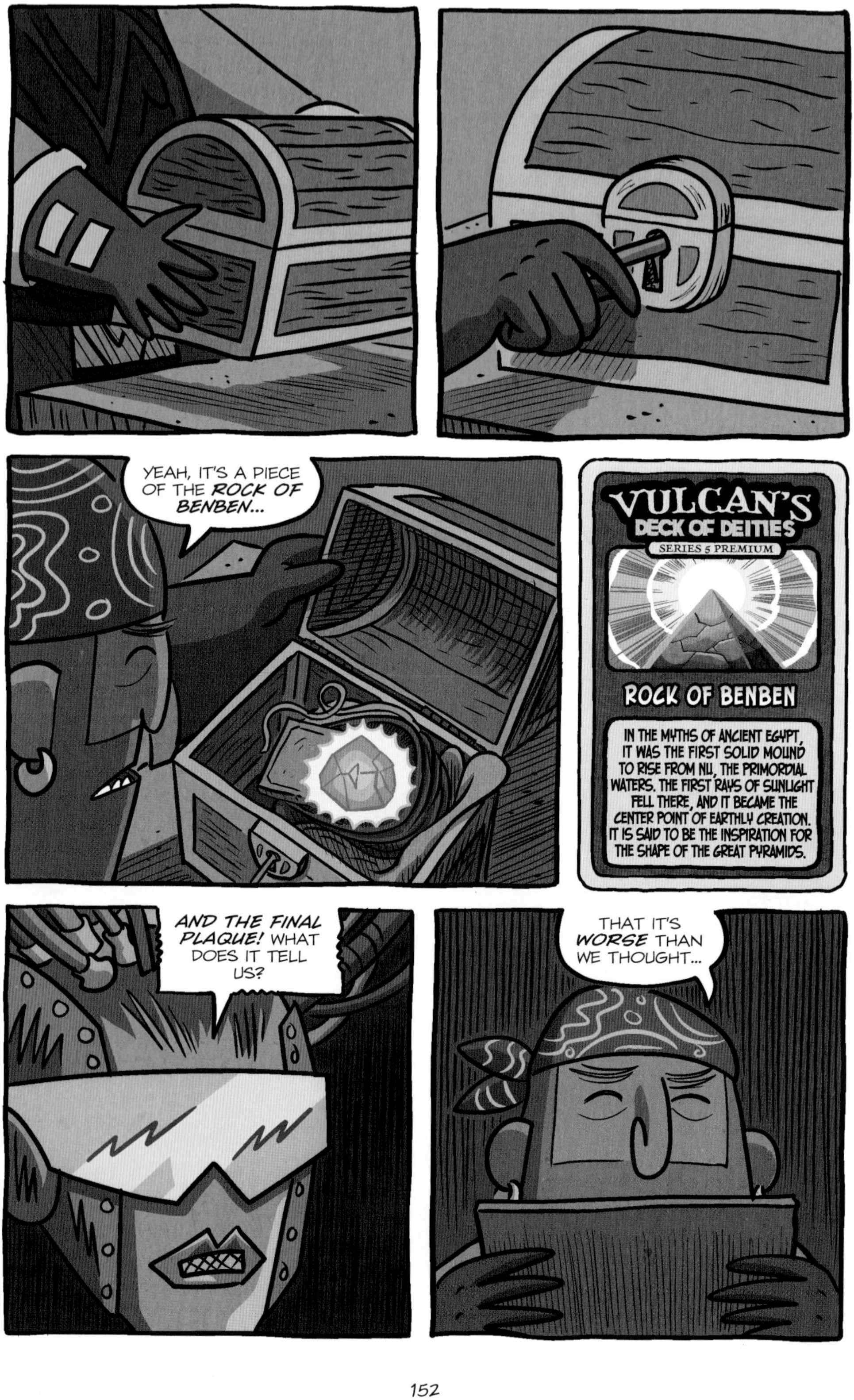
YEAH, IT'S A PIECE OF THE ROCK OF BENBEN...
VULCAN'S DECK OF DEITIES
SERIES 5 PREMIUM
ROCK OF BENBEN
IN THE MYTHS OF ANCIENT EGYPT, IT WAS THE FIRST SOLID MOUND TO RISE FROM NU, THE PRIMORDIAL WATERS. THE FIRST RAYS OF SUNLIGHT FELL THERE, AND IT BECAME THE CENTER POINT OF EARTHLY CREATION. IT IS SAID TO BE THE INSPIRATION FOR THE SHAPE OF THE GREAT PYRAMIDS.
AND THE FINAL PLAQUE! WHAT DOES IT TELL US?
THAT IT'S WORSE THAN WE THOUGHT...

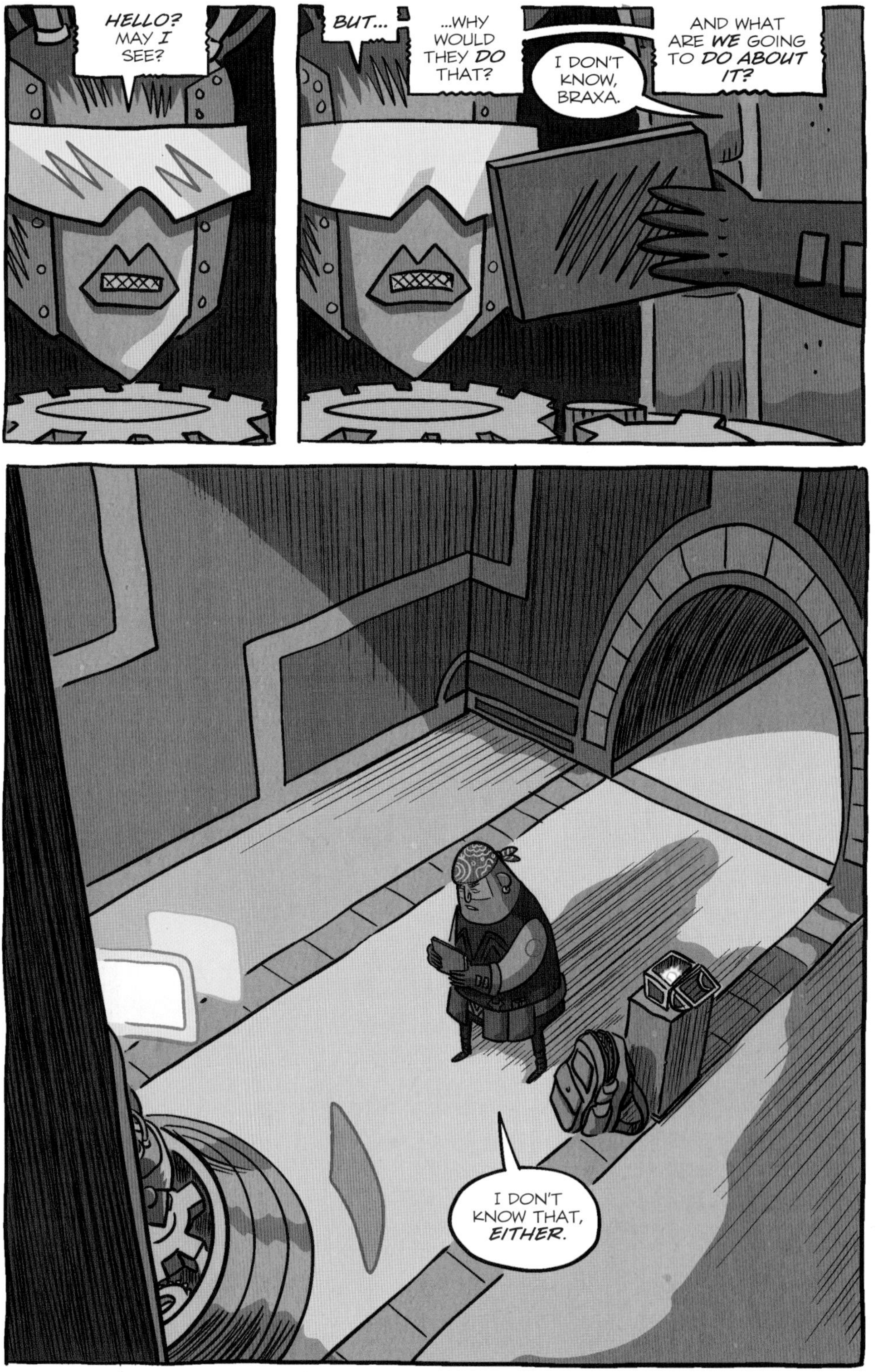
HELLO? MAY I SEE?
BUT...
...WHY WOULD THEY DO THAT?
I DON'T KNOW, BRAXA.
AND WHAT ARE WE GOING TO DO ABOUT IT?
I DON'T KNOW THAT, EITHER.

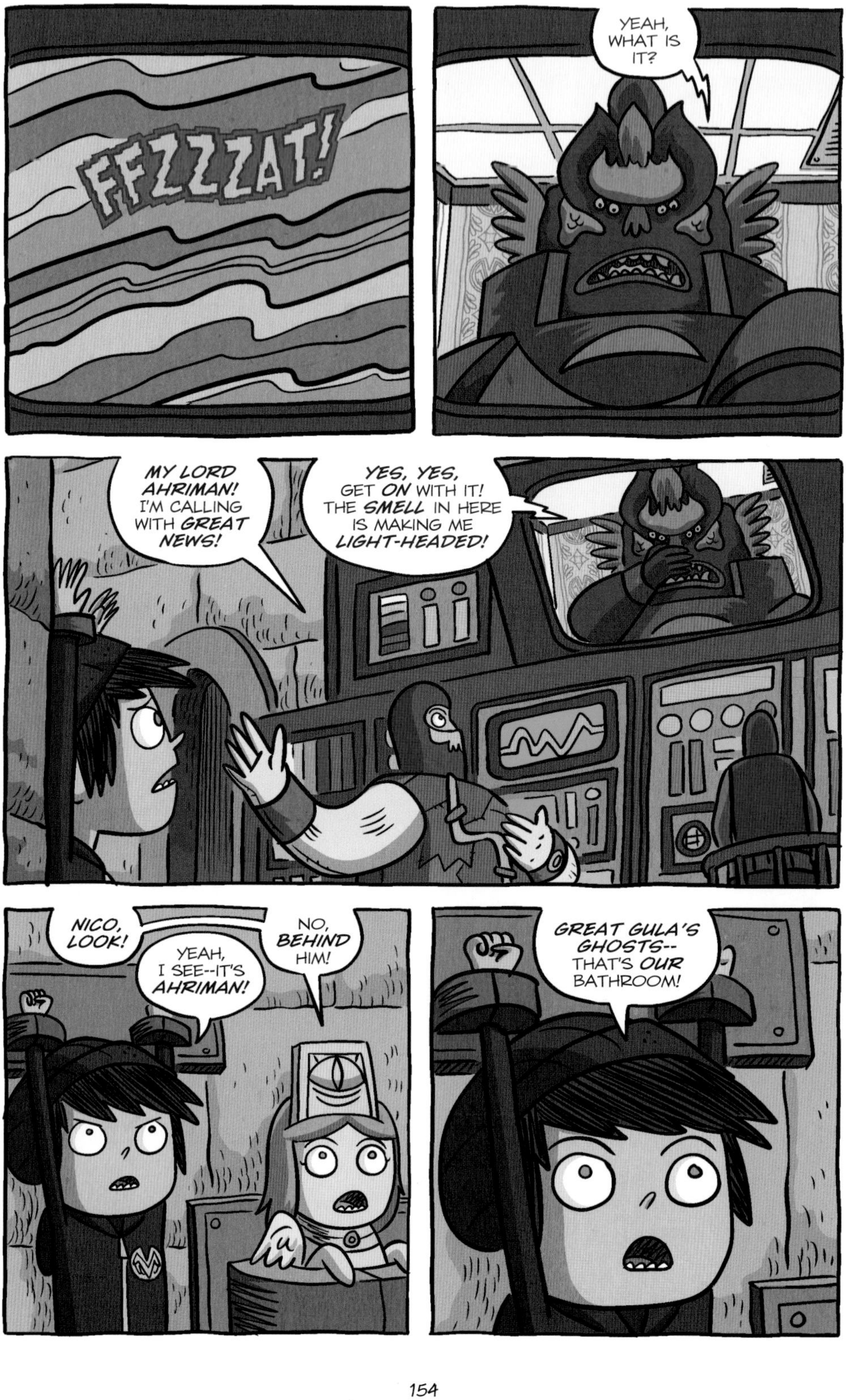
FFZZZAT!
YEAH, WHAT IS IT?
MY LORD AHRIMAN! I'M CALLING WITH GREAT NEWS!
YES, YES, GET ON WITH IT! THE SMELL IN HERE IS MAKING ME LIGHT-HEADED!
NICO, LOOK!
YEAH, I SEE--IT'S AHRIMAN!
NO, BEHIND HIM!
GREAT GULA'S GHOSTS-- THAT'S OUR BATHROOM!

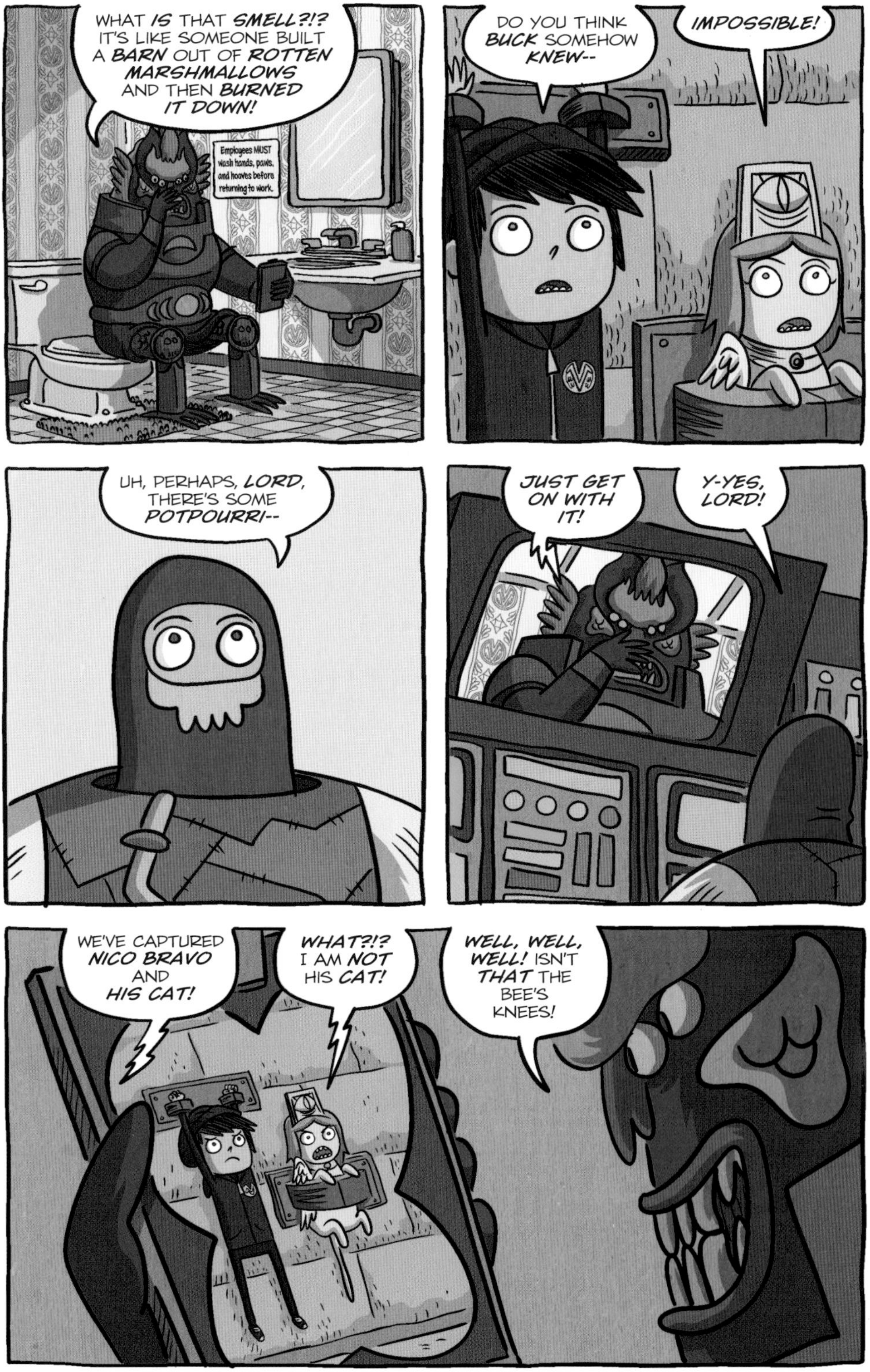
WHAT IS THAT SMELL?!? IT'S LIKE SOMEONE BUILT A BARN OUT OF ROTTEN MARSHMALLOWS AND THEN BURNED IT DOWN!
Employees MUST wash hands, paws, and hooves before returning to work.
DO YOU THINK BUCK SOMEHOW KNEW--
IMPOSSIBLE!
UH, PERHAPS, LORD, THERE'S SOME POTPOURRI--
JUST GET ON WITH IT!
Y-YES, LORD!
WE'VE CAPTURED NICO BRAVO AND HIS CAT!
WHAT?!? I AM NOT HIS CAT!
WELL, WELL, WELL! ISN'T THAT THE BEE'S KNEES!

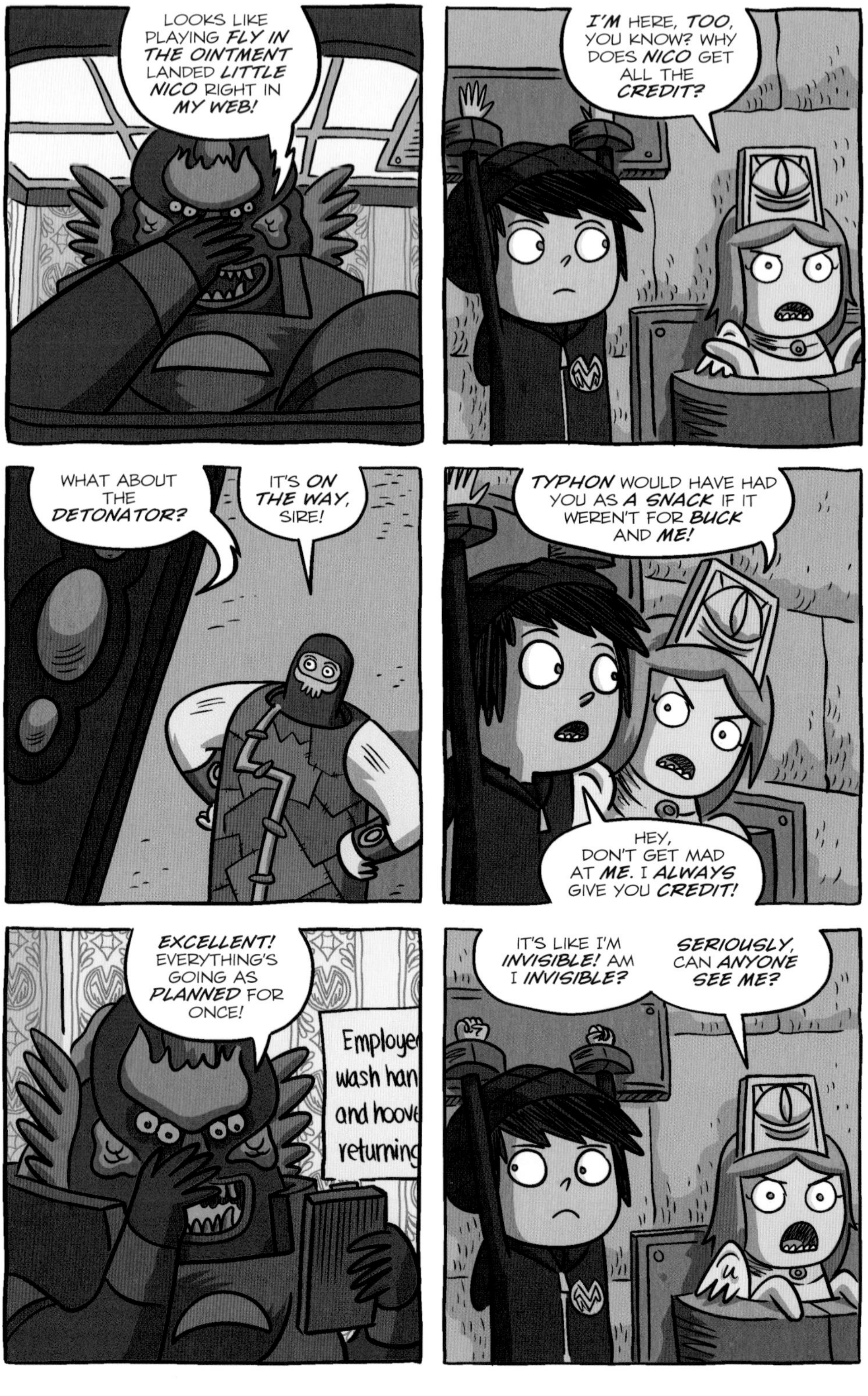
LOOKS LIKE PLAYING FLY IN THE OINTMENT LANDED LITTLE NICO RIGHT IN MY WEB!
I'M HERE, TOO, YOU KNOW? WHY DOES NICO GET ALL THE CREDIT?
WHAT ABOUT THE DETONATOR?
IT'S ON THE WAY, SIRE!
TYPHON WOULD HAVE HAD YOU AS A SNACK IF IT WEREN'T FOR BUCK AND ME!
HEY, DON'T GET MAD AT ME. I ALWAYS GIVE YOU CREDIT!
EXCELLENT! EVERYTHING'S GOING AS PLANNED FOR ONCE!
IT'S LIKE I'M INVISIBLE! AM I INVISIBLE?
SERIOUSLY, CAN ANYONE SEE ME?

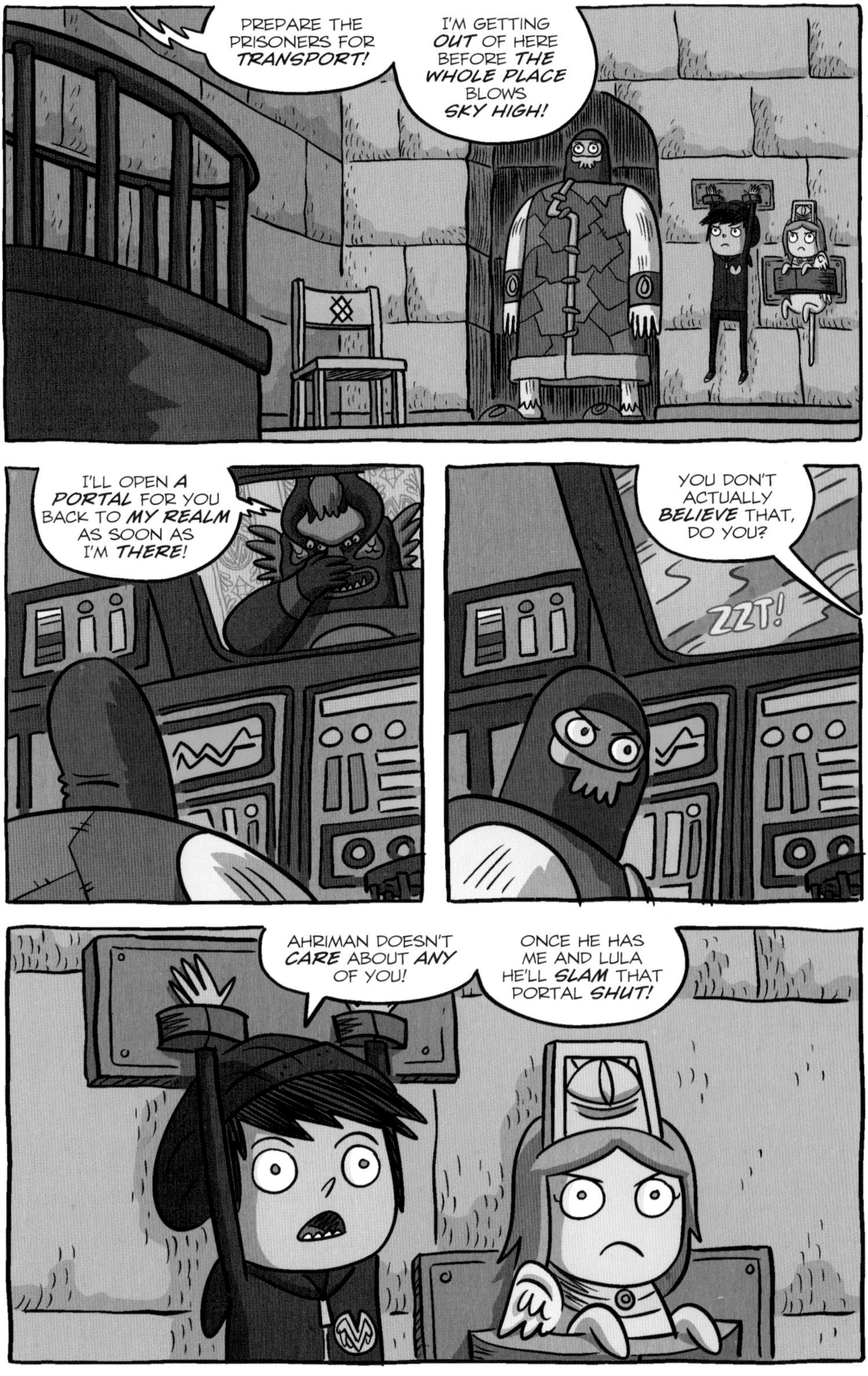
PREPARE THE PRISONERS FOR TRANSPORT!
I'M GETTING OUT OF HERE BEFORE THE WHOLE PLACE BLOWS SKY HIGH!
I'LL OPEN A PORTAL FOR YOU BACK TO MY REALM AS SOON AS I'M THERE!
YOU DON'T ACTUALLY BELIEVE THAT, DO YOU?
ZZT!
AHRIMAN DOESN'T CARE ABOUT ANY OF YOU!
ONCE HE HAS ME AND LULA HE'LL SLAM THAT PORTAL SHUT!

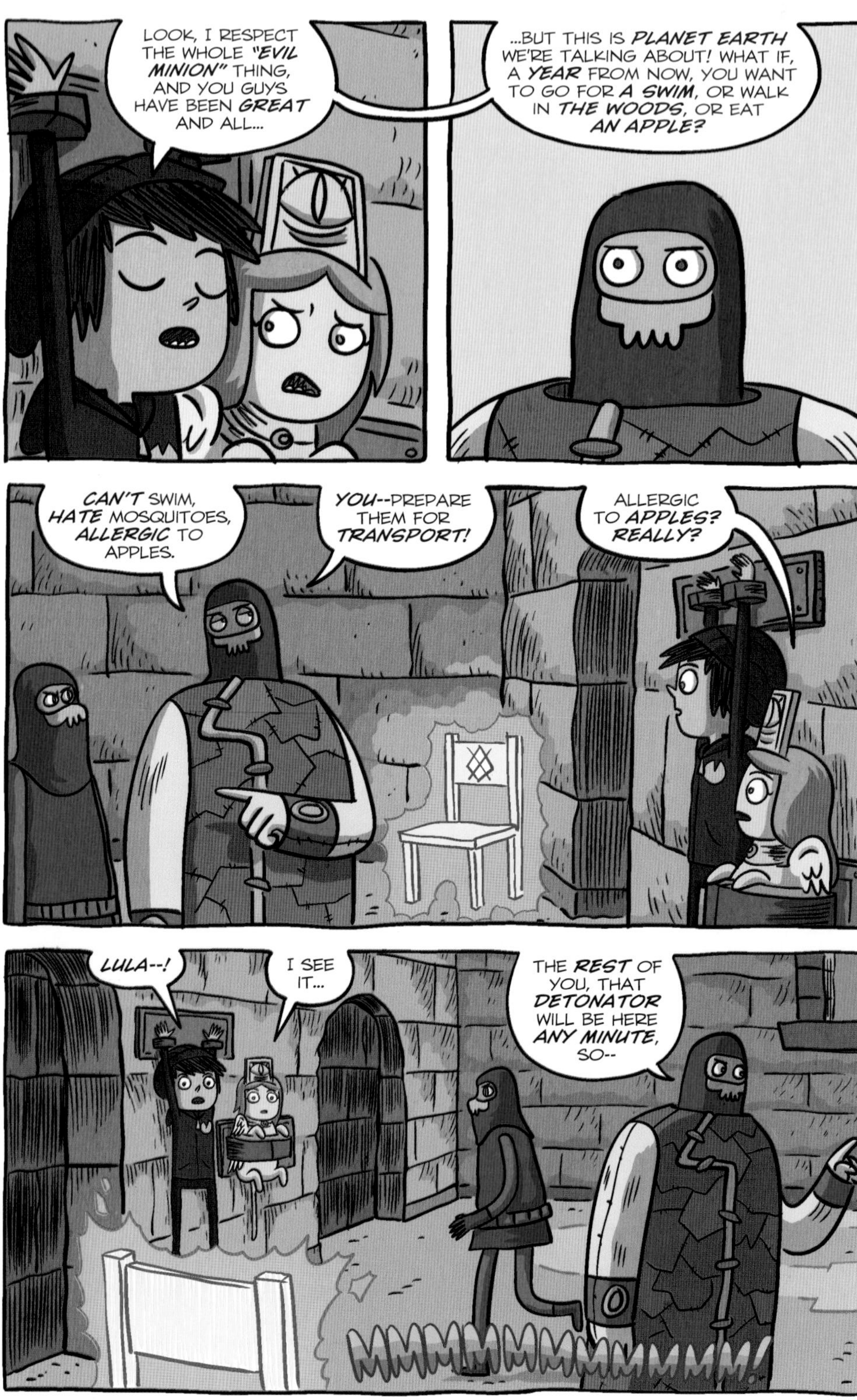
LOOK, I RESPECT THE WHOLE "EVIL MINION" THING, AND YOU GUYS HAVE BEEN GREAT AND ALL...
...BUT THIS IS PLANET EARTH WE'RE TALKING ABOUT! WHAT IF, A YEAR FROM NOW, YOU WANT TO GO FOR A SWIM, OR WALK IN THE WOODS, OR EAT AN APPLE?
CAN'T SWIM, HATE MOSQUITOES, ALLERGIC TO APPLES.
YOU--PREPARE THEM FOR TRANSPORT!
ALLERGIC TO APPLES? REALLY?
LULA--!
I SEE IT...
THE REST OF YOU, THAT DETONATOR WILL BE HERE ANY MINUTE, SO--
MMMMMMMMMMMMMM!

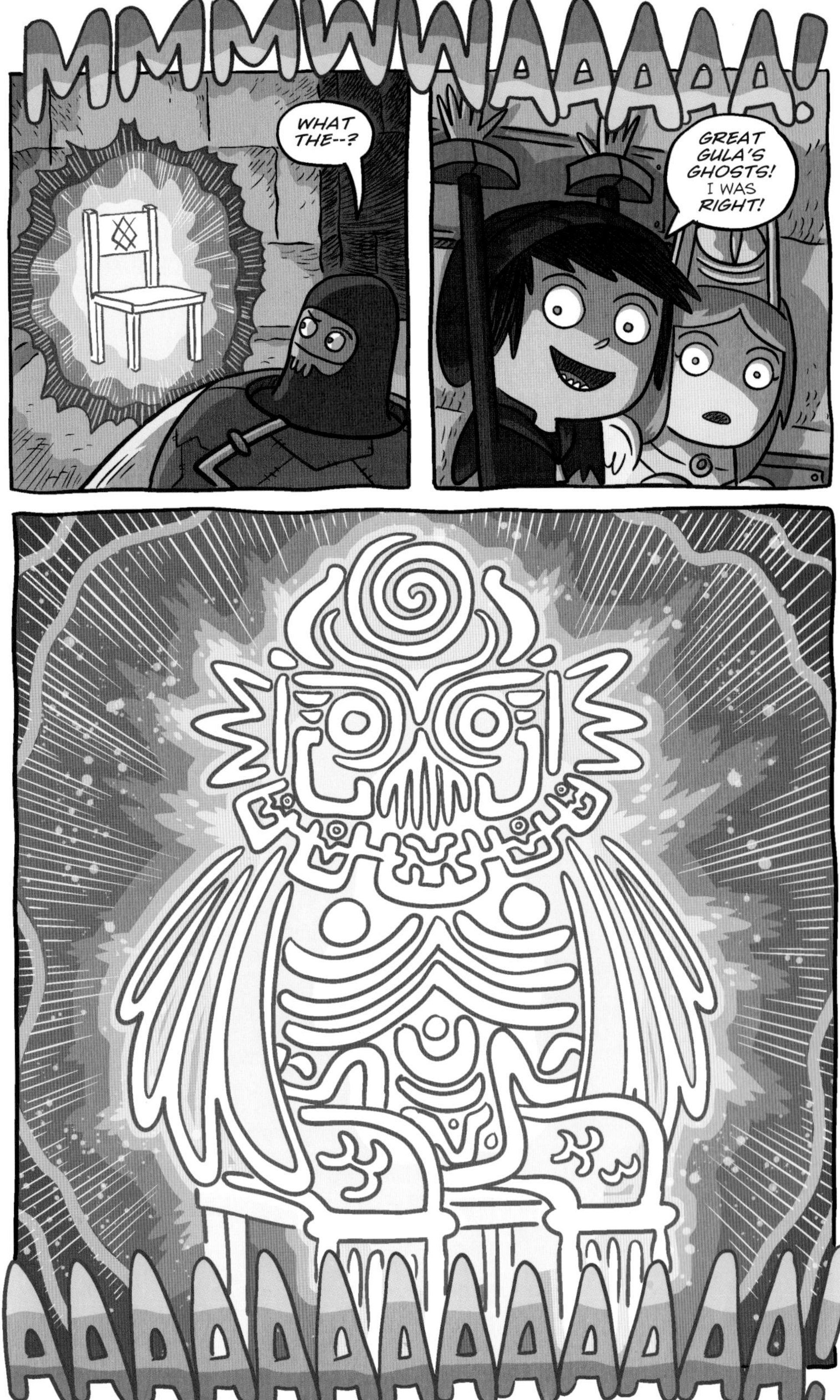
MMMWWAAAAA!
WHAT THE--?
GREAT GULA'S GHOSTS! I WAS RIGHT!
AAAAAAAAAAAAA!

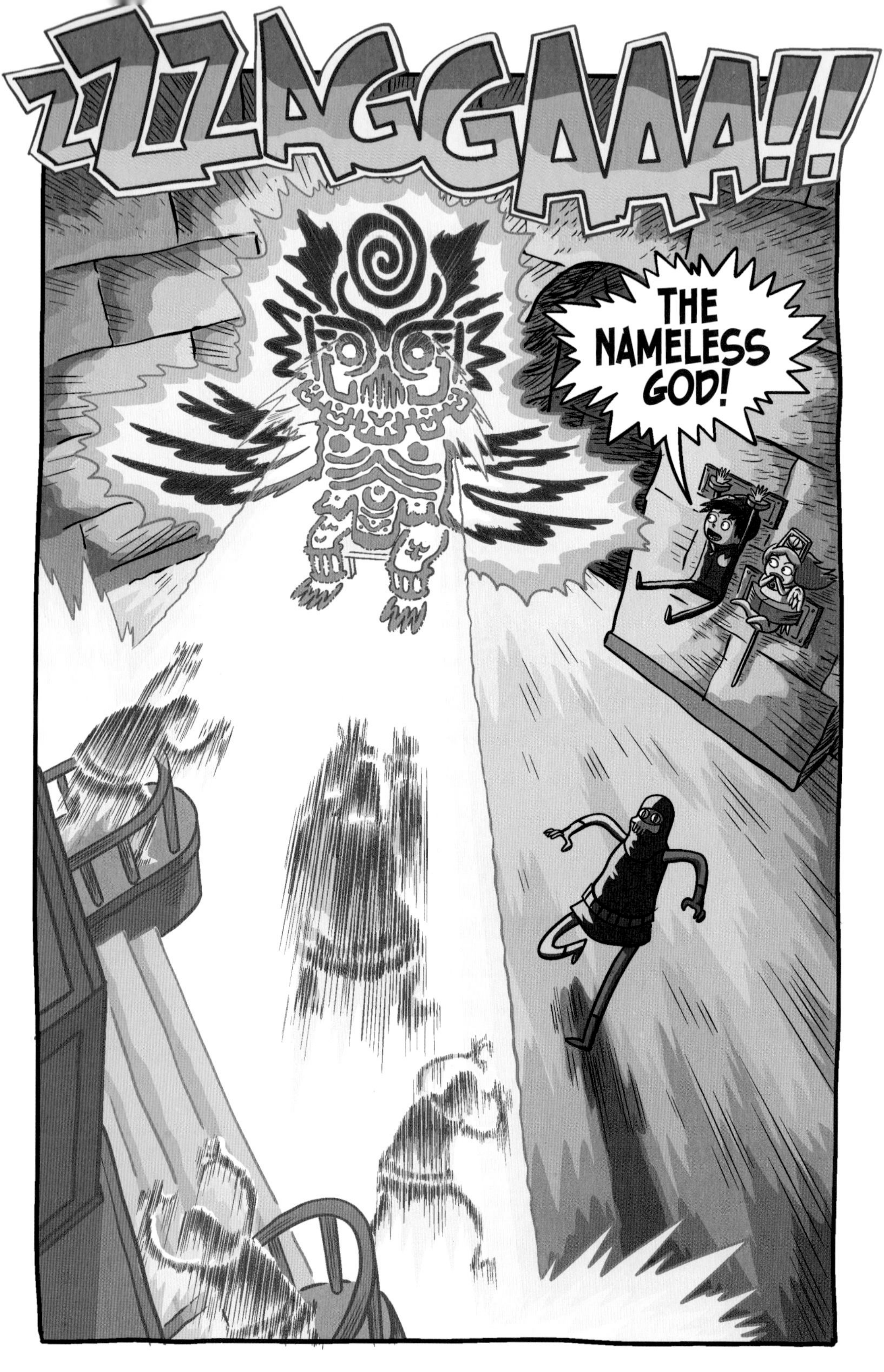
ZZZAGGAAA!!
THE NAMELESS GOD!

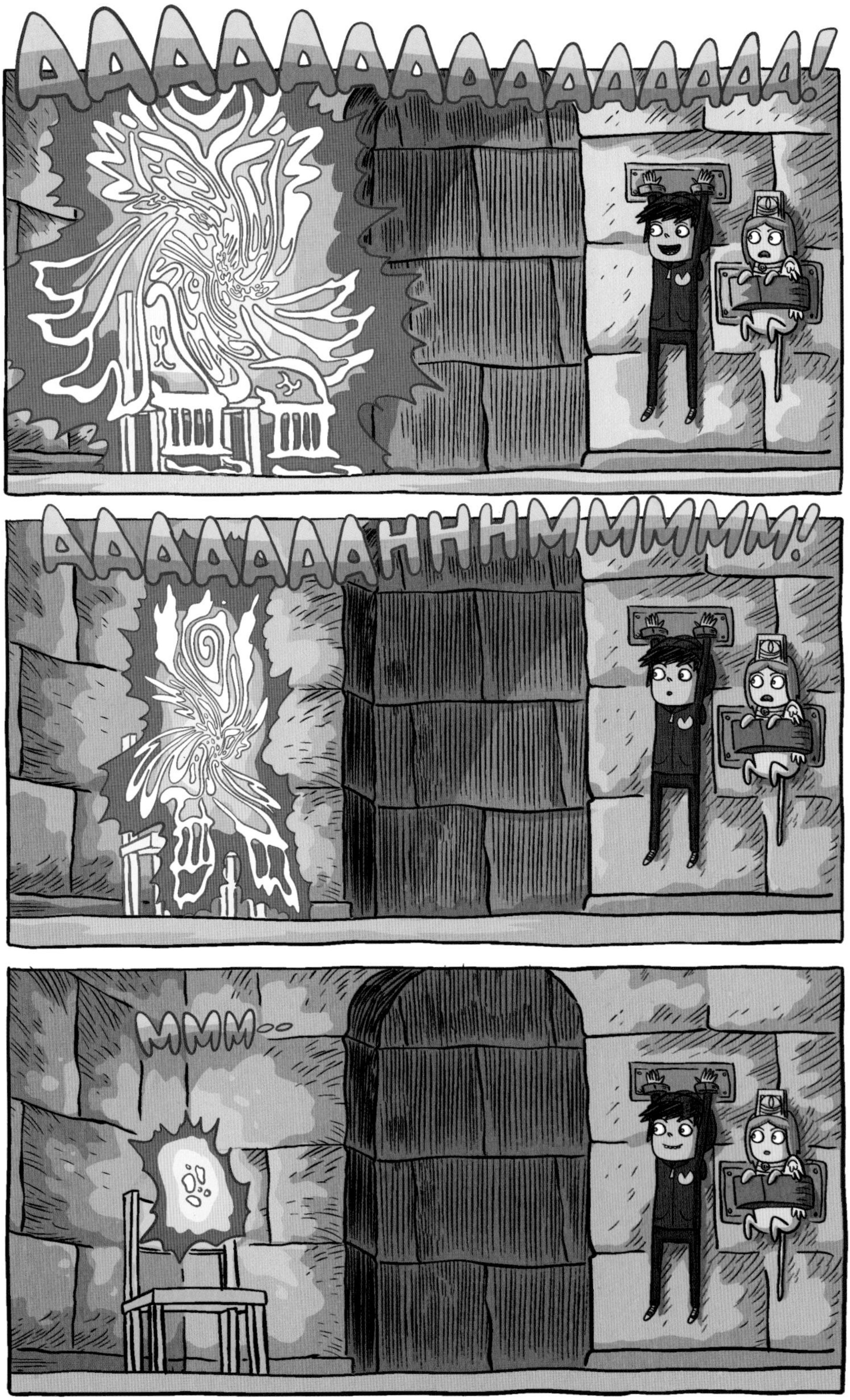
AAAAAAAAAAAAAAA!
AAAAAAAHHHMMMMM!
MMM..

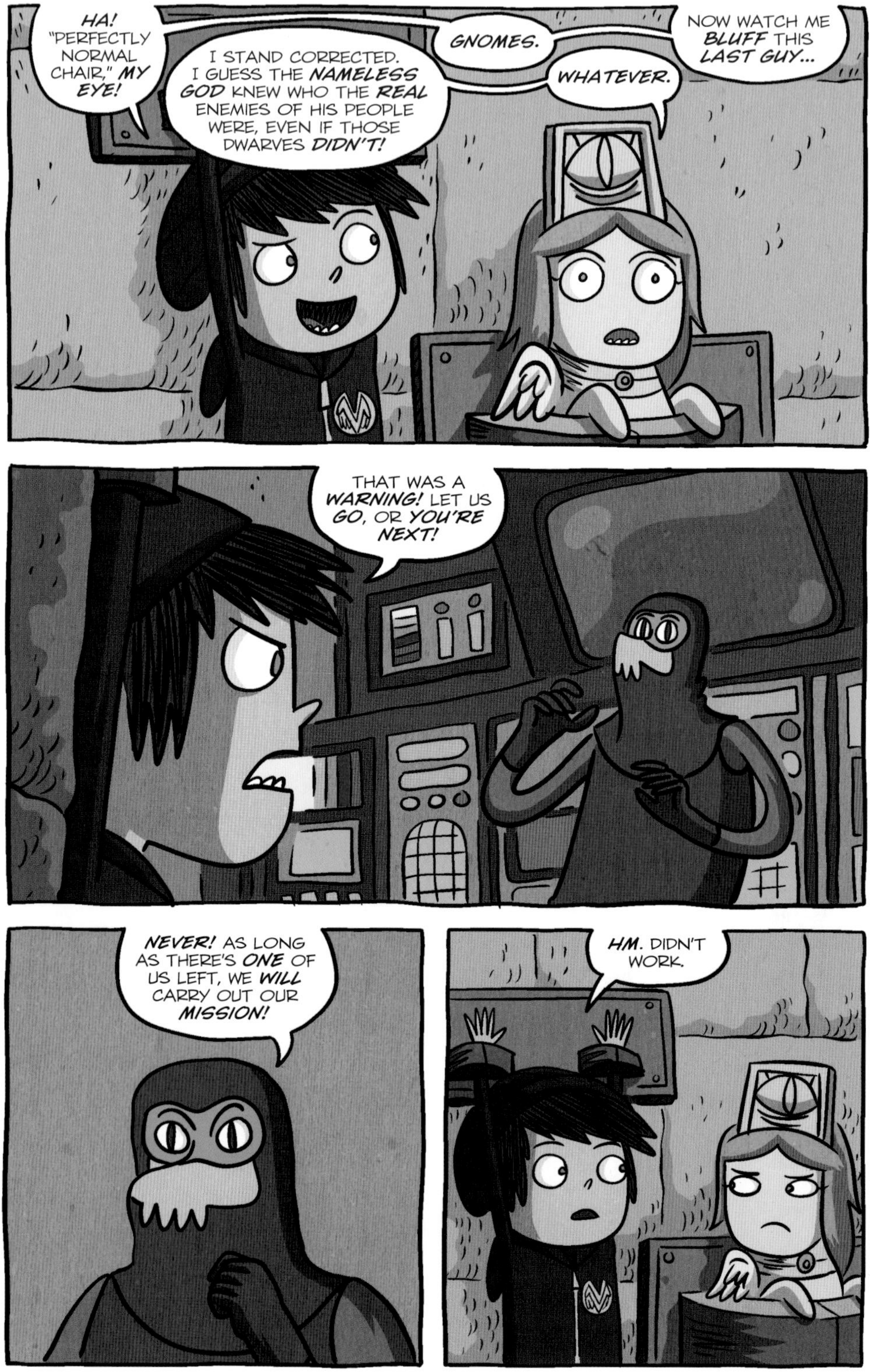
HA! "PERFECTLY NORMAL CHAIR," MY EYE!
I STAND CORRECTED. I GUESS THE NAMELESS GOD KNEW WHO THE REAL ENEMIES OF HIS PEOPLE WERE, EVEN IF THOSE DWARVES DIDN'T!
GNOMES.
WHATEVER.
NOW WATCH ME BLUFF THIS LAST GUY...
THAT WAS A WARNING! LET US GO, OR YOU'RE NEXT!
NEVER! AS LONG AS THERE'S ONE OF US LEFT, WE WILL CARRY OUT OUR MISSION!
HM. DIDN'T WORK.

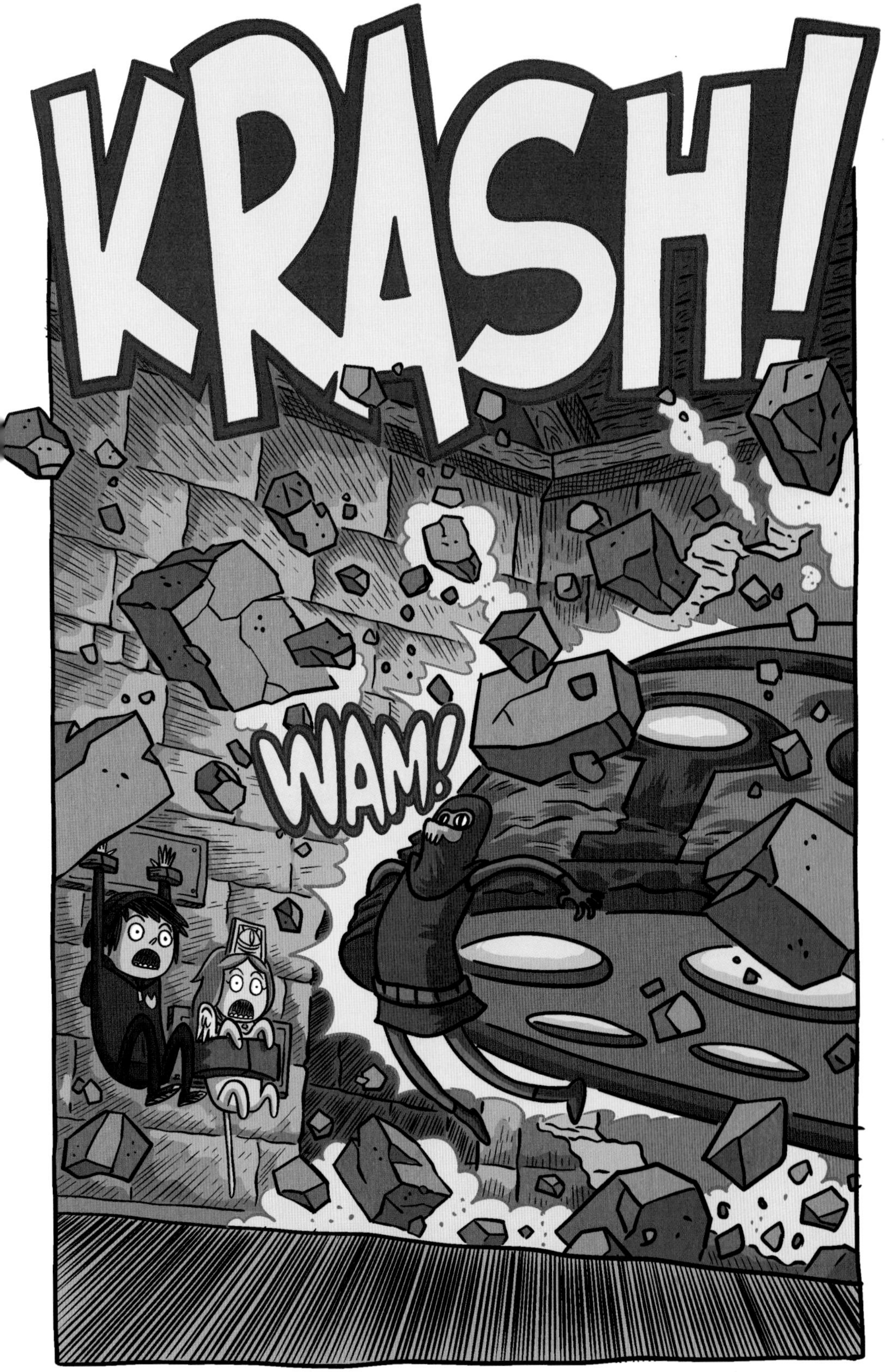
KRASH!
WAM!

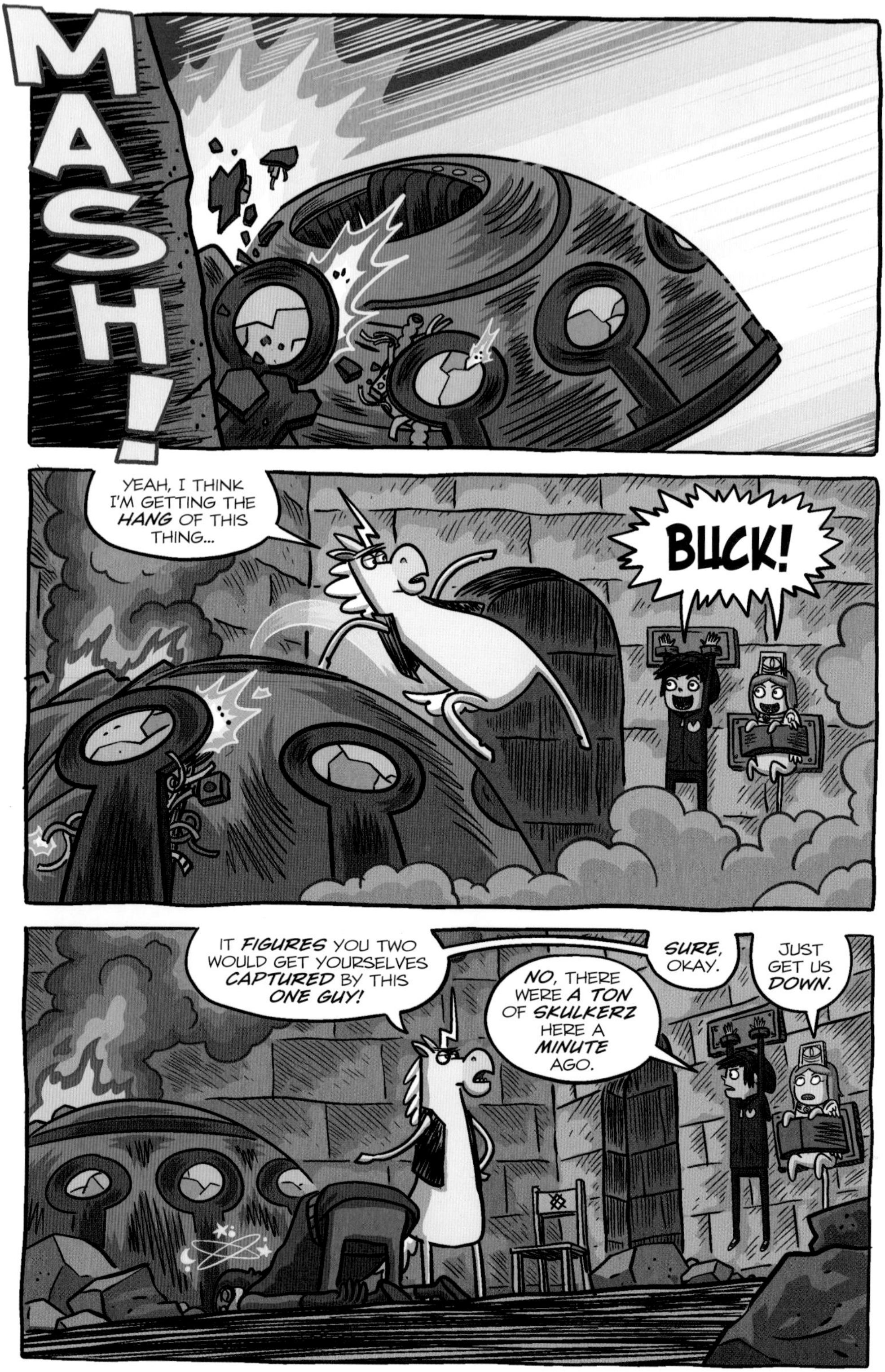
MASH!
YEAH, I THINK I'M GETTING THE HANG OF THIS THING...
BUCK!
IT FIGURES YOU TWO WOULD GET YOURSELVES CAPTURED BY THIS ONE GUY!
NO, THERE WERE A TON OF SKULKERZ HERE A MINUTE AGO.
SURE, OKAY.
JUST GET US DOWN.

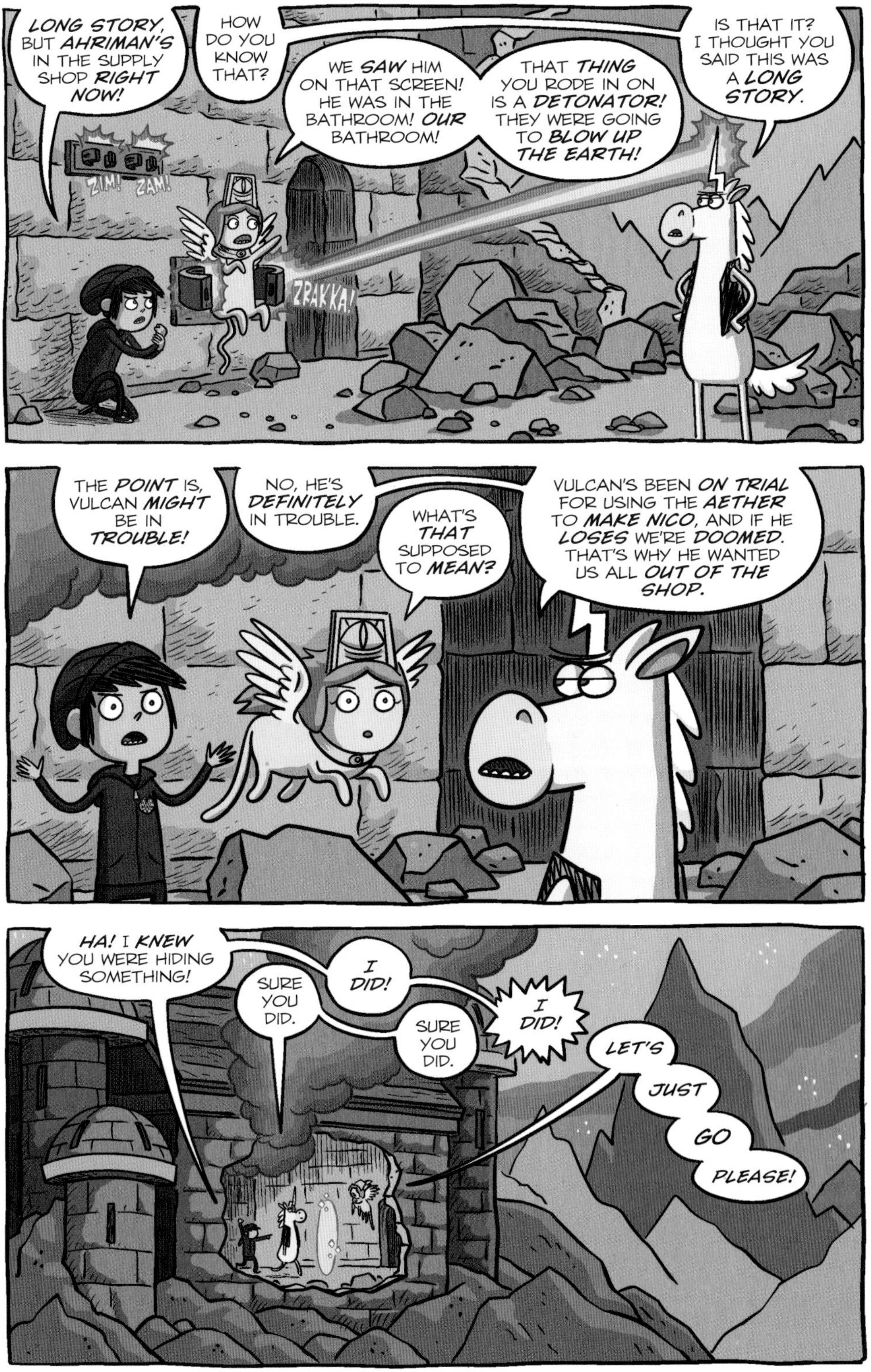
LONG STORY, BUT AHRIMAN'S IN THE SUPPLY SHOP RIGHT NOW!
HOW DO YOU KNOW THAT?
WE SAW HIM ON THAT SCREEN! HE WAS IN THE BATHROOM! OUR BATHROOM!
THAT THING YOU RODE IN ON IS A DETONATOR! THEY WERE GOING TO BLOW UP THE EARTH!
IS THAT IT? I THOUGHT YOU SAID THIS WAS A LONG STORY.
ZIM!
ZAM!
ZRAKKA!
THE POINT IS, VULCAN MIGHT BE IN TROUBLE!
NO, HE'S DEFINITELY IN TROUBLE.
WHAT'S THAT SUPPOSED TO MEAN?
VULCAN'S BEEN ON TRIAL FOR USING THE AETHER TO MAKE NICO, AND IF HE LOSES WE'RE DOOMED. THAT'S WHY HE WANTED US ALL OUT OF THE SHOP.
HA! I KNEW YOU WERE HIDING SOMETHING!
I DID!
SURE YOU DID.
I DID!
SURE YOU DID.
LET'S JUST GO PLEASE!

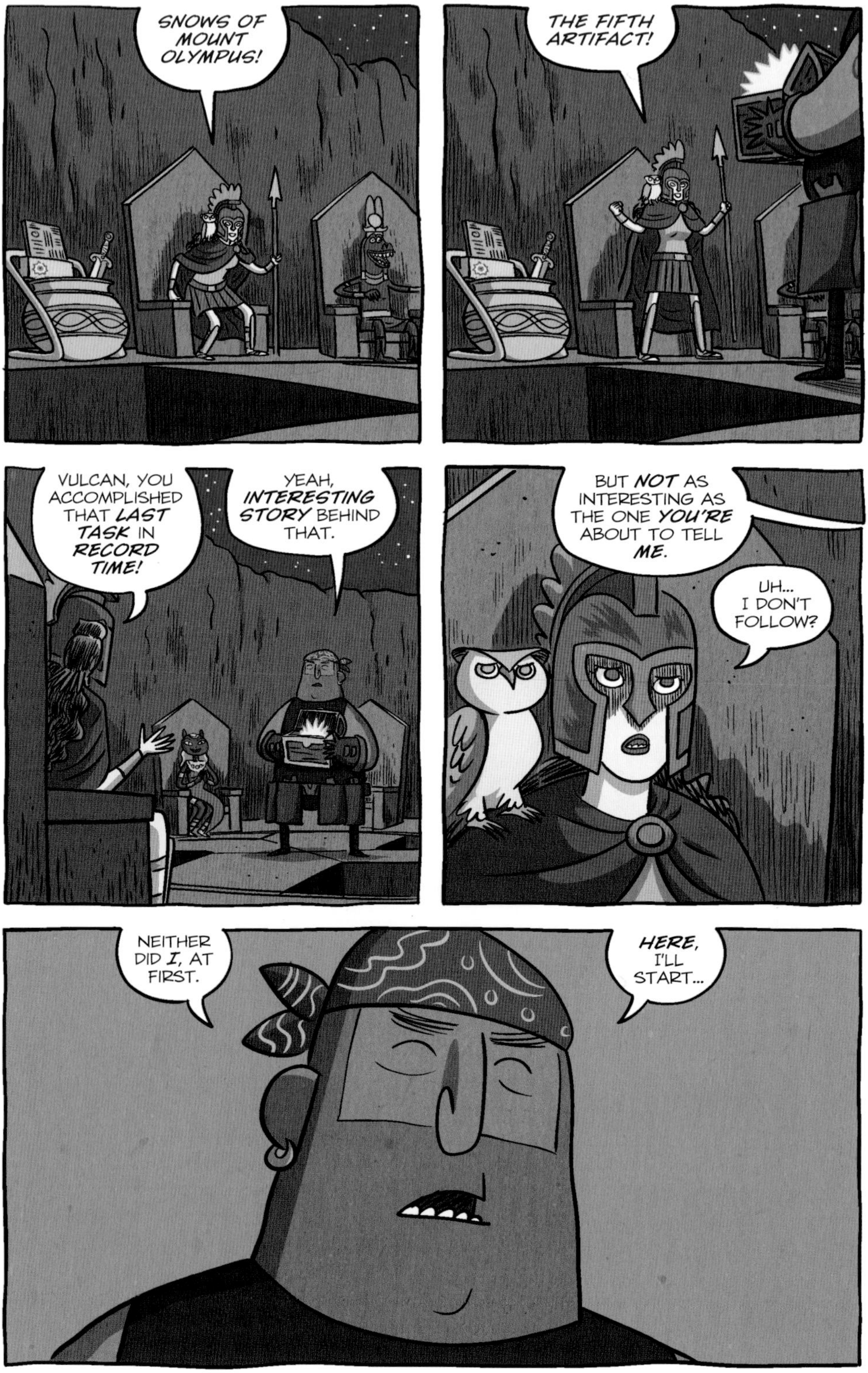
SNOWS OF MOUNT OLYMPUS!
THE FIFTH ARTIFACT!
VULCAN, YOU ACCOMPLISHED THAT LAST TASK IN RECORD TIME!
YEAH, INTERESTING STORY BEHIND THAT.
BUT NOT AS INTERESTING AS THE ONE YOU'RE ABOUT TO TELL ME.
UH... I DON'T FOLLOW?
NEITHER DID I, AT FIRST.
HERE, I'LL START...

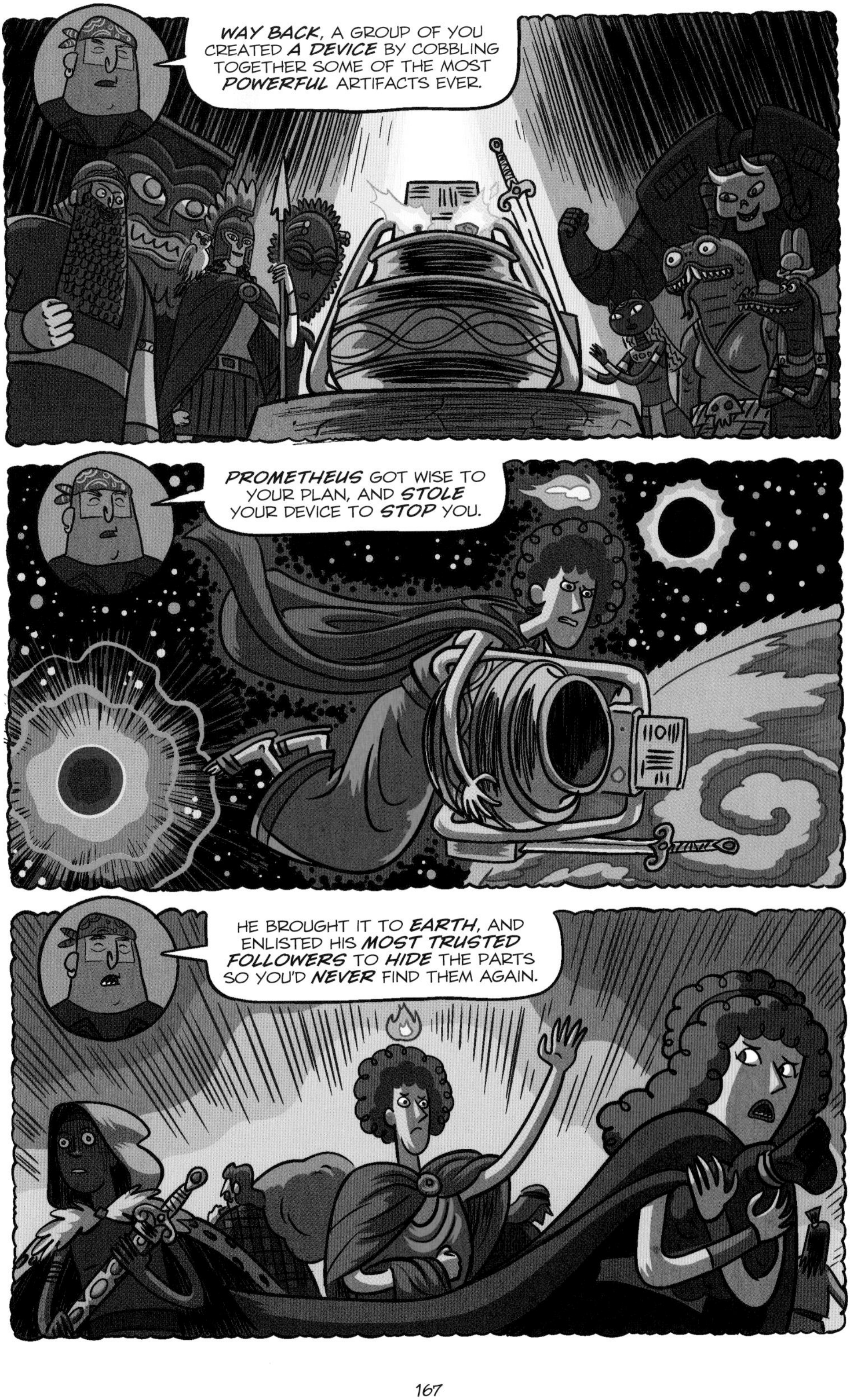
WAY BACK, A GROUP OF YOU CREATED A DEVICE BY COBBLING TOGETHER SOME OF THE MOST POWERFUL ARTIFACTS EVER.
PROMETHEUS GOT WISE TO YOUR PLAN, AND STOLE YOUR DEVICE TO STOP YOU.
HE BROUGHT IT TO EARTH, AND ENLISTED HIS MOST TRUSTED FOLLOWERS TO HIDE THE PARTS SO YOU'D NEVER FIND THEM AGAIN.

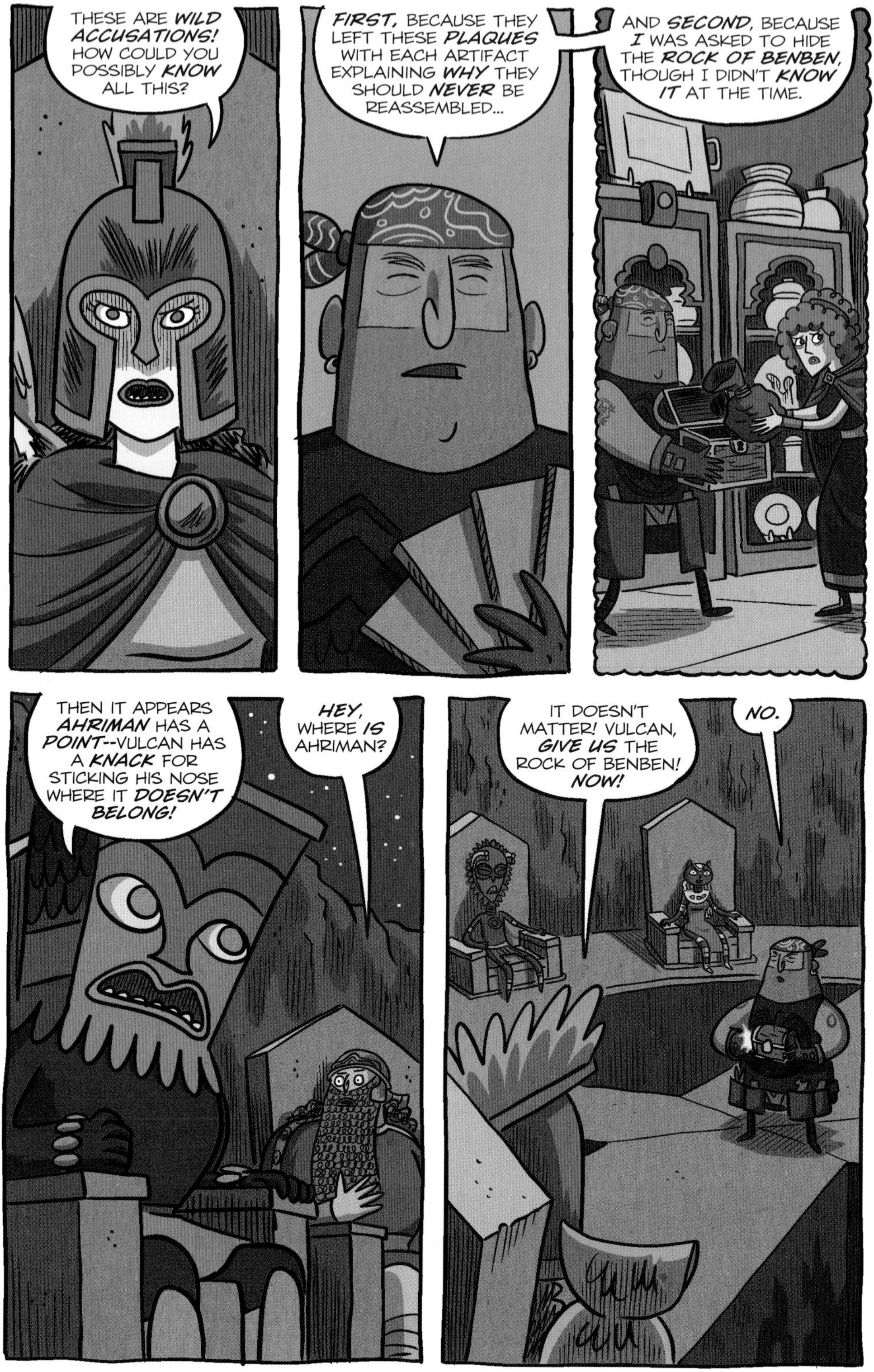
THESE ARE WILD ACCUSATIONS! HOW COULD YOU POSSIBLY KNOW ALL THIS?
FIRST, BECAUSE THEY LEFT THESE PLAQUES WITH EACH ARTIFACT EXPLAINING WHY THEY SHOULD NEVER BE REASSEMBLED...
AND SECOND, BECAUSE I WAS ASKED TO HIDE THE ROCK OF BENBEN, THOUGH I DIDN'T KNOW IT AT THE TIME.
THEN IT APPEARS AHRIMAN HAS A POINT--VULCAN HAS A KNACK FOR STICKING HIS NOSE WHERE IT DOESN'T BELONG!
HEY, WHERE IS AHRIMAN?
IT DOESN'T MATTER! VULCAN, GIVE US THE ROCK OF BENBEN! NOW!
NO.

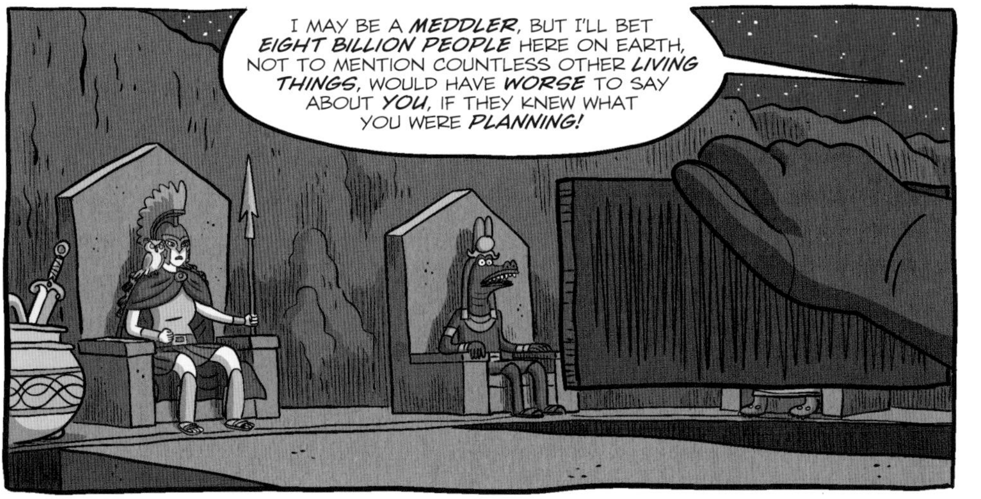
I MAY BE A MEDDLER, BUT I'LL BET EIGHT BILLION PEOPLE HERE ON EARTH, NOT TO MENTION COUNTLESS OTHER LIVING THINGS, WOULD HAVE WORSE TO SAY ABOUT YOU, IF THEY KNEW WHAT YOU WERE PLANNING!

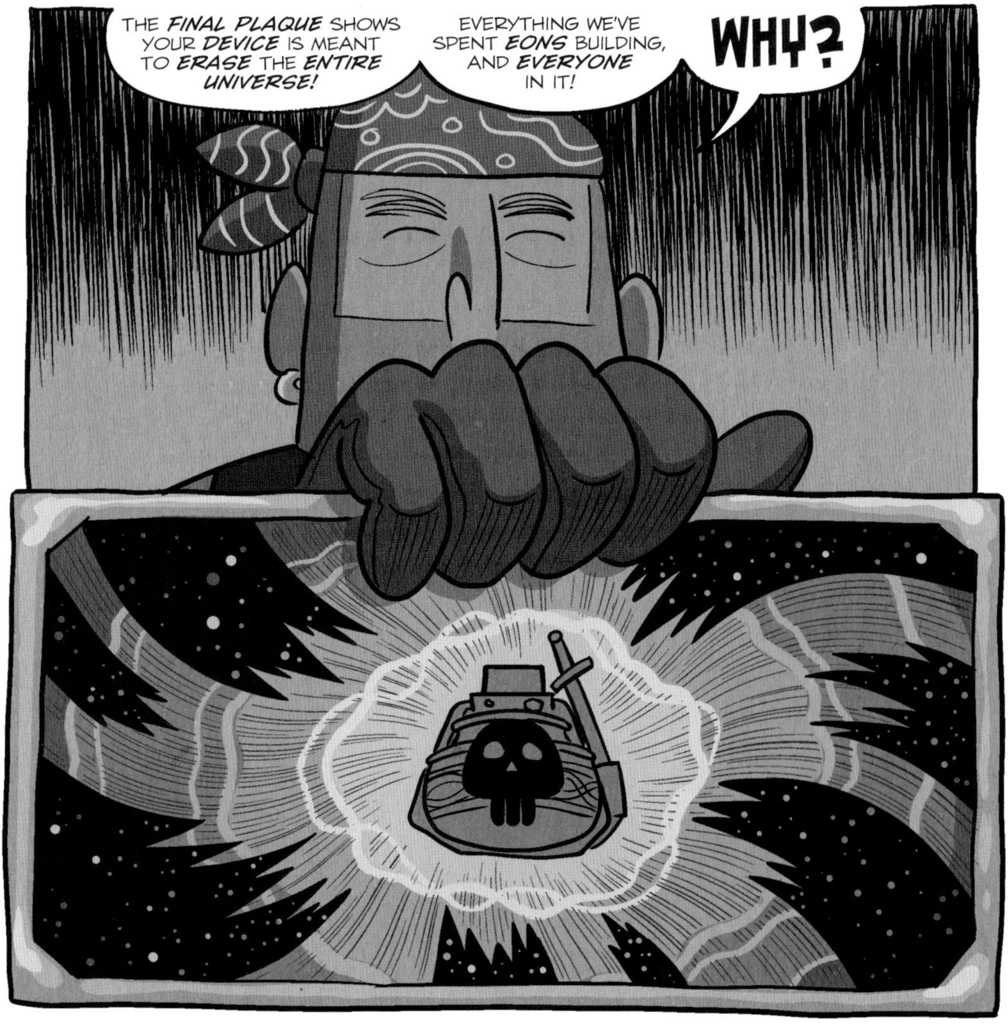
THE FINAL PLAQUE SHOWS YOUR DEVICE IS MEANT TO ERASE THE ENTIRE UNIVERSE!
EVERYTHING WE'VE SPENT EONS BUILDING, AND EVERYONE IN IT!
WHY?

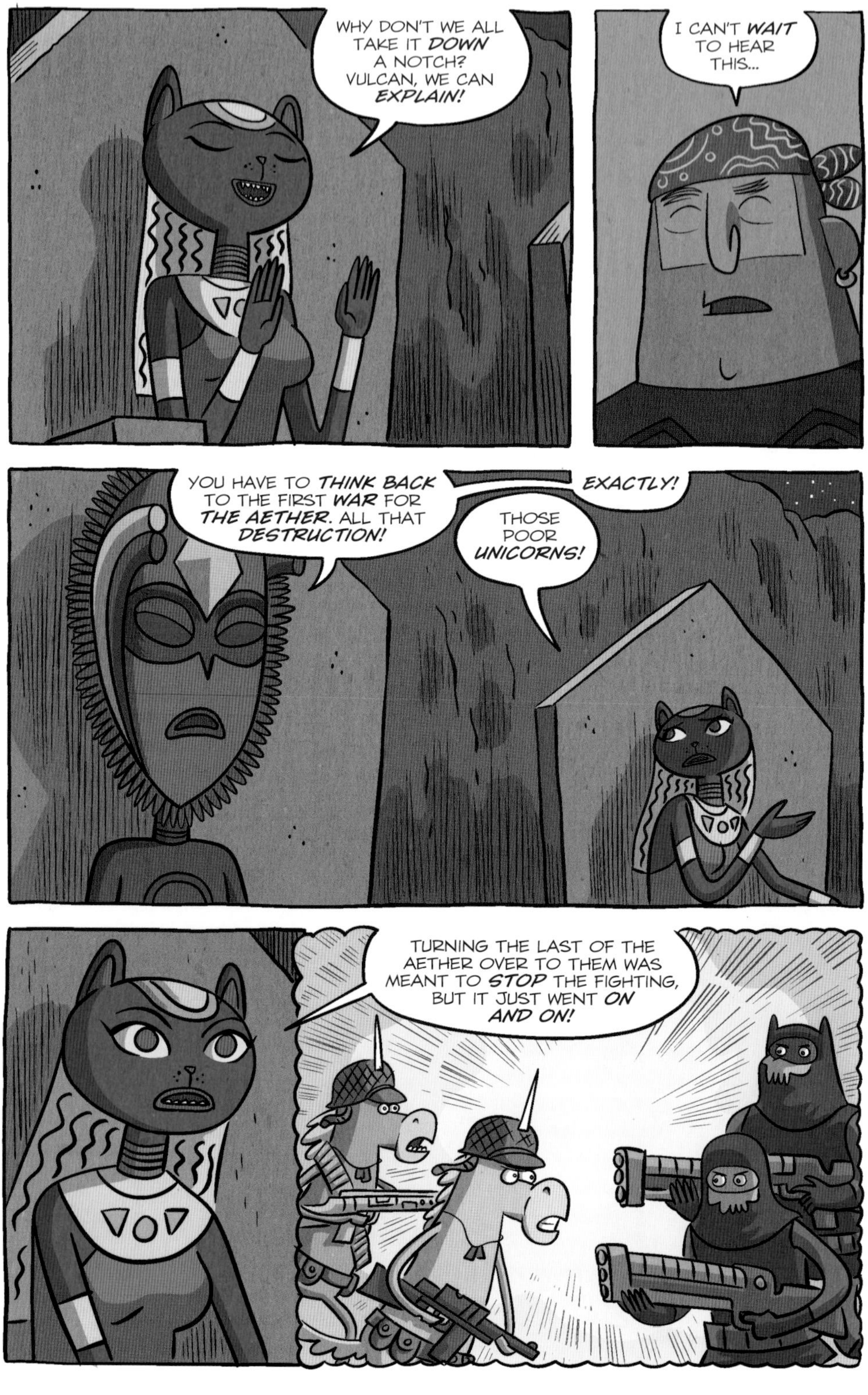
WHY DON'T WE ALL TAKE IT DOWN A NOTCH? VULCAN, WE CAN EXPLAIN!
I CAN'T WAIT TO HEAR THIS...
YOU HAVE TO THINK BACK TO THE FIRST WAR FOR THE AETHER. ALL THAT DESTRUCTION!
EXACTLY!
THOSE POOR UNICORNS!
TURNING THE LAST OF THE AETHER OVER TO THEM WAS MEANT TO STOP THE FIGHTING, BUT IT JUST WENT ON AND ON!

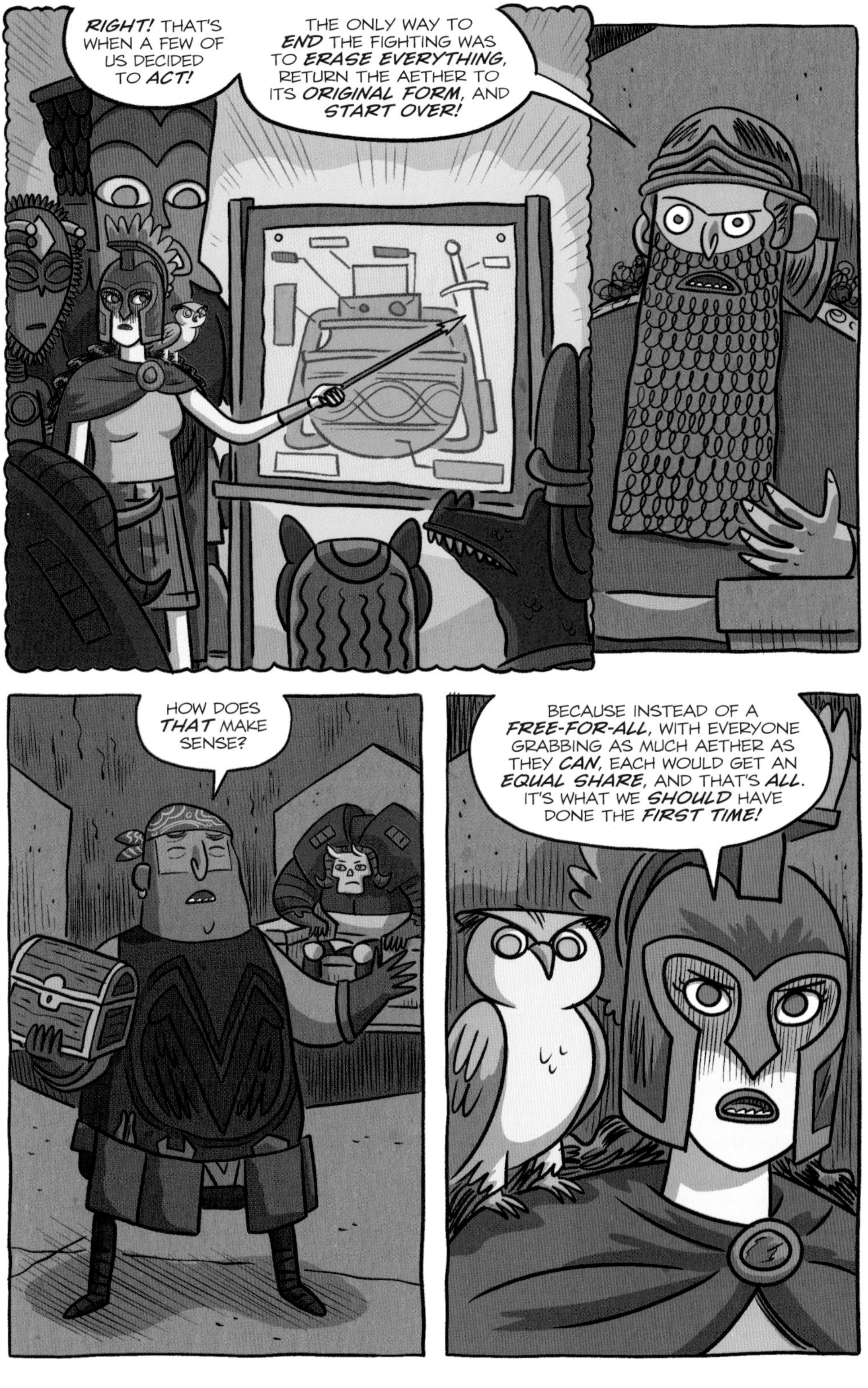
RIGHT! THAT'S WHEN A FEW OF US DECIDED TO ACT!
THE ONLY WAY TO END THE FIGHTING WAS TO ERASE EVERYTHING, RETURN THE AETHER TO ITS ORIGINAL FORM, AND START OVER!
HOW DOES THAT MAKE SENSE?
BECAUSE INSTEAD OF A FREE-FOR-ALL, WITH EVERYONE GRABBING AS MUCH AETHER AS THEY CAN, EACH WOULD GET AN EQUAL SHARE, AND THAT'S ALL. IT'S WHAT WE SHOULD HAVE DONE THE FIRST TIME!

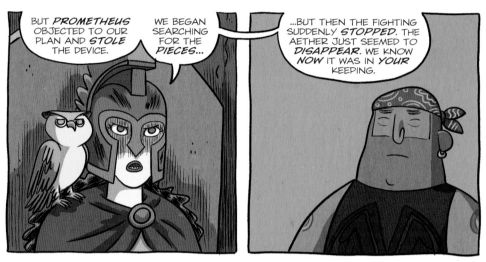

BUT *PROMETHEUS* OBJECTED TO OUR PLAN AND *STOLE* THE DEVICE.

WE BEGAN SEARCHING FOR THE *PIECES*...

...BUT THEN THE FIGHTING SUDDENLY *STOPPED*. THE AETHER JUST SEEMED TO *DISAPPEAR*. WE KNOW *NOW* IT WAS IN *YOUR* KEEPING.

SO WE LET THE WHOLE THING *DROP*.

BUT *NOW* IT'S ALL *FLARED UP* AGAIN!

YOUR OWN BELOVED *CELESTINA* WAS ALMOST *WIPED OFF THE MAP!*

DID YOU THINK WE HADN'T *NOTICED?*

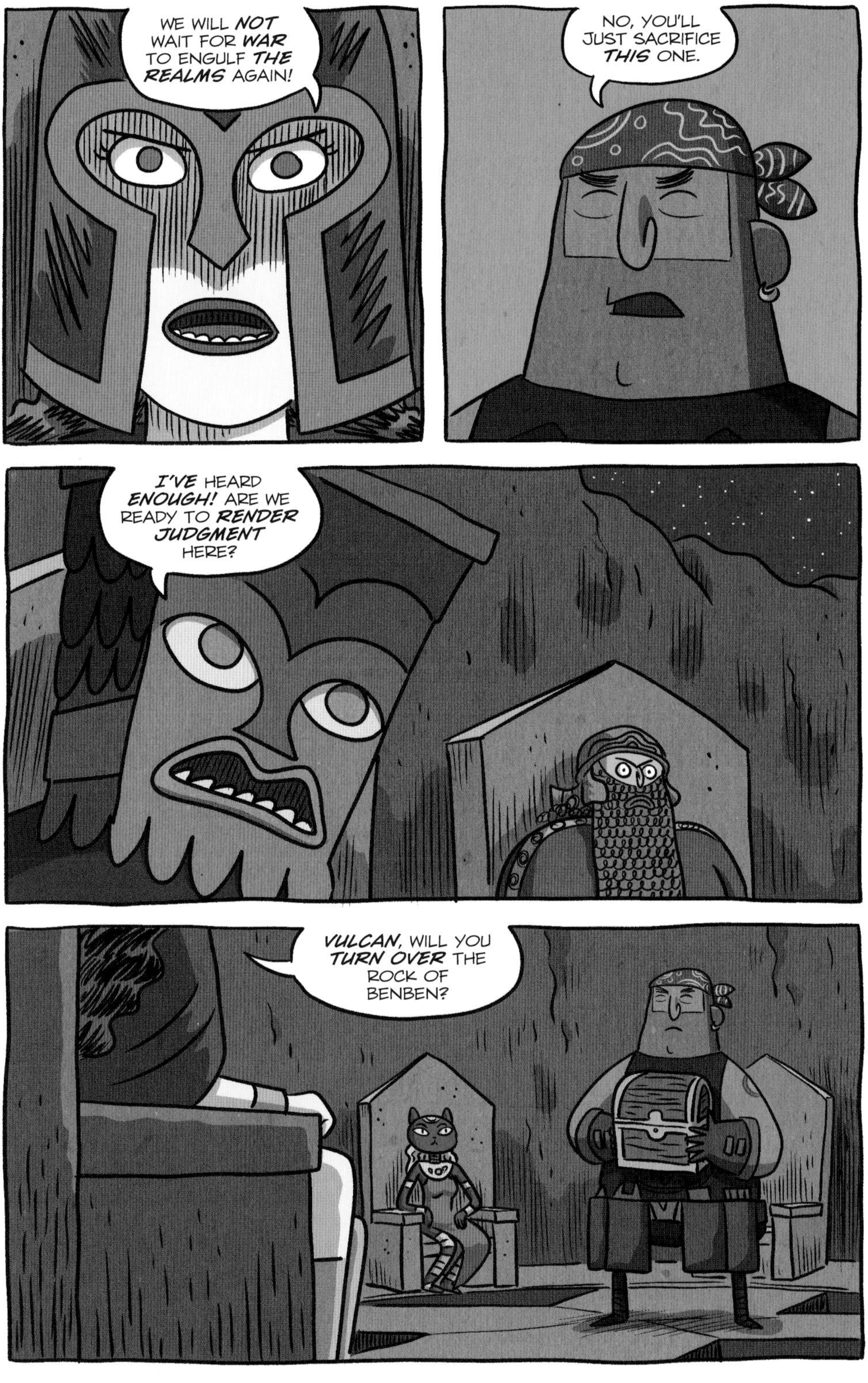
WE WILL NOT WAIT FOR WAR TO ENGULF THE REALMS AGAIN!
NO, YOU'LL JUST SACRIFICE THIS ONE.
I'VE HEARD ENOUGH! ARE WE READY TO RENDER JUDGMENT HERE?
VULCAN, WILL YOU TURN OVER THE ROCK OF BENBEN?

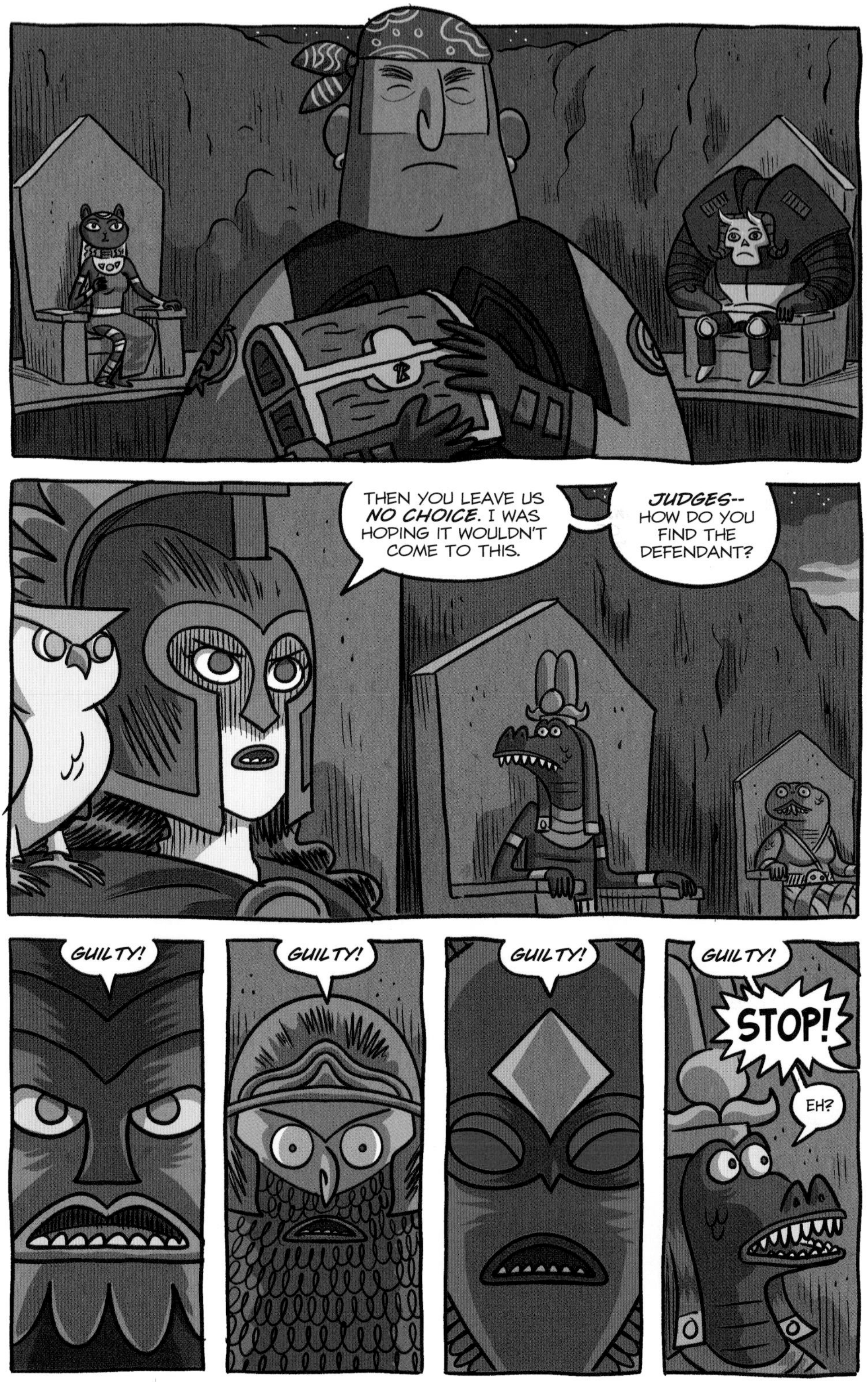
THEN YOU LEAVE US ***NO CHOICE***. I WAS HOPING IT WOULDN'T COME TO THIS.
JUDGES-- HOW DO YOU FIND THE DEFENDANT?
GUILTY!
GUILTY!
GUILTY!
GUILTY!
STOP!
EH?

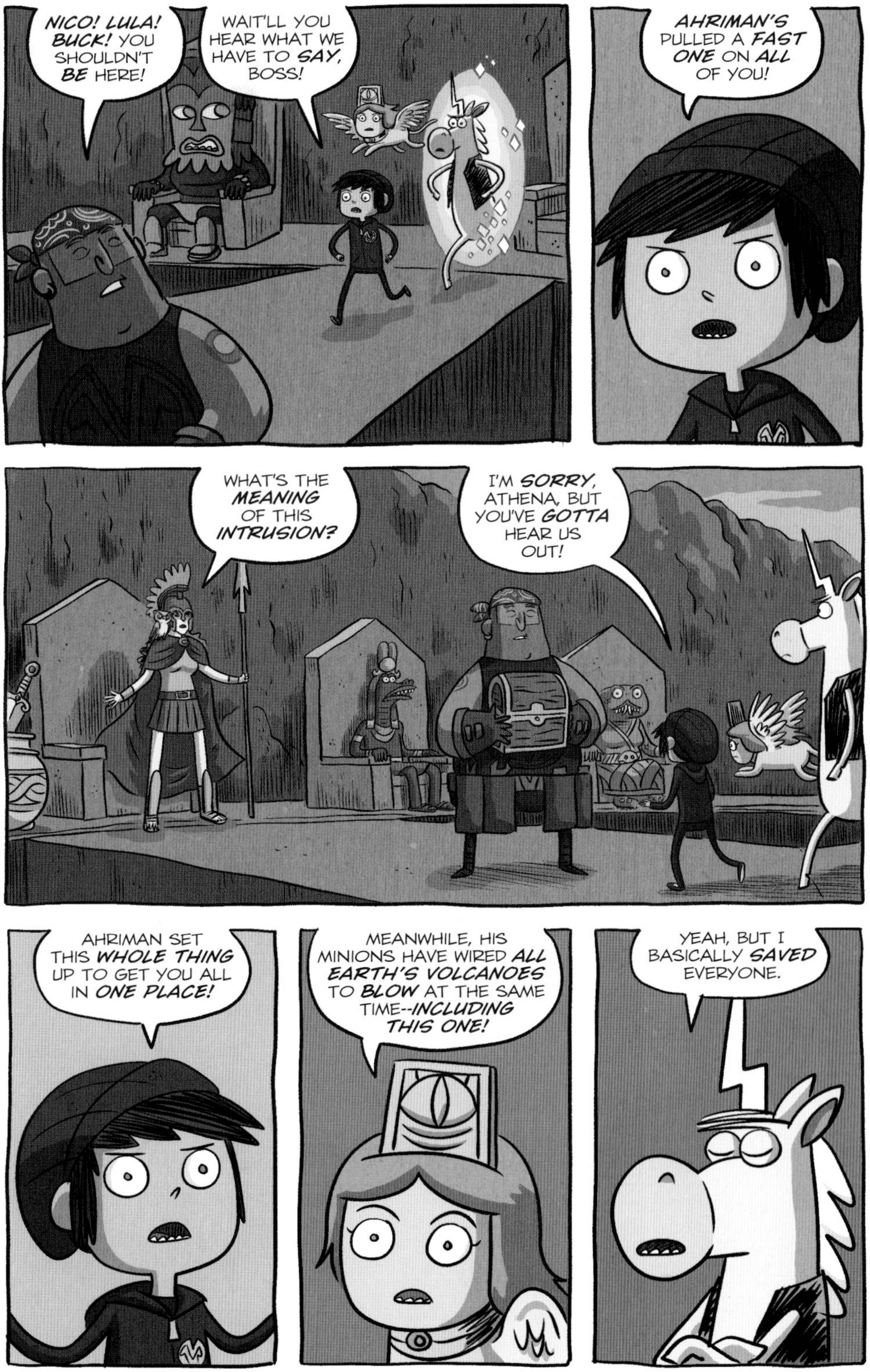
NICO! LULA! BUCK! YOU SHOULDN'T BE HERE!
WAIT'LL YOU HEAR WHAT WE HAVE TO SAY, BOSS!
AHRIMAN'S PULLED A FAST ONE ON ALL OF YOU!
WHAT'S THE MEANING OF THIS INTRUSION?
I'M SORRY, ATHENA, BUT YOU'VE GOTTA HEAR US OUT!
AHRIMAN SET THIS WHOLE THING UP TO GET YOU ALL IN ONE PLACE!
MEANWHILE, HIS MINIONS HAVE WIRED ALL EARTH'S VOLCANOES TO BLOW AT THE SAME TIME--INCLUDING THIS ONE!
YEAH, BUT I BASICALLY SAVED EVERYONE.

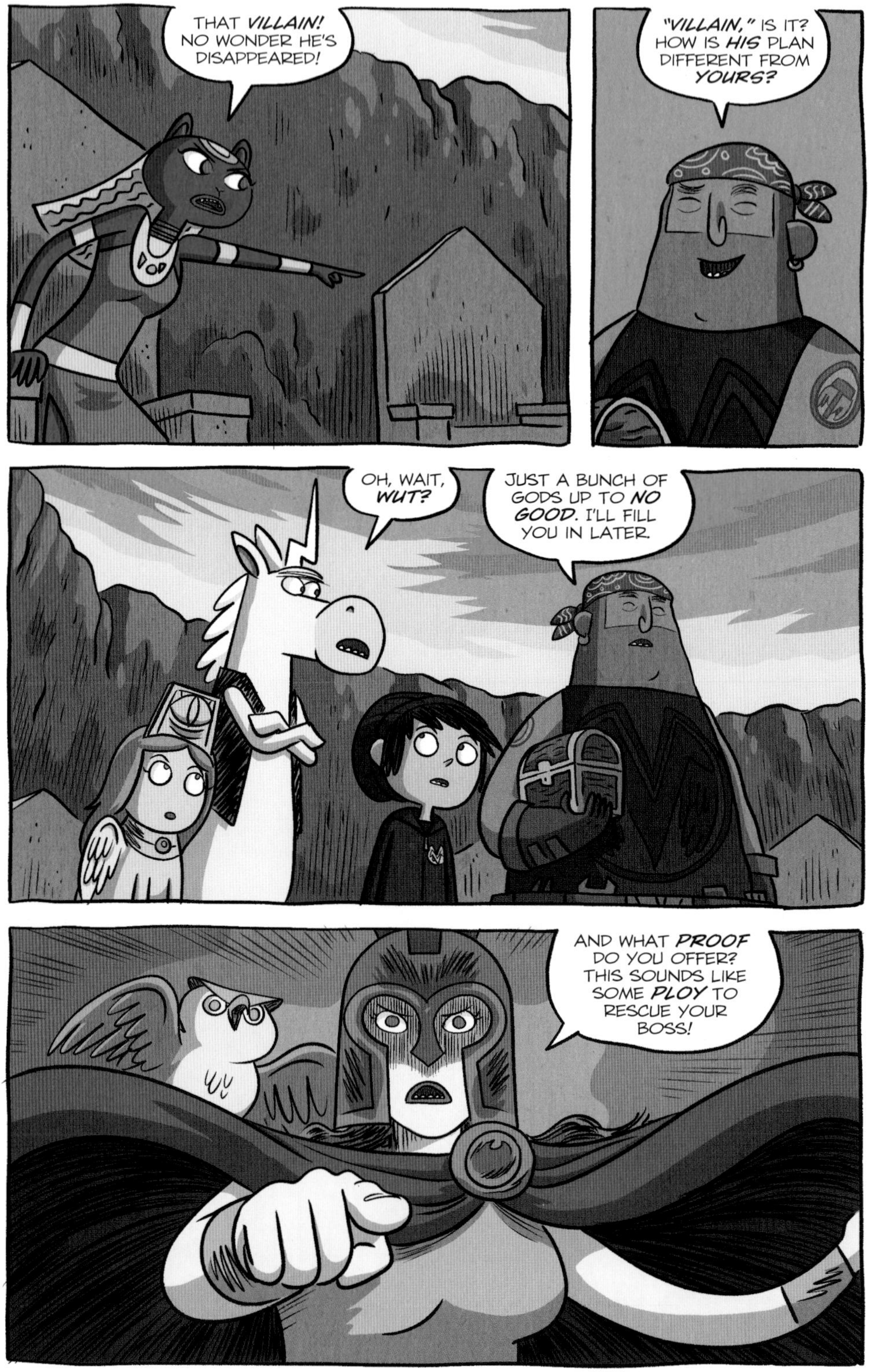
THAT VILLAIN! NO WONDER HE'S DISAPPEARED!
"VILLAIN," IS IT? HOW IS HIS PLAN DIFFERENT FROM YOURS?
OH, WAIT, WUT?
JUST A BUNCH OF GODS UP TO NO GOOD. I'LL FILL YOU IN LATER.
AND WHAT PROOF DO YOU OFFER? THIS SOUNDS LIKE SOME PLOY TO RESCUE YOUR BOSS!

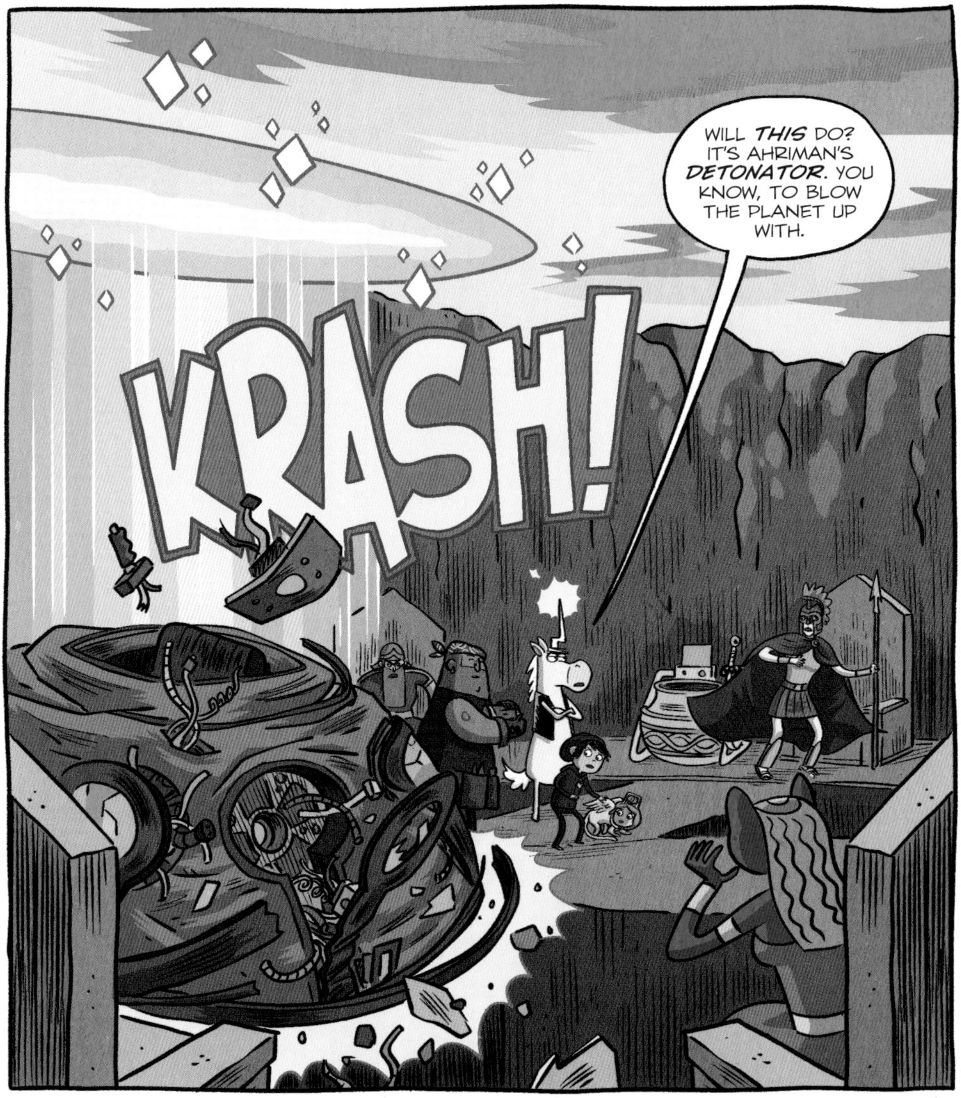
KRASH!
WILL THIS DO? IT'S AHRIMAN'S DETONATOR. YOU KNOW, TO BLOW THE PLANET UP WITH.

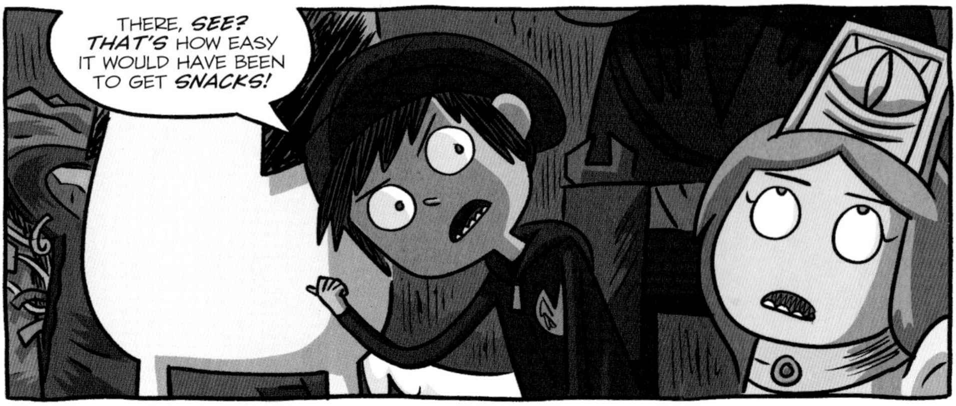
THERE, SEE? THAT'S HOW EASY IT WOULD HAVE BEEN TO GET SNACKS!

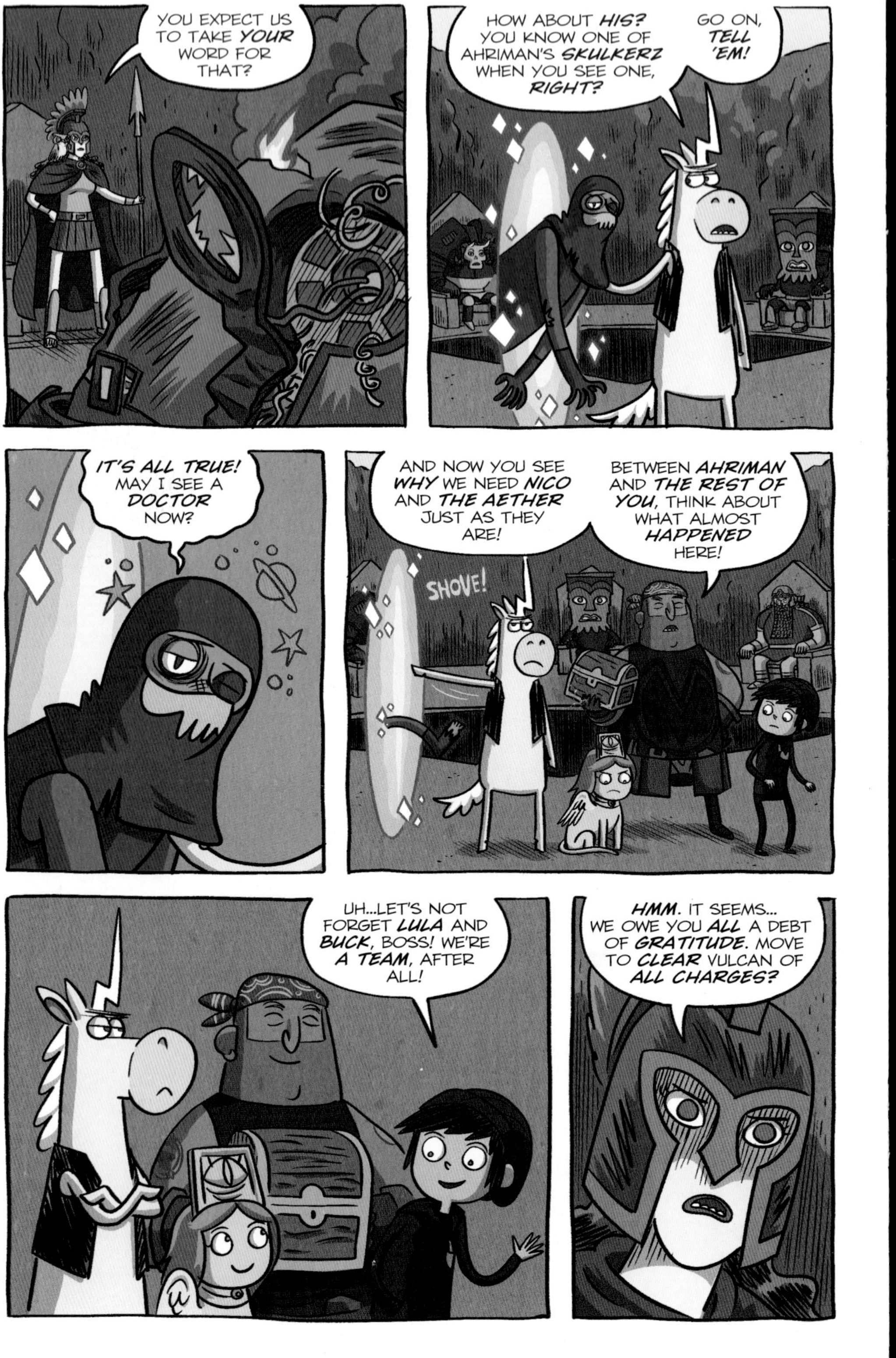
YOU EXPECT US TO TAKE YOUR WORD FOR THAT?
HOW ABOUT HIS? YOU KNOW ONE OF AHRIMAN'S SKULKERZ WHEN YOU SEE ONE, RIGHT?
GO ON, TELL 'EM!
IT'S ALL TRUE! MAY I SEE A DOCTOR NOW?
AND NOW YOU SEE WHY WE NEED NICO AND THE AETHER JUST AS THEY ARE!
BETWEEN AHRIMAN AND THE REST OF YOU, THINK ABOUT WHAT ALMOST HAPPENED HERE!
SHOVE!
UH...LET'S NOT FORGET LULA AND BUCK, BOSS! WE'RE A TEAM, AFTER ALL!
HMM. IT SEEMS... WE OWE YOU ALL A DEBT OF GRATITUDE. MOVE TO CLEAR VULCAN OF ALL CHARGES?

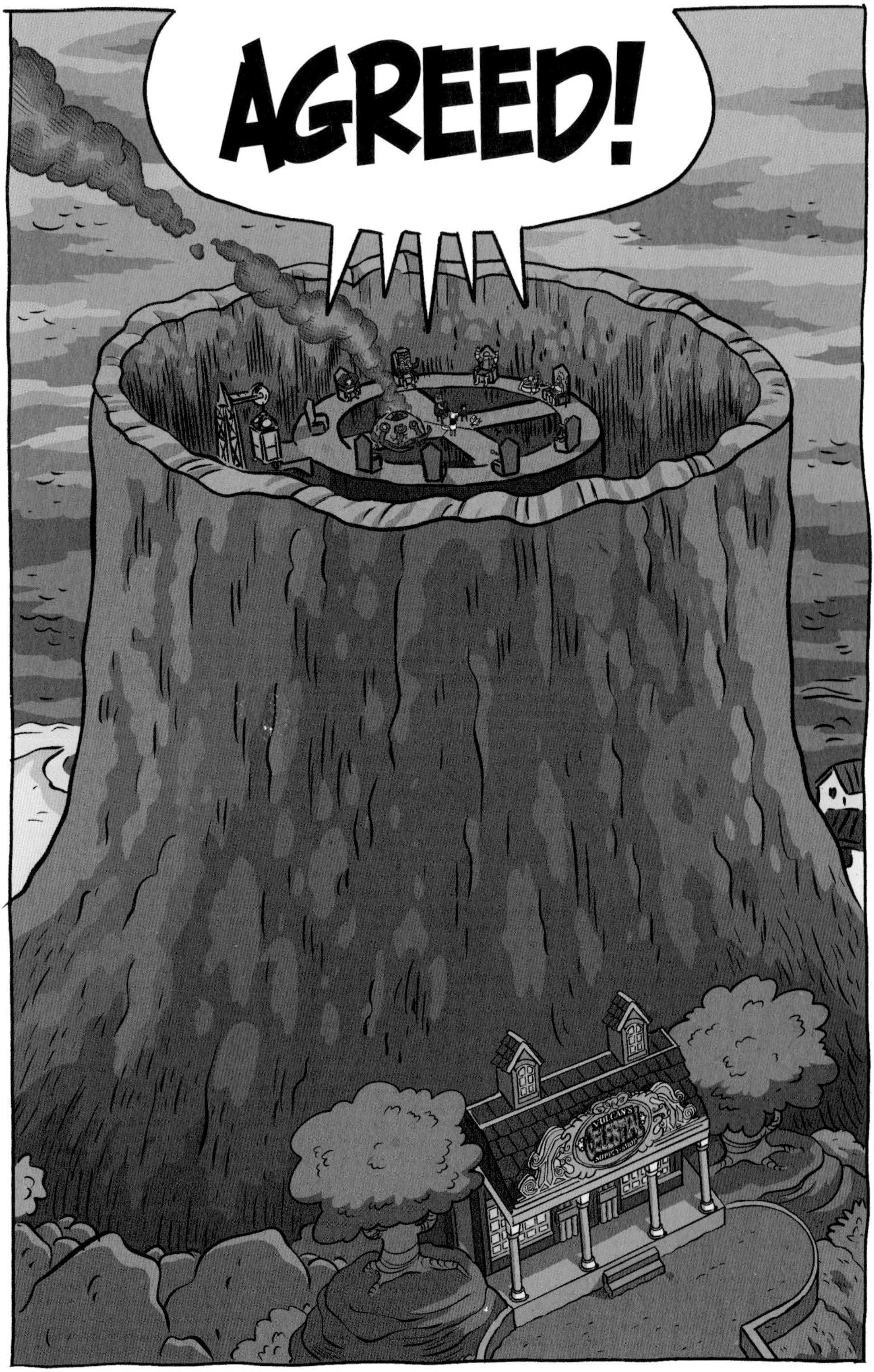
AGREED!
VULCAN'S

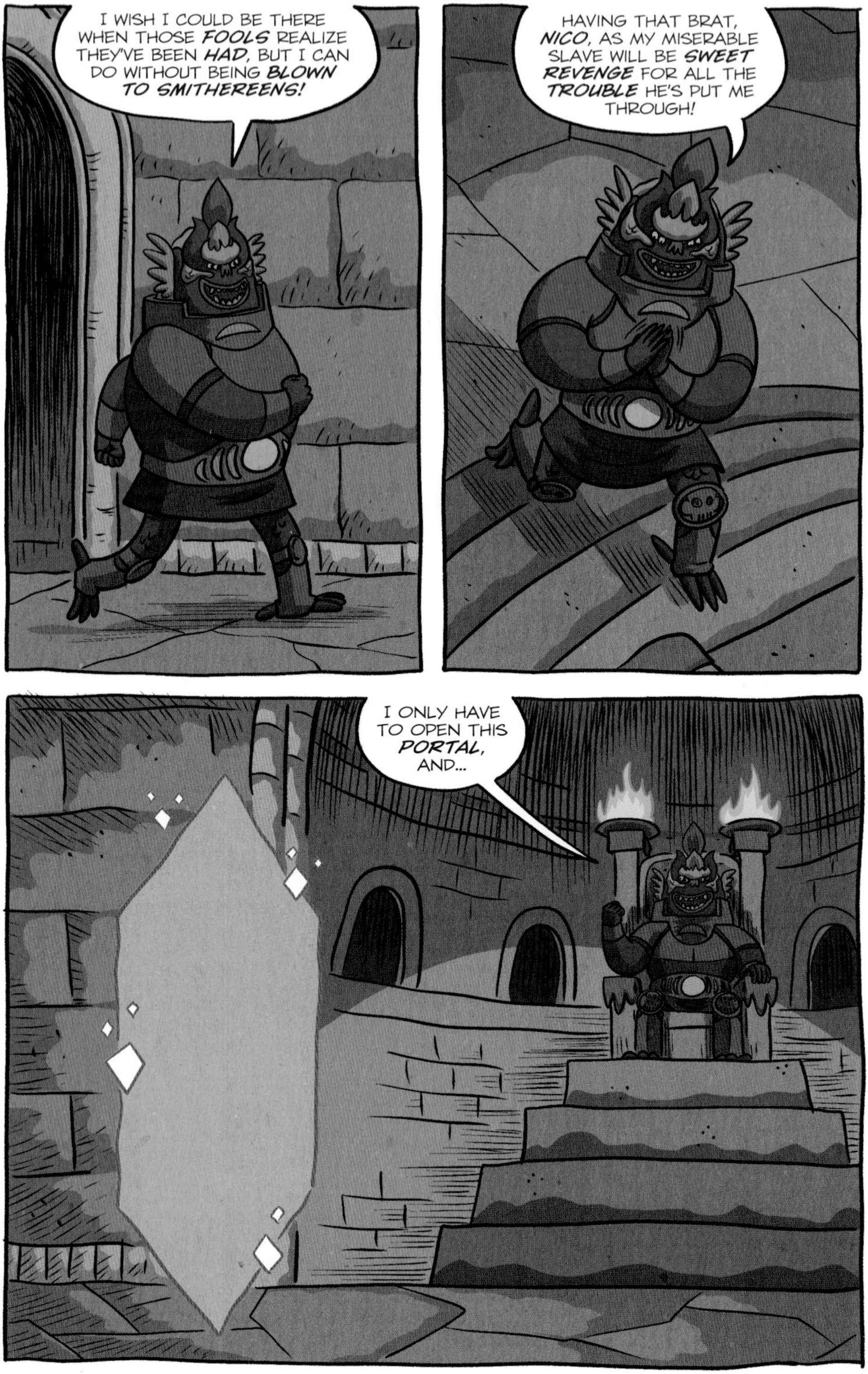
I WISH I COULD BE THERE WHEN THOSE FOOLS REALIZE THEY'VE BEEN HAD, BUT I CAN DO WITHOUT BEING BLOWN TO SMITHEREENS!
HAVING THAT BRAT, NICO, AS MY MISERABLE SLAVE WILL BE SWEET REVENGE FOR ALL THE TROUBLE HE'S PUT ME THROUGH!
I ONLY HAVE TO OPEN THIS PORTAL, AND...

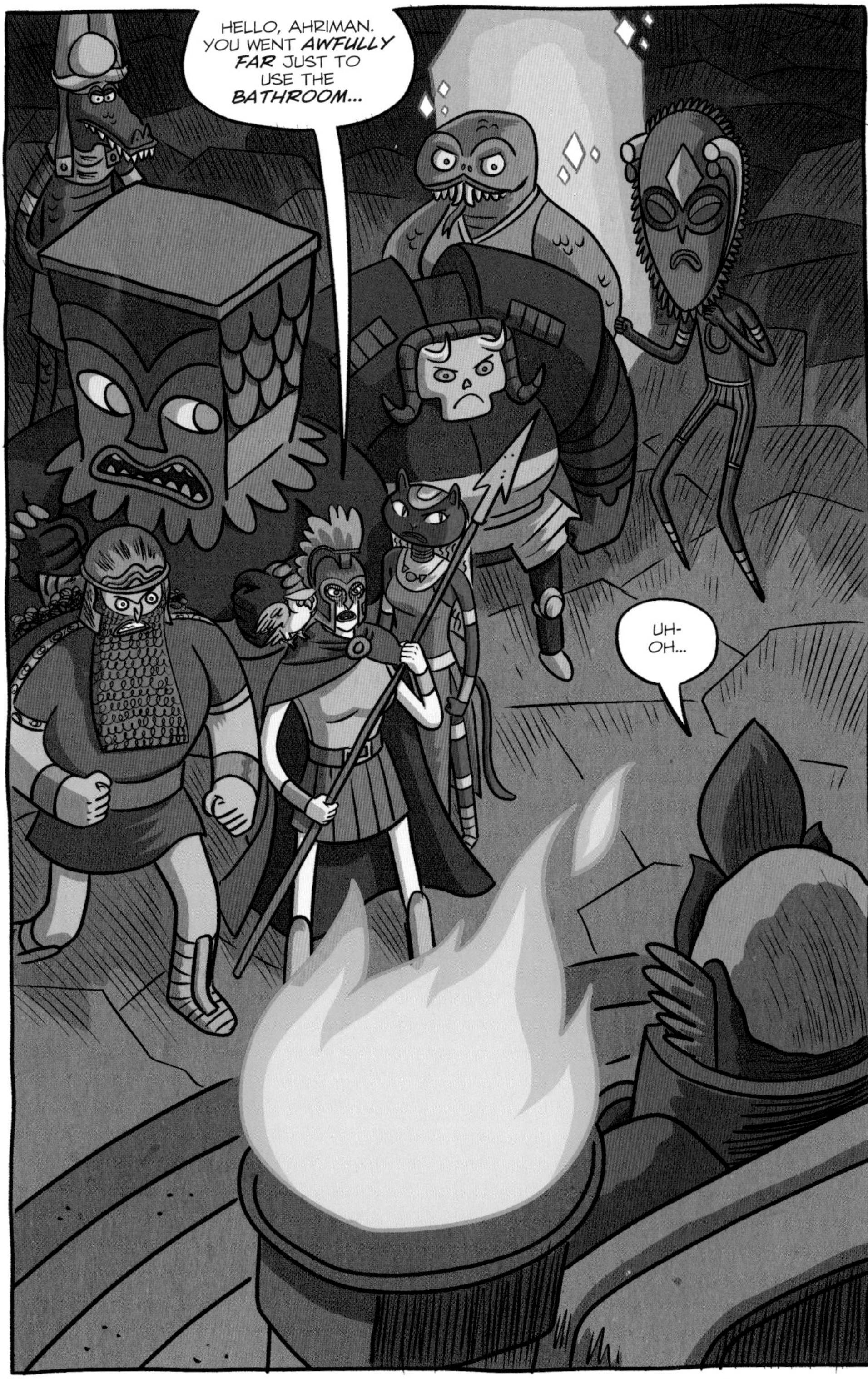
HELLO, AHRIMAN. YOU WENT AWFULLY FAR JUST TO USE THE BATHROOM...
UH-OH...

Epilogue

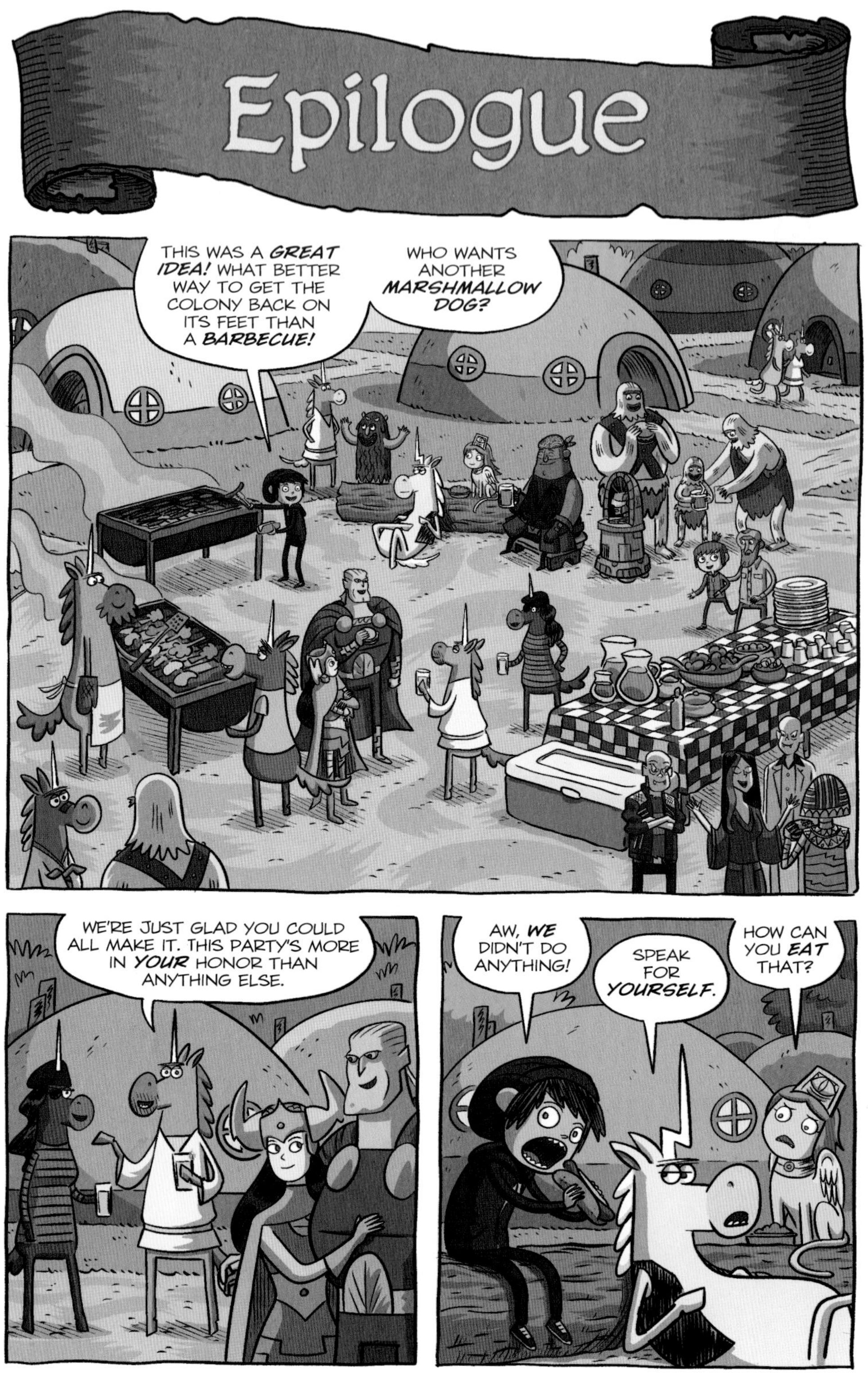
THIS WAS A GREAT IDEA! WHAT BETTER WAY TO GET THE COLONY BACK ON ITS FEET THAN A BARBECUE!
WHO WANTS ANOTHER MARSHMALLOW DOG?
WE'RE JUST GLAD YOU COULD ALL MAKE IT. THIS PARTY'S MORE IN YOUR HONOR THAN ANYTHING ELSE.
AW, WE DIDN'T DO ANYTHING!
SPEAK FOR YOURSELF.
HOW CAN YOU EAT THAT?

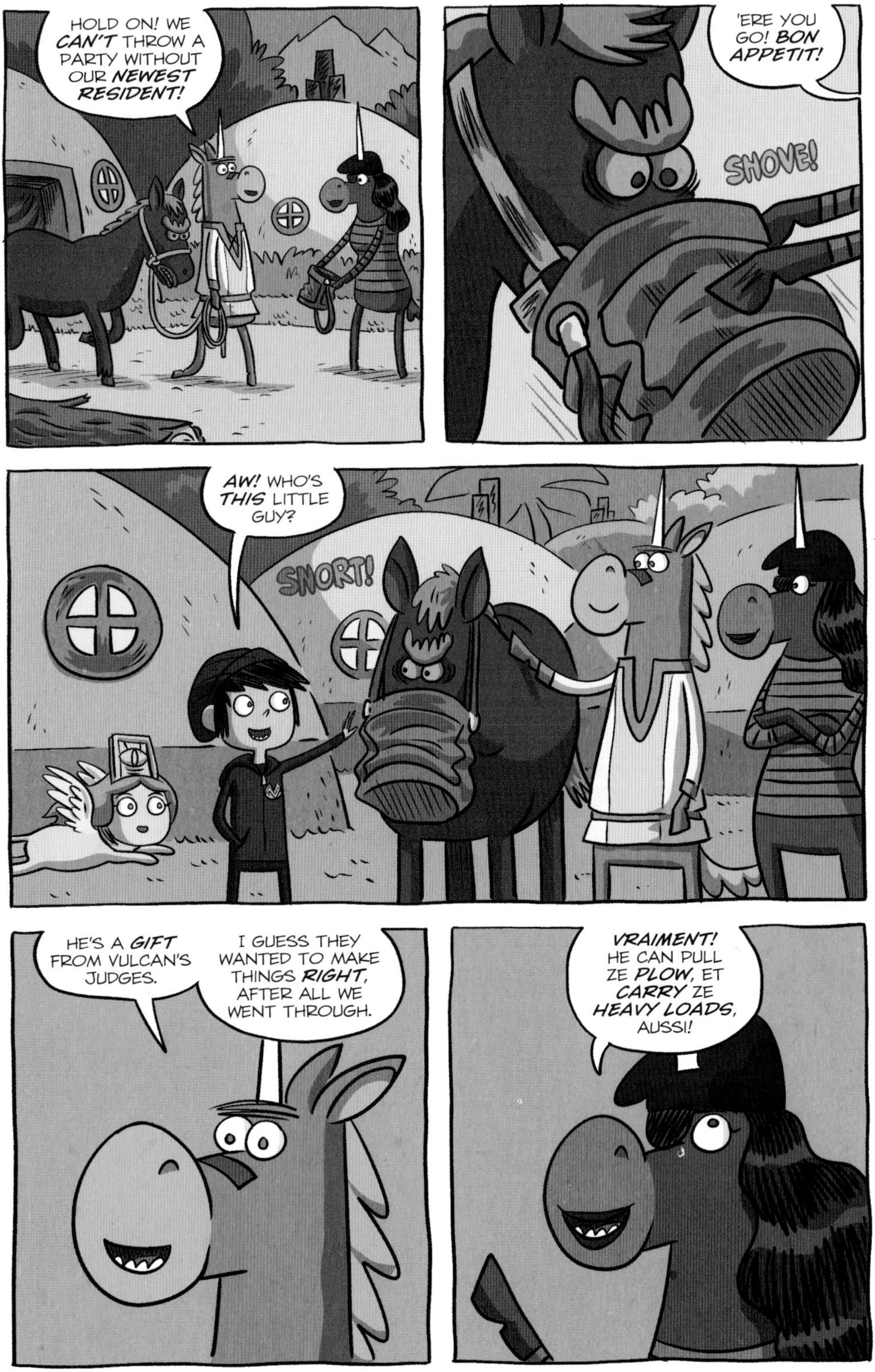
HOLD ON! WE CAN'T THROW A PARTY WITHOUT OUR NEWEST RESIDENT!
'ERE YOU GO! BON APPETIT!
SHOVE!
AW! WHO'S THIS LITTLE GUY?
SNORT!
HE'S A GIFT FROM VULCAN'S JUDGES.
I GUESS THEY WANTED TO MAKE THINGS RIGHT, AFTER ALL WE WENT THROUGH.
VRAIMENT! HE CAN PULL ZE PLOW, ET CARRY ZE HEAVY LOADS, AUSSI!

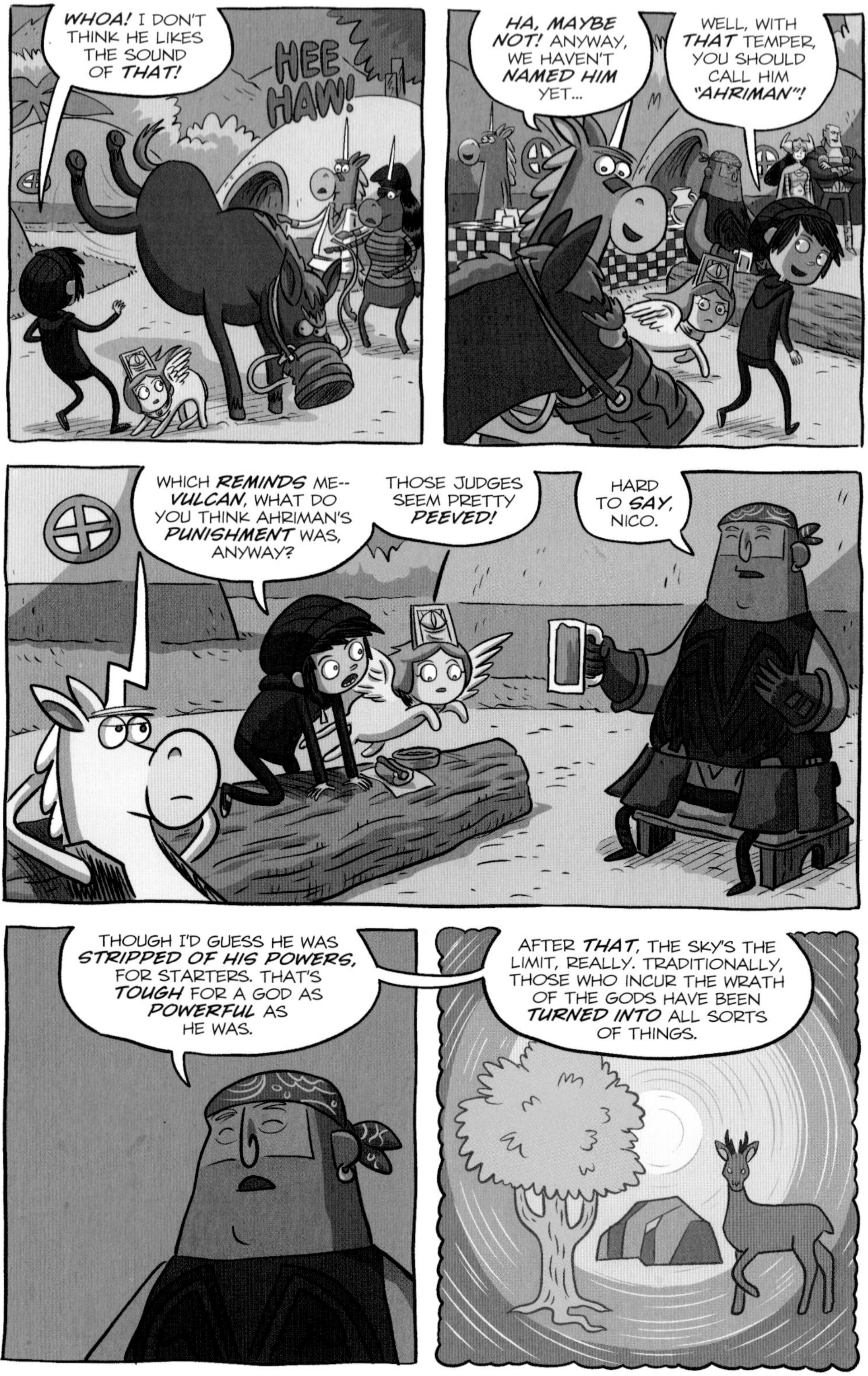
WHOA! I DON'T THINK HE LIKES THE SOUND OF THAT!
HEE HAW!
HA, MAYBE NOT! ANYWAY, WE HAVEN'T NAMED HIM YET...
WELL, WITH THAT TEMPER, YOU SHOULD CALL HIM "AHRIMAN"!
WHICH REMINDS ME-- VULCAN, WHAT DO YOU THINK AHRIMAN'S PUNISHMENT WAS, ANYWAY?
THOSE JUDGES SEEM PRETTY PEEVED!
HARD TO SAY, NICO.
THOUGH I'D GUESS HE WAS STRIPPED OF HIS POWERS, FOR STARTERS. THAT'S TOUGH FOR A GOD AS POWERFUL AS HE WAS.
AFTER THAT, THE SKY'S THE LIMIT, REALLY. TRADITIONALLY, THOSE WHO INCUR THE WRATH OF THE GODS HAVE BEEN TURNED INTO ALL SORTS OF THINGS.

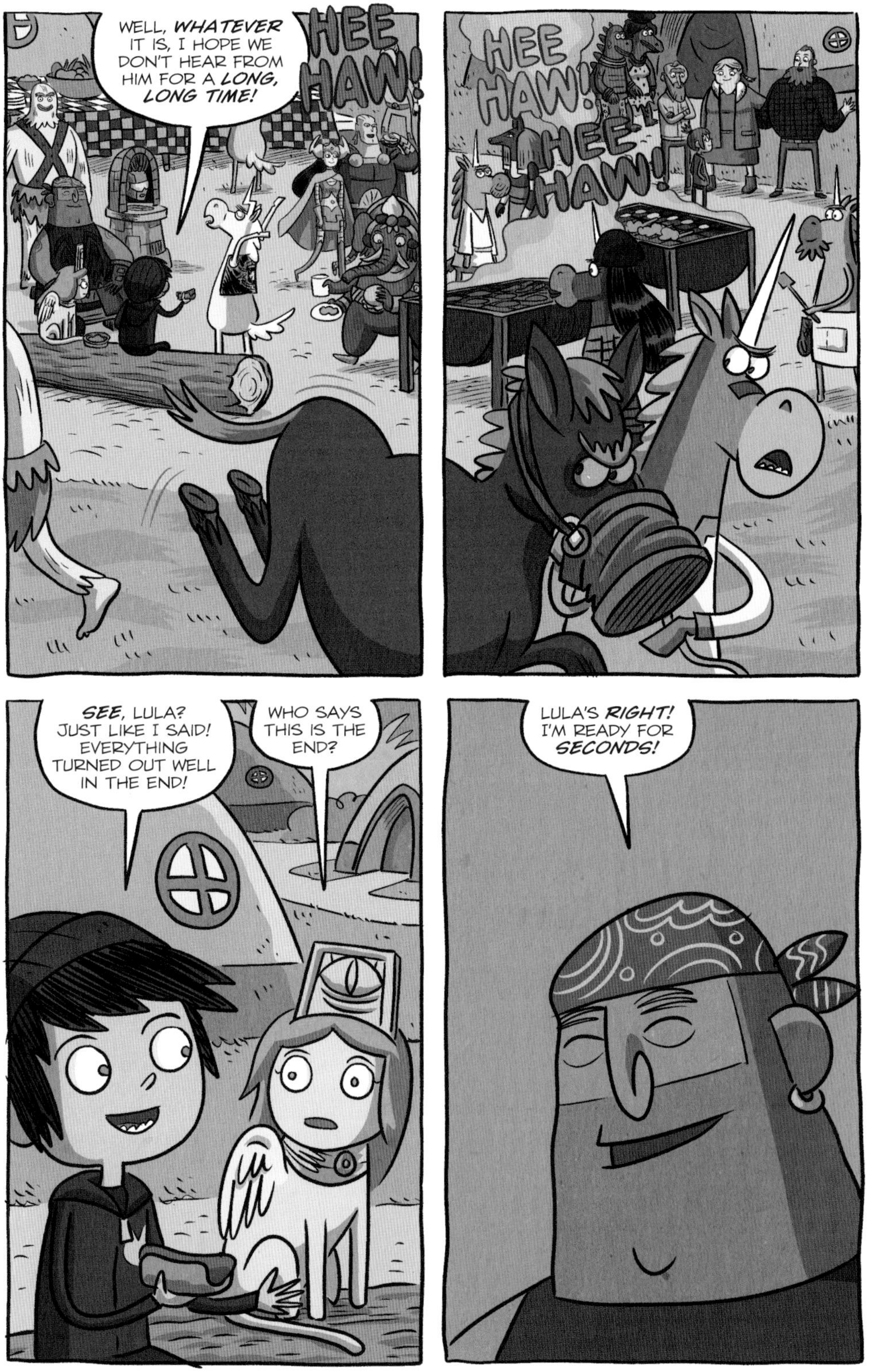
WELL, WHATEVER IT IS, I HOPE WE DON'T HEAR FROM HIM FOR A LONG, LONG TIME!
HEE HAW!
HEE HAW! HEE HAW!
SEE, LULA? JUST LIKE I SAID! EVERYTHING TURNED OUT WELL IN THE END!
WHO SAYS THIS IS THE END?
LULA'S RIGHT! I'M READY FOR SECONDS!

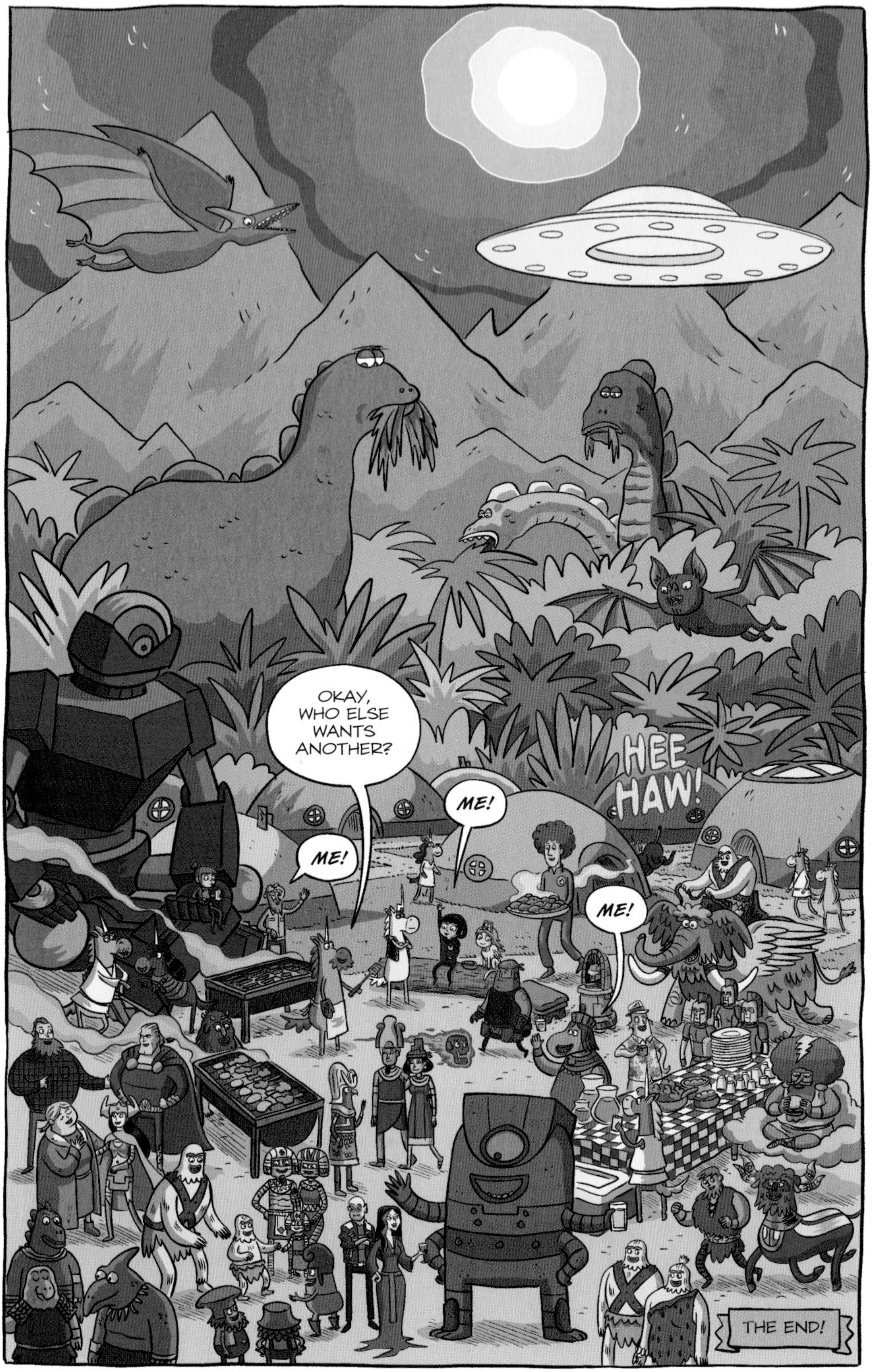
OKAY, WHO ELSE WANTS ANOTHER?
ME!
ME!
HEE HAW!
ME!
THE END!

COMING SOON!

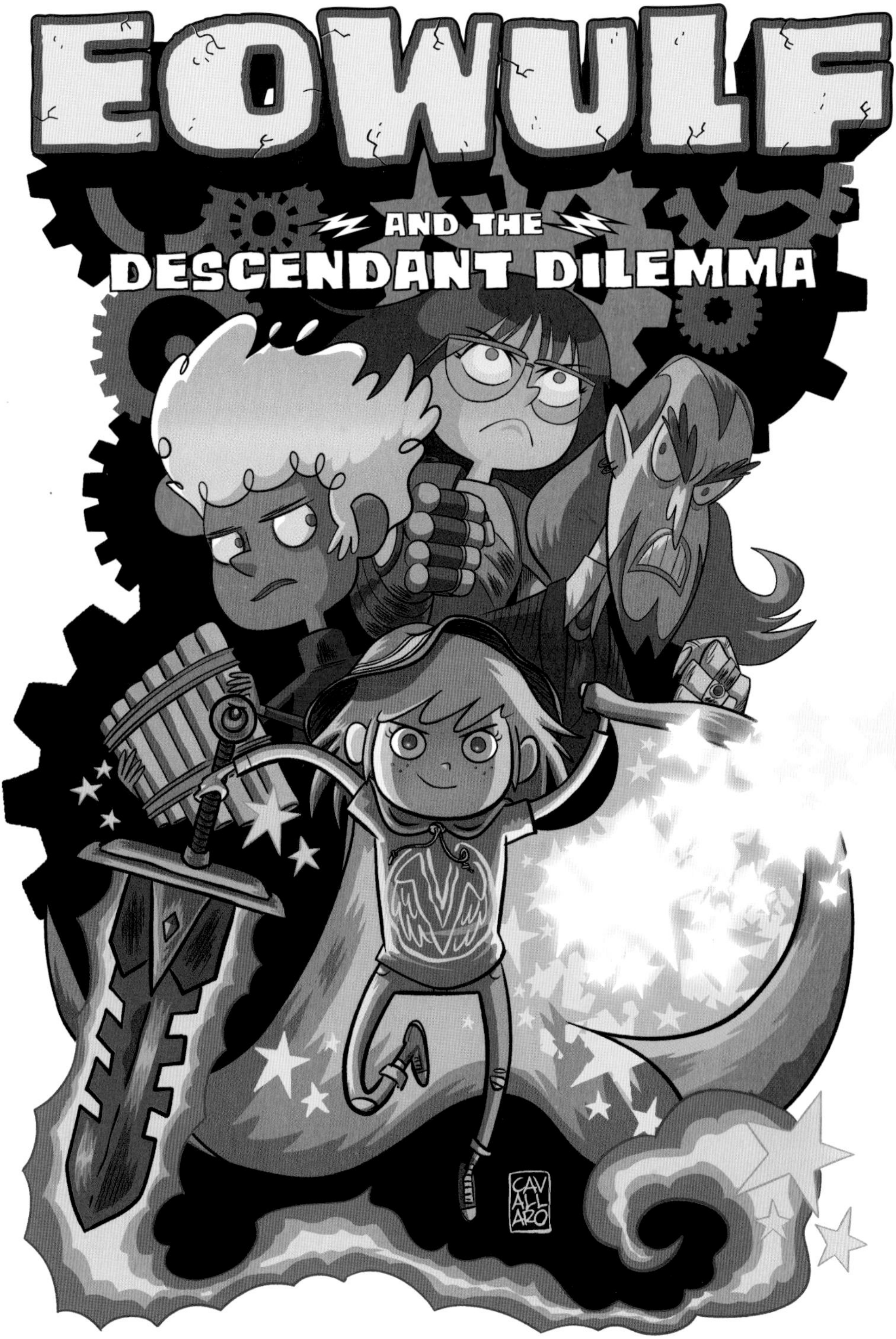
EOWULF
AND THE
DESCENDANT DILEMMA
CAVALLARO

THANK YOU

GIORGIA & FRANK CAVALLARO, PAUL CAVALLARO & FAMILY, ANNA WINCHOCK & FAMILY, LISA NATOLI, NICK ABADZIS, ANDREW ARNOLD, KIRK BENSHOFF, J.M. DEMATTEIS, KRISTIN DULANEY, SCOTT FRIEDLANDER, MOLLY JOHANSON, JEREMY LAWSON, SUNNY LEE, GEORGE O'CONNOR, BEN SHARPE, MARK SIEGEL, GABE SORIA, ED STECKLEY, NICOLE SWIFT, KIARA VALDEZ, SARA VARON, CARYN WISEMAN AT ANDREA BROWN LITERARY AGENCY, AND THE NATIONAL CARTOONISTS SOCIETY.